Living Apart Together

Also by Elise Darcy

It Takes 2 to Tango

Dear John

Love on the Rooftop

AUTHOR'S NOTE

The events in 'Living Apart Together' precede those in the
follow-on novels listed above.

Living Apart Together

Book I

ELISE DARCY

Penny Lane Press

To Isabelle

1

'Mrs Baxter, I'm so sorry to call you at this hour.'

They had never apologised before when they phoned. Sylvie waited for the person on the end of the line to say something more, until realisation surfaced in the awkward silence that followed.

'What is it?' John's voice startled her from the stairs. 'What's happened?'

Sylvie had been standing in the hall for some time, the phone cradled in her hand, the line dead. She felt numb. She looked up at her husband as he walked down the stairs in his red and blue striped pyjamas, the mug of tea she had handed him not five minutes ago in one hand, and the newspaper in the other. His reading glasses were still perched on the end of his nose. His face was a picture of concern as he said, 'I thought you were going to visit your mother?'

She had been anxiously counting down the hours until she could visit her mother again and resume the conversation they had only yesterday. She was just leaving when the phone rang.

Sylvie slowly replaced the handset. 'She...died.'

'Oh Sylvie, I'm so sorry.'

She wished she hadn't answered the phone. If that were the case, she would be sitting on the bus right now in blissful ignorance. Sylvie stared miserably at the phone thinking what a difference a day makes. Now she wasn't going to visit her mother or resume that conversation to find out what her mother was so desperately trying to tell her.

Reluctantly, Sylvie put her handbag and house keys down next to the phone on the sideboard.

John left his mug and newspaper on the bottom stair. 'Here, let me take that,' he said, helping her out of her coat. He hung it up on the coat stand by the door and then turned to Sylvie, holding out his arms.

She stepped into her husband's warm embrace. He held her protectively while she sobbed over the unfairness of it all. The fact that her mother had died was not in itself a great surprise; the doctors had given her a week, a month at most. She was on her way out, Sylvie was well aware of that. But it was the timing that had upset her the most. All she needed was one more day, one more visit. It had been going on for weeks, her mother residing in that care home waiting for the inevitable, and just when her mother seemed on the verge of telling her something that appeared of great importance, it had all been taken away by a phone call.

'Why now?' moaned Sylvie, her face buried in John's cotton pyjama top, her voice muffled. She knew her husband couldn't answer that; it was one of life's unanswerable questions.

John hugged her close as she stared at the phone thinking of the last two words her mother had spoken to her.

'How about a nice cup of tea?' John cut across her thoughts.

Sylvie nodded as John released her from his embrace.

He looked at her solemnly, tried to find some words of comfort, failed miserably, and dashed off to make some tea.

Sylvie stood in the hall listening to the sound of her husband pottering about in the kitchen. She could hear him filling the kettle with water, and the chink of china cups as he arranged the cups and saucers on the tea tray. Her eyes drifted back to the phone. She recalled the last time she saw her mother.

Forgive me. They were the last words her mother had spoken. Sylvie wanted to believe that was the dementia talking, not some secret she had kept all these years and taken to her grave.

'The tea's made,' John called out.

She kicked off her shoes, walked down the narrow flight of stairs to the floor below and took a seat at the table in the basement kitchen of their London home. She glanced through the french doors into the garden. The big elm tree at the end of the garden was ablaze with autumnal colours, its red, yellow and rust-coloured leaves a veritable rainbow of colour against the backdrop of a cloudless blue sky. The rays of sunshine streaming through the glass doors made her feel all the sadder that her mother had passed away on such a beautiful morning.

Sylvie shifted her attention from the garden to John who was sitting across the table drinking his tea in muted silence. She said, 'We have to tell the girls.' Harriet, Jessica, and Chloe had always been close to their maternal grandmother. Sylvie felt too emotional to talk to their daughters and break the news. She couldn't bear to hear their tears down the phone.

John reached across the table and took her hand giving it an affectionate squeeze. 'I'll do it,' he said as if reading her mind.

She watched him head upstairs before turning to look out the garden once more. She sat there recalling, with sadness, a snippet of an earlier conversation she'd had with her mother a little over a week ago when the fog of dementia had temporarily lifted.

'I want you to be happy,' her mother had said out of the blue during one of her rare lucid moments.

'I *am* happy,' said Sylvie, offering up a belated smile.

'Are you?'

Sylvie's smile had faded at that comment. It was true she wasn't happy. She hadn't been happy for some time. With both her parents now gone, Sylvie was acutely aware of the passage of time. She was moving up life's escalator. A baby boomer, she was the next generation on God's hit list. As she approached another big birthday – she was sixty years old this year – Sylvie was questioning her life choices. She didn't feel she had achieved anything significant with her life.

Sylvie knew her family would beg to differ. She had a stable marriage, a lovely home, three wonderful daughters and a longed-for first grandchild. Even so, she felt there was something missing in her life. Some part of her still unfulfilled. Perhaps it didn't help that she lived with a family of high achievers. Her husband had reached the pinnacle of his career as an accountant and was now a financial controller overseeing the accounts department of the company he worked for.

Their daughters had turned out just as successful in their own way. Chloe, their youngest, had always loved computers. She was now a computer software engineer commanding extortionate sums of money for contract work in London. Harriet, their eldest, was a writer and worked as the editor of a prominent women's magazine. She was the only one of her daughters so far to get married. Two years ago she had her first child, Gertie.

And then there was Jessica. Jess as she was affectionately known to family and friends. She was the most independent, free-spirited and adventurous of their three daughters. Maybe that was why, unlike Sylvie, Jess never stopped looking for what she wanted out of life, for what would make her happy. She wouldn't settle for anything less. Eventually, Jess found her niche in life and, in so doing, the life that was waiting for her. But she had to travel halfway around the world to find it.

It turned out to be a change of scene, a move Down Under, that kick-started her life. She never looked back. That was where she met her partner, completed a Zoology degree, and started work as a conservationist and wildlife expert at Melbourne Zoo. This was no surprise to Sylvie as Jess always loved animals, even though John did not share their daughter's enthusiasm for the animal kingdom and would never allow the girls to have a pet when they were growing up. Not even a hamster.

Thinking of her family's achievements, Sylvie resolved to make some changes in her own life before it was too late. Perhaps she would also find her niche in life and discover something that made her happy. Sylvie hoped that, unlike her middle daughter Jess, she didn't have to travel halfway around the world to find it.

Sylvie was staring into space when she heard the sound of John's voice coming from the hallway upstairs. He was talking to one of the girls on the phone. Sylvie rose from the table and started to pace the kitchen floor. She desperately wanted to do something, anything to keep her mind occupied. She needed a refuge from her grief. Searching through the kitchen drawers, Sylvie found what she was looking for in the shape of a notepad.

She sat down at the kitchen table with the small notepad that she normally used to make her grocery shopping lists, opened it to a blank page, and wrote the words: *Sylvie's life-changing to-do list*. Sylvie liked the sound of that and underlined it three times as if to emphasize the fact that she was going to see it through – no matter what. If anything was going to jolt her into action, she couldn't think of a more fundamental event in her life, at this moment, than the loss of her mother. It was a turning point in her life, Sylvie knew that. But she also knew her mother would not want to see that loss, that grief, overtaking her life.

Although it was tough to let go and think about something else, Sylvie forced herself to concentrate on the list. She was afraid that if she didn't, she might fall apart and John would return from making the phone calls to find an emotional wreck sitting at the kitchen table. She knew he wouldn't want that so, for his sake, she made a supreme effort to stay focused on the list; she was determined to think about the future and the changes she wanted to make in her life. It helped that she knew the first thing she wanted to change in her life. She wrote it down with an exclamation mark just as John walked back into the kitchen.

Sylvie looked up. The list she had been conscientiously writing suddenly all but forgotten as the events of this morning rushed back into her consciousness. That feeling of emotional numbness settled over her once more. Her mother's passing didn't come as a shock or even a surprise, but that didn't dull the pain when she was gone.

'Are you all right?' he asked as soon as he stepped into the kitchen. He walked over to the table and placed a comforting hand on her shoulder.

She turned in her chair and gave John a reassuring smile that she wasn't about to fall to pieces. She had her life-changing to-do list, and that was going to help her get through this. It was something to focus on, something to force her to think about the future. 'What about the girls? How did they take the news?'

John pulled out a chair and sat down at the kitchen table. 'I haven't managed to get hold of Jess or Chloe.'

'Oh.' Sylvie was disappointed but not all that surprised. The time difference between Melbourne and London meant it was about four in the afternoon in Australia, and knowing her sporty daughter Jess, she would not be sitting at home. She was most likely out and about doing something adventurous like canoeing or white water rafting that she was so fond of.

As for Chloe, it was Sunday morning here in London and a few streets away she could be found in her flat, still comatose under the duvet fast asleep. Sylvie knew all about Chloe's Saturday nights on the town, partying until the early hours; that was her favourite past time when she was a teenager still living at home. Ten years on, Chloe hadn't changed a bit. Her idea of recreation was very different from her older sister in Australia.

'I did speak to Harriet.' He offered Sylvie a reassuring smile that she was okay.

It came as no surprise that Harriet was up and about very early on Sunday morning to answer the phone – after all, she had a toddler.

'She asked after you.'

'Did she?' Sylvie managed a smile. Her eldest daughter had mellowed considerably in the two years since having her first child. Harriet had always been very careerist, very driven, but she had surprised everyone by choosing to take some time off work to be a stay-at-home mum for Gertie. It had changed their own mother-daughter relationship for the better.

Harriet was returning to work soon to resume her career in journalism. Sylvie was immensely proud of her, especially as she had never achieved anything remotely resembling a career like her daughters. Thinking of which, Sylvie glanced at what she had written down in her notepad. It was time to make some changes. She looked across the table at John and announced, 'I want to try something new.'

'Sounds interesting,' said John in a bored tone of voice which did not escape her notice.

Sylvie put her pen down, leaned back in her chair and folded her arms across her chest. Her hazel-brown eyes studied John. They had known each other for nearly forty years, getting married soon after they first met. She had been instantly attracted to the tall, slim young man who stood at over six feet tall, with piercing blue eyes and a shock of blonde wavy hair which had long-since faded to pepper grey. John was a year older than her, and back then they were both very young and very much in love.

They say opposites attract; they were undoubtedly quite the opposite in appearance. Sylvie was short and stocky, with a classic pear-shaped figure and problem thighs, accentuated by being small in stature at barely five feet tall. She had often wondered what it was about her that first attracted John. She couldn't imagine it was her figure.

Despite outward appearances, they used to have a lot in common. They had the same goals and aspirations for their future and they used to make time to talk to each other. However, sitting here at the kitchen table in the home they had lived in most of their married lives, Sylvie couldn't remember the last time they had sat down and shared their hopes and dreams, and made plans for their future. That seemed to come to an end once they had settled into their respective jobs, finished renovating the house, and brought up their children.

It made her wonder if that had something to do with why she was so unhappy. Sylvie couldn't remember the last time John showed even the remotest interest in what she was doing. When she told him she wanted to make some changes in her life, what surprised her was not his reaction but how hurt she still felt by his apparent indifference.

Sylvie sat at the table staring at John intently. She was making him feel uncomfortable under her gaze, she could tell.

He glanced nervously in her direction. 'So…what is it you plan to do?' John asked half-heartedly, his attention was drawn to the Sunday supplements sitting unopened on the kitchen table.

Sylvie knew he was just asking out of politeness, but she told him anyway, 'I'm leaving my job.'

John looked at her curiously as he reached for the sports supplement. He didn't seem all that surprised because he was well aware Sylvie had never particularly liked secretarial work. She had drifted into it when she left school and returned part-time once the children reached school age.

'I think that's a marvellous idea.' He was still looking her way as he pulled the supplement towards him and tried to do the impossible; pay attention to Sylvie and read an article at the same time. 'Marvellous,' he repeated as his eyes scanned the page.

She waited for him to ask her how she felt about leaving a job she had spent the last eighteen years of her life slaving away in. She waited for her husband to ask her what her plans were for the future. She waited for him to ask her why she wasn't happy.

John looked up briefly. 'Just marvellous,' he said once more before turning the page.

A feeling of *déjà vu* settled over her. It reminded Sylvie of her childhood when nobody listened or paid her any attention. She realised somewhat belatedly that she had fallen into the same trap with her own family. Something had to change. Leaving her job was a start. Sylvie knew it was long overdue. At least she would have some time while John was at work to figure out what she wanted to do next.

Sylvie glanced at him engrossed in reading the paper under the misapprehension that everything was all right in the Baxter household. Well, it wasn't. It made Sylvie wonder what the fallout would be when she started to take the initiative and change her life.

2

John was sitting in the lounge in his favourite chair holding the daily newspaper open in front of him. He wasn't reading the paper however, but staring out of the Georgian bay window lost in thought. John was surprised when he arrived home from work to find Sylvie had not returned. He found this rather troubling.

He looked at his watch wondering how long it took for a solicitor to read a will. It seemed to be taking an age. John wished he could have been there with Sylvie to offer his support but it was immediate family only on this occasion, unlike the funeral they had attended two days ago.

The funeral had been a muted affair, as to be expected, and somewhat perfunctory. There had been an assortment of relatives and a few family friends in attendance, but the numbers were thin on the ground. The family wanted to keep it simple so a wake had not been organised, much to John and Sylvie's relief. Unlike John, who was close to his two brothers, he knew that Sylvie never really got along with her four older siblings. He couldn't imagine trying to keep up the small talk with virtual strangers, which is what her brothers and sisters had become over the years as they rarely saw them. It would never surprise

John if they had arranged a small get-together after the funeral without including Sylvie. He wouldn't dream of hurting her feelings by voicing that thought.

John closed his newspaper as he reflected on the fact that perhaps it was the considerable age gap between Sylvie and her four older siblings which had driven a permanent wedge between them, or maybe it was merely the differences in personality. Sylvie appeared quieter and more introspective than her older, louder, more theatrical family.

Whenever John had met any of them over the years – which wasn't that often – John had observed how different his Sylvie was to the rest of them. For that reason, John was only too pleased to have the funeral out of the way with very little fanfare. He imagined Sylvie felt the same way.

John looked at his watch once more trying to speculate what exactly was taking so long. They both knew there would be little in the way of possessions left in the will. Neither John nor Sylvie would come into any inheritance to speak of; it was never on the cards. Whatever they had, they worked for. That was the lay of the land and nothing was going to change that.

John folded his unread newspaper neatly in two, deposited it in the wicker magazine basket beside his chair, and got up to stand by the window. He was looking for any sign of a black London taxi-cab that would be ferrying his wife back from the solicitor's office in Grosvenor Square. John hadn't been standing by the window for long when he spotted a black cab making its way down the street towards their house.

'At last!' exclaimed John as it stopped outside and Sylvie climbed out.

She took a moment to pay the taxi driver and then turned

towards the house. The expression etched on her features immediately told John that something was up.

John rushed downstairs to the kitchen to put the kettle on and made it back in time to open the front door for her. He offered up an empathetic smile as she walked in. John had been through all this before with both his parents and understood what she was going through.

He took her coat and hung it on the coat stand by the door. Only then did John notice Sylvie had brought something home with her from the solicitors. How odd. 'What's in the bag, Sylvie?'

Sylvie opened the bag and retrieved the box inside.

John took an involuntary step back the moment he saw it.

Sylvie sighed. 'It's my mother's ashes.'

'I can see that,' said John in alarm. 'But what in god's name—'

'Don't swear,' admonished Sylvie as she turned around to put the box down on the telephone table in the hall.

'Not there!' John darted to the table and nearly knocked the box right out of Sylvie's hands. He didn't want Sylvie to leave that box in the hall. In fact, John didn't want that box anywhere in the house.

'Sylvie, what do you intend to do with it . . . them . . . her?' John was having a problem dropping in the right pronoun. This wasn't exactly an everyday line of conversation you normally had with your wife. The last thing he expected was Sylvie to return home with her mother's remains. 'Don't they have places for that sort of thing?' John was trying very hard to be understanding but what he really wanted to know was what on earth was going on?

Sylvie sighed, kicked off her black patent shoes and walked into the lounge carrying the box.

'Sylvie?' John followed hot on her heels.

Sylvie turned around looking exasperated and held up the box in John's line of vision. She couldn't carry it around all day. She needed to put it down somewhere.

John hastily looked around the room until his eyes settled on the empty coal scuttle on the hearth beside the fireplace; out of sight, out of mind was John's only thought right now.

Sylvie narrowed her eyes. She knew what he was about to suggest. Did he know how disrespectful that was?

'You're right, that's not one of my better ideas,' said John reading her disapproving scowl.

Sylvie placed the box on one of the shelves in the alcove beside the fireplace. She regarded the box solemnly for a brief moment before she turned around and sat down on one of the two-seater sofas adjacent to the fireplace.

Taking his cue, John sat down on the sofa opposite Sylvie, the cup of tea he was going to make all but forgotten by this unusual turn of events. He hadn't expected Sylvie to return from the solicitors with anything, let alone her mother – or her mother's ashes to be precise.

'Well?' John asked expectantly, still waiting for an explanation. His eyes kept drifting to that box making him inwardly shudder. He wished he could swap seats with Sylvie so at least it wouldn't be in his line of vision. Instead, John did the next best thing and got up intending to go and sit next to Sylvie, with his back to the box. He edged his way around the glass coffee table, wondering in passing why the table had looked just the right size on the shop floor when he bought it, until they got it home and it swallowed up most of the floor space between the sofas.

John was just about to sit down when he remembered the tea. Five minutes later John sat down next to Sylvie and put two cups of tea down on the coffee table in front of them.

Sylvie made no move to pick hers up. She was unusually quiet. John waited patiently for Sylvie to explain why she had returned home with the box.

There was little of value in terms of possessions that had been bequeathed in her mother's will. Sylvie's father had been a vicar. Her parents had lived all their married lives in the church vicarage, living out their latter years in the church almshouses. Her father's first post was in London. That's where they stayed and where Sylvie and her siblings were born and brought up. However, Sylvie always knew her mother's heart belonged to Cornwall, where she had been born and raised. Sylvie wasn't surprised by her mother's final request to scatter her ashes in Cornwall.

The solicitor produced a handwritten note from her mother giving these express wishes. He passed the note to Sylvie.

She gave it no more than a cursory glance, quite happy to take the solicitor's word for it.

When Sylvie attempted to pass the note on to one of her siblings, the solicitor leaned forward and told her to stop. 'Please read the letter, Mrs Baxter. It is addressed to you.'

Sylvie looked at him in surprise and then glanced at her four siblings, in turn, who were staring at her suspiciously. None of the others had been left a handwritten note from their mother in her will. She knew what they were thinking: what made Sylvie so special? Sylvie was wondering the exact same thing.

Sylvie's hand shook as she turned her attention back to the letter. When she finished reading the short note, the solicitor made it clear for the benefit of the others gathered at the reading of the will that it was Sylvie's responsibility, and hers alone, to carry out her mother's wishes. The hand-written note offered no explanation as to why Sylvie had been chosen to carry out her final request to scatter her ashes in the garden of a cottage in Cornwall.

John sat drinking his cup of tea listening intently as Sylvie recounted word for word what had happened at the solicitor's office this morning.

When she had finished, John put his empty cup back on the saucer and turned to Sylvie with a question, 'Why you?'

Sylvie hadn't touched her tea. 'I suppose it was to be expected.' She sighed. 'As if my brothers and sisters don't hate me enough as it is.'

'Oh, I'm sure that's not true,' John said lamely.

Sylvie wished it wasn't. She glanced over her shoulder at the box on the shelf and knew exactly why her mother had chosen her. Out of all of them, it could only have been Sylvie.

'There's something you don't know about my childhood, John,' began Sylvie, about to tell him what she had kept to herself all these years because she didn't think it mattered – until now.

John listened intently once more as Sylvie told him an extraordinary tale, made all the more extraordinary because he assumed, after all these years together, that he knew everything there was to know about the woman he had married.

Growing up in a large family there was never any money for holidays, apart from day trips to the seaside. But this was not so for Sylvie. Every summer her mother had taken only Sylvie with her on the steam train to a magical place called Cornwall. Sylvie vividly recalled the soft sandy beaches as far as the eye could see and the cottage they always stayed in by the sea. She loved it there, and she knew her mother felt the same way too.

Sylvie didn't care a jot that she spent those summers on her own with no one to play with. Her older brothers and sisters would never let her join in and play with them anyway. Sylvie didn't even ask if she could bring her best friend, Julia. She would have loved Julia to see Cornwall, but this was the only opportunity for Sylvie to have her mother all to herself, just the two of them. Unfortunately, not even her best friend was going to get in the way of that.

Sylvie had often wondered why the trips suddenly stopped when she was eleven years old. At first, Sylvie had begged and pleaded to return. Sylvie loved visiting Cornwall and staying in the cottage by the sea. But it was not to be. Sylvie and her mother never returned to Cornwall together again. As Sylvie's life moved on, those summers in Cornwall became but a sweet memory of things past.

'Now you see why it's up to me to do this.'

'Wow, I had no idea,' exclaimed John, raising an eyebrow. 'That explains . . .' He trailed off staring at the carpet in muted silence.

Sylvie knew what he was thinking: that's why her brothers

and sisters always hated her so. Sylvie hadn't thought about those summers for many, many years. It was only when she became a mother herself that she thought back to her own childhood and couldn't imagine showing such favouritism, singling out one child over the others. It was, in hindsight, so wrong.

Perhaps that's why her mother was asking for her forgiveness because Sylvie paid the price of spending those summers with her mother in Cornwall, living with four older siblings who despised her for it. But to a child like Sylvie who would have preferred to have grown up in a smaller, quieter household, she saw nothing wrong with going away to Cornwall on her own without them.

'Why do you think she only took you on holiday?' asked John, intrigued. 'If your parents couldn't afford to take you all on a family holiday together, then why didn't she at least take one of your siblings on occasion?'

Sylvie stood up without answering John's question. She walked over to the box and stared at it sadly. She suddenly had so much she wanted to say to her mother, so many questions. John was right: why did she take only her and not one of the others? Whatever her reasons, whatever secret she had yet to reveal, had gone with her to her grave, Or, more specifically, to a box on a bookshelf in the corner of the living room.

Sylvie turned to John ignoring his last question; a question that Sylvie was painfully aware would never be answered. All that mattered now was that her mother had chosen her to carry out this final request. It was up to Sylvie to return to Cornwall and find the cottage that her mother had chosen as her last resting place.

'I haven't set foot in that part of the world since I was eleven years old, almost fifty years ago,' mused Sylvie. She couldn't approach her siblings to help her because the resentments still cut deep. Sylvie was afraid of opening up old wounds.

'What are you going to do?'

Sylvie looked at John and replied, 'I'm going to return to Cornwall, find that cottage, and do as she asked,' sounding a lot more confident than she was feeling.

That wasn't the only thing Sylvie intended to do. She still had the little notepad where she had jotted down her life-changing to-do list. Sylvie thought of that list and knew exactly what she had to do first thing tomorrow morning.

3

Sylvie checked her resignation letter was in her handbag three times before leaving for work. However, Sylvie's resolve had abandoned her by the time she walked into the office. Although she kept reminding herself that she was doing the right thing, it wasn't working. Sylvie kept stalling when it came to handing the letter to her boss. Eventually, she bottled out and shredded it later that day in the office shredding machine.

Sylvie had discovered that the act of writing it down at the kitchen table at home was one thing, but when it came down to doing something about it and going through with making those changes on her list, that was a whole other ball game.

On the face of it, it wasn't as though she had anything much to lose. They didn't need her income because John paid the bills. And it wasn't as though she loved her job – far from it. So why had she stayed working there for so many years? That was not a mystery. Over time Sylvie had got stuck in a comfortable rut that gave her some financial independence, refusing to acknowledge that it was making her unhappy – miserable even.

When Sylvie first returned to work, when the children were small, it was all part of John's plan. John was still in the throes of renovating the house, and they needed her income. It had been John's idea to buy the house, an idea that paid off because they were now living in a lovely home in Holland Park.

It wasn't always so in the beginning when they took the biggest gamble of their lives, back in the seventies, to move into a four-storey townhouse in a street full of squatters. Sylvie remembered she was afraid to walk down the street in broad daylight, let alone at night. However, since then things had turned out very well indeed all thanks to John and the plan.

They had finished renovating the house some time ago and with no financial commitments towards their children – the girls were all independent – she was now free to make her own choices. For the first time in her life, Sylvie was going to find herself. She should have done it years ago, but as she grew older it became more difficult to get out of her comfortable rut and make that leap to change her life, even though there really was nothing stopping her.

Sylvie was sitting at her desk with all this going through her mind fervently wishing she hadn't been so quick to shred her resignation letter. Then fate stepped in and offered Sylvie a gentle push in the right direction. That afternoon, soon after Sylvie had backed out of handing in her resignation letter, everyone in the office had been called into an emergency meeting. There was an announcement that job cuts were imminent and employees were being invited to volunteer to take redundancy or early retirement. The timing was fortuitous.

Sylvie knew she wouldn't get much after working for the firm of solicitors as a part-time secretary for eighteen years – a modest lump sum and a small pension – but it was more than she would have got if she'd simply done them a favour and resigned. Sylvie thought of her resignation letter going through the shredder and was the first to raise her hand and eagerly volunteer to take early retirement right there in the middle of the meeting.

She was politely told to put her hand down and wait to go through the proper channels.

Although Sylvie discussed it with John that evening because that's what married couples do, this time her mind was made up. John still had five years left until he retired but he was supportive of Sylvie's decision to leave her job.

It didn't mean that once Sylvie left her job, she would idly sit around all day doing nothing. Sylvie liked to keep herself busy. It had crossed her mind that if she left work now she might not get another job any time soon, even if she wanted one. After all, she was approaching the big six O.

Sylvie wouldn't mope around feeling sorry for herself. On the contrary, she believed in the old mantra: work cures everything. It's just that Sylvie didn't want to work in her job any longer. She didn't even like her job. She just liked the feeling that she was contributing financially, albeit in a small way, to their lives together. However, her mother's death had put things into perspective. Time was short, and she didn't want to waste another minute.

Sylvie could feel the anticipation reminiscent of years gone by when her world hadn't become quite so routine and life could still surprise her. It was as though she was about to set off on a journey into the unknown, unravelling the mystery of where the next chapter in her life might lead.

It was a strange sensation that for once in her life Sylvie didn't have a destination in mind like a job, or marriage, or motherhood. It was simply about finding herself. Sylvie knew she was fortunate to have this opportunity. Her only regret was that she hadn't done it sooner.

The following Monday Sylvie put her name forward for early retirement and signed the necessary paperwork to release her from her job. With a mixture of excitement and trepidation, Sylvie ticked off the first entry on her life-changing to-do list. There was nothing else on that list because for the first time in Sylvie's life her future was not yet written. She found that thought surprisingly scary.

'Honestly, I don't know what you're so afraid of,' Julia had said over the phone when Sylvie told her best friend what she was doing.

Sylvie was afraid that if she started the ball rolling by letting go of her job, where would it lead? What else would she discover she wanted to change in her life that was making her unhappy? Sylvie didn't tell Julia her secret fears. Instead, she told Julia about her mother's last request.

As much as she wanted to carry out her mother's wishes, there was something so final about making that last journey with her back to Cornwall. In a way, Sylvie knew it would be a journey to accepting she was truly gone. Sylvie would have to be ready for that, for the happiness of reliving those childhood memories and the sadness that this time had come.

Sylvie told Julia there were times she wished the cottage no longer existed so she wouldn't have to go through with it. Or better still, that something would happen to disrupt her plans, forcing her to put that return trip to Cornwall on hold.

Sylvie cast her eyes heavenward in response to her superstitious best friend telling her – in no uncertain terms – to stop that right now, warning Sylvie to take care to listen to the old saying: be careful what you wish for.

4

Sylvie had a spring in her step since signing the paperwork. Her initial apprehension at the thought of leaving her job had given way to relief that she had made the right decision. Sylvie was already counting down the days to her newfound freedom and the start of something new, even though she hadn't figured out what that something new would be.

It was a Wednesday, Sylvie's half-day at work, and the morning had flown by. It was nearly the end of her shift, and Sylvie was uncharacteristically watching the clock. She had already put on her coat and picked up her handbag ready to leave work dead on twelve. Sylvie had always been very conscientious, working more hours than she was paid to do. She was always one of the last secretaries to leave the office. However, since taking early retirement Sylvie had changed. She decided it was about time she put herself first. Today Sylvie would be home earlier than usual for lunch because she saw no reason to stay behind at work.

By one o'clock Sylvie got off the bus around the corner from where she lived, her free afternoon already planned. She mentally ticked off what she was intending to do with the rest of her day as she strolled along the pavement, glancing in the boutique shop windows as she passed by. As soon as she arrived home, she would change out of her work clothes into something more comfortable, have some lunch, and then head out to do some shopping in Camden Town. Perhaps she would buy some groceries and make John something special for dinner tonight.

Sylvie wouldn't normally do grocery shopping midweek but she was feeling really good about the first decision she had made on her life-changing to-do list, and she fancied preparing a special meal tonight to celebrate. In hindsight, it made Sylvie wonder why she had been so anxious about leaving her job. She knew she had made the right decision.

Sylvie opened the wrought iron gate and walked along the garden path and up the short flight of stone steps to their house. She unlocked the front door and stepped inside.

After taking off her coat, she briefly checked her appearance in the hallway mirror. Sylvie caught a lock of chestnut shoulder length hair that had fallen in front of her face and tucked it behind her ear. Her hair hadn't always been this colour. Sylvie's natural hair colour was jet black. But when Sylvie spotted her first grey hairs, her immediate reaction was to dye her hair back to its original colour. Sylvie's hairdresser had another idea, suggesting a softer shade to match her hazel-brown eyes. Sylvie had taken her advice and never looked back.

As Sylvie stared at her reflection in the mirror, she recalled the hairdresser commenting on how she kept her thick, glossy hair in great condition. Sylvie appreciated the compliment even though she didn't do anything in particular to warrant it. On the contrary, she felt her hair always looked slightly unkempt, a bit too wavy and out of control. Even using straighteners, Sylvie couldn't quite pull off the sleek, smooth look she desired.

Today that didn't bother Sylvie. Nothing was going to spoil her happy disposition as she looked forward to what she had planned for this afternoon. Sylvie tried smoothing her hair down, gave up, kicked off her shoes and padded across the hall in her bare feet. Walking through the lounge, Sylvie continued down the stairs to the kitchen. She stopped dead on the last stair. Her breath caught in her throat. Sylvie was not alone.

'John?' She called out his name even though she was unsure it was him. Sylvie hovered on the bottom stair, her heart racing, as she stared into the kitchen waiting for her eyes to adjust to the gloom.

It *was* John! He had given her quite a fright; he was a dark figure sitting in the shadows.

The back of the house was north facing which meant every afternoon the natural light in the basement kitchen was so poor that you always needed a light on in the kitchen for the rest of the day. John had not switched on the lights. For a split second, Sylvie thought they had burglars until she realised it was her husband sitting stock-still at the kitchen table. John was never home from work this early. Had she forgotten he was taking annual leave this afternoon or wasn't he feeling well?

Sylvie switched on the lights, casting a worried look in his direction. 'John, I didn't expect you home so soon.'

Neither did John. He had been sitting in the kitchen for the last hour wondering how he was going to break the news.

John had neglected to tell Sylvie that at the same time as she was offered early retirement, there had been talk of people losing their jobs at his place of work. Not long after those rumours surfaced, the first wave of job cuts began when people had been asked to step forward voluntarily.

Unlike Sylvie, John loved his job. He wouldn't dream of volunteering to leave. And he certainly wasn't ready to retire. John was well aware that whenever Sylvie broached the subject of how they planned to spend their retirement, he always managed to sidestep the issue, doing his level best to avoid talking about it. A word came to mind when he thought about retirement: denial. It was as though it would never happen to him. John didn't think he'd ever willingly retire because he wouldn't know what to do with himself. He had no hobbies and few friends that were not work-related. John knew he would be completely lost without a job.

John looked sheepishly at Sylvie. He had not brought up the issue of what was going on at work because he didn't think it had anything to do with him. John believed he was indispensable.

He was wrong.

And now a very nervous John was sitting contrite at the kitchen table waiting for Sylvie to return home from work on her half-day and tell her the news. He felt a failure. He felt he had let them both down. But above all, he knew he should have told her what was going on at work. She would not be expecting him home at this hour or have the faintest clue what he was about to tell her.

John bit his lip and nodded when Sylvie offered to make him a cup of tea. His eyes followed her around the kitchen as she filled the kettle with water and got out the cups and saucers, milk and sugar, and put them in front of him on the kitchen table. She obviously sensed something was up because she did all this in silence. John waited for Sylvie to make the tea as he sat thinking about exactly how he was going to tell Sylvie about his eventful morning at work.

John had been called into his boss's office and given two choices: redundancy or early retirement. When he had barely got over the shock, John did a quick mental calculation and opted for the early retirement package because that was by far the better offer on the table. He signed the paperwork there and then.

They said he was lucky to be chosen. How did they figure that? John was aware that some of his colleagues, who had also worked at the firm for decades, wanted to leave. But he didn't. He had said as much in the meeting, not that it made any difference.

After an apologetic handshake from his boss, John had been escorted out of the building. This did not surprise him in the least. John was an accountant, and because of the nature of his work he could do some serious financial damage to the firm before he left. He could cook the books. In short, he could screw them over. John wouldn't do that. His boss knew he wouldn't dream of doing that under normal circumstances. However, the people upstairs, who made the overriding decisions, had placed John on gardening leave to see out his notice until he officially retired in a month's time.

John had left that morning for work and returned home that afternoon retired, five years ahead of plan. John was in shock.

Sylvie calmly sat down at the kitchen table and poured them both a cup of tea from the teapot. She listened as John nervously recounted his morning at work.

When he finished, Sylvie set her empty cup down on the saucer and looked at John. As if it wasn't bad enough that John had not told her they were laying off people at his job too, he was also avoiding eye-contact, which meant John was hiding something. 'What are you not telling me, John?'

John stole a glance at Sylvie across the table. He knew Sylvie was going to hit the roof when she found out he hadn't been exactly straight with her about what was going on at work. He should have told her sooner, at least brought it up when they were discussing her early retirement before she went ahead and gave up her job. He knew why he hadn't. John didn't want to worry her unnecessarily because he genuinely believed the job losses would not affect him. Now John didn't want to make matters worse by telling her he was on gardening leave. If Sylvie hadn't hit the roof already, she surely would if she found out he was not even returning to work for four weeks to serve out a notice period. This was it. This was now.

John knew how much Sylvie was looking forward to having some time to herself to figure out what she wanted to do next. He imagined that having her husband at home all day under her feet was not quite what Sylvie had in mind when she decided to leave her job.

Sylvie repeated her question, 'What are you not telling me?'

'Nothing,' John quickly replied.

Sylvie got up from the table and walked across the kitchen to the butler sink. She turned on the tap, running some fresh water into the washing up bowl.

Although John was relieved the worst was over now he had told Sylvie, he was still waiting for her reaction. 'Aren't you going to say something?' He watched her intently as she put the cups and saucers in the sink. 'You do know we've got a dishwasher,' quipped John without thinking.

'Oh do shut up and let me think.' Sylvie started washing up the cups and saucers. 'So how long have we got until you leave the job?'

John fidgeted in his chair and randomly said, 'Oh er one month . . . I think.'

'You *think*?' Sylvie glanced at John in surprise. 'Didn't they at least have the decency to give you a leaving date?' Sylvie shook her head in disgust and turned back to the sink to continue the washing up. 'After everything you've done for that firm, after all you're hard work, I still can't believe they just showed you the door when you were so close to retirement.'

Much to John's relief, he realised Sylvie wasn't mad at him but angry at the firm for letting him go. He nodded in agreement.

Sylvie placed the cups and saucers on to the draining board. She brushed her hair out of her eyes with a wet marigold glove leaving a soapy smear down her left cheek. Sylvie turned from the sink to look at her husband.

John stared at her soapy cheek hoping she didn't lift off.

Sylvie regarded John a long moment. She didn't see the point in lifting off and rowing about it. He should have told her what was going on at work, especially when she was in the throes of making decisions of her own on the work front. He should have brought it up when she told him that she was leaving her job, but he didn't. There was no use crying over spilt milk, thought Sylvie. It was all water under the bridge now. All the same, it must have come as quite a blow. She could well imagine he thought his job was safe. Nothing like this had ever happened to them in the past. John always had a plan in life. That's what kept him going. That's what made him tick. This was the first time John's plan had gone awry. And there was nothing he could do about it.

Sylvie took off the marigold rubber gloves and said simply, 'Let's assume we've got one month before you leave your job to figure this out.'

It wasn't their financial situation that was bothering either of them. Despite the money they had poured into the house over the years, John and Sylvie were savers. Perhaps it was part of their generations psyche, or maybe it was just down to their upbringing. Both Sylvie and John had come from large families and had seen first-hand their parents work hard for everything they had. With no access to credit or loans, their parents had to scrimp and save for the least little thing, or simply do without.

This had rubbed off on both of them. Despite living in a large house in an exclusive part of London, John and Sylvie did not lead an extravagant lifestyle by any means. The upshot of being relatively frugal over the years was that John could afford to take early retirement. On paper, they were one of the lucky ones; they could choose to retire together. How many times had Sylvie heard about people of their generation with all these grand plans for their retirement, only to stay in their jobs until the bitter end and then drop dead of a heart attack, or some other serious illness, their retirement plans put on hold forever? That didn't have to happen to them.

In another household, a couple might have this discussion and concluded that for all the extra money another five years in work was going to give them, what it couldn't buy was that extra time spent together in their twilight years. Who knew what lurked unseen in anyone's future – good or bad?

Wasn't this a sign? Wasn't it telling them they were meant to spend this time together? Sylvie sighed heavily as she imagined John's reaction if she asked that question.

Sylvie made some sandwiches. Over lunch, she tried having this conversation with John, but it did not go well. Sylvie wasn't in the least bit surprised. This was the reason Sylvie knew that if she wanted any chance of finding herself, she had to leave her job first because once John retired he would not be a happy camper stuck at home all day without a job. He was used to the cut and thrust of a high-flying career. It would take him some time to adjust to life outside work – if he ever could.

She already envisaged him moping around at home all day without the first clue what to do with himself. Sylvie was not looking forward to being the one in the firing line when John inevitably got depressed and frustrated with his very changed circumstances.

The irony was not lost on Sylvie that it had taken this long and the shock of losing her mother to budge her out of her inertia, only to find the goal posts had moved and John had pipped her at the post. She hadn't even served out her notice. John's early retirement couldn't have come at a worse time for either of them. However, arguing about it wasn't going to change a thing.

Sylvie tried to remain positive. She had already worked two weeks of her notice period, which meant she could look forward to a couple of weeks by herself at home when her job ended to figure this out before John was forced into early retirement in a month's time. John was never going to be ready to retire even if they had kept him on until the age of sixty-five. But at least if they had, there would have been five more years to prepare for it and not just one month. Sylvie was already dreading that day. What was it going to be like with John at home all the time?

Maybe he would surprise her and move on to the next stage of his life with the good grace and humility of somebody who has had a very good innings. They were, after all, probably the last generation to enjoy the sort of stable work lives and decent pensions that their children and grandchildren could only dream of. Would John accept that? Would John look on the bright side and believe he was one of the lucky ones? Probably not, thought Sylvie. She sighed heavily.

They finished their lunch in silence.

Sylvie sat watching John staring forlornly out of the kitchen window. He already looked depressed, and he hadn't even left his job yet. Sylvie had a sinking feeling in the pit of her stomach that there was trouble ahead.

She glanced at the clock on the kitchen wall above John's head and asked him, 'What time have you got to get back to the office?' It was now well past his lunch hour. Although Sylvie appreciated John coming home to break the news of his impending retirement straight away, she didn't want John to have any more aggravation at work. He had enough on his plate right now.

John slowly turned his head in Sylvie's direction. He looked distracted. 'Pardon?'

'The time!' Sylvie gestured at the clock. 'Isn't it about time you made a move?'

John looked at her perplexed.

'Don't you have to go back to work this afternoon?' Sylvie was trying to remain calm. It had started already; she could see it written all over his face – John was giving up.

'What? Oh yes, of course, back to work for the afternoon.' John sounded peculiar.

'Are you okay? Perhaps I should ring them up and tell them you're not feeling well and you need to take the afternoon off.'

'*No!*' John suddenly jumped out of his chair.

Sylvie looked up at him in surprise. 'I just thought after the shock of—'

'No really, I'm fine. I'll best be off.'

34

Sylvie followed John up the stairs and into the hall where she helped him into his coat. She opened the front door and stood on tiptoes to kiss him goodbye, squeezing his hand reassuringly. She was well aware John wasn't used to surprises. John didn't like surprises. He had coasted through life with most things going according to plan – *his* plan. Their life together had revolved around following through with John's plans. It had worked so far, but now all that was about to change at the wrong time of their lives – for John at any rate.

For John to get through this, Sylvie realised he had to face the fact that he wasn't getting any younger. One way or another, these changes – whether they were today, tomorrow, next month, or in five years' time – were not going to go away, no matter how much John wanted them to. Perhaps when he accepted the inevitable, then this would prove to be just the beginning of a new chapter in their lives together, and hopefully the start of something better for the both of them. He just couldn't see it yet.

Sylvie tried to keep that thought in mind as she stood at the door watching John slowly walk down the garden path. He looked like a man who had lost everything. Sylvie shook her head and closed the front door.

She was standing in the hall staring into space, wondering what she was going to do with the rest of her afternoon, when her eyes settled on John's briefcase on the sideboard.

Sylvie scooped it up, opened the front door, and ran down the steps and along the path to the gate. She spotted John only a short distance away ambling along the street as though he had nowhere to be. Sylvie called out, 'John!' She watched him turn around. 'Darling, you've forgotten something.' Sylvie held his briefcase aloft.

John trudged back to the house and looked at the briefcase in Sylvie's hand. He offered Sylvie a tight smile as she handed it to him. He was beginning to realise that not telling Sylvie the whole story was probably a bad idea.

'Are you sure you've got everything?'

'Yes, dear.'

'Good.' She took in his grim expression. 'Let's not forget that although you've had some bad news today, it is not the end of the world.'

'But what on earth am I going to do when—'

Sylvie held up a finger to his lips. She knew what he was about to ask: what on earth was he going to do with himself when he retired? Ignoring John's question, Sylvie said, 'At least there are no more surprises, heh?'

He watched Sylvie walk back to the house. She turned around and gave him a jolly wave before closing the front door.

John stood at the garden gate debating whether to tell Sylvie that as of today he might as well toss the briefcase in the bin for all the use it was to him now. His job was gone. His professional life was over. On top of which, John was already at a loss as to what to do with himself, and that was just for a few hours this afternoon. What about tomorrow, and the next day, and the day after that? However, he couldn't tell Sylvie he was really on gardening leave. What was it she had just said? "No more surprises."

He realised he had made his bed and for the next four weeks he had to get on with it. John reminded himself that he was doing it for Sylvie. She needed some time to acclimatize to the fact that very soon her husband would be at home all day. Perhaps John needed that too. He shuddered at the thought. He honestly couldn't imagine what he was going to do all day without a job. John brushed that thought aside. Right now he had more pressing concerns. How was he going to make sure he didn't bump into Sylvie this afternoon when she thought he was at work?

John ambled down the street wondering what Sylvie would normally do on a Wednesday afternoon. He didn't have a clue. In hindsight, John wished he had taken more of an interest in how Sylvie spent her time. He mentally ticked off all those places he thought Sylvie might go, like her favourite bookshop called Foyles on Charing Cross Road. Or perhaps she visited the little café in Baker Street opposite the Sherlock Holmes museum. It was where they used to take the girls for tea and a bun before walking into Regent's Park to feed the ducks.

Sylvie was also rather fond of window shopping in Camden Town, which was another possibility. John thought she might pick up some groceries to cook him a special meal tonight to cheer him up, even though she didn't usually go grocery shopping midweek.

All these places that Sylvie might frequent were, incidentally, all the places John could think of that would be perfect to spend an afternoon. Another idea popped into John's head: what about the London museums? They were huge. Surely he could go to South Kensington and look around the Natural History Museum or the Science Museum without bumping into Sylvie?

John thought he had a plan until he mulled it over some more and factored in Sod's law. What if that's how Sylvie decided to spend her afternoon and she spotted him wandering around the exhibits? No matter how unlikely that scenario was, it just wasn't worth the risk. John realised that trying to avoid his wife was going to prove far more difficult than he thought. Although there was one place in London John could go that he knew, without a shadow of a doubt, he would not bump into his wife.

John stood on the platform of Holland Park Tube Station smiling to himself as he watched the train hurtle out of the tunnel towards the station. Sylvie had spent her entire life living and working in London, but she refused to use the tube. There wasn't any significant reason for this; she didn't like being underground even if it was quicker and more convenient to get from A to B. Sylvie preferred to be outside, sitting on the top deck of a bus, seeing the sky. She told him this once, many years ago when they first met. It's just the way she was. John was going to use this knowledge to his advantage.

John randomly picked a platform on the Central Line.

Within minutes he was sitting in a crowded carriage, his briefcase resting on his lap, heading in the direction of Notting Hill Gate. He looked at his watch. It was only two o'clock. John didn't usually arrive home from work before six.

John stared at the large tube map stuck on the wall inside the carriage before turning his attention on the hordes of people entering and exiting at the next tube station. John wished that he had somewhere to be, a destination in mind; he'd never been without one until today. His boss had seen to that. He had no job and no five-year plan. It had all gone in one morning and now here he was spending the afternoon on the tube, hiding from his wife because he thought it was a good idea not to tell her he was on gardening leave.

When John's knees began to ache from sitting in the same position for too long, he exited the tube at Oxford Circus. He looked at his watch in surprise; only fifteen minutes had passed.

John walked to another platform to stretch his legs and waste more time. He had a feeling this was going to be a long afternoon. At least he could hang around the house when Sylvie was at work. However, Sylvie only worked part-time, and for the next two days she was not at work. John couldn't imagine doing all this again tomorrow. He would just have to find out what Sylvie was planning to do with her days off so that he could plan his.

Now that was a plan, thought John as he boarded another tube – destination unknown.

5

Sylvie did not go to Camden Town to look around the shops that afternoon or buy groceries to cook something special for their evening meal. What was there to celebrate? John had already broached the very subject Sylvie was afraid of: what was he going to do all day with no job, no interests and no hobbies outside of work?

Just when Sylvie was starting to think about herself for a change and all the things she might want to do when she left her job, she found herself preoccupied with John instead. So that afternoon, rather than go shopping, Sylvie sat down with her little notepad, turned to a fresh page and wrote another list.

She came up with an array of possibilities to fill John's time and even added some things they might do together. Sylvie remembered when they first started going out together, before they married, John used to take her to a dance at the local community hall. Sylvie rather fancied dancing again. What she had in mind was something old-fashioned and romantic like dancing with a partner, with John.

In the past, she had suggested they do things together like they used to when they were young, but John always came up with excuses. He was always too busy with his job or renovating the house. John could have found the time if he really wanted to, thought Sylvie shaking her head.

Sylvie put her pen down and looked at the list. She then tore out the piece of paper from the notepad and ripped it in half. What was the point? There was nothing wrong with what she had written down. The list wasn't the problem. John was the problem. Unless John changed, unless he surprised her by showing a modicum of interest in taking up some hobbies or, heaven forbid, doing something together, the list was a pointless exercise.

Sylvie flipped the page and turned back to her own list. She had already ticked off the first thing on her life-changing to-do list which was leaving her job. Perhaps she should tear up that page too. After all, it hadn't exactly got off to a good start with John's surprise visit home at lunchtime to tell her his news. In fact, it just made her feel anxious about what other unwelcome surprises might be lying in wait.

After an exhausting three hours travelling around the London underground, John couldn't stand it any longer and exited the tube two stops before Holland Park. He walked the rest of the way home wondering if that little exercise had put him off travelling on the London underground for life.

'You're early,' observed Sylvie as soon as John walked through the door.

'I didn't see the point of hanging around any longer.'

Sylvie took that as a reference to work. She could empathise. 'I have been doing the same thing since I started working my notice, leaving dead on time. Good for you,' said Sylvie and she meant it. Maybe this was a sign that John was letting go.

'Did you have a nice afternoon?' said John conversationally as he put his briefcase on the floor in the hall and slipped off his shoes.

'Yes, quite nice, thank you for asking,' Sylvie replied with a smile. She was pleased to discover that John wasn't completely preoccupied with his own situation that he couldn't ask her about her afternoon. Once again Sylvie thought that was a good sign.

John felt dog-tired. It was exhausting hanging around doing nothing all afternoon. John headed straight for the lounge feeling the floor swimming under his feet as though he had just got off a long boat ride. He was about to slump on the sofa when he caught sight of that box on the shelf in the alcove by the fireplace. He walked around the coffee table and sat down on the other sofa with his back to that box, so he didn't have to be reminded of Sylvie's mother.

'Did you go anywhere in particular?' asked John, interested to find out how Sylvie had spent her afternoon, and rather anxious to know that he had not wasted three hours of his life on the tube for nothing.

'Nope, I didn't end up going anywhere,' replied Sylvie, standing in the lounge doorway. 'I stayed at home for the afternoon.'

'What?' John looked at her in bewilderment. 'Are you telling me you didn't go out at all?'

Sylvie shrugged. 'It's no big deal.' Little realising it was a big deal for John. 'Now, would you like me to cook some dinner?'

John nodded his head vigorously. He was famished.

An hour later they were sitting in silence at the dining-room table busy eating large platefuls of spaghetti bolognese. Sylvie always liked Italian food. She never skimped on the rich sauces or the Parmesan cheese topping, which probably explained why Sylvie and John had always carried around a few extra pounds than was good for them.

'What are your plans for tomorrow?'

Sylvie was just about to pop a forkful of spaghetti in her mouth when John's question took her by surprise. He never asked how she spent her time. In fact, he never showed the slightest bit of interest in what she did or where she went. This was new. Sylvie put her fork down and smiled across the table at John. 'Tomorrow is Thursday, and I always do the weekly shop on a Thursday.'

'Of course you do,' said John. When he came home from work on a Thursday, the kitchen cupboards were always stocked up with groceries.

Sylvie's weekly shopping expedition to the supermarket was one of the rare occasions when one of them took the car out for a spin. If John was honest with himself, he should have got rid of it years ago. They really didn't need a car living in the heart of London. However, John was too attached to that car to let it go. It had been part of John's original plan: along with buying a house, John wanted a car. He had always dreamed of owning a Reliant Scimitar. It was a second-hand car when he bought it, and now ridiculously old, but once a week that old car roared to life and never once let them down on its weekly outing to the supermarket.

John recalled that one time his car was nearly made redundant when Sylvie tried grocery shopping online. That didn't last long because she got fed up with finding items in her virtual shopping trolley that weren't on her grocery list.

John really should have owned up at the time. He kept sneaking on to the computer and adding things he fancied when Sylvie wasn't looking, foolishly thinking she wouldn't notice. Eventually, Sylvie had had enough, calling online shopping a scam. She believed the store was adding things to her shopping cart without her knowledge.

'Did they honestly think I wouldn't notice?' John recollected Sylvie remarking crossly one day.

John had kept quiet, and Sylvie resumed doing the weekly shop the old-fashioned way. The unexpected upshot was that John's car got a reprieve from ending up in the scrapyard.

'So where exactly do you go shopping?' asked John, with a mouthful of spaghetti.

'You want to know where I do the weekly shop?'

'Yep,' replied John innocently. 'Perhaps . . .' He stalled trying to think of what to say next. He wanted to know where she went shopping to get some idea how long she would be out of the house.

'Perhaps . . .' Sylvie prompted.

'Perhaps I could . . . er help you with the shopping? We could um . . . do it together when I'm no longer at work.' John felt like kicking himself for making that suggestion. He couldn't think of a more boring way to spend his free time, apart from travelling around on the London Underground all afternoon. That would definitely come top of the list.

'Are you saying you want to do things with *me*?'

'Yes – why not,' John said off-hand, shrugging his shoulders and tucking into more of his meal.

Sylvie looked at him in astonishment. She wished she hadn't been so quick to tear up that list she had written earlier with her ideas for what John could do in retirement, especially all the things she thought they would like to do together.

John sprinkled some more Parmesan cheese on his spaghetti bolognese and glanced at Sylvie. 'So, are you going to tell me all about the day you have planned tomorrow?'

Sylvie quickly finished her meal, pushed the plate to one side, and told John how she usually spent her Thursdays. He seemed so attentive that Sylvie went on to tell him about her other day off too. 'On Fridays, I meet the girls.'

'The girls?'

'Yes, my small circle of friends. We usually meet up in the morning and—'

'What time exactly?' interrupted John, forgetting himself.

Sylvie let out a little laugh. 'Why John, what's with all the questions?' But Sylvie wasn't annoyed by his question, not at all. On the contrary, she was enjoying herself immensely sitting at the dinner table talking to her husband, who was suddenly, inexplicably interested in her day, interested in her.

Had somebody switched him at work and sent back a new and improved John? Sylvie studied him intently. Was this how it was going to be when he retired? Was John really going to pay attention to her for a change? This was not what Sylvie had anticipated. It had certainly taken her by surprise but in a good way. It made Sylvie wonder whether John's early retirement wasn't going to turn out half as bad as she first thought.

Sylvie felt like pinching herself in case she was dreaming. Instead, she leaned forward and said, 'Well, if you really want to know all the details about my day . . . '

'Of course I do.'

Sylvie met her friends every Friday morning for coffee. It

had become a weekly ritual over the years. Their conversation usually revolved around their jobs, their home lives and their children, just as it had when they first met at the school gate in their twenties. All their children were grown up now. Two years ago Sylvie was the last one of her circle of friends to become a grandparent, news she remembered she couldn't wait to share with them. Sylvie didn't feel quite so eager to share the news of John's impending retirement.

It's not that she didn't want to tell them because she feared they would feel sorry for her. On the contrary, she knew they would eagerly congratulate them on their retirement, under the misapprehension that it meant Sylvie would be jetting off on holidays with her husband whenever they fancied and spending time together. Isn't that what retired couples do?

None of their husbands were retired yet. She wouldn't be at all surprised if they even admitted to feeling a bit envious. And it wasn't as though Sylvie and John had the responsibility of looking after their grandchild to curtail their newfound freedom. On paper, they were free to spend their time enjoying retirement together – at least that's what her friends would think.

The problem was, although her friends had met John, they didn't really know John. They didn't know he wasn't the retiring type. However, sitting up the dinner table that evening with the conversation taking an unexpected turn, even Sylvie was beginning to wonder just how well she knew her own husband. He had certainly surprised her by showing an interest in what she was doing and where she was going; this wasn't the John she was used to. It pleased Sylvie no end because it started to dispel her fears about John's impending retirement.

'Where do you meet your friends for coffee?'

'We normally meet up at Convent Garden,' Sylvie replied.

As Sylvie was giving him all the details, John made a mental note just in case he fancied nipping out for coffee himself on Friday morning. He now knew where *not* to go if he wanted to avoid Sylvie and her pals. John still had no idea how he was going to spend the next couple of days until the weekend, but he had no intention of spending another minute wasting his time on the London underground.

6

John kept up appearances by ostensibly leaving for work the next morning. Loitering up a side street, he doubled back as soon as he spied Sylvie leaving in the car to go shopping. John spent the morning hanging around the house at a total loss as to what to do with himself. As he wandered from room to room feeling bored and looking for something to do to pass the time, he couldn't help but notice the house looked like a train wreck. He had no idea Sylvie left the place in such a mess when he was out.

The first things he found were her dirty breakfast dishes on the kitchen table. John scratched his head wondering why she hadn't bothered to wash them up or load the dishwasher before she went shopping. John would never leave dirty dishes lying around. Even when he was working long hours in his job, John didn't expect his wife to run around clearing up after him.

He always washed up his breakfast dishes before he left for work in the morning. He always put his dirty laundry in the linen bin; John never left it strewn around the bedroom floor as Sylvie evidently did. And the bed was unmade, which John soon discovered when he meandered upstairs. He wished he hadn't ventured into their bedroom and seen the state Sylvie had left the en-suite bathroom in. He didn't expect to be clearing up after Sylvie. John resisted the urge to do just that, reminding himself that Sylvie wasn't aware he was at home right now.

From what he'd seen, it was obvious she must do a quick whip around to tidy up before he returned home from work. Evidently, it didn't bother her to walk out and leave the house looking like a pigsty. John always liked to see the house neat and shipshape; he assumed Sylvie felt the same way. John stood in the bedroom doorway shaking his head in disbelief. He didn't realise she was so disorganised and untidy. If this was what she was really like when he wasn't around, it was beginning to make John wonder how well he knew his wife.

He walked downstairs into the lounge to find yesterday's newspaper had been leafed through and left dishevelled on the coffee table. John frowned. He remembered leaving it neatly folded in the wicker basket beside his favourite chair. His eyes drifted to the sofa. The scatter cushions had not been puffed up and straightened, and Sylvie had failed to vacuum the carpet; John could still see biscuit crumbs where Sylvie was sitting last night.

John caught himself involuntarily folding the newspaper neatly in two before he realised what he was doing. He put the newspaper back where he found it and retreated to the study at the back of the house, closing the door out of harm's way.

John sat down in the swivel office chair behind his desk. He leaned back with his hands behind his head and stared vacantly out of the study window. He watched the branches of the old elm tree in the back garden gently swaying in the wind as he mentally calculated how long he had until Sylvie returned from her shopping trip. He could hear the clock ticking on the wall behind him. John had never known the house to be this quiet because he was rarely home alone.

He spent the next few minutes tidying his desk, fondly recalling many a happy hour sat right here making plans: plans for this house, plans for his career and plans for their future. Suddenly a wave of sadness engulfed him. For the first time in his adult life, he had no job and no plans for the future.

John suddenly swivelled around in his chair and glanced at the clock on the wall. He had lost track of time. He knew he had to start thinking about how he was going to spend the afternoon when Sylvie returned home from shopping, but the thought of wasting more time pointlessly hanging around doing nothing filled him with dread.

That evening he was less communicative at the dinner table. John had not enjoyed his day. He didn't know where to go to fill what felt like an interminable afternoon. Unfortunately, the reality of his situation had finally hit home; this was just the first of many days stretching out in front of him with nothing to do but sit at home and vegetate.

John listened in silence as Sylvie recounted her day. She sounded as though she'd had a much better time.

At John's prompting, Sylvie once again went over her plans for the following day – in detail. John not only wanted to know where she was going so he could avoid crossing paths with Sylvie, but he was also tapping her for ideas regarding how to spend his free time. John decided he would follow her lead and plan his day in a similar fashion.

Unlike Sylvie, who was meeting her small circle of friends

for coffee, John didn't have any close friends he could call on to spend a morning with. That wouldn't stop him paying a visit the local café on his own to break up the tedium. He knew exactly where Sylvie would be tomorrow morning, so as long as he avoided Convent Garden, nothing could go wrong with his plan.

John left the house the next day, on the pretext of going to work, with a newspaper tucked out of sight in his briefcase. He headed straight for the local coffee shop intending to have more than just a cup of coffee. John was starving. He noticed his appetite had increased since losing his job and had a pretty good idea why – it was boredom. That didn't stop him ordering a full English cooked breakfast as soon as he arrived, even though he had already eaten cereal and toast at home.

John's mouth watered as he sat in the café anticipating his second breakfast that morning. To keep himself occupied while he waited for the food to arrive, John opened his briefcase and retrieved his newspaper. He placed the empty briefcase on the floor by his chair and started to read, trying his utmost not to think about the tempting cakes and pastries on the counter right in his line of vision.

Sylvie was heading out the door to catch the bus when the phone rang. She did an about-turn and reached for the phone. It was one of her friends sounding relieved that Sylvie hadn't left yet, which was just as well because they weren't meeting in Convent Garden as planned. This happened from time to time, but it wasn't normally at such short notice.

It turned out that her friends were having trouble with the tube this morning because the Piccadilly line to Convent Garden had been temporarily closed. They wanted to know whether they could all meet up at Sylvie's local coffee shop instead as it was easier for them to get to.

Sylvie avoided a smart remark that they should have taken the bus to Convent Garden, but she did say she had no problem with the change of venue. It saved her a bus ride. The café was only a short walk from her house.

Paul was their local branch of the lovely French café chain found across London. Sylvie adored their coffee, and they had the best pastries and éclairs Sylvie had ever tasted. It was also very convenient for her friends travelling by tube because the coffee shop was virtually next door to Holland Park tube station. The only thing Sylvie was concerned about was whether the place would be too crowded to seat the four of them at a table. The coffee shop was quite small and it might be a squeeze. Sylvie decided to set off straight away to secure a table.

As soon as Sylvie arrived, she glanced through the window hoping she wasn't too late to get a table. She knew it was popular. Not surprisingly it was already filling up with customers. Sylvie stepped inside and noted a young couple sitting at a table for two by the window, a large party of mothers and toddlers in the corner on the left, and a single gentleman – his face obscured by the newspaper he was reading – seated at the far end of the café opposite the pastry counter.

Sylvie hurried over to the nearest table just inside the door. It was a table for two, but she was sure they could manage. The staff helpfully provided an extra couple of chairs. Sylvie sat down and stared out the window watching the world go by. She was trying not to think about those tempting chocolate éclairs that were usually on the pastry counter. Sylvie willed herself not to turn around and take a look otherwise she might be tempted. She hadn't long had breakfast with John.

The waitress appeared. Sylvie ordered a large cafetière of coffee while she waited.

It wasn't long before her three friends arrived. They greeted one another with affectionate hugs before sitting down at the table. By this time the café was full, a low murmur of conversation filled the room. Sylvie looked around the table at her friends and thought she might tell them the news about John's retirement after all.

She was about to make the announcement when one of her friends pointed across the crowded café, and said, 'Sylvie, isn't that your husband?'

'No, I'm afraid you must be mistaken,' replied Sylvie, not even bothering to turn around and look in the direction her friend was pointing. She poured herself another cup of coffee from the cafetière. 'John's at work today,' Sylvie added offhand.

'Really?' She gave Sylvie a sideways glance. 'I'm pretty sure that's him.'

Sylvie was pretty sure it wasn't. All the same, she turned in her seat and looked into the crowded room, curious to see who bore a striking resemblance to her husband.

At first, she didn't see a familiar face, but she spied a familiar briefcase sitting on the floor beside a table. Sylvie raised her eyes from the briefcase to look at the gentleman who had been sitting in the corner behind a newspaper when she first arrived.

He raised his hand requesting the bill.

Sylvie did a double take as her friend said, 'It *is* him!' And before Sylvie could stop her, she stood up and waved her hand in the air calling out, 'John!'

John had just requested the bill when he could have sworn he heard somebody call his name. John scanned the room and saw a woman he didn't recognise waving at him theatrically from across the crowded café.

'I was right,' she said to Sylvie triumphantly when he turned to look in their direction. 'I thought I recognised him. You know me, I never forget a face.'

John thought it was a case of mistaken identity until he glanced at the woman sitting next to her and recognised a familiar face scowling back at him.

John froze.

He had listened to Sylvie intently over dinner last night, and he was sure Sylvie and her friends were meeting up in Convent Garden this morning. What in hell were they doing here?

What in heavens name was he doing here thought Sylvie, as she watched him pay his bill?

Sylvie continued to watch him avidly as he approached their table. He could hardly avoid them as they were seated at a table adjacent to the door.

One of Sylvie's friends reached over and touched her arm to get her attention. 'John's been made redundant, hasn't he.'

'Early retirement,' confessed Sylvie.

'I knew it!' She shook her head solemnly. Her husband worked for a rival firm and predicted there would be job cuts. 'If it's any consolation, Sylvie, it happened to one of my husband's colleagues. He was offered redundancy or early retirement and opted for early retirement. Good for them if they can get it. Why hang on until the bitter end if you can afford to go early and enjoy more time together?' She squeezed Sylvie's hand making her feel guilty for even thinking of not telling them.

'So how is he enjoying gardening leave?'

Sylvie looked at her perplexed. 'Pardon me?'

'You do know what gardening leave is?'

Of course Sylvie knew what gardening leave was; she didn't know what that had to do with John.

'I think it's very distrustful of them to do that, don't you?' Sylvie's friend added, 'My husband's colleague went through the same experience. They wouldn't dream of letting him near the office once he had signed the paperwork, so they escorted him right out of the building that very same day, never to return. He was home by lunchtime.'

'Is that a fact,' said Sylvie flatly, turning her attention back to John.

As John approached the table, they both said in unison, 'What are you doing here?'

Sylvie folded her arms and looked up at John hovering in front of her. He looked surprised to see her. Sylvie narrowed her eyes waiting to hear it straight from the horse's mouth.

Sylvie's friend stepped into the uncomfortable silence. 'Why don't you join us?' She got up to fetch another chair.

John looked at Sylvie. 'No, I don't think—'

'Yes, please do,' said Sylvie indicating the chair next to her and smiling sweetly at him.

John offered Sylvie a tentative smile, still unsure how he was going to explain what he was doing here. Then he remembered the briefcase in his hand. He held it up. 'I'd really love to stay,' he lied, 'but I ought to get going. I . . . I've got to . . . um . . . get back to work.'

Sylvie caught one of her friends staring at him sadly. Sylvie shifted her attention back to John and patted the seat of the

55

chair beside her. 'Take a seat, John. We want to hear all about your day, don't we girls.' Sylvie added, 'On *gardening leave.*'

John's smile faded the second he heard those two words. He slumped down in the chair clutching his briefcase to his chest, facing three smiling women who were quite happy to see him. And one that clearly wasn't.

7

'I can't believe you didn't tell me!' Sylvie was standing in the kitchen staring at John, waiting for an explanation.

John shrugged. 'I thought that if I told you I was going to be at home all day from now on, it would make things worse.' John turned around and opened the fridge door to look inside; he was already thinking about lunch.

Sylvie put her hands on her hips. 'And by not telling me, it made things better – how?'

John couldn't answer that. Instead, he reached inside the fridge and found a slab of cheese, a packet of ham, some limp lettuce, a big juicy vine-ripened tomato and a large tub of mayonnaise.

'And another thing,' said Sylvie to his back, 'all this business about wanting to know what I was doing, where I was going.' She paused to take a breath. 'That wasn't because you were interested in my day. It wasn't because you were interested in me – was it? It was because you wanted to make sure you didn't bump into me when you were pretending to be at work.' Sylvie's voice was getting louder. 'In case I found out about your little charade.' Sylvie stamped her foot like a petulant child.

John glanced over his shoulder. She was preparing to lift off, he could tell.

John thought back to the beginning of the week when he told Sylvie he had lost his job. She had been very understanding and quite empathetic under the circumstances. And she had not made a point of the fact that John should have told her what was going on at work a lot sooner, so at least she would have been forewarned. On the contrary, she had overlooked all that and simply been supportive. He should have told her everything. Instead, like the fool he was, John assumed he was doing the right thing by not telling Sylvie he was on gardening leave. Now it had backfired, Sylvie was on the warpath.

John was busying himself in the kitchen avoiding her gaze.

'Well? Haven't you got anything to say?'

John turned around, his arms laden with the makings of a monster ploughman's lunch. 'Would you like a sandwich?'

'Would I like a sandwich?' Sylvie gaped at him. 'Is that all you have to say?'

'Well, I'm hungry, and I thought as I was making myself one, you might want one too?'

Sylvie threw her arms in the air in frustration. 'No, I do not want a bloody sandwich!' She turned around and marched up to the french doors, opened them, and stormed out.

Five minutes later Sylvie was furiously digging up some weeds in the back garden. Kneeling on the damp grass, Sylvie didn't notice the morning dew leaving a wet patch on the knees of her trousers. All that was on her mind was next week. It was her last week at work and she was starting to feel she had made a terrible mistake leaving her job. She knew it wasn't going to work with both of them at home all day together.

Sylvie felt the damp ground beneath her soaking through her trousers. She stood up and looked around the garden. Her eyes settled on the large elm tree that shielded their house from the neighbouring property whose garden backed on to theirs. It was the only feature of their garden that had not changed over the years. As for the rest, Sylvie remembered when they moved in, and you couldn't see the garden for the overgrown weeds almost as tall as the first storey of the house.

When they cut it back, they found all manner of assorted junk, from a clapped-out rusting tumble drier to a child's bike beyond repair. There was even a pile of car tyres in the exact spot Sylvie had been digging.

It wasn't a large back garden by any means, but it had been Sylvie's project to transform the garden after she had cajoled John into letting her have free rein outside. She didn't get a look-in with the rest of the house because John had insisted on choosing everything, right down to the fixtures and fittings, and the colour scheme throughout the house.

Sylvie didn't even get to decide on the new kitchen that was installed in the basement. John had already gone ahead and ordered the kitchen units he wanted. This had infuriated her not least because she was the one who would be spending the most time in the kitchen. It turned out that the back garden was the only place left through which Sylvie could put her own stamp on the house. Sylvie thought she had done a splendid job. She adored her garden, fondly referring to it as a cottage garden. Sylvie loved flowers. Her garden was so full of them that to the untrained eye it looked like a wild garden.

John did not share her enthusiasm. He would have preferred a neat square lawn with small planting borders and a large patio outside the kitchen french doors on which to sit and look out over the lawn on lazy summer afternoons. When it came to her ideas for the garden, they disagreed on everything. John even wanted to get rid of the proud old elm tree at the bottom of the garden that Sylvie was so fond of. Sylvie wouldn't hear of it. She did not want to lose that beautiful tree. Although she doubted John could do anything about it because she imagined the tree was protected by a tree preservation order.

She remembered John smugly telling her that if the tree had already come down, what could the local council do about it? Sylvie was so furious over that remark that she had gone straight to the local planning office and discovered she was absolutely right: there was a tree preservation order. She walked home with the paperwork that afternoon, put it in a plastic wallet and attached it to the tree. It served as a warning to anybody who came near it, including John, that there would be big trouble if they so much as breathed on that tree. Short of felling it himself, nobody was going to risk a hefty fine to do the job. Consequently, Sylvie kept her elm tree. Ignoring John's wishes for a lawn, she went ahead with her own vision for the garden, growing an abundance of plants and shrubs instead.

A narrow cobbled path now wound its way up the garden in between a huge variety of established plants and flowers – some even taller than John – an array of colours and fragrances bombarding the senses, making for an impressive display.

John was always complaining that the garden was not in keeping with the style of the house. Sylvie knew that, but she didn't care. From the start, her project wasn't about the house, and it wasn't about John. This garden was for Sylvie and her alone; it was about what she wanted. All these years later she still couldn't understand why John didn't get that.

Sylvie did make one small concession for John. She gave him a paved patio outside the french doors, with a set of four garden chairs, a matching table and umbrella. For herself, she wanted a small cobbled patio to match the garden path at the other end of the garden. Here she placed a long wooden garden bench. Sylvie imagined they would sit on that bench together in the shade of the elm tree on a hot summer's day and look out on the garden she had nurtured over the years, just as John had nurtured the house. But if memory served, John had never once sat with her on that bench.

He preferred his comfortable cushioned reclining garden chairs on the patio just outside the kitchen door because it was much more convenient to nip into the kitchen and get a drink or a bite to eat. Sylvie preferred her bench at the back of the garden where it was more peaceful. She could barely hear the cars going by at the front of the house, or John's radio tuned into Classic FM coming from the kitchen.

Over the years, Sylvie often found herself in the garden late on a summer's evening. She would sit on her bench, lost in a book, oblivious to dusk fast approaching until she could barely see the page in front of her. It was her favourite spot.

Sylvie stared wistfully at the damp bench littered with autumn leaves. Unfortunately, it wasn't summer and storm clouds were gathering, the sky turning dark with the promise of rain. Sylvie quickly gathered up her gardening tools and returned them to the shed. When she closed the shed door, she noticed some flaking paint. Sylvie made a mental note to paint the shed come spring; perhaps a different colour this time.

John always called it the beach hut. He was being sarcastic because he didn't like the fact that Sylvie had chosen to paint the shed at all, let alone paint it pastel blue. Henceforth, John had called it the beach hut. He was right: it did look like a beach hut, but that didn't mean she liked the colour any less. Sylvie closed the shed door and smiled. As always, just stepping out into her garden acted like a tonic. It was an oasis from life's ups and downs that always lifted her spirits.

Sylvie locked the shed and turned towards the house. As she made her way down the narrow cobbled path her smile faded the minute she saw John sitting in the kitchen still eating. Sylvie heaved a sigh. Unfortunately, she didn't feel any better about the start of another week with the prospect of John at home all day.

John was not looking forward to the reception when Sylvie finished gardening and came back inside. She didn't usually do a lot of gardening this time of year. John glanced at the clock on the kitchen wall. She had been out in the garden an awfully long time, which meant only one thing: he was definitely not in her good books. John decided he'd better keep a low profile.

As soon as John saw her walking down the garden path, he quickly polished off the remains of his triple sandwich and got up from the table.

Sylvie opened the french doors and walked into the kitchen as John was loading the dishwasher. Out of the corner of his eye, John saw Sylvie walk straight past him and up the stairs. Sylvie was ignoring him, he could tell.

John did his best to stay out of her way for the rest of the day. He tiptoed around her and left it until much later in the evening, after they had hardly exchanged a word over dinner, to offer to make her a cup of tea.

Sylvie declined the tea; that was always a bad sign.

John made her a cup anyway, deposited it on the coffee table in the lounge, and said in a small voice, 'I'm off to bed.' He hovered for a moment and risked a quick peck on Sylvie's cheek with another lame apology. 'Sorry,' he whispered in her ear before disappearing upstairs with his mug of tea.

By ten o'clock John closed the book he was reading. He put his reading glasses and the book on the bedside table, and leaned over to switch off the table lamp. He left Sylvie's bedside table lamp on and the duvet pulled down her side. John lay down, pulled the duvet up to his chin and stared at the ceiling.

John dozed off and was woken by the sound of the creaky floorboard outside their bedroom door. He opened one eye and saw Sylvie creeping into the bedroom and slowly closing the door behind her. She must have seen him lying there under the duvet and thought he was asleep. He closed his eyes and heard Sylvie walk into the en-suite bathroom and shut the door.

A short time later John felt the movement of the mattress as Sylvie climbed into bed next to him. The next thing he heard was the click of the bedside table lamp on her side. He opened his eyes in darkness. Before she came to bed he had visions of Sylvie moving into the spare bedroom. John smiled in relief. He turned over in bed and went back to sleep.

In the morning, Sylvie got out of bed to make the first cup of tea of the day like she normally did. She could tell by the look on John's face that he was surprised when she handed him his morning cuppa, considering yesterday.

John eagerly took the tea and watched her climb back into bed. He kept glancing her way as he drank his tea. She seemed a bit subdued. He wondered what she was thinking . . .

Sylvie sat in silence drinking her tea thinking back to the events of a fortnight ago. Was it only the Sunday before last that she was already up looking forward to visiting her mother until she got that phone call informing her she had passed away? Sylvie couldn't believe that in just two weeks she had been to her mother's funeral, attended the reading of the will, given up her job, and told her best friend, Julia, that she wished something would happen to put her planned visit to Cornwall, to scatter her mother's ashes, on hold.

Julia had warned her not to say things like that. Sylvie, not superstitious by nature, now wished she could take that back because since then John had lost his job and, to add insult to injury, he had been put on gardening leave. Sylvie didn't even have a few precious weeks without him under her feet to acclimatize to their new situation. It wasn't John's fault he had lost his job, but she would have preferred it if he had told her about the gardening leave and not embarrassed her yesterday in front of her friends.

She finished her tea and got out of bed. 'What would you like for breakfast?'

John stared at her for a long moment before replying, 'I don't mind, whatever you're having.'

Sylvie looked at him quizzically. 'You don't like porridge, or toast and Marmite.'

That was very true. 'Anything other than—'

Sylvie groaned loudly. She knew what he was up to. 'John, you don't have to pussyfoot around me. Just tell me what you want for breakfast, and I'll go and prepare it.'

John did just that. He knew this was Sylvie's way of saying all is forgiven.

When Sylvie left the room, John put on his reading glasses and picked up the daily newspaper that Sylvie remembered to bring up with his cup of tea every morning. John opened the paper and then looked over the top of his reading glasses at the bedroom door. He was debating whether to break with routine, fold his newspaper away for later, and go downstairs to help Sylvie prepare breakfast. John thought about this for all of two seconds and then turned his attention back to his newspaper.

The weekend passed by as it normally did with Sylvie doing her thing and John doing his. They had settled back into their familiar routine, although both of them had Monday on their mind and the beginning of a new routine with John out of work. John was not looking forward to being at home all day, every day. He had already asked Sylvie several times what her plans were for the following week.

A few days ago Sylvie was delighted that John appeared to be taking such an interest in her. But that was before she found out what he was really up to, hiding the fact that he wasn't at work. Now his incessant questions were getting on her nerves.

He tried to palm it off by explaining that he was genuinely interested in how she spends her days off. Sylvie wasn't fooled this time. She knew there was more to it than that; she suspected John was fishing for ideas regarding what he could do with his free time.

As the weekend drew to a close, John became less talkative and more withdrawn, and Sylvie became more anxious about what lay ahead when she left her job in a weeks' time and they were both at home all day together.

65

8

Sylvie returned home from work on Monday evening to find John in surprisingly good spirits. This was not what she had been expecting. She was relieved and cautiously optimistic that John had turned a corner. On the other hand, she didn't expect John to have cleaned the house from top to bottom either. Sylvie found this a tad concerning, not because it was out of character – Sylvie knew her husband and knew how tidy he was – but because he had nearly cleaned the entire house in just two days.

Sylvie should have been grateful to return home to a tidy home and dinner on the table. Other husbands might have sat around all day and not bothered to lift a finger to do the washing up, hang out the laundry, sweep the front path, hoover, polish, and dust.

Not so John.

When Sylvie walked into the lounge, intending to slump on the sofa and put her feet up, she discovered the cushions were so neatly arranged that she was almost afraid to sit down. Casting her eye around the room, Sylvie shook her head in dismay. It was all so spotlessly clean that it was making her feel uncomfortable. But that wasn't the worst of it. Up the dinner table, she had barely finished her meal when John whisked her plate away and started loading the dishwasher. Within seconds of finishing her dessert, John was already wiping the table clean. Sylvie hadn't even risen from her seat.

When John got out the furniture polish – that was the last straw.

'What on earth are you doing now?' hissed Sylvie. She was exasperated by John's incessant cleaning.

John pointed at the table. 'There's a stain – right there. I thought I'd try some furniture polish.'

'Right now?' Sylvie glanced at the time. It was seven o'clock in the evening, and they had just finished dinner. She thought they might retire to the lounge upstairs with a glass of wine and watch the news, not get out the furniture polish and start polishing the kitchen table for heaven's sake.

John insisted, so Sylvie left him to it and retreated upstairs to watch the seven o'clock news.

As soon as she sat down with a wine glass in hand, and put her feet up on the sofa, John appeared at the door. Sylvie glanced over at him and rolled her eyes wearily. He had *that* look. That sheepish expression Sylvie recognised which said: *I had an idea, but I'm not sure you're going to like it.*

Sylvie's shoulders sagged as she watched John walk into the lounge carrying two large shopping bags. Sylvie wondered what on earth he'd been up to while she was at work.

John sat down opposite her with the bags. 'I had an idea.'

Sylvie put her wine glass down on the coffee table and looked at the shopping bags. She wasn't aware he had been shopping today; he hadn't mentioned it at dinner.

'What have you bought, John?' she asked impatiently.

'Ah, hang on a minute.' John bounced off the sofa and darted out of the room without answering Sylvie's question. He quickly returned carrying a box of coasters that Sylvie didn't even remember they had; he must have found them when he had been cleaning the house from top to bottom. Sylvie sighed as he got some out of the box and studiously distributed them around the coffee table, picking Sylvie's wine glass up and putting it down on one of the coasters.

Sylvie looked up at John and down at the coasters. All her fears about John being at home all day suddenly resurfaced like a ghastly premonition. Sylvie picked up her glass of wine and drunk it in three large gulps.

'I had an idea,' repeated John. He sat down opposite Sylvie and picked up one of the bags. 'It came to me when I was vacuuming the sofas this morning . . .'

Vacuuming the sofas? Sylvie hoped he was joking.

'I thought that perhaps we need some throws.' John opened the bag in front of him and got out a large beige throw, almost the same colour as the sofa. He held it up. 'It took a bit of time to find a good colour match.'

Sylvie's eyes glazed over.

John looked at Sylvie expectantly as if seeking her approval. When she didn't respond, he added, 'Perhaps we need to see it on the sofa, eh?' John stood up to unfold the throw and then placed it on the sofa in front of him. He spent several minutes arranging the throw, tucking it around each seat cushion, before he was finally satisfied. John stood back to survey his handiwork.

Sylvie watched him in silence.

John turned around. 'What do you think?'

Sylvie wasn't looking at the throw but staring fixedly at John.

She was beginning to wonder if he wasn't coping as well as she thought. She wanted to ask John if he had been offered any counselling over the sudden loss of his job.

'I thought it was a good idea to buy the throws because if we are going to put our feet on the sofa—'

Sylvie glanced down at her feet on the sofa and looked back at John.

'—then the throws are going to come in handy.' John opened the other bag and unpacked the second throw. He walked around the coffee table towards Sylvie with the throw. 'If you don't mind shifting off the sofa for a minute . . .'

Sylvie folded her arms.

'Or I could do it later . . . if you'd prefer.' John placed the throw on the arm of Sylvie's sofa by her feet.

Sylvie scratched her head, picked up the remote control and turned the volume up on the television. When Sylvie got up to visit the loo, she returned to find John had draped the throw on her sofa when she was out of the room.

He smiled at her with a twinkle in his eye as though he had just given her a nice surprise.

Sylvie did an about-turn and took herself off to bed.

The following day Sylvie needed to go shopping for groceries. It wasn't Thursday, her normal shopping day, but with John hanging around the house all day bored he was eating more, and it had not gone unnoticed. It was Sylvie's half day at work. She had returned home at lunchtime to discover there was nothing left for lunch. Sylvie promptly collected the car keys and told John she was going shopping.

John insisted on coming too.

'Fine,' said Sylvie, although it wasn't fine. She was used to getting things done without John tagging along, on top of the fact that Sylvie had a routine which John was already disrupting. Since when did she have to go shopping twice in one week? John was virtually eating them out of house and home. It was like having a ravenous teenager living at home.

Sylvie sighed and handed John the car keys. If he insisted on coming, he might as well be useful and drive her to the supermarket.

Sylvie locked the front door and waited for John to back the car out of the drive before climbing in beside him. She glanced at John as they set off in the car. This felt strange. They never went shopping together. But at least she would have an extra pair of hands to help her get the shopping done as quickly as possible. Sylvie did not particularly enjoy grocery shopping.

It had been her idea to shop online and have it delivered straight to their door. She thought it was the perfect solution to wasting two hours of her life each and every week traipsing up and down supermarket aisles. What a fiasco that turned out to be. The supermarket would not accept there was something wrong with their system. She had written a strongly worded letter telling them that they must cease and desist from adding items to peoples' shopping carts without their knowledge.

They had swiftly written a response denying this was the case and even had the cheek to suggest it was somebody in her household who was adding extra groceries to her shopping basket without her knowledge. Sylvie had written back and told them that it was a ridiculous suggestion since she no longer had children living at home who would do such a thing, there was only her husband. She never got a reply back. Sylvie was left with no choice but to resume her weekly shopping trips to the supermarket.

Sylvie checked her shopping list as John drove them to the supermarket. She debated whether to divide the list up between them so she could send John off on his own with a list, but decided against that idea on this occasion. Instead, she thought it would be a good idea to show John around the store first so he could familiarise himself with where things were.

'Good god!' exclaimed John as soon as they walked through the supermarket entrance with their shopping trolley. 'This store is mammoth.'

Sylvie gave him a sideways glance. As impossible as it sounds, apart from their smaller counterpart the city metro supermarket, John had not set foot in a proper full-size supermarket – ever.

Sylvie looked at her watch and set herself a target to walk out of the store in forty-five minutes. It was fifteen minutes less than she usually gave herself to do the shopping because this time Sylvie had help. She glanced down at her list and then took charge of the trolley, walking briskly through the shop.

John kept his hand glued to the side of the trolley, afraid that if he let go he might get lost, swallowed up down one of the huge supermarket aisles that seemed to stretch as far as the eye can see. John thought it was more like a cavernous warehouse than a shop.

A small boy, also holding on to the side of a shopping trolley, passed them by on the other side of an aisle and stared at John.

Sylvie stopped down one aisle to pick up the first thing on her list. She asked John to fetch a jar of pickle across the way. When she turned around, John was still standing in front of the pickle jars.

Sylvie steered the trolley over to John. 'Where's the jar of pickle I asked for?'

John turned to Sylvie, eyes wide, his hands empty. 'Isn't it amazing? I had no idea there were so many different varieties of pickle.' He pointed at the shelf stocking row after row of every pickle imaginable.

Sylvie tutted. 'Never mind that, you know the one we always have.' Sylvie reached straight for the jar and put it in her trolley. 'Now let's get a move on.'

But John didn't get a move on. Every time she asked him to go and fetch something, she would find him idly standing around reading labels, before sharing a useless piece of information like the salt content of one brand as opposed to another. Sylvie kept reminding him to stick to the one they usually buy, but all she got was a running commentary on the pros and cons of their normal brand as opposed to the competition.

Sylvie was getting tired of John's incessant yacking while she was trying to do the shopping. At this rate, they were going to be here all day.

At one point she couldn't stand it any longer. Abandoning John down aisle ten, Sylvie left him to get some gravy granules while she sped down several aisles picking up a good few items on her list, before returning to retrieve her husband.

He was still standing there in front of the gravy granules empty-handed.

She came to an abrupt halt and watched him pick up a jar and studiously study the label on the back. Sylvie groaned and went to fetch him.

'But I want this one,' whined John when Sylvie took it out of his hands and put it back on the shelf.

'I said *no!*' Honestly, thought Sylvie, it was like having a five-year-old child in tow. Although to be fair, she had seen children who were more help than him. At least they did as they were told. Sylvie had had enough. She left him standing with the trolley and went to pick the items off the supermarket shelves herself.

By the time they reached the check-out, Sylvie had glanced at her watch and discovered the shopping had taken almost twice as long with John's so-called help.

Never again.

Sylvie was busy loading the shopping on to the conveyor belt when she suddenly stopped and turned to John. 'What's this?' She held up a packet of chocolate digestive biscuits that she knew was not on her shopping list. 'And this?' Sylvie pointed at some Camembert cheese before searching through the shopping only to discover a number of other items that had mysteriously appeared in her shopping trolley. She turned to John, her arms laden with the offending items.

John looked at his feet and shrugged.

'Honestly!' Sylvie couldn't believe he had sneaked things into her shopping trolley when she wasn't looking. Sylvie glared at him before turning to the lady at the check-out. 'Excuse me, I'm so sorry but I don't want these items.'

John looked up sharply. 'Sylvie, I fancied that . . . and that.' He watched Sylvie hand over the items to the lady on the check-out, one at a time. 'Oh, can't I at least have those?' He snatched the packet of chocolate biscuits out of Sylvie's hand.

Sylvie put her hands on her hips and glared at her husband. 'John, give those back right now,' she said with a firm *this is your final warning* voice, a tone she hadn't used since the girls were small.

73

'But I want it!' whined John.

A young boy helping his mother pack groceries at the check-out next door stopped and stared wide-eyed at John.

Sylvie caught him staring and gave in. John was having a temper tantrum at the check-out. Sylvie was finding it all highly embarrassing. She turned to the check-out girl who was also staring at John. 'We'll take the biscuits.'

'Do you want these too?' she asked, holding up the other items and glancing furtively at John.

John was about to start whingeing again when Sylvie grabbed the items out of the girl's hand and threw them in with the other shopping. 'Yes, we'll take the lot,' replied Sylvie, trying to save herself further embarrassment. She glared at her husband.

John shut his mouth.

Sylvie opened a plastic carrier bag and started packing up the groceries, throwing John a disapproving look.

John gathered up the items that Sylvie had tried to confiscate and handed them to the check-out girl before Sylvie changed her mind.

She scanned them in, giving John a nervous smile.

Sylvie was furiously packing the shopping. As soon as an item was scanned, she was virtually snatching it out of the girl's hand. She knew it was incredibly rude but she couldn't wait to get out of the store.

John picked up a plastic carrier bag and carefully packed his own groceries in his own bag.

Sylvie scowled at him.

When the check-out girl rung up the total, Sylvie discovered it had not only taken much longer to do the shopping, but it had also cost a lot more too. She grudgingly handed over the cash.

Sylvie pushed the trolley out of the store with John trailing behind her carrying his own bag of goodies.

John kept lagging behind to look inside his plastic carrier bag like a child who had been bought a new toy and couldn't wait to get home and play with it.

Sylvie stopped the trolley abruptly and waited for John to catch up. 'Give me that!' She grabbed the bag out of John's hand and threw it on top of the other shopping bags in the trolley. Then she set off in the direction of the car at a brisk pace. Sylvie had already made up her mind this was her first and last shopping trip with John.

Things did not improve when they got home. All Sylvie wanted to do was leave the shopping bags piled on the kitchen table and make a cup of tea.

Never mind what Sylvie wanted, John insisted on unpacking the shopping and putting it away immediately.

Despite Sylvie protesting that she was quite capable of doing it herself, reminding him sarcastically that she has had plenty of practice over the last thirty-nine years of their marriage, John did not get the message. Sylvie gave up and left him to it while she put the kettle on.

Sylvie sat down at the kitchen table with a mug of tea and one of John's chocolate digestive biscuits, and watched John unpack the shopping.

While he was at it, he decided now was the time to rearrange the entire contents of the kitchen cupboards. He also gave Sylvie a running commentary on why it was infinitely preferable to have the cereal boxes in the kitchen cupboard over here and the tins in the cupboard over there, ad nauseam.

Sylvie rolled her eyes.

When John asked Sylvie to pass him the last bag of shopping and got no response, he turned around to discover his wife was no longer sitting at the kitchen table. He wondered how long he had been standing there unpacking the shopping talking to himself.

Sylvie had finished her cup of tea and wandered upstairs.

In no time at all John was at her heels again asking what happens next.

'What do you mean: what happens next?'

'Well, what are we going to do now?'

Sylvie opened her mouth with a sarcastic retort on the tip of her tongue and then sighed heavily. John was only trying to be helpful. Besides, she wasn't used to her husband being around during the weekday. That wasn't his fault.

Be nice, thought Sylvie. 'Well let me see . . .' Sylvie mused under John's intent gaze.

By the weekend, after two full days at home with John, Sylvie was done with playing nice. Sylvie had had enough of John insisting on doing everything together. Every time he asked her what *we* were doing next, Sylvie wanted to scream. That old adage came to mind: be careful what you wish for. Sylvie had wished they would do more things together because she thought she would enjoy spending time with her husband once he retired.

She couldn't have been more wrong.

All Sylvie felt was that she didn't have a minute to herself. They had suddenly gone from practically leading separate lives to being joined at the hip, and Sylvie was not enjoying it one bit. And she knew why. John had no hobbies. John had few friends.

He was at a complete loss as to what to do with himself. For some incomprehensible reason he was looking to Sylvie to tell him what to do. She was already sick and tired of it. And that was only after one week, two and half days of which Sylvie had been at work.

At least when he was out of the house at work all day, she could be herself. It didn't matter if she hadn't cleared the dishes away, or the newspaper she had idly leafed through was left dishevelled on the coffee table. Now he seemed to spend his day following her around, clearing up after her, and constantly asking what they were doing next. It was like having a whining dog at her heels.

That wasn't the only change she noticed. As the first week of John's retirement progressed so did his mood, from being in a positive frame of mind on Monday, to being moody, short-tempered and depressed by Friday. If this was what it was like at home with John now, what was it going to be like when she stopped work altogether? Sylvie couldn't imagine being around John all day, every day, without the refuge of her part-time job. Not only that, Sylvie didn't know how she was going to find the time to think about what she wanted to do with herself once she left work, if she had her husband under her feet all day, moping around and depressed? The answer was simple: it wasn't going to happen.

After a sleepless night tossing and turning, with all this weighing heavy on her mind, Sylvie woke up the next morning to her last day at work knowing exactly what she had to do.

9

Sylvie sat at her desk on her final day at work debating how she was going to approach her boss and tell him there had been a change of plan; she no longer wanted to leave her job, and she would be very, very grateful if he could see fit to accept the retraction of her early retirement. Sylvie had worked hard for the firm of solicitors over the last eighteen years, and she thought if they knew she'd had a change of circumstances they might understand.

'But I don't understand,' said her boss. 'I seem to recall that you were quick to raise your hand and volunteer to take early retirement right there in the meeting.'

Despite requesting a private word with her boss the moment she arrived at work, Sylvie had waited all day to be called into his office, by which time her nerves were standing on end. Sylvie stared at her boss. She didn't know what to say in response to that rather sarcastic remark.

'And you were the first person to sign the paperwork,' he reminded her, sounding every inch the lawyer.

Sylvie felt as though she was in a court of law being cross-examined, not sitting on an expensive leather couch in the senior

78

partner's office as he continued his interrogation. 'In fact, it appears to me that you were only too eager to leave our firm.'

Sylvie was trying very hard not to feel intimidated. It was only on the rare occasion at work that she was made to feel the lowest of the low working as a secretary; it was normally by some pretentious trainee solicitor, rarely by a senior partner in the law firm – until now.

Sylvie tried to explain. 'There have been some changes in my personal life since I made the decision to leave your firm.' Sylvie bit her lip nervously. She knew her boss was married, a family man, so she hoped he might sympathise.

'My husband lost his job,' confided Sylvie, wanting to add that he was driving her crazy and she really needed to stay in work for her own sanity. Instead, she let him make his own summation. She could have said they needed the money; perhaps then he would be more understanding. However, Sylvie couldn't say that, simply because it wasn't true. Sylvie always told the truth.

'Truthfully . . .' the solicitor began.

Sylvie liked the sound of that.

'Truthfully, I'm afraid there really is nothing I can do. You *have* signed the paperwork.'

'But . . . but can't you just rip it up?'

'May I remind you that we are *solicitors*,' he exclaimed in a condescending tone of voice. 'We are not in the habit of tearing up official documents.'

'No, of course not,' said Sylvie in a small voice, thinking what a stupid, stupid thing to say.

The solicitor stood up and smiled at Sylvie. 'Now, will there be anything else?'

Sylvie shook her head.

The solicitor held out his hand as if they had come to some sort of agreement.

Sylvie supposed they had. She got up and shook his hand.

'Goodbye Sylvie.'

Sylvie walked out of his office not at all surprised by the outcome of that meeting. They were letting people go, and she had already signed on the dotted line. Sylvie thought her boss was being quite reasonable considering she was wasting his time.

In the corridor, Sylvie passed by four young women seated outside his office. They were all very young and smartly dressed. Each one nervously glanced her way as though they were expecting to be called into his office for an interview. Sylvie gave them a curious look as she walked by. They didn't normally take on trainee solicitors this time of the year.

Sylvie returned to her desk for the final time. She was about to collect her coat and handbag to leave when she noticed a pink envelope, a bouquet of flowers and a large box of Thornton's chocolates on her chair. Sylvie stared at the gifts and felt quite overcome with emotion by such an unexpected gesture.

The other secretaries gathered around her desk as Sylvie opened the envelope and read the card. It brought tears to her eyes as her colleagues wished her all the best for the future.

As Sylvie put the card in her handbag and gathered up the flowers and chocolates, the secretarial team drifted back to their desks, leaving Linda and Jane whom Sylvie had worked alongside for nearly two decades. They both offered Sylvie a goodbye hug, telling her how envious they were that she was lucky enough to quit her job five years short of retirement.

Sylvie wished she hadn't been quite so fortunate. This wasn't the note she expected to leave on – regret.

They made her promise to meet them for lunch on occasion.

'Who were those girls waiting outside the boss's office?' asked Sylvie casually as they walked her to the door.

Linda and Jane exchanged glances. 'They are interviewing for a position.'

'Oh really?' replied Sylvie, not all that interested now she had left the firm, although she did comment, 'I wasn't aware they were hiring trainee solicitors at the moment.'

Linda said, 'They're not taking on a trainee solicitor.'

Jane turned on Linda and said crossly, 'I thought we agreed not to tell Sylvie.'

'But she already found out they were interviewing today.'

'What's going on?' asked Sylvie, shifting her gaze from Linda to Jane. 'What are you two not telling me?'

'They're taking on a new secretary.'

'Pardon me?' Sylvie said in surprise. 'They're interviewing for somebody to fill *my* position?'

'I'm sorry you had to find out this way,' remarked Linda.

'That's why we never volunteered to go,' Jane added. 'Don't you see?'

Sylvie did not see until they explained it to her. The firm wanted to get rid of the employees approaching retirement age who were just hanging on in until they got their pension.

Sylvie was stunned. She hadn't just been biding her time until she retired. She was a grafter, unlike her two colleagues who found any excuse to be away from their desks, spending far too much time chatting and not enough time working.

Sylvie had worked hard for the firm. Didn't they realise they were getting rid of the wrong person?

'Now don't be a stranger,' said Linda

'Yes, you must keep in touch,' agreed Jane.

Sylvie was already outside. She stood there with the box of chocolates in one hand and the flowers in the other, and watched them walk slowly back into the office doing their utmost to waste as much time as possible.

Sylvie felt a fool. If only she had known, she would not have gone begging for her job back.

'A silly fool,' said Sylvie out loud. 'Well, I'll show them,' she said defiantly. 'I'll show them there's more to Sylvie Baxter than meets the eye.' She caught a passer-by staring at her and coloured in embarrassment.

Sylvie set off towards the bus stop for her last journey home from work. She got off the bus outside the small parade of shops in Holland Park Avenue and called into the local paper shop to buy a newspaper.

When Sylvie arrived home, she walked straight downstairs to the kitchen followed by John hot on her heels like an excitable puppy whose master had just arrived home.

'How was your last day at work?' John asked, before he spotted the box of chocolates. 'Are those chocolates? May I have one? Please?' Unlike Sylvie who preferred savoury foods, John always did have a sweet tooth.

Sylvie handed over the chocolates and left the newspaper on the kitchen table. She walked over to the butler sink with the flowers and placed them on the draining board before pouring some fresh water into a glass vase. Sylvie found a pair of scissors in the kitchen drawer and started to trim the stems of the flowers.

The silence was punctuated by John smacking his lips as he scoffed a chocolate. 'Hmm these are nice, do you want one?'

Sylvie shook her head without turning around.

'What's this?' asked John with his mouth full.

Sylvie glanced over her shoulder as John picked up the newspaper she had bought on her way home. He looked at her quizzically. 'We don't normally get the local paper.'

'That's mine,' snapped Sylvie.

John raised an eyebrow and put the newspaper back on the kitchen table where he found it. He popped two more chocolates in his mouth in quick succession, and asked Sylvie, 'So how did it go today?'

'Fine,' she replied curtly, and carried on arranging the flowers in the vase. Sylvie did not want to talk about her last day at work.

When she finished arranging the flowers, Sylvie picked up the vase and carried it over to the table, setting it down in the centre. Sylvie loved fresh flowers in the house. John did not. He suffered from hayfever which made him sneeze and his eyes water. As if on cue, John sneezed.

Sylvie caught him frowning at the flowers as he wiped his nose. She wondered if that's why he never bought her flowers, not even on Valentine's Day. Or perhaps it was simply the case that he couldn't be bothered. Sylvie looked at the flowers and suddenly felt like confronting him about it.

He sneezed again and the moment was lost. Sylvie rolled her eyes. 'I'm going upstairs to change,' she said unnecessarily. She wouldn't normally tell him that. However, with John at home all day, Sylvie had fallen into the irritating habit of feeling obliged to tell him every single thing she was about to do next so he wouldn't follow her every move.

'John, why don't you put the dinner on?' Sylvie had already prepared a casserole earlier in the week. All John had to do was pop it in the oven to heat up.

Sylvie left him to it and decided to take a nice relaxing bath before dinner. Sylvie was going to mull over the events of her last day at work and make plans for tomorrow.

Sylvie had just lowered herself into the fragrant bath water when she heard a faint knock at the bathroom door. She threw her hands up in exasperation. Couldn't she even use the bathroom in peace?

'It's only me. I just wanted to check you're all right.'

'Of course I'm all right, John.'

'Can I come in?' John poked his head around the bathroom door before Sylvie had a chance to say no.

'What do you want?' hissed Sylvie. She was trying to have a relaxing bath *on her own*.

'I was wondering why you bought that newspaper . . .'

Sylvie threw a wet flannel in John's direction.

He shut the door just in the nick of time. The wet flannel splat against the bathroom door and fell to the floor.

Dinner consisted of the usual game of twenty questions as John probed Sylvie to find out what they were going to do tomorrow. Sylvie was not playing ball. Their meal together eventually proceeded in near silence.

After dinner, Sylvie watched television.

John took himself off to bed early. He looked depressed.

Sylvie wasn't surprised. Every evening John eagerly sat down and listened to Sylvie's plans for the following day, but not this evening. This evening Sylvie wanted to think about herself for a change, so she gave John the silent treatment. What Sylvie wanted above all was some time on her own.

The following morning Sylvie's prayers were answered. They had run out of bread, yet again, because John was still snacking in between meals. John went out to the local bakery leaving Sylvie with some precious time alone.

Sylvie made a cup of tea and sat down at the kitchen table. She sat in silence for several minutes savouring this rare moment of solitude. She was trying to think about the future, and what she would like to do now she was no longer in work, but all Sylvie could think about was their immediate situation. She had not been prepared for John's early retirement and certainly not finding out, in the aftermath, that it wasn't going to work with both of them at home all day unless something changed. Unless John changed. Sylvie couldn't see that happening any time soon. She had a sinking feeling that if she didn't sort this situation out pronto being around John all day was not going to end well.

Sylvie finished her cup of tea and reached for the local newspaper she had bought yesterday. It was still unopened on the kitchen table. She leafed through the pages until she found the classifieds section. Sylvie took a deep breath. It had been a long time since she searched for a new job.

She was well aware that everybody in this economic climate was hanging on to their jobs for dear life. You couldn't walk out of one job and into another on a whim. This wasn't the sixties, and she wasn't some fresh-faced school-leaver with the world at her feet. Consequently, Sylvie thought her chances of finding another job were probably slim to none. But at least she had to try because, as crazy as it sounded, this was the only thing she could think of to get her out of the house and away from John. Sylvie picked up a red pen and proceeded to circle all the secretarial and administrative jobs advertised in the paper.

Finding a refuge from John wasn't the only reason she was intent on looking for another job. Sylvie was still angry at her boss's attitude towards her when she found out they were interviewing for her position. Evidently, he believed she was worth less to him as an employee than somebody half her age. In his estimation, her experience and maturity counted for nothing. Sylvie was livid. She sat there staring at the newspaper thinking, how dare they assume that because I'm approaching sixty, I am no longer capable of working hard and making a valuable contribution to society. What a cheek! That, more than anything, had galvanized Sylvie into looking for another job just to prove them wrong.

She continued to scan the job ads until one in particular caught her eye. It was a vacancy for a writer and trainee journalist. Sylvie's pen hovered over it as she sat silently contemplating whether to circle that ad. She knew she didn't exactly have any experience and she was fast approaching official retirement age. She probably had no business thinking she could start a new career at her age . . . Sylvie's pen was already circling that ad.

'What are you doing?' John startled her. He unceremoniously dumped two loaves of bread down on the kitchen counter and quickly darted around the table to look over her shoulder.

Sylvie had been so engrossed in the task at hand that she didn't hear John arrive home and walk down the stairs to the kitchen. Sylvie tried to cover the newspaper with her hand but it was too late, John had already spotted the newspaper open at the classified ads, along with the job vacancies Sylvie had circled in red pen.

'Are you looking for another job?' exclaimed John in surprise.

'Yes.' Sylvie saw no pointing denying it.

John was clearly taken aback. 'I don't understand. You just left your job yesterday, why would you want to go back to work?' He stared at the paper open in front of her, and added, 'If you get another job, what am I supposed to do all day?'

And there, in all its glory, was the real crux of the matter. At least he was honest, thought Sylvie shaking her head in dismay. Perhaps it would do them both a favour if she did get another job. If she was out all day, then he would have to learn to fend for himself. Maybe he could find new interests, take up a hobby, and start getting to grips with what he wanted to do with his retirement. It wasn't up to Sylvie to provide him with the answers.

Sylvie didn't tell John what she was thinking. It wasn't that she was being dishonest. She just didn't want to hurt his feelings. Instead, she told him about her last day at work when she found out it wasn't her position that was being made redundant, but her person.

At first, John didn't grasp the significance of the distinction until Sylvie told him about the young women who were being interviewed for her job.

'I want to prove to them there's still life in the old dog yet,' said Sylvie. 'I'm not passed it. I can still work and do a bloody decent job of it too. I'm going to be a success at something.'

That's exactly what Sylvie had been thinking with her pen hovering over the last ad that was not for a secretarial position but for something entirely different – a writer and trainee journalist – something Sylvie had once dreamed about doing a lifetime ago.

Of course she only told him half the story. She wasn't about to mention the fact that getting another job was the only way she could think of right now to have some time out from John.

John sat there listening intently without interrupting once, which made a refreshing change.

Finally, he said, 'I understand completely.' He paused. 'By the way, what is the name of that local newspaper?'

'Why do you ask?'

John gave her an unexpected hug followed by a sloppy kiss on the side of her cheek.

'What was that for?' asked Sylvie in surprise, bewildered by the sudden display of affection.

'Because you are amazing. I don't know why I didn't think of it myself.'

Sylvie eyed him dubiously.

He sat down opposite her grinning from ear to ear. Sylvie found it unnerving. One minute he was feeling down, the next minute he was as high as a kite. She knew they had a name for that sort of thing. Was John depressed? Is that what John was suffering from? She wouldn't be surprised. A big shock, a big change in one's life could bring on something like that, couldn't it?

John leaned back in his chair and puffed out his chest. 'You know what I'm going to do?'

Sylvie had a pretty good idea what was coming next.

'I am going to get another job,' he said triumphantly.

'No kidding,' replied Sylvie sarcastically. She slapped the red pen down on the newspaper and slid them both across the table in his direction. 'Here.'

He looked at her in surprise. 'Don't you need them?'

Sylvie had already written down the jobs she was interested in applying for in her notepad. She had to flick to the second page after her life-changing to-do list. The irony was not lost on Sylvie that she might as well scrub that list because she wasn't going to do anything remotely meaningful for herself with John at home hounding her all day.

'Look, I know what you're thinking, Sylvie. That I'm a silly old fool.' He leaned forward to take the newspaper and pen.

Sylvie looked across the table at John and thought, you have no idea. He *was* a silly old fool who should just accept what had happened, put his feet up, and start enjoying his retirement – after all, he'd earned it.

'I'm not going to accept everybody thinking that I'm over-the-hill, passed it, or redundant – economically speaking.'

Sylvie cast her eyes heavenward.

'I feel exactly like you, Sylvie. Why should my boss tell me I can't work any longer?'

Sylvie sighed. She wished she hadn't told John what had happened on her last day at work. Sylvie knew what this was really about: John couldn't accept he was nearing retirement and entering a new stage in his life. He probably never would.

'I'll show them, Sylvie, just you wait and see.'

Sylvie tried to explain to John that her circumstances were different; she would still have a job today if she hadn't just volunteered to go.

'I hear you, Sylvie, I do. But here's what I don't understand: you volunteered to leave your job, so why are you looking for another one?'

When she didn't respond, John said pointedly, 'Weren't you going to try and find that cottage in Cornwall in order to, you know . . .' He glanced up at the ceiling, indicating that box containing her mother's ashes upstairs in the lounge. John fixed his pale blue eyes on Sylvie. 'I thought after your mother passed you needed some time to yourself to figure things out?'

89

Sylvie, not normally a physical person, and always one to shy away from confrontation, suddenly had the urge to throw something at him. Since he lost his job, Sylvie felt as though she didn't have a minute to herself. Find that cottage? Figure things out? Was he out of his mind?

Sylvie was just about to tell him what she was really thinking at this moment – his feelings be damned – when John suggested something that stopped her in her tracks.

'Doesn't it make sense if I was the one who returned to work? Then I wouldn't be under your feet all day.' John studied her face as Sylvie mulled this over. He understood the situation more than she gave him credit for.

Sylvie had to concede this was probably the most sensible thing he'd said all week. It wouldn't stop Sylvie applying for work. But it did start her thinking about being more selective and applying for positions she really wanted this time. The ad for the trainee journalist came to mind.

'Ah you see it too,' said John. 'It makes perfect sense.'

It did at that, although she was loath to admit it. Sylvie didn't want to return to secretarial work, and John didn't want to be out of work. He was absolutely right: it made perfect sense.

John nodded his head as if reading Sylvie's thoughts.

Sylvie was just about to agree that this was by far the better solution until she saw a fly in the ointment, a flaw in John's plan.

Sylvie opened her mouth to say something, saw John avidly scouring the newspaper for suitable vacancies, and thought the better of it. Nothing she said now was going to deter John from his new plan. John would just have to find out for himself.

10

For the first time since John was forced to retire things had settled down into some sort of routine that, to Sylvie's relief, did not revolve around John smothering her all day. John threw himself with gusto into applying for jobs. He had a focus, he had a plan, and for a brief interlude Sylvie realised she had the old John back.

He approached the task of finding a job, like a job in itself. He had set himself a schedule, bought a new diary and arranged to see an advisor at the local jobcentre who helped people get back into work. John also cleared his study of all the clutter and bought an array of fancy stationery to fill in his job applications.

The days drifted into a familiar pattern. John spent the mornings out and about delivering completed application forms by hand before stopping by the jobcentre. This was followed by a pit stop at a café where he sat over lunch scanning the newspaper for new job vacancies, before arriving home early afternoon to start the next batch of application forms.

John had found a direction. What bothered Sylvie was what would happen when the penny finally dropped, and John realised his job search was futile? It was on her mind because she was having no luck on the job front despite filling in dozens of applications for work. And John wasn't faring any better. Just as she feared, John was getting rejection after rejection too.

'Is it any surprise?' she barked at John one day after a particularly gruelling half-hour rant, during which John went on and on about the injustice of not even being offered an interview.

Sylvie realised belatedly that this idea of applying for work had actually made things worse. Not only did his old job not want him, but John had rubbed salt in the wound by proving nobody else wanted him either. He had just confirmed all those things he was feeling, that he was over-the-hill, passed it, redundant – in short too old. Of course the rejection letters said no such thing – they couldn't could they? You just had to read between the lines.

John had finally figured out the flaw in his plan. No matter how much legwork he did. No matter how much time he spent meticulously filling in job application forms or dressing up smart-as-you-please to personally hand in said forms to a disinterested secretary who gave him no more than a cursory glance. The fact was, a sixty-year-old overqualified accountant was not going to get a job any time soon – if ever. His age and the realities of the current economic climate would see to that. When was John going to face the fact that he was retired and there was nothing he could do about it?

John was sitting at the kitchen table half-heartedly filling out another job application form.

Sitting opposite John, Sylvie was doing the same, except her form didn't have a splodge of coffee staining the top right-hand corner where John had scrawled his name. Sylvie was staring at the coffee stain thinking that he can't possibly hand in a job application form in that condition when it suddenly dawned on her that this was crazy.

They were both crazy.

If John had just accepted he was retired, then neither of them would be sitting here wasting their precious time filling in applications for jobs they didn't need, and jobs they didn't want. Enough was enough.

Sylvie stood up. She picked up the application form she had been conscientiously filling in not a moment ago and walked over to the pedal bin in the corner of the kitchen. She tapped the lever with her foot and threw it in the bin without a second thought, before turning on her heel and heading for the stairs.

John was busy filling in his form when the sound of the bin lid banging shut interrupted his flow. He looked up, surprised to find Sylvie was no longer sitting at the kitchen table. 'Where are you going?'

'Out.'

'But what am I supposed to do with this?' John held up the coffee-stained form that Sylvie was meant to proofread.

Sylvie walked back to the table, snatched the form out of John's hand, and told him, 'This is what you can do with it . . .' Sylvie scrunched it up into a tight round paper ball right in front of his nose.

'What did you do that for?' said John in astonishment.

Sylvie rolled her eyes. 'Now, shall I throw it in the bin, or are you going to do the honours?'

He stared at Sylvie dumbfounded.

She shrugged her shoulders and deposited it with hers in the pedal bin before heading back to the stairs. She was about to walk upstairs when she heard the sound of the bin opening. Sylvie turned around to find John on his knees in front of the bin with his sleeves rolled up. He was retrieving his application form from among the empty milk cartons and leftovers.

Sylvie shook her head in disbelief. 'John, don't you get it? How many more rejections is it going to take for you to grasp the fact that we are both wasting our time?'

John, still on his knees, looked at the screwed up application form in his hand, glanced at Sylvie, and then dropped it back in the bin. John had finally got the message. He needed a new plan.

It was Sylvie who came up with a new plan. She wondered why she hadn't thought of it before. There were plenty of jobs out there for the taking, dozens of positions waiting to be filled. She could start work today, and they would welcome her with open arms. It wasn't paid of course. That's why they called it voluntary work. You were still remunerated just not in hard cash but in the satisfaction of knowing that at the end of a few hours work you had given something back. Sylvie liked the thought of that.

Sylvie had noticed an advertisement placed in a local charity shop window for volunteers. She intended to call in after breakfast to see if they still had a vacancy. Sylvie was determined to start the new day on a positive note – unlike John.

Breakfast had been a tense affair. John was down in the dumps because all that effort on the job front had amounted to nothing. Sylvie could understand that. What she couldn't understand was why John wouldn't accept it and move on. She said as much over breakfast, and wish she hadn't.

'But what am I going to do now?'

'I don't know.' Sylvie glanced out the garden trying to ignore John's constant whining as she ate her porridge. 'Why don't you take up a hobby or something?'

'I don't want a hobby,' John said irritably. 'They're a waste of time.' John had finished his tea and toast but remained seated at the kitchen table opposite Sylvie, watching her intently.

Sylvie continued to eat her breakfast waiting for the inevitable question.

'So, what are we going to do today?'

Sylvie finished eating her porridge. She looked at John and sighed. He was impatiently drumming his fingertips on the kitchen table waiting for an answer.

Finally, Sylvie said, '*We* are not doing anything.'

'What's that supposed to mean?'

'It means that I have got something to do this morning.' She got up from the table and took her empty bowl over to the sink to rinse out before loading the dishwasher. Sylvie normally left her dirty dishes in the sink until later, but she wasn't in the mood for another petty gripe about it. Sylvie dutifully loaded the dishwasher under John's watchful gaze.

John pushed his chair away from the table and stood up. 'Can I come too?'

Sylvie slammed the door of the dishwasher shut and turned around, trying to remain calm. She knew he was at a loss as to how to spend his time. It was to be expected after a lifetime at work. But what she didn't expect was John to make both their lives a misery because of it. After he had discovered she was applying for jobs, he had done the same thing with disastrous results. Now he was more depressed and needy than ever.

Sylvie decided it was time to instigate some changes of her own for John's benefit. He had to learn to find his own way of filling the void that retirement had created. Nobody else could do that for him. The only way to force him to see that was for Sylvie to find things to fill her own time, without letting John tag along just because he couldn't think of anything better to do. It was time to be cruel to be kind.

Sylvie resolved to start today so, without further ado, she went upstairs to their bedroom to get ready to go out. A short time later she walked downstairs carrying her handbag to find John hovering in the hall holding her coat.

'Do you need a lift?' John asked, helping Sylvie into her coat. 'I could run you in the car.'

Nice try, Sherlock. 'No thank you.'

'Are you catching the bus?'

Ignoring John, Sylvie slipped on her comfortable shoes.

'You're walking,' concluded John, glancing at her shoes as she walked over to the front door.

Sylvie wasn't giving anything away. 'I'll see you later, John.' She opened the door and stepped outside into a bright, blustery autumnal morning. Sylvie smiled to herself as she made her way down the front steps. She waved goodbye at the garden gate.

John was still watching as she turned left, in the opposite direction to the bus stop, and started walking.

Sylvie didn't frequent her local parade of shops that often. It was always too tempting to nip into Kensington or Oxford Street for the big high street stores. However, on this occasion, she had good reason not to venture far. A couple of weeks ago Sylvie had been making her way home from work on the bus when it stopped in traffic and a sign in a charity shop window caught her eye: *Volunteers needed.* She hoped they still had a vacancy.

Although Sylvie was anxious to get there and find out, she didn't regret walking instead of catching a bus. The gentle stroll through the leafy London streets lifted her spirits. By the time she walked to the charity shop, all thoughts of John and the aggravation at home had been carried away on the autumn breeze. Sylvie stopped outside the shop feeling confident she was about to make some positive changes in her life and John's.

'Volunteers needed,' said Sylvie, smiling as she read the sign in the shop window. She was excited at the prospect of doing something for herself for a change. This was just what she needed.

Sylvie heard the tinkle of the bell above the shop door as she stepped inside. She was already familiar with the charity shop because she had visited before, not to volunteer but to browse the neatly arranged racks of clothes. Sylvie liked a bargain, and there was always something in the shop window to tempt her inside. The outfits, shoes, handbags, and accessories were so meticulously arranged in the shop window that if you didn't read the small sign above the door, you would be forgiven for thinking this was a designer boutique, not a charity shop.

Sylvie avoided the temptation to look through the clothes. She walked straight past the clothes racks heading for the person standing behind the counter at the far end of the shop who was busy serving a customer. Sylvie stood in the queue observing. The volunteer, who was around her own age, wore a figure-hugging floral dress and a tailored jacket. She looked very chic. Sylvie wished she had been blessed with a figure like that.

Sylvie stepped up to the counter when the customer left and

introduced herself. 'Hello there, I'm Sylvia Baxter. I've come about the advert in your window. I want to volunteer.'

'You do? That's wonderful. When can you start?'

'Right now,' replied Sylvie, taking off her coat.

'Right now?' The lady behind the counter looked delighted. That ad had been in the shop window for quite some time. 'I'm Brenda, by the way. Welcome aboard!'

Sylvie couldn't operate the till and serve customers on her own until they had taken up references for the voluntary position. However, they were desperate for help. Until the necessary formalities were out of the way, Sylvie could shadow Brenda and help her sort through some of the bags of new donations.

'If that's all right with you?' Brenda asked, hoping she hadn't put off her much-needed volunteer.

'It's just perfect,' said Sylvie, breathing a sigh of relief.

Brenda made two mugs of tea in the small kitchen at the back of the shop. With no customers to serve, they both sat behind the counter swapping life stories.

Sylvie was enjoying herself. She finished her tea and handed her empty mug to Brenda with a smile.

Brenda was intending to take the empty mugs back to the kitchen when she noticed a man loitering outside the shop.

Sylvie saw him too. She didn't think it was anything to worry about. Holland Park, the residential area where Sylvie lived, was close to Notting Hill and renowned for being a safe neighbourhood. It had an almost village feel. Sylvie could still understand Brenda's concerns; anybody used to living in a city was always on their guard against the vagaries of a stranger.

The stranger was standing outside, his back to the window. They both watched him walk past the window and disappear out of sight. But a few minutes later he was back again. Brenda was right: his behaviour seemed a little odd.

'Do you think he intends to rob us?' asked Brenda in alarm.

Sylvie agreed it was strange behaviour. 'Perhaps he's waiting for someone?'

They were still staring at him when he turned around and cupped his hands to the window, peering in. From the back of the shop, it was hard to make out his features.

Brenda reached for the phone. 'I'm calling the police.'

'Wait!' Sylvie could no longer see him loitering outside the shop. She turned to Brenda with a reassuring smile. 'I think he's gone.'

'Thank heavens!'

The bell suddenly tinkled above the front door making them jump. They turned in unison to see the stranger walk into the shop.

He closed the door behind him and started browsing through the clothes.

Sylvie sighed in relief. 'There, you see? There's nothing to worry about, Brenda. It's just another customer.'

That's what Sylvie thought until he drew closer and she recognised the strange man instantly. She couldn't believe John had followed her here. Sylvie was livid. She ignored him hoping he would get the message and go away.

John casually rifled through some clothes. He was looking in her direction and not paying attention to what he was doing. If he had been paying attention, he would have realised he was rifling through ladies skirts.

This had not gone unnoticed.

'I'm definitely calling the police.' Brenda picked up the phone.

Sylvie placed a hand on her arm. 'Let me deal with it.' Before Brenda could protest, Sylvie was already marching towards the front of the shop.

John saw Sylvie coming and ducked behind one of the clothes racks in the centre of the store trying to avoid her. He then quickly made his way to the back of the shop, heading straight for Brenda.

Sylvie turned around to follow John. She registered the look of alarm on Brenda's face as the stranger made his approach.

Brenda backed away from the counter as he came towards her.

John came to a halt and leaned casually on the counter in front of Brenda. 'Excuse me, but I noticed your advertisement in the window.' He smiled at Brenda.

Brenda visibly relaxed and came closer.

'You see, I've just retired. I was looking for something to fill my time.'

Oh no you don't! Sylvie overheard John's remark. She marched up behind him and said sharply, 'The vacancy was filled this morning.' Sylvie joined Brenda on the other side of the counter.

Brenda stared at John. 'As a matter of fact, there were two vacancies.'

John glanced at Sylvie. 'Well fancy that.'

Sylvie grasped Brenda's hand and took her to one side. 'Let me get this straight, you thought he was going to rob the store not five minutes ago, and now you want to offer him a voluntary position?'

'Well, he looks a nice sort – don't you think?'

Sylvie glanced at her husband who was throwing a charming smile in Brenda's direction.

Sylvie turned to Brenda and said, 'Excuse me a moment.'

Sylvie skirted the counter, grabbed hold of John's arm, and marched him out of the store. When the door was firmly closed behind them, Sylvie rounded on John. 'No! Absolutely and unequivocally *no*!'

'Oh Sylvie – why ever not?'

'Because . . . because . . .' Because if Sylvie didn't get some time on her own away from John, she was going to explode. 'If you go back through that door, I am not coming with you. I mean it, John. I need some time to myself. And this—' Sylvie pointed at the shop. 'This is it!'

John thought about that. 'I'm sure we can come to some sort of arrangement, Sylvie. We could do different hours, different days. It doesn't mean I can't—'

'Oh for heaven's sake! You just don't get it, do you? You keep following me around, waiting for me to tell you what to do next. I don't get a minute to myself. Well, I'm sick of it, John.' Sylvie glared at him. 'I'm sick of you!'

John took an involuntary step back in surprise.

'This was meant to be mine!' Sylvie prodded herself in the chest theatrically. 'All mine! Do. You. Understand?'

John understood perfectly: his wife was being melodramatic and quite unreasonable under the circumstances. He decided against voicing that opinion in case he made matters worse. A passer-by was already staring at them after Sylvie's embarrassing outburst. John turned around to look through the charity shop window hoping she would calm down.

'I mean it, John. If you walk through that door, I'm leaving.'

John turned to face her. 'Oh come on, Sylvie. Just because you found it first, that doesn't mean I can't work here too. It will give me something to do.' He didn't know why Sylvie was making such a fuss about it. There were enough hours to accommodate both of them, working part-time. 'Besides, you did say you wanted some time to yourself with me out of the way.' John glanced at the shop. 'Well, here it is. We've found the perfect solution.'

Sylvie scowled. '*We* haven't found anything.' He was making her blood boil.

John opened the shop door.

'I'm warning you, John. Don't do it.'

He put one foot inside the shop, teasing her.

Sylvie shook her head, turned on her heel, and marched up the street in the direction of home. There was something she needed to do.

11

John walked home later that day feeling surprisingly refreshed after a change of scene volunteering in the charity shop. The patrons who frequented the establishment were decent enough folk, and some even struck up a conversation here and there which temporarily stalled the tedium. John was used to a hectic schedule at work. He found the relaxed pace certainly a challenge. However, it had given him some time out of the house and a chance to think about what Sylvie had said.

She was right when she said he was smothering her. He knew what was going on: he wasn't coping with being retired and he was making Sylvie's life a misery because of it. No wonder she wanted to go back to work just to get away from him. From this point forward John resolved to change. He was not going to question Sylvie any more about what she was doing or where she was going. John was going to back off because, apart from anything else, he was concerned about Sylvie's over-the-top reaction when he turned up at the charity shop. John raised an eyebrow. Perhaps she wasn't coping with her retirement either.

When John arrived home, instead of calling out for Sylvie the moment he got in and going to find her, John reminded himself that he was turning over a new leaf. He walked into the lounge, picked up the newspaper from the coffee table where Sylvie had left it, and settled into his favourite chair by the bay window. He knew she was home because her coat and shoes were in the hall.

John opened the newspaper and called out, 'Honey, I'm home.' There was no response, which didn't surprise him. The walls were so thick in these old properties that she probably wouldn't have heard him if she was in the next room, let alone on one of the other three floors of the house. Either that or she was ignoring him. That was more than likely considering she was probably still cross with him over that episode at the charity shop. John still thought it was Sylvie who was being unreasonable.

John heard movement on the ceiling above him, suggesting Sylvie was upstairs in one of the spare bedrooms. He fought the urge to go upstairs and find out what she was up to. Instead, he scanned the newspaper and found an article of interest. John began to read.

A short time later, Sylvie appeared in the lounge doorway. 'You're home.'

John glanced over the top of his newspaper and registered her surprise. 'Just reading the paper,' he said nonchalantly, keeping up the act.

Sylvie walked into the room and sat down on the matching upholstered chair opposite him.

John ignored her and continued reading the newspaper, or trying to. He had a feeling Sylvie had something on her mind. John resisted the urge to ask her what it was. He hoped she wasn't going to start another row over his decision to volunteer in the charity shop.

'John, I've been thinking . . .'

John furtively glanced her way.

'I've been thinking about doing something . . . new.'

'Really,' said John from behind the newspaper, doing his level best to sound totally disinterested. He was guessing she had been true to her word and decided not to return to the charity shop. Perhaps that was for the best. 'I think trying something new will do you the world of good,' added John, careful not to ask any specifics.

'You think so?'

John peered over the top of his newspaper. 'Absolutely.'

'You haven't even asked me what I'm going to do yet.'

'Oh haven't I?' said John innocently. 'Well, I'm sure whatever you decide to do will be for the best.' He turned his attention back to the newspaper and made every effort to concentrate on the article in front of him.

'So you'll be supportive.'

'Yes of course.' John stole a glance at Sylvie as he turned the page to the sports section, dying to know what she had in mind. The charity shop would only take up so much of his time. He needed another idea, another project to keep him busy. If John was honest, he was already bored with the charity shop, even though he had only spent half a day there.

'I've decided to take a break.'

'A holiday?' John lowered his newspaper and gave Sylvie his full attention. Now there was an idea. He tried to restrain himself from getting too involved. This was her idea, her baby. He really shouldn't interfere, but this was an interesting proposition. 'We could start planning—'

'No,' Sylvie cut in, thinking of that word *we* again. Sylvie frowned at John. Why did he always do that? Why did he always take charge without giving her a chance? And why on earth would he assume she'd go on holiday with him when all she wanted was some time on her own?

'A short-break then,' said John, leaning forward in his chair, surprisingly excited about Sylvie's idea. 'We could go on the internet and find a nice hotel.'

'No.'

John was getting frustrated by the conversation. 'Do you want a break or not?' Why was she being so cryptic? 'Look, Sylvie, why don't you tell me what it is you want to do, and I'll just go along with it?' He couldn't be fairer than that, could he?

'I want a break – from us.'

John took a minute to process that. He couldn't. John looked at his wife in bewilderment. 'Sylvie, I don't understand . . .'

Sylvie got up from her chair and announced, 'I'm moving into the spare bedroom.'

John gaped at her. 'You're leaving me?'

'Don't be so melodramatic, John. I only said I'm moving into the spare bedroom.' Sylvie walked across the room and out the door.

John stared after her. This had never happened in the Baxter household before. John tossed his newspaper on the floor, bolted out of his chair and hurried after Sylvie. 'But what does that mean?' asked John, following her up the stairs.

Sylvie turned around on the landing to face him. 'It means that I have decided to try something new.'

'In the spare bedroom?' John shook his head in confusion.

'No John, in our lives. Well, in my life to be precise. I don't think I can go on like this.' Sylvie turned around and made her way along the landing towards one of the spare bedrooms, leaving John standing there trying to fathom out what had just happened. Once again he couldn't. He thought they were discussing a holiday.

John was on her heels again. 'What do you mean: you don't think you can go on like this?'

Sylvie stopped in the doorway of the spare bedroom and turned to John. That very question just proved to her that he didn't have the first clue how she was feeling.

When John retired, she thought that for the first time in their married lives they would have the opportunity to do things together which did not revolve around work or the girls or the house. She wanted to rekindle that special relationship they once had all those years ago before it got lost in the minutiae of raising a family, putting food on the table and keeping a roof over their heads. However, increasingly over time Sylvie had become painfully aware they had nothing in common.

It almost felt like they had been leading separate lives, John with his career, and Sylvie with her part-time job, her friends and the time she devoted to her garden. Two individuals living under the same roof pretending they were still in a relationship. They shared the same house, they shared the same bed, and they jogged along quite amicably in each other's company. But that was it.

Over the years, Sylvie put it down to the fact that John was always busy with work, or some project on the house, which meant they rarely found time for each other. They used to do things together once upon a time. Sylvie wasn't thinking about the ordinary, everyday, mundane tasks like going shopping, but the meaningful things, the romantic things. They used to be a couple once, and Sylvie mistakenly believed that when John retired they would finally get the chance to recapture some of that magic from their youth when they used to enjoy the simple pleasure of one another's company.

Sylvie wasn't even going to attempt to explain all this to John. What was the point? She had tried to make it work. Sylvie had even gone so far as to rewrite that list she had torn up, with all her ideas for meaningful things they could do, just the two of them. But John didn't want that. John didn't want to retire and spend time together – that much was obvious. All John really wanted was to stick to the five-year plan and work until he was sixty-five. Nothing else mattered. Spending time with his wife didn't matter. It dawned on Sylvie that something had happened in those intervening years of working hard, raising children, and renovating the house: they had grown apart.

Did they still have a future together? That was the question at the forefront of Sylvie's mind. Sylvie needed some time on her own to figure this out. To figure *them* out. For tonight, the spare-bedroom would have to do. Sylvie didn't want to think any further than that, hoping that by morning something miraculous would happen to make all this go away.

John stood staring at Sylvie lost in thought until he suddenly had an idea what all this was about. 'All right then, have the job for all I care.'

Sylvie hit the roof. 'It's not about the charity shop, John.' Couldn't he see that? The episode at the charity shop had only brought matters to a head.

John held up his hands in defeat. 'Just tell me what it is you want?'

'I want a trial separation,' Sylvie blurted, surprising herself.

She didn't even know where that came from. It felt like someone else had put those words into her mouth. It made her wonder how long that idea had been stored at the back of her mind, deep in her subconscious, festering, waiting for the right moment to be unleashed on to an unsuspecting John.

Sylvie stared wide-eyed at her husband waiting for a reaction. She expected him to say something but he didn't say a word. She watched him turn around and walk slowly back along the landing towards the stairs.

Sylvie stepped into the spare bedroom and shut the door. She stood there staring at the overnight bag she had packed earlier, and cast her mind back to the events of that morning . . .

Sylvie had returned home after the row with John outside the charity shop and went straight upstairs to their bedroom to find her overnight bag. She packed her nightie, dressing gown, slippers and reading glasses, and remembered to pick up the novel she had been reading from the bedside table. Next, she raided the en-suite bathroom, filling up her toiletry bag with all the essentials. Sylvie had then stuffed it all into her overnight bag, along with a clean set of clothes and underwear.

When she walked out of their bedroom with the bag, Sylvie wasn't heading for the spare bedroom down the hall. She was intending to stay with her best friend, Julia.

Lucky she phoned first.

Sylvie was just about to tell Julia what was going on at home, and ask if she could come over and stay the night, when Julia told Sylvie some news of her own.

'I'm moving, darling. Can you believe it?'

Sylvie didn't even know that Julia had put her place on the market. 'I wish you'd told me sooner,' said Sylvie, feeling a bit put out that Julia had not mentioned her plans.

'Well, that's just it,' Julia had replied. 'I only visited the estate agent to get a valuation. I hadn't even made up my mind I wanted to sell.'

That sounded like Julia.

'And would you believe that a couple came into the estate agents at the same time and wanted to view it straight away. I swear my feet haven't touched the ground, Sylvie. They made an offer there and then, and . . . well I just haven't had a chance to tell you. Things have been moving so fast, excuse the pun, darling.'

Sylvie thought it must be so nice when things fall into place like that. She could do with a bit of that herself right now, rather than the other extreme – things seemed to be falling apart.

'I'm sorry to bombard you with my news, darling. I'm so excited. What about your end? How are things with you?'

'Fine,' Sylvie replied stiffly, not wanting to spoil the moment by sharing her woes with Julia when she sounded so happy.

Julia quickly returned to the subject of her sale, telling Sylvie she was moving at the end of the week.

Sylvie eyed her overnight bag perched on the kitchen table. She knew if she asked Julia whether she could come and stay, her best friend would welcome her with open arms. But Julia was in the middle of packing boxes and trying to sort out her place. It would be unfair to impose at a time like this. So instead of asking Julia if she could stay the night, Sylvie had offered to help her with her move.

Julia was delighted.

Sylvie pencilled the date into her diary as soon as she got off the phone. The next thing she did was run her overnight bag upstairs and dump it on the unmade bed in one of the spare bedrooms. That's when John returned home from his afternoon at the charity shop. She had heard the faint sound of his voice from directly below her in the lounge when he called out her name. Sylvie had ignored him. She had been pacing the floor wondering what John's reaction would be when she told him she was moving into the spare bedroom.

Now it was over, and she had told him, Sylvie was back to pacing the floor once more, this time wondering how he was taking the news. Her mind was racing as she thought of all sorts of troublesome scenarios. Was he going to reappear at her bedroom door crying, sobbing and begging her not to leave him? Or was he going to get angry that he had worked hard to provide her with a comfortable lifestyle and accuse her of being ungrateful, demanding to know what more she could possibly want? Finally, the most worrisome of all, Sylvie imagined her husband driving off in the car and finding some deserted spot – albeit a bit difficult in the heart of London – to gas himself.

Her imagination was running so wild that Sylvie had to find John and stop him from doing whatever crazy thing he was about to do right now. She rushed to the bedroom door, flung it open, and caught herself just in time from careering into her husband. He had been standing just the other side of the door with his hand raised, about to knock.

Feeling flushed from all that emotion, Sylvie looked him over to check he was all right. He certainly looked okay. After pacing the floor and getting increasingly anxious over her husband's reaction to this trial separation, it turned out that John wasn't standing there pleading or sobbing or begging, or even angry. He didn't even ask her why.

All John said was, 'One pillow or two?'

John had been in the laundry cupboard upstairs the whole time searching for sheets, blankets, and pillows to make up the spare bed.

Sylvie stepped to one side and watched John walk into the room. He deposited the folded sheets and blankets on to the bed, and said conversationally, 'You wouldn't believe how long it took to find them in the laundry cupboard. I had to burrow under a mountain of towels, but I found them eventually.' John turned to Sylvie looking rather pleased with himself. 'Now, would you like some help making up the bed?'

'Would I like some help making up the bed?' Sylvie repeated incredulously. Was he joking? She stared at him in disbelief. Sylvie hadn't anticipated this cool indifference. She didn't expect him to agree so readily to what might turn out to be the end of their marriage. Sylvie thought he'd at least do something, anything to try and save their relationship.

'One pillow or two?' said John for the second time, holding them both up.

Sylvie grabbed one out of his hand, threw it on the bed and then steered John, and the other pillow, towards the door and out of the room. She slammed the door behind him.

'I take it,' said John from the other side of the door, 'that you don't want my help with making up the bed.'

Sylvie threw the pillow at the door. John wasn't taking her seriously, she could tell. Sylvie knew what he was thinking: he was under the misapprehension that all this will blow over and she would come around in the morning.

Sylvie shook her head. If that's what John was really thinking, then he was in for a rude awakening. How could she make John understand that sleeping in the spare room wasn't just a knee-jerk reaction to all the sudden changes in her life, like her mother's death, or John's surprise retirement? It had only served to reinforce how desperately unhappy she was. Sylvie sat down on the unmade bed with her chin in her hands, deep in thought. She was thinking about the last thirty-nine years since she got married. There had always been the nagging doubt that this wasn't meant to be the sum total of her life. It was as though there was something missing; some part of her life as yet unfulfilled.

Sylvie frowned wondering what she was going to do about it until a daunting thought occurred to her. What if she had to make some significant changes in her life in order to find what she was looking for? Was she prepared for that? Was John?

This already felt like a significant change in her life. She had never, ever done anything like this before. Of course, they both had their moments, what relationship isn't without its ups and downs? It came with the territory; it was, by definition, marriage. But neither of them had moved into the spare bedroom. Neither of them would ever have contemplated leaving – until now.

As Sylvie made up the spare bed, a rather troubling thought stopped her in her tracks: what if she was looking at this all wrong? What if she wasn't the only one in their marriage who wanted this? It certainly didn't seem to bother John that she had moved into the spare bedroom. His reaction was not what she had expected – *one pillow or two?*

Sylvie stood staring into space, her thoughts consumed with her husband. John was a creature of habit. John had routines. John was too set in his ways to even contemplate leaving her. He wouldn't have it in him – would he?

Looking back, even as a young man John had always been conservative. In the seventies, her friends were enjoying themselves going to parties. Some of her more adventurous friends, like Julia, even travelled the hippie trail. That was never John's idea of fun. John lived for the plan. He went to work, saved money and bought this house, and then set about spending what little spare cash they had on renovating it. As their house rose from the dying embers of the decaying seventies, so did the other houses on the street, transformed from near-derelict bedsits and squats into the fine Georgian homes they were today. These grand homes now housed city professionals and celebrities, barristers and businessmen – and Sylvie and John.

They didn't know it back then, but the area they bought into was to become one of the most fashionable and sought-after addresses in London. It was a stone's throw from Central London and a short walk from the beautiful London Park of the same name, Holland Park. And that's where John and Sylvie still lived today, all thanks to John and the plan.

John, ever astute and sensible with money, had provided them with a beautiful home in an affluent part of London. They had an adequate income from John's pension and a tidy nest egg they had squirrelled away over the years. There was enough money to live comfortably in retirement without selling their home if they didn't splash out on new cars or foreign holidays.

Thinking back on all this, Sylvie was only too glad John didn't ask her why she really wanted a trial separation. How could she tell her husband that deep down she felt the life they had built together wasn't enough? They'd never had a helping hand because neither of their parents had any money to speak of, but thanks to John they had both come a long way over the course of their life together. So why did she feel her journey wasn't over? Sylvie shook her head. Why now, when things were more comfortable than ever, did she have to stir things up, unable to quash the desperate feeling that she needed to move on with her life before it was too late?

Sylvie finished making up the single bed. She picked up the pillow and stood staring at it feeling all at sea over her move into the spare bedroom, not to mention John's flippant attitude toward her. Sylvie lay down on the bed, tucked the pillow under her head, and hoped by some miracle that things looked better in the morning.

12

Sylvie woke up the next morning in some confusion. Not an early riser, on waking Sylvie always suffered from brain fog. Today was no exception but made worse by the fact that she was in a strange bed, in a strange room, and she had not slept well. Sylvie had missed the warmth of her sleeping companion. And she was not used to sleeping in a single bed. She kept rolling over dangerously close to the edge of the bed. At some point in the early hours, she rolled over and unintentionally deposited all her covers on the floor.

Sylvie sat up in bed shivering with cold. She got out of bed, traipsed over the bed covers on the floor, and put on her dressing gown intending to go downstairs and make some tea. She was always the first to get up and make them both a cup of tea in the morning. Old habits die hard, thought Sylvie.

As she wandered out of the bedroom, walking along the landing in her slippers and yawning as she made her way down to the kitchen, Sylvie was debating whether today she would make an exception to that unwritten rule and just make herself a cup of tea for a change. The thought of sneaking back to bed with it, and sitting in peace and quiet deciding how she wanted to spend her day, was very appealing. Not to mention the thought of John having to get out of bed and make his own tea for once in his life. Sylvie smiled wickedly.

As Sylvie was walking down the stairs she noticed the light was on in the kitchen. She must have forgotten to switch it off last night. It certainly wouldn't be John up and about making tea and preparing breakfast. In fact, she wouldn't be at all surprised if he had heard her emerge from the spare bedroom, and he was sitting upstairs in bed at this very moment waiting for Sylvie to bring him up a cup of tea and his morning newspaper like she always did, even though she had moved into the spare bedroom. Sylvie shook her head. If that was the case, John was in for a long wait.

Sylvie walked into the kitchen and was almost accosted by her husband the moment she stepped foot in the room.

'Ah, there you are,' said John, sounding in high spirits. 'That's for you,' he said, handing her a mug of tea and guiding her to the kitchen table. He pulled out a chair. 'Sit,' he said light-heartedly, placing a gentle hand on her shoulder.

It wasn't exactly an order but Sylvie did as she was told, too stunned to do or say anything else. If memory served, in all their married life John had never, ever made her a cup of tea first thing in the morning. She looked at the mug in her hands and didn't know what to make of it. Her first thought was that John had also had a rough night because he too missed his sleeping companion. Perhaps this was his way of trying to make amends.

John sat down at the kitchen table and confessed, 'I hardly got a wink of sleep last night.'

Sylvie suppressed the urge to nod in agreement.

'And then it came to me . . .' John was staring vacantly into space, his expression full of wonder, 'like a bolt out of the blue.' It sounded as though he'd had some kind of epiphany.

Sylvie sipped her tea eyeing John cautiously. She still didn't know what to make of the fact that John had made her a cup of tea first thing in the morning.

He turned to Sylvie wide-eyed. 'I realise now what I need to do.'

Sylvie looked at him intently. John had already surprised her this morning with a mug of tea; that was no small thing in Sylvie's book. She couldn't imagine what was coming next.

John was never one for spontaneity – far from it. Usually, by the time something that started off as an exciting idea – like booking a holiday – had been researched and analysed and planned to distraction, Sylvie would be so tired and drained that the excitement of actually going ahead with it had evaporated. Inevitably, when those ideas were fully realised into hard cash and the cost of a fleeting experience, like a holiday, was compared to the long-term benefits of spending the money on a new bathroom or redecorating the house, the outcome was always the same: the original idea was shelved for later and the money spent on the house.

As far as John was concerned, there was always *later*, *another time*, or *in the future*. What this came to mean, was that over the years the house became their plans, their holidays, their memories and their future. Was all that about to change?

Sylvie stared fixedly at her husband. After her announcement last night, had it dawned on him that she might be serious about a trial separation and he needed to do something about it other than offer to make up the spare bed? What if, after all these years, John was about to do something completely out of character and tell her that he had booked a table for two at a nice restaurant, or a romantic weekend away together, even a Mediterranean cruise. Perhaps all of the aforementioned? What lengths would he go to, to save their marriage, to win back his wife? It had started with a mug of tea, where could it lead?

Sylvie finished her tea and set the mug down on the kitchen table. She waited with baited breath in anticipation of what was coming next.

'I've got something to show you, Sylvie.'

It had never occurred to her that he might do something like this. It didn't even cross her mind that as a consequence of suggesting this trial separation, overnight something miraculous might happen and John would start thinking about their future together and how he could change things for the better.

John produced a beige manila folder that had been sitting on his lap out of sight under the table. John smiled at her. 'In light of last night . . .'

Sylvie glanced at the folder and smiled back at him.

'Why stop at the spare bedroom?' John held up the folder. 'What about an apartment?' He placed the folder on the table and grinned at Sylvie.

'Pardon me?' Sylvie's smile faded.

'This is just some rudimentary research I printed off the internet.' John opened the folder. 'Here are some plans and ideas for converting the house into two apartments.'

'You want to convert the house into two apartments?' Sylvie said in astonishment. Was this some kind of joke? Sylvie wasn't looking at the paperwork that John had spread out on the kitchen table in front of her. And she wasn't listening to the plan. All she was focused on was the beige manila folder. Sylvie couldn't believe he had found a folder and organised this stuff like it was the start of another project on the house. Suddenly it was thirty-odd years ago and John hadn't been on the internet but to a local architect's office, returning home with a beige manila folder, just like this one, full of drawings and plans for the renovations he wanted to do on the house.

Sylvie stared forlornly at the paperwork realising that things hadn't changed. He hadn't changed. It was just like before: they were never *their* ideas, *their* plans, they were always his. She could kiss goodbye to any thoughts of a restaurant meal or a romantic weekend away for two. John wasn't thinking about their future together. He wasn't thinking about his wife at all. All that was on his mind was his precious house.

John never knew this, but if Sylvie had her way they would never have bought this house in the first place. If she'd had a choice, Sylvie would have preferred to buy somewhere smaller and cheaper. Then maybe over the years, they would have had some money over to spend on really living, like throwing parties for their friends and going out more. When their children came along, they might have had the money to buy them the latest toys they craved and taken them on foreign holidays.

They might even have accrued a debt or two along the way; the battle scars of a moment of excess that John would never dream of, like buying a brand new car or taking a romantic break away in a fancy hotel in Paris or New York.

Sylvie would be the first to admit that John's plans had paid off in spades but at what price? Sylvie knew all too well. The true cost was thirty-nine years of really living; the experiences and the treasured moments with their children, with each other, they could have shared but they didn't because they were so wrapped up in the house.

Now it was starting again, John's obsession with the house, with *the plan*. Sylvie looked down at the paperwork John had spread out on the kitchen table. It occurred to her that what she was really looking at was, quite possibly, the beginning of the end of their marriage. Despite that, Sylvie still sat there waiting to hear the words *restaurant* or *cruise* suddenly pop out of his mouth, hoping that John's new plan for the house was just a wind-up before he told her what he really had planned for them.

'I can see I've surprised you,' said John, cutting across her thoughts. 'But it's a really good plan.'

Sylvie shook her head in disbelief when she realised he really wasn't planning to take her out to a restaurant or surprise her with a weekend away together. This was it. This was the surprise.

'It would involve some work on the house, naturally,' John continued unaware of Sylvie's complete lack of interest in anything more he had to say on the subject. 'The plan would be to divide the house into two apartments and then rent one out to subsidise our retirement income.' John glanced at Sylvie. He took her silence as a cue to continue explaining the plan. 'The girls have moved out. We've got far too much space than we need. With the rental income, we wouldn't have to be so careful with money.'

Sylvie scoffed at that. When was John ever *not* careful with money? And had John forgotten the events of last night? Sylvie thought it was about time she reminded him. 'John, in case it has slipped your mind, I *have* moved into the spare bedroom.'

'Yes – isn't it great? If it wasn't for that, I would never have got this fantastic idea. I must say though it did give me rather a sleepless night.'

Sylvie gaped at John. Was he serious? There she was thinking that John had missed her last night, and those dark rings under his eyes were because John had had a restless night trying to think up ways to save their marriage, when all he was thinking about was the blasted house. She was right: he wasn't taking this trial separation seriously at all.

'They'd be an awful lot of planning to get it right,' he went on, 'however, I think it will be worth it in the end.'

John wasn't looking at Sylvie. He was too engrossed in his potential new project waiting to take off from the kitchen table. John hadn't asked her opinion and he didn't even notice Sylvie get up from the kitchen table, deposit her mug in the sink, and head for the door.

She stopped at the foot of the stairs and turned around. His lips were still moving, but she wasn't listening to him blathering on about his new idea; what was on her mind were some real concerns over John's plan for the house. She couldn't believe at a time like this, when they were both out of work, that John was proposing spending more money and causing a lot of upheaval to convert the house into two apartments. Why now?

Sylvie could think of only one explanation. Over the years, John had two things in his life he loved besides his family: his job and this house. Both involved a lot of work. Both took up a lot of his time. Now he had neither. Quite simply, John needed a project. He had failed to find another job. Sylvie doubted the charity work would suit John. That left the house. And the house was finished, much like their marriage.

That thought had crept unbidden into her mind. She swiftly brushed it aside to mull over later. Sylvie was trying to stay focused on the issue at hand. Didn't they have enough on their plate, with John losing his job and Sylvie moving into the spare bedroom, without adding something else to the mix just because John was bored and needed something to do?

Sylvie attempted to raise her concerns, but John was having none of it. He wasn't going to back down. Unable to hide his excitement and enthusiasm at the prospect of starting a new project on the house, he wouldn't hear another word on the potential pitfalls. John had a new plan, and nobody – not even Sylvie – was going to take that away from him.

She stood there watching John leafing through the paper-work, scribbling down ideas, totally engrossed in the plan and totally ignoring her. Seeing John like this suddenly made Sylvie aware of the potential benefits of John's new project – and it had nothing to do with the financial gains from converting the house.

Sylvie was sick and tired of John moping around the house all day looking depressed, the sight of his hangdog expression making her feel depressed too. Sylvie wasn't that type of person. She liked to look on the bright side of life wherever possible, but John was dragging her down. Sylvie knew he needed something to focus on. Despite her misgivings, she had to grudgingly acknowledge that perhaps converting the house was it.

She would have to trust him to take one more gamble on the house and maybe things would pay off in the end. Or maybe they wouldn't. Quite frankly, Sylvie was past caring. As long as whatever John did, it kept him occupied and out of her hair so she could think about herself for a change. Like John, she too wanted to find something that puts a spring in her step and filled her with enthusiasm. Perhaps Sylvie was beginning to appreciate why this new project on the house was so important to John.

But then, in the face of Sylvie's receding scepticism over John's proposed plan for the house, he suggested something which made her suspicious there was more to this conversion than creating a project to focus on and an apartment to rent out for the extra income.

'I'll tell you what,' said John, finally looking up as Sylvie was about to walk upstairs. 'If you still need some time on your own, you could always move into one of the apartments as soon as the work is complete.' John paused. 'Now I come to think of it, that wouldn't be a bad idea,' he added, nodding enthusiastically. 'We could each test-run an apartment to iron out the wrinkles, so to speak. If anything cropped up, I could get the builder in to fix things before we get a tenant.'

Sylvie stood there staring at John trying to second-guess his real motives. Was he trying to win her over, attempting to convince her it was a good plan by making this proposal to get her to go along with it? Perhaps it shouldn't come as a surprise that he was suggesting she could spend some time in one of the apartments. After all, she had made a point of showing John how much she needed some time on her own; she *had* moved into the spare bedroom.

Or was there more to it than that? Sylvie frowned as she thought of another possibility. Was John planning ahead in the eventuality that this trial separation became permanent? Maybe she had got it wrong and he was taking her move into the spare bedroom very seriously indeed.

John knew if they split up he would have to sell the house and divide the proceeds so Sylvie could get a place of her own. The problem was John would never sell this house, and there wasn't the money to buy her out. Converting the house into two apartments was the only solution. On paper, it was a win-win situation. If they didn't split up, then they would have the extra money from the rental income. If they did split up, John still kept the house – or half of it at any rate. Sylvie narrowed her eyes thinking how very clever of John to cover all the bases.

Sylvie was back to trying to second-guess his motives. What if this was something John secretly wanted all along – for them to go their separate ways – but he was just too nice to make the first move? Sylvie thought she was the one doing the separating; it never occurred to her that he might feel the same way. Why did that bother Sylvie so much when she was the one who wanted this trial separation? It was her idea to have a break from *us*. Even so, Sylvie didn't know if she wanted that break to be permanent. In fact, Sylvie wasn't sure about anything in her life at this moment.

Suddenly, inexplicably, she started to feel anxious that she had set a train in motion that wasn't entirely of her own making. She was afraid that if she asked John outright what converting the house was really all about, he might turn around and tell her that he didn't love her and he wanted a divorce. Right now, Sylvie wasn't prepared for that.

Her thoughts turned to their children. How was she going to explain to the girls what was going on at home? Especially what John was proposing to do to the house they grew up in, their childhood home. As soon as she thought about the girls, Sylvie started on a guilt trip convincing herself this was all her fault. If she hadn't moved into the spare bedroom, John wouldn't have got this crazy idea in his head to convert the house. Despite the guilt trip, Sylvie was not about to move out of the spare bedroom which meant somebody had to tell the girls.

Sylvie reluctantly turned from the stairs and walked over to the table where John was still seated. She picked up one of the sheets of paper with information about house conversions that John had printed off the internet.

John was watching her avidly. 'Well, what do you think?'

Sylvie didn't bother answering that question. It didn't matter what she thought. With a sigh, Sylvie put the piece of paper back on the table next to the manila folder. She sat down at the kitchen table opposite John. 'If you're going ahead with this, who's going to tell the girls?' Sylvie didn't relish the thought of telling them herself.

'I'll take care of it,' John volunteered eagerly. 'I'll phone them up and tell them all about our plans.'

Our plans. Sylvie winced at those words. There was no *our* or *we* or *us*. Didn't he get that?

'In fact, I think I'll speak to them right now.'

Evidently, John couldn't wait to tell them *our plans.* Sylvie didn't know what she resented the most, the fact that her idea of a trial separation had provided John with a new project on the house. Or the possibility that she had played right into his hands and this was what he wanted all along, for them to split up, he just didn't have the guts to take the initiative and end it himself.

Sylvie sat at the table watching John organise the paperwork back into the manila folder before racing upstairs to make those calls. Sylvie was not sharing John's enthusiasm. She didn't think telling them over the phone was such a good idea. However, she didn't feel that inclined to look them in the eye and tell them she had moved into the spare bedroom either. She knew there would be massive resistance to this trial separation in the shape of three daughters for whom their father could do no wrong. It was better if it came from him in the first instance, and let the dust settle on the debris of their marriage before she told them herself it was, quite conceivably, over. Besides, with John's newfound optimism borne of his new plan for the house, he was bound to put a positive spin on the situation somehow.

What Sylvie wasn't aware of, was exactly what the content of that spin would be . . .

John walked into his study, picked up the phone and proceeded to explain to his daughters, one by one, that their mother was just going through a phase.

The way he saw it, Sylvie was feeling a bit fragile after the death of her mother. She needed something to focus on, like a project to keep her busy. He didn't think it was relevant to mention she had moved into the spare bedroom. As far as he was concerned that was just a reaction to his own idiotic behaviour since he lost his job – he could see that now. Once he proved he had changed, it would all blow over very soon.

His daughters had asked why they had to go through all the upheaval of converting the house into two apartments just to keep her occupied, raising their concerns that at the end of it, all the work, expense and hassle would have been for nothing.

'Not so,' John had countered, proceeding to explain to each of them, in turn, his brilliant idea of asking Sylvie to test-run an apartment because the whole point of the plan was to rent out one of the apartments to tenants for a second income. With the extra money, they could do all the things they couldn't afford in the past because the cost of living in their substantial home swallowed up a sizeable chunk of their income. John believed it was about time the house, which they had poured so much effort and money into over the years, paid them back for a change.

One last investment in the house to convert it into two apartments would give them a small apartment of their own to live in, with substantially reduced overheads, and a generous rental income from the other to spend on frivolous things they would never dream of doing in the past. John was thinking of meals out at restaurants or weekends away together. Perhaps a foreign holiday. Or better still, a cruise. Sylvie appeared so dead-set against the idea of the house conversion that she never gave him a chance to explain all this. John was looking forward to surprising her with all these things he had planned for them to do together once the work was complete, a tenant was found, and the rental income rolled in.

John also believed his plan was the perfect solution to get Sylvie out of the spare bedroom and things back to normal in the Baxter household. He had given this a good deal of thought. He was awake most of the night thinking of Sylvie sleeping in another bedroom, on another floor, still unable to comprehend what was going on. And, more worryingly, what he could do about it. Until it came to him – *the plan*.

'Things always seemed okay when we had a plan and were busy working on the house,' mused John thinking aloud. 'But ever since we put the finishing touches on the house some time ago, your mother has been . . .'

John had paused here during his phone conversation with each of the girls, realising belatedly that, try as he might, he was still unable to put his finger on the crux of the matter.

Chloe suggested she was bored. Typical Chloe. She was the youngest of their trio, always flitting from one job to the next and from one relationship to the next. Always getting bored and moving on.

Their eldest daughter, Harriet, had suggested her mother was frustrated. John had cringed at the use of that word hoping it wasn't a reference to what he thought it was. Everything was fine in that department as far as he was concerned, although not a line of conversation he intended to pursue with his own daughter. Besides, she was probably referring to something else entirely: frustration at not having had a successful career.

Perhaps it was understandable that Harriet might think that. Unlike Sylvie, Harriet had juggled motherhood with a very successful career as a journalist. She was now an editor working for a prominent women's magazine based in London and New York. Still living in London with her family, but with frequent trips across the pond, little wonder she thought her mother might be frustrated career-wise.

John had one more phone call to make. He flicked through his rolodex to find Jessica's phone number. As he did so, he thought about his middle daughter . . .

Affectionately known as Jess, she had always been the odd one out. Sporty and athletic, growing up she didn't have the same interests or aspirations as her two sisters. She also looked remarkably different from them too. Whereas the other two took after John's side of the family with their slim builds, blonde hair and blue eyes, Jess looked like a younger version of her mother. She was small in stature with jet black hair, hazel-brown eyes and skin that tanned at the first hint of summer.

Never one to follow the crowd, Jess had disappointed her parents by not going to university after school like Harriet and Chloe. She went travelling instead and never came back. The long-distance phone call to Australia, where she had settled, was saved until last. John picked up the phone. He would never admit to a living soul that he had a favourite child – what parent would? But in his heart, Jess was his. Ever since she was a little girl she was brave, a risk-taker, grabbing life by the horns and going for it.

Always pushing the boundaries growing up, she never settled for the ordinary. Even as a child she wasn't satisfied with the local swing-park, she always wanted to do something more adventurous. Their lives were all the richer for it. Maybe she was his favourite because she was so different. It was still a mystery to him where her spontaneity and taste for adventure came from because John and his middle daughter couldn't have been more different.

'Unhappy,' Jess concluded when he paused at the same point in the conversation for the third time that evening.

'You think your mother is unhappy?' John frowned. That was a bit of a stretch considering Jess lived half way around the world and was barely on speaking terms with her mother. Perhaps it was because they were so alike in temperament that caused so much friction between them, John pondered. He was well aware that Jess had never developed the same easy-going, close relationship with her mother that the other girls had, so how would she know that Sylvie was unhappy?

With the other two girls, John had proceeded to explain the plan. As far as John was concerned, whatever the problem was with Sylvie, converting the house was the answer. Especially in light of the fact that he intended to rent out one of the apartments as an extra source of income to guarantee a comfortable retirement. What more could Sylvie possibly want?

It was such a perfect plan he wondered why he hadn't thought of it sooner. John knew Sylvie loved this house as much as he did. She would never sell up and move somewhere smaller to release some equity. Now they were retired, this conversion would be the perfect solution to fit their new circumstances. Why would the two of them want to rattle around in this large four-storey, five-bedroomed townhouse, when half of it would be ample for the both of them to live in, with the added bonus of another apartment providing an income?

The other girls, once they had heard the plan, sounded very enthusiastic. It had to be Jess who threw a spanner into the works of a seemingly perfect plan.

'Daddy, are you still there?'

John had proceeded to tell her the plan, reasoning that if Sylvie was bored, frustrated, or unhappy, the project was just what she needed. It didn't mean she was unhappy with her life per se. It didn't mean she was unhappy with him. The problem with the word *unhappy* was that it was so open-ended. It could mean any number of things. But then wasn't that Jess all over? You could never quite pin her down: today Australia, tomorrow – who knows?

'Daddy, did you hear me?'

Yes, he heard her all right. She had made a suggestion that the other girls had not even thought of. That *he* had not thought of.

Jess repeated herself. 'What if, when the apartments are completed, she moves into one on her own – and stays there?'

It hadn't even crossed his mind. 'Well, that's just ridiculous.'

'Is it?'

13

It was Julia's moving day. Sylvie's best friend had sold her flat and was moving on with her life. Julia had lived in her flat for almost as long as Sylvie and John had lived in their house. Over the years it had almost become like a second home to Sylvie. It was where she had often called on her best friend, sharing with her all the highs and the lows of the last three decades.

Sylvie felt she needed to be there to say goodbye to the flat almost as much as Julia. She was glad she had offered to help Julia with her move. Although the removal men were doing most of the work, Julia had some personal items she wanted to pack herself, with Sylvie's help.

'You're very quiet Sylvie, what's going on?'

Sylvie really shouldn't have brought it up on Julia's moving day, but she couldn't keep it bottled up any longer. She had resisted the urge to phone Julia and tell her what had been going on in her life of late. However, as soon as she arrived at the flat, Julia knew something was up and eventually wheedled it out of her.

As they sat together in the bedroom packing boxes, Sylvie told her everything, recounting the whole sorry affair of John losing his job and being at home all day driving her crazy.

Finally, she told Julia all about the house conversion, including John's suggestion that she could move into one of the apartments if she wanted to and iron out the wrinkles, which sounded suspiciously like something he'd made up on the spot.

'He said what?' Julia had been carrying a box down the stairs. She stopped abruptly halfway down and turned around to look at Sylvie behind her.

Sylvie registered the look of surprise on Julia's face at the mention of the house conversion.

'At first, I believed him,' confided Sylvie as they continued down the stairs. 'The house is far too big for the two of us. I could see his thinking when he said he wanted to convert the house and rent out one of the apartments for some extra income, now I'm not so sure . . .' Sylvie trailed off.

'But you don't need the extra money.'

'Exactly. It's not as though we splash out on fancy restaurant meals and foreign holidays. I can't see that changing any time soon. He certainly hasn't mentioned anything of the sort.' Sylvie couldn't help thinking there was more to it than that.

As she followed Julia down the stairs of the split-level apartment and into the lounge, Sylvie was still mulling over the possibility that she wasn't the only one who wanted a trial separation.

'You did what!' exclaimed Julia, momentarily forgetting what she was doing and taping over Sylvie's finger.

They were sitting together on the floor in the lounge and Sylvie was helping Julia do up the last cardboard storage box when she casually let slip that she had moved into the spare bedroom.

Julia reached for the scissors to cut free Sylvie's finger.

Once the last box was taped up, Julia sat back on her heels in the empty lounge and studied Sylvie thoughtfully. 'You moved into the spare bedroom and told John you want a trial separation? I don't believe it.'

Sylvie knew that everybody assumed their marriage was rock solid. She had been too embarrassed to admit that something was wrong, even to her best friend. Sylvie could feel the tears welling up as she confided in Julia that she had been unhappy for quite some time.

'Oh Sylvie!' Julia leaned forward and wrapped her arms around Sylvie's shoulders, giving her best friend a sympathetic hug. 'Please don't cry.'

Sylvie couldn't help herself. It was as though by telling Julia, it made the trial separation all the more real. Her emotions were still raw over losing her mother, without the prospect of losing John too, even though she was the one who had instigated the trial separation. She felt so confused.

Julia let go of Sylvie and fumbled in her pocket for a packet of Kleenex tissues she had on hand. Julia had bought them in case she came over tearful at the prospect of saying goodbye to the flat that she had happily called home for so many years. So far, Julia didn't need a tissue. She offered them to Sylvie.

Sylvie took one and wiped her eyes dry. 'I'm so sorry for dumping all this on you Julia, especially on your moving day – of all days. This should be a happy occasion for you, and I've gone and ruined it by telling you all my problems.'

Julia shook her head profusely from side to side. 'Don't you dare say that,' Julia admonished her sternly. 'Never mind all this,' she gestured at the boxes and then fixed her gaze on Sylvie. 'You're my best friend. I wish you'd told me sooner.'

'I know. It's just that John's plans for the house have taken me completely by surprise. After John suggested I could have my own apartment for a while to figure myself out, I agreed to the house conversion. Not because I want a whole apartment; the spare bedroom is just fine. I agreed to it because I don't know what this is really all about, Julia. I don't know if John is being completely honest about the plan for the house, or he's got some hidden agenda, like leaving me.'

Julia regarded Sylvie a long moment. She didn't have the answers, but she did ask Sylvie, 'Are you going to do it?'

Sylvie tucked the tissue in the sleeve of her jumper and looked up at Julia. 'Do what?'

'When the house has been converted, are you going to move into one of the apartments on your own?'

'Don't be silly. Of course not,' Sylvie replied, although she didn't tell Julia it had crossed her mind.

'These boxes too, Luv?' The removal men walked into the lounge and pointed at the last two boxes on the floor.

Julia nodded.

Sylvie and Julia watched the removal men take a box each and walk out of the room, leaving the lounge empty. They stood there in muted silence.

Sylvie cast her eyes around the room. The lounge looked cavernous now all Julia's furniture had gone. It made Sylvie feel worse to think that another part of her life was drawing to a close when Julia moved out of this flat. It was as though all her familiar benchmarks were slipping away, leaving her adrift in a sea of uncertainty.

Julia squeezed Sylvie's hand. 'I'm going to miss the flat too,' she said as if reading her mind. 'But once I've unpacked and got things organised at the other end, you can come over and see my new home. You'll love it, just you wait and see.'

'At least give me your new address so that I can write it in my diary,' suggested Sylvie, rummaging in her bag for a pen. So far, Julia had been vague about where she was moving to, unwilling to divulge her new address. This had upset Sylvie.

'As soon as I'm settled in, you'll be the first person I call. I promise.'

Sylvie held up the pen. 'But—'

'Not just yet. I want it to be a surprise.' Julia was still holding out on giving Sylvie any details.

Sylvie reluctantly put her pen back in her handbag and then looked up sharply as a horrid thought occurred to her. 'You're not leaving London, are you?' What if she was moving miles away to Cornwall or Scotland, or Australia like Jess? Sylvie was about to burst into tears again.

'You daft brush,' Julia said playfully. 'You know me better than that. The only way I'm leaving London is in a box.' Julia's hand flew to her mouth. 'I'm so sorry, Sylvie, that was really insensitive of me.'

Sylvie thought of her mother's remains in a box sitting on a shelf at home waiting to be taken to Cornwall. She gave Julia a sideways glance. Her best friend always had an uncanny ability to come out with the most inappropriate things at the most inopportune moment. This was a case in point. Sylvie once jokingly called it a gift. Although it wasn't much fun being on the receiving end if you didn't have a sense of humour or a sense of irony. Fortunately, Sylvie had both.

Sylvie couldn't help but smile when she caught the look of horror on Julia's face at her unintentional gaffe.

Staring at Sylvie, noting her smile, Julia's horror-stricken expression abruptly changed into a cheeky grin, one that took Sylvie back more than fifty years to her childhood. And now, as then, it only served to make Sylvie laugh.

Together they stood in Julia's empty lounge – which wasn't in point of fact her lounge any longer – and laughed and laughed. Their laughter reminding them of all the good times they'd shared and all the happy memories Julia would take with her from this flat. It was a good note to end on, thought Sylvie, as the laughter ebbed away. They both fell silent.

She glanced at Julia who was looking around the room for the final time before she closed the door on this chapter of her life. The last time they both stood in this room together, when it was devoid of all furniture, was over three decades ago when Julia was moving in. They had both stood for a moment in quiet contemplation wondering what the future had in store.

Sylvie guessed that's what Julia was doing now, what they were both doing now. Except back then things were very different. Sylvie had John with the plan for their future together. They were in the throes of renovating their family home. And Sylvie was a mother to two small children and a baby on the way. Her future seemed all mapped out.

Today, Sylvie didn't know what she had. Today, Sylvie didn't know what the future held.

'I'm ready,' said Julia with a smile. Julia was ready for the next chapter in her life. Julia was ready for the future she had planned.

Sylvie wasn't. Although she knew it was time to change that. She glanced at Julia standing beside her, smiling happily. If she wanted any chance of finding happiness like her best friend, Sylvie knew she had to make her own plans and map out her own future. Regardless of John's real motivations for converting the house, Sylvie didn't know whether she wanted John to be a part of her future or not.

Julia closed the front door and turned to Sylvie, giving her an affectionate hug. 'Thanks for being here today, darling. I couldn't have done it without you.'

Sylvie smiled as they walked down the front steps to the street where Julia's old mini was parked at the kerb. Sylvie glanced down the street. The removal men had already set off in the van, making their way to Julia's new home.

Sylvie watched Julia get in her car and look up at the flat one last time, silently bidding it a fond farewell before setting off to her new life.

Sylvie waved as Julia departed and then reluctantly turned towards home, towards an uncertain future.

14

The builder arrived outside the house dead on eight o'clock. Sylvie had been standing by the bay window in the lounge for the last half an hour, with butterflies in her stomach, awaiting his arrival. She was not looking forward to his visit and the start of what she believed was John's ill-conceived plan. Sylvie was still not convinced that John was doing the right thing going ahead with the house conversion, even though it was keeping him occupied and out of her hair.

Sylvie stood by the window in silence, arms folded, watching a young man get out of a shiny blue Porsche. If it wasn't for John suddenly appearing behind her exclaiming, 'That's him!' making her nearly jump out of her skin, Sylvie would not have pegged him for the builder. He wasn't at all what she had been expecting. He seemed very young to be at the helm of his own building company. Sylvie thought he wouldn't have looked out of place dressed in a suit driving his Porsche to work in the City.

The young man stopped to open the front gate.

Sylvie suddenly felt self-conscious standing at the window staring at him. Even so, she remained rooted to the spot studying the young builder.

Dressed casually in blue chinos and a white cotton shirt, he was smart in appearance, clean shaven, with neatly trimmed blonde hair swept back with hair gel. He was carrying what appeared to be a laptop case, giving the impression that he was on his way to a board meeting rather than a building job.

For some reason he brought to mind some of the young men Chloe had dated in the past before all those relationships fizzled out. Chloe wasn't seeing anybody at the moment. For a split second, Sylvie stopped thinking about the conversion and saw the young man walking up their garden path as a rather nice prospect for her daughter.

The young man suddenly stopped and waved.

To Sylvie's embarrassment, she realised she had lingered too long; he had spotted her standing at the window. She gave him a limp wave back and scuttled away from the window, wondering why she was suddenly thinking about playing matchmaker. The thought had never crossed her mind before. That was normally Julia's territory, trying to fix up her single, available friends.

Sylvie hoped her best friend wasn't getting any ideas because Julia seemed very interested to know whether she was moving into one of the apartments on her own after the conversion.

Sylvie dismissed that thought as she disappeared downstairs to put the kettle on, leaving John to answer the front door. She still had butterflies in her stomach at the prospect of what lay ahead when the building work began.

John brought the young man down to the kitchen to introduce him to Sylvie. John was well aware that Sylvie still had reservations about his plans for the house. To put her mind at rest, he had insisted that the sceptic – meaning Sylvie – met the builder who would be overseeing the conversion.

Sylvie took to Declan straight away. In terms of first impressions, Sylvie wasn't far off the mark. He used to work in the City but traded in his suit and tie for the family business. It turned out that his father had run the building firm for years and his son, Declan, had recently taken over when he retired. Sadly, Declan had lost his mother shortly before his father retired. This had given Declan pause to consider his future and what he really wanted to do with his life.

He had attended university straight from school, graduating with a first in economics, and then drifted into the City to work in finance because that's what his friends were doing. But his heart wasn't in it. Losing his mother had been the catalyst to make him stop and re-evaluate his life.

Sylvie could empathise.

'I didn't want to work in finance for the rest of my life and reach retirement regretting that I never had the courage to try something else,' explained Declan. 'My father was going to sell the family business. He was so surprised when I asked him if I could take over the reins that I thought he was going to have a heart-attack!'

Sylvie and John both laughed at that.

'You see, I never showed the slightest interest in the family business growing up. My father was concerned that I didn't know what I was getting myself into. However, now I've been in the business for almost five years, I've really found my feet. I can't imagine doing anything else.'

John had already shown Sylvie the glowing recommendation letters from other satisfied customers. Now she had met Declan, Sylvie was starting to feel more confident about John's idea.

'Now down to business,' said John, once the pleasantries

were out of the way. John was already prepared with his yellow manila folder containing his proposed plans for the conversion of the house.

Declan got out a clipboard, pen and a tape measure from his black shoulder bag. 'Right, the first thing we need to do, Mr Baxter, is for you to take me on a quick tour of the house.'

'Of course, of course,' said John leading the way.

'I'll make some tea,' said Sylvie to the empty room.

Fifteen minutes later Sylvie heard the creak of the stairs as they made their way back downstairs to the kitchen.

'Declan has come up with a clever idea,' said John, walking into the kitchen.

Sylvie handed Declan a cup of tea and listened to his clever idea.

'After looking round your property and drawing up some rudimentary plans of the layout, I think it is quite feasible for you both to remain living in your home during the conversion.'

John turned to Sylvie. 'Isn't that marvellous?'

Sylvie didn't think so. She frowned at him. Trust John to think of ways to save money from the outset. Sylvie envisaged that they would move out and stay in a London hotel or a bed and breakfast. She even had visions of the two of them going away together for a few weeks, leaving the builder to get on with it. Sylvie knew that was out of the question; John would want to oversee the project every step of the way. This didn't surprise her. But what did, was the prospect of having to live in the house while the conversion went on around them.

She would never forget the last round of building work they had done to the house years ago when they first moved in. It was messy. It was disruptive. And Sylvie remembered she seemed to walk around with a permanent taste of cement dust in her mouth. It wasn't pleasant. Sylvie was not looking forward to going through all that again, and they shouldn't have to. This time around they had the money to find alternative accommodation. Perhaps John had to face the fact that they weren't in their twenties; they were too old to rough it. They needed their creature comforts. Sylvie needed her creature comforts. Sylvie thought they should move out once the conversion work went ahead. She broached it with John.

'Move out?' John wouldn't hear of it. 'Just give it a try. This will work – you'll see.'

'And if it doesn't?' Sylvie said sceptically.

'I can understand your concerns, Mrs Baxter,' Declan said smoothly. 'Your husband was telling me all about the extensive work you've had done to the house over the years. I bet the thought of living on a building site tasting that cement dust in your mouth again doesn't sound too palatable, does it?'

He had practically read her mind. Sylvie nodded at him and smiled warmly thinking, what a lovely young man.

'This is the clever part,' noted John, butting in before Declan had a chance to finish what he was about to say.

'I wouldn't call it clever,' said Declan with a self-deprecating smile. 'It's just common sense.'

Declan had made some rough sketches of the layout of the house during his tour with John. He spread them out on the kitchen table for Sylvie to see. With a pencil to hand, he pointed at the sketch of the lower ground floor where they were standing, and then the floor directly above comprising the lounge, the dining room at the back and John's study. 'What I propose is this . . .' Declan proceeded to explain his clever idea in detail.

Sylvie nodded here and there as she listened attentively to Declan. By the time he finished, she had concluded that Declan's idea for them to remain living in the house while the conversion went ahead was surprisingly feasible.

Their townhouse was spread over four floors so Declan proposed that, to begin with, John and Sylvie could move downstairs and live on the lower two floors of the house consisting of the basement and the ground-floor.

'I can seal off the two lower floors from the rest of the house while we work upstairs,' explained Declan. 'You would still have your own entrance by way of the back garden through the french patio doors.'

Declan pointed at the french doors in the kitchen. 'You would effectively have a self-contained apartment where you could live quite adequately, and come and go independently of the workmen carrying out the conversion on the top two floors. The workmen will enter the house by way of the front door and then proceed straight up the stairs from the entrance hall.' He paused, glancing at Sylvie. 'We will seal off the door from the entrance hall to the lounge for now, so there's no dust. I promise.'

Sylvie managed a smile.

Declan returned her smile, confident that Mrs Baxter was warming to the idea. He knew from past experience with clients that, unbeknown to most husbands, it really was the wife who made the decisions. If she vetoed John's plans, then he was out of a job. He could tell the moment he arrived, when Mr Baxter was keen to introduce him to this wife, that this couple was not the exception to that rule. It had been the same for his own parents when his mother was still alive.

Declan couldn't comment from personal experience as he

wasn't married and had never been in a long-term relationship. Single again, Declan was still looking for the one.

He hoped one day to meet a young lady he could confidently say he wanted to spend the rest of his life with. So far, that hadn't happened. He hoped it happened soon. Declan was sensitive about the fact that he was pushing thirty, and he still hadn't settled down when a surprising number of his friends were already married.

Always competitive, he was the first among his mates to reach milestones: a girlfriend at the tender age of fifteen; passing his driving test at seventeen; a midlife crisis at twenty-five when he chucked in the towel on a lucrative but stressful city job to run his own business. But now Declan was feeling left behind and, if he was honest, a bit unnerved that for all he had going for him he couldn't seem to go the distance with any of his previous girlfriends. He was beginning to wonder what the hell was wrong with him that he couldn't commit.

'Declan?'

'Oh sorry, Mrs Baxter, I was lost in thought there for a moment. Now, where was I?'

Sylvie reminded him, 'You were talking about temporarily sealing off the lower two floors of the house for us to live in . . .'

'Ah yes.' Declan turned his attention to the sketches in front of him. 'I think the only inconvenience for you is that there won't be a bathroom or en-suite. However, I've noted on these plans that you do have a wet room.'

Sylvie nodded, glancing at the door in the kitchen that led through to a small lobby housing the washing machine and tumble-drier. From the small lobby, another door opened into the wet room which was fully tiled with a shower, vanity basin and toilet. It was put in when they had their new kitchen installed years ago. They had rarely used it.

John turned to Sylvie. 'I think we could make do with the wet room for a little while – don't you?'

Declan looked across at Sylvie, waiting for confirmation that she was happy to go along with that.

Sylvie considered it for a moment. Sometimes she liked a bath, but it would not be any great inconvenience to live with only a shower for a short time. Sylvie nodded her head in agreement.

'On the next floor you have a lounge on the front,' Declan continued as he studied the layout of their house. 'If you don't have any objections, you could use the dining room at the back as a temporary bedroom until we finish the conversion upstairs.'

'What more do we need,' said John, clearly delighted with Declan's idea. He picked up his mug of tea and grinned at Sylvie.

Sylvie frowned. John had forgotten something. She decided to remind him. 'What about the spare bedroom?'

John spluttered into his mug. He wiped the tea dripping from his chin and glanced at Declan, throwing him a lop-sided smile before turning to Sylvie. 'Do we still need a spare bedroom, dearest?'

Sylvie stood there with her arms folded tapping her foot impatiently. Did he really want her to spell it out in front of Declan? More to the point, did he really think just because she had agreed to the house conversion that anything had changed? It didn't mean she was moving out of the spare bedroom. If they were going along with Declan's idea and moving downstairs, Sylvie was taking the spare bedroom with her.

Declan looked from John to Sylvie and coughed into the

uncomfortable silence. 'I don't think that will be a problem.' At least he hoped it wouldn't. Declan studied the sketches of the layout looking for a solution. So far, Declan thought things were going well. He wanted this job because, although he had no shortage of work, converting a townhouse into two apartments was certainly a little different to the usual extensions and house renovations that he normally worked on. And he liked his potential new clients.

John had told Declan the reason for the conversion. They had lived in this house most of their married lives, and raised their children in this house, but now their home was far too large for them. Most people their age would sell up, downsize and bank some money. They were a little different. Declan liked that they were prepared to think out of the box. Clearly, they didn't want to move house, so they had come up with an alternative solution. He admired their sense of adventure taking on a project like this when they retired. He wished he could tell them how lucky they were to be making these plans together. His parents hadn't been quite so fortunate. Perhaps that's why Declan really wanted to help this couple realise their dreams for the future.

Declan tapped his pencil on the plans indicating the study. 'There you see – problem solved. The study could be used as the spare bedroom while you're living downstairs.'

Sylvie smiled at Declan. 'Perfect.'

'But I need my study,' whined John.

Sylvie grabbed John's arm. 'Excuse us a moment.'

'Of course.' Declan held up his tape-measure and picked up his clipboard. 'I'll just erm pop upstairs and start taking some detailed measurements if that's okay with you?' Sensing the atmosphere in the room, he didn't wait for a reply.

As soon as Declan disappeared up the stairs, Sylvie turned to John. 'Now look here, I'm going along with all this despite my reservations, so the least you can do is give up your study. What do you need it for anyway?' Sylvie had a good mind to go and get a hotel room. The problem was John would have to agree to spend the money, and that was like getting blood from a stone.

Five minutes later John and Sylvie were standing in silence waiting for Declan. They had reached a compromise. Although Sylvie still preferred to stay in a hotel, she was prepared to move downstairs on the proviso that the study was turned into a spare bedroom.

Declan appeared at the bottom of the stairs and knocked on the door to the kitchen even though the door was open.

'Come in,' said Sylvie, glancing at John.

Declan sidled into the room hoping Mrs Baxter hadn't changed her mind and the whole thing was off.

'We have decided to go ahead with your plan,' said Sylvie. 'We will use the study as my—' Sylvie hastily rephrased, '—the spare bedroom.'

'In case we have guests,' John added quickly.

Sylvie turned around and glared at John; did he want to make it any more obvious what was going on here?

John caught her meaning and swiftly looked at his shoes in embarrassment.

Sylvie shifted her gaze and smiled at the nice young man. 'Now tell me Declan, what happens when the conversion upstairs is complete?'

'Ah,' said Declan brightening, 'that's the easy part. Once we have completed the work to turn the upper two floors of the house into a self-contained apartment, you simply move upstairs into your newly converted apartment while we work on the necessary alterations downstairs.'

The plan sounded as though it was foolproof – on paper. Sylvie was no stranger to the reality of a building project. They rarely, if ever, went without a hitch.

As Sylvie predicted, it wasn't long before the cracks started to appear in the builder's carefully conceived plan. However, the problem was not quite what Sylvie had envisaged.

15

Sylvie wasn't walking around with the taste of cement dust in her mouth, as she had feared, or sprinkled liberally in her hair so it appeared she was turning prematurely grey like the last time. Sealing off their downstairs living quarters from the rest of the house had sealed off the dust and debris, and even the strong odour of wet paint drying. Sylvie had expected some teething problems, in the beginning. However, she would be the first to admit that it had worked better than she imagined, in terms of disruption and cost.

What Sylvie had not anticipated was the unexpected side-effect of their new living arrangements, which had nothing to do with the building work. Used to having plenty of room in their large four-storey townhouse, Sylvie did not stop to consider what it would be like living in such close quarters with John. She didn't realise how much all that extra space made a difference until the builders sealed off half the house, in effect forcing them into apartment-style living much sooner than Sylvie was prepared for.

There were times when Sylvie seriously wished that, along with sealing off the upper two floors of the house, they'd sealed John upstairs too. Since moving downstairs, everything he said and did was getting on her nerves, especially when John kept reminding her that they were living in a much smaller space now.

'In order to keep the flat tidy, we have to strive to put everything away in its proper place.'

How many times had she heard him say that in the course of just one day? Sylvie found it irritating beyond belief. He was treating her like a child who had to obey his house rules, not a grown woman who just wanted to relax in her own home. It didn't bother Sylvie if some washing up was left in the sink. It didn't bother Sylvie if she just wanted to kick back at the end of the day, wine glass in hand, and ignore the pile of ironing on the ironing board. But it bothered John.

If she thought he was a bit pernickety before they started the conversion, their much-reduced living space only seemed to accentuate John's irritating penchant for tidying up. Sylvie couldn't put anything down without finding it had been put away when she wasn't looking. Her novel disappeared from the coffee table. Her magazines disappeared from the kitchen worktop. Sylvie seemed to spend an inordinate amount of time searching for things John had "helpfully" tidied away that she was in the middle of using or reading. Even the spare bedroom, which was meant to be her own personal space, was not immune to John's obsessive tidying up. The more it went on, the more it made Sylvie wonder if they would live to regret converting the house.

Sylvie imagined that things would improve when the first part of the conversion was complete and they moved upstairs. Perhaps when they both had time to acclimatize to living in an apartment, John would get off his high horse and stop being so fussy. She hoped so for both their sakes. At the moment, the only positive thing she could glean from the situation was that John was preoccupied all day with the project on the house. He was far too busy with the plan to even ask Sylvie what she was up to of late. The days of John following her like a shadow were but a distant memory. Sylvie finally had some time to herself to figure out what she wanted to do next.

The first thing she decided to do was pay another visit to the charity shop, on her own. John had quickly lost interest in volunteer work in favour of overseeing the conversion on the house. This left Sylvie feeling duty-bound to return to the charity shop cap-in-hand in order to apologise profusely for walking out on her first day and not coming back. That was all John's fault. Even so, her behaviour, letting them down like that really was inexcusable. She was not that kind of person. Besides, it just felt like the right thing to do.

Sylvie stood outside the charity shop and took a deep breath before she opened the door. The sign was still in the window, *Volunteers needed*, but somebody had scrawled the word *urgent* in red ink across the sign. It made her feel terribly guilty for abandoning the shop on her very first day.

Sylvie stepped inside the shop and immediately recognised the woman serving at the counter. It was the same friendly volunteer called Brenda who had welcomed her with open arms a short time ago. Sylvie wondered what sort of reception she would receive today. She headed straight for the counter at the back of the shop before she bottled out.

Brenda's friendly expression wilted as Sylvie approached. 'You again!' Brenda folded her arms and regarded her coolly.

'I . . . I've come to apologise.' Sylvie pointed towards the ad in the window. 'I notice you still have a vacancy.' Sylvie was hoping she could still volunteer.

'You are joking,' Brenda shot back. 'We need volunteers who are committed. *Reliable*,' she emphasised. 'Not flit in on a whim, then change their mind and leave us in the lurch.'

'Oh, I can assure you I wouldn't do that.'

'But you already did!' Brenda barked irritably. 'You both did.' She shook her head as if to say *it's no use*. 'I'm sorry but—'

'Look, my husband has been having some issues,' admitted Sylvie. 'John lost his job recently, and I'm afraid he hasn't been coping very well.'

'I see,' said Brenda, meaning *do tell*.

'He's been driving me around the bend, Brenda. So when he followed me here, I just sort of . . . lost it.' Sylvie felt her face colour in embarrassment. She did not appreciate having to air their dirty linen in public, telling a virtual stranger all their problems. Nonetheless, Sylvie felt she owed Brenda an explanation.

Brenda's expression softened as Sylvie told her all this.

'Just give me a chance,' Sylvie pleaded. 'I really want to make it up to you. I can see by the sign outside that you still need volunteers. And I'm more than happy to come back, really I am. I promise I won't let you down this time.'

Perhaps, in hindsight, Sylvie realised she had laid it on a bit too thick because when Brenda admitted they were in desperate need of volunteers, Sylvie added, 'Whatever you want me to do is fine by me, anything at all.'

Brenda considered this for a moment. 'You originally agreed to volunteer two days per week. Your husband volunteered the rest of the week – and Saturday.'

Sylvie nodded even though she had no idea John was going

to work Saturdays as well.

'Are we going to see your husband return any time soon?' Brenda glanced towards the door as though she was expecting John to make an appearance.

Sylvie looked at the floor in embarrassment.

'I thought not.' Brenda offered Sylvie another disapproving glare. 'It would have been nice if your husband had at least informed us he wasn't coming back.' She let that statement hang in the air.

Sylvie mumbled, 'I'm sorry.' She glanced at the door wishing she had dragged John along too. I'm going to murder him when I get home, thought Sylvie. She was already aware that John wouldn't be returning to work in the charity shop once the project on the house got underway. She knew this for a fact because she had asked him outright. She just didn't realise he had neglected to tell Brenda.

'Now, if you really want to be of help . . .' began Brenda.

'Yes, anything,' Sylvie replied a bit too quickly.

'Perhaps you would consider doing your husband's hours until we find a replacement? That would be an enormous help.'

Sylvie smiled. 'Brenda, I'm delighted to help in any way I can.' Even though Sylvie wasn't keen on the idea of working on Saturdays, she thought that was the least she could do under the circumstances. Sylvie had been prepared to stay and work today if they would have her back, but John's hours weren't until the latter part of the week. 'You can count on me,' said Sylvie buttoning up her coat.

'You're leaving?' Brenda looked at Sylvie in surprise as she turned to go.

'Well yes. John's hours aren't until—'

'Oh dear, I can see where I've confused you,' observed Brenda. 'You are quite right: John volunteered on Thursday, Friday, and Saturday.'

Sylvie could feel her patience wearing thin. She knew that, that's why she was leaving.

Brenda explained, 'Your hours, on the other hand, were the first half of the week, which includes today.' Brenda looked at her expectantly. 'You are still committed to your hours, aren't you?'

Sylvie offered Brenda a tight smile realising she had just backed herself into a corner. She didn't realise she was also volunteering to cover John's hours on top of her own. Sylvie unbuttoned her coat under Brenda's watchful eye.

When Sylvie walked into the charity shop this morning, she did not envisage that she would end up committed to working six days per week – almost twice the hours she was working in her part-time job. Sylvie sighed heavily. Her first foray into doing something for herself had not gone well. And Sylvie knew who she had to thank for that.

John was now fully occupied by the project on the house which should have left Sylvie with lots of free time on her hands to do her own thing. On the contrary, she found herself working all hours in the charity shop covering for John, while he was clearly enjoying himself overseeing the conversion and making himself at home in the apartment.

She knew it suited John down to the ground that she was out of the apartment all day, so he had the run of the place. Not to mention the fact that without Sylvie around he could keep the apartment pristine, just the way he liked it. In fact, John had his daily routine finely tuned. She had seen the calendar on the wall

155

in the kitchen. His days consisted of meetings with Declan and the architect, visiting DIY stores for paint samples and the like, and plenty of R&R listening to classical music and reading his newspaper.

R&R? Sylvie had bristled when she saw that written on his calendar. As far as she was concerned, John's whole day was one long R&R. She could do with a bit of rest and relaxation herself. Sylvie was starting to resent their new routine whereby she was out all day working in the charity shop and John was at home.

At least the conversion was running smoothly. The building work on the house had progressed rapidly, thanks to Declan and his hard-working team. It wasn't long before they were en-sconced on the upper two floors of the house that had been fully converted into an apartment. Sylvie assumed that once they moved upstairs things would be different between them, but to her surprise nothing changed. What really rankled Sylvie was that despite giving it a chance, living in an apartment with John wasn't getting any easier. In fact, it was getting harder.

Every time Sylvie returned home after a long day at work, feeling tired and a little bit disillusioned, she had John to contend with. He was acting like her mere presence was upsetting his equilibrium, as though she was purposely messing up the apartment and being a general nuisance like an unwanted house-guest. It felt like she was invading his own private space, as though it was his apartment, not theirs.

Was it little wonder John was making her feel this way? As with the original building work on the house, Sylvie had no input in the design, layout, or even the colour schemes of both apartments. It was all what John wanted. Not surprisingly, it was decorated in neutral magnolia paint. And let us not forget John's favourite colour for almost everything else – white. The whole upstairs apartment reminded Sylvie of a rather bland show-home. The way it was decorated and furnished, and so spotlessly clean and tidy, made it appear as though it had been staged for a photo-shoot. This might be nice on the cover of a magazine, but not so nice when you just wanted to relax in the comfort of your own home – at least not for Sylvie.

Sylvie had said as much on numerous occasions until John finally snapped. 'Perhaps if you made an effort to get involved, you could have voiced your opinions before I went ahead with all this!'

They were both standing in the brand new kitchen in the apartment upstairs. It was a much smaller kitchen than Sylvie was used to and it had white flush kitchen cupboard doors that didn't appear to have any door handles.

Sylvie looked angrily at John after that rather snide remark. If she could figure out how to open one of John's new kitchen cupboards, she would reach inside and hurl the first thing she could lay her hands on right at John's head.

She gave up and shouted back, 'Perhaps if I wasn't working so many hours covering for you,' she pointed a rude finger at John, 'then maybe I'd have some free time to get involved.'

That wasn't the real issue, and they both knew it. John wouldn't have wanted her to get involved in the conversion whether she had the time or not. This was his plan, not hers. This was his apartment, not hers. At least that's the way John was making her feel.

Sylvie was well aware she wasn't helping the situation. She had continued to sleep in the spare bedroom, first downstairs and then in the upstairs apartment. But that didn't excuse the fact that Sylvie no longer felt welcome in her own home. Was John even aware of the way he was making her feel? Did he even care? Or was this the master plan to get her to move out? If that was the case, he was succeeding. Sylvie was at her wit's end.

A few days after that heated argument with John, Sylvie's best friend Julia phoned with her new address. It seemed to have taken Julia an age to settle in before making that call. As soon as Sylvie heard her voice on the phone, she was mentally packing her travel bag to get out of the apartment and away from John. She just hoped Julia's new home could accommodate her. It couldn't.

It turned out that Julia's life wasn't all plain sailing at the moment either. There had been a hitch with her house move. It sounded as though there was a leak and the place had flooded, which had temporarily forestalled her moving in. Julia didn't feel like going into details, but she sounded bitterly disappointed that it might be another month at least before she would be settled in her new home. In the meantime, Julia's brother was putting her up in his spare bedroom.

Sylvie was very sorry to hear Julia's bad news, doubly so because her escape plan had just evaporated. She was still stuck living in the apartment with John.

Sylvie knew she should have it out with him, but at this point, she was just past caring. Instead, she couldn't help thinking about the conversion taking place below, and what it might be like to pack her bags and move into the apartment downstairs – alone.

16

The building work downstairs had proceeded better than expected and was completed ahead of schedule. Unfortunately, as far as Sylvie was concerned, things had only gone from bad to worse on the domestic front.

By the time the conversion was finished, Sylvie wished John had never come up with the plan. She had a feeling it was a bad idea from the outset. Sylvie didn't know how bad until she had experienced living in an apartment with John for three months. How was she going to survive the next ten, twenty, or even thirty-plus years living like this, if they stayed together? And right now, for Sylvie, that was a big *if*.

At least Sylvie knew, once the renovations were complete, there was always the option to move into the apartment downstairs for a short time while she figured out what to do.

Sylvie remembered John's exact words when he had made this proposal before she went along with his plan to convert the house. John had said she could spend a few days in the garden apartment to iron out any wrinkles, so to speak, before the first tenants moved in. Sylvie was beginning to think she might have to take him up on that, if for no other reason than her own sanity. She needed some time to herself now all the building work was over, in order to digest all this and put things into perspective.

It had crossed her mind that perhaps she was overreacting. There had been so many changes in her life in such a short space of time. It had started with her mother passing, swiftly followed by John's surprise retirement, and then their family home being dismantled around her. Even her best friend moving house hadn't helped the situation. In hindsight, it just felt like one loss on top of another. Little wonder she had the urge to run away from everything, from her mother's final request still gnawing away at her because she hadn't done anything about it, from the house, from John.

Maybe, moving into the downstairs apartment to get away from her husband wasn't really the answer. Perhaps John wasn't the problem at all. What if she needed to see somebody, like a counsellor, and talk things through?

Sylvie left the charity shop on Saturday evening with these thoughts weighing heavy on her mind. She hadn't walked far when she found herself preoccupied with John.

As soon as the conversion was complete, John immediately launched himself into his next project which was planning a grand opening. John was throwing a small party to show off the completed apartments. He had invited as many people as he could think of, which wasn't that many. Sylvie couldn't see why her youngest daughter Chloe would be all that interested in coming or their eldest daughter Harriet and her husband, Dominic. And why Jess would fly all the way home from Australia for this was beyond Sylvie. They had converted the house into two apartments – big deal.

John had also asked Sylvie to invite her friends to the party, but she couldn't do that. Since starting work at the charity shop, Sylvie didn't have time to meet them for coffee and a catch-up which meant she had not got around to telling her friends about the house conversion.

Sylvie knew that was just an excuse. She could have phoned them up and told them. But unlike John, Sylvie didn't relish the thought of telling people about the house conversion. Her friends were all living comfortable middle-class lives in their large family homes. If Sylvie was honest, she felt embarrassed that her own circumstances were very different now they had downsized to a two-bedroomed apartment. Not to mention the fact that at some point soon they would be living with tenants below them. When she really thought about it, it almost felt like a step back, not a step forward in their lives. Was it really worth all this upheaval for a few extra pounds swelling their bank account?

Sylvie didn't feel inclined to tell her friends about her new living arrangements, or the fact that she was sleeping in the spare bedroom. The only friend who knew about everything was her best friend, Julia. Disappointingly, Julia had been so up to her eyes in sorting out the unforeseen glitches with her new place that Sylvie hadn't had a chance to see her.

Thankfully, that was about to change. Julia was moving into her new home very soon. Sylvie couldn't wait for Julia to get in touch with her new address because she was feeling quite down and in desperate need of a friend right now. In the meantime, she had made a point of not getting involved in John's grand opening. Sylvie didn't feel like celebrating. At the forefront of her mind was what would happen when the party was over and John came back down to earth? The conversion project on the house was finished. The party was tonight. And then that too would be over. What would John do afterwards? Sylvie couldn't possibly go back to the way things were in the aftermath of John losing his job, especially now they were living together in a small apartment. There would be no getting away from John then.

Sylvie tried very hard not to dwell on that as she walked home from her day at work in the charity shop. Approaching the house, Sylvie opened the wrought iron gate and made her way along the short garden path and up the stone steps to the front door. She was thinking how the house no longer felt like home. It was just a place where they lived and, very soon, a place where other people would live too. Tenants. Strangers.

Sylvie stood for a moment on the porch and looked up at the house. She thought she would spend the rest of her life here. Now she wasn't so sure. Sylvie shook her head sadly as she rummaged in her handbag looking for the house keys. She now had two keys, one key to the main front door leading into the communal entrance hall, the other to the apartment upstairs. Sylvie was still getting used to the changes.

It was John's idea to have a communal entrance hall to both apartments. He said he wanted to preserve a feeling of space in the property, although Sylvie had an idea he wanted to keep an eye on the comings and goings of the tenants downstairs.

Declan's plan was to use the french doors in the basement kitchen as the main entrance to the rental apartment downstairs. He wanted to take advantage of the fact that their property was an end-terrace which meant tenants could easily access their apartment through the side gate from the street into the back garden. Declan then proposed to keep the main front door of the house as the entrance to John and Sylvie's apartment upstairs, effectively sealing off both apartments as completely separate entities, as was the case during the conversion.

This was the only part of the project that Sylvie distinctly remembered John and Declan disagreed on. John vetoed Declan's idea in favour of a more communal arrangement whereby the occupants of both apartments would use the main front door of the house that still led into the original entrance hall. From the hall, the tenants would enter their apartment through a door on the right at the foot of the stairs. This door now served as the front door to the garden apartment and led straight into the original lounge overlooking the front garden.

The occupants of the apartment upstairs, being Sylvie and John the landlords, would take the staircase leading to the first-floor landing and enter their apartment through a door on the right at the top of the stairs. The door to their apartment led directly into a small lobby area for hats, coats and shoes, and then into their open plan living space. The lounge had a bay window identical to the apartment below, overlooking the street at the front. At the other end of the living area was a small kitchenette with a sash window overlooking the garden two storeys below and just enough room for a small bistro table and two chairs.

Their kitchen was much smaller than anticipated because John insisted on having a study. This meant that the original plan for a large double-aspect kitchen was shelved in favour of an additional room next door to the lounge on the front. Sylvie would have preferred a larger separate kitchen rather than a small kitchenette but, as with everything else, her views were not taken into consideration.

They accessed the second floor of their apartment, formerly the top floor of the house, through a new inner staircase from their lounge. This floor now comprised of two bedrooms and a bathroom. The original staircase that led up to the top floor of the house had been removed making the first-floor landing outside their apartment a dead end. Once inside their apartment, as with the apartment below, it was completely self-contained.

Sylvie closed the front door and stood in the communal hall outside the door to the rental apartment. She was thinking about the conversion of the lower two floors of the house. It turned out that very little in the way of alterations were necessary to the layout of the ground floor and basement of the house to create the rental apartment.

The apartment consisted of a lounge-diner entered directly from the door to the apartment Sylvie was standing in front of. The two bedrooms on this floor were originally the dining room and John's study at the back of the house. The only addition was a small bathroom. The lower ground floor of the apartment was accessed by the original staircase from the lounge, leading down into the large basement kitchen with the original french doors on to the back garden. A door on the other side of the kitchen led into a utility area, with a further door through to the wet room which had an obscured basement window at eye level with the front garden.

Sylvie frowned at the apartment door. She had let John get on with the conversion without interfering once. However, there was one part of John's plan that they most definitely did not agree on. When it came down to the decision over which apartment they would live in, and which one they would rent out, John had already made up his mind. He wanted to live in the apartment upstairs. Sylvie did not. Sylvie would miss her garden.

John insisted he wanted to live over the tenants, rather than downstairs, in case he heard people walking around above him. Sylvie thought it would be doubtful they would have any noise issues because of the stringent building regulations they had to adhere to regarding soundproofing. Sylvie imagined the tenants would have to be quite noisy and inconsiderate for them to hear anything. When Sylvie pointed this out, she got to the bottom of the real reason John's preference was to rent out that apartment in particular. It was all because he could call it a *garden* apartment and consequently he believed they would get more rental income for it. As usual, everything boiled down to the bottom line – money.

Sylvie recalled that conversation with John as she stood in the hall at the bottom of the stairs outside the door to the garden apartment. She stared at the door wondering what it would feel like to have the key to that apartment in her hand right now. She imagined opening that door, walking inside, throwing herself on the deep-cushioned sofa in the lounge and putting her feet up on the cushions without John pestering her to use a throw. The thought of doing whatever she fancied, whenever she fancied it, without having to answer to anybody – without having to answer to John – was very, very appealing.

Unfortunately, Sylvie didn't have the key to that apartment. She sighed as she turned from the door and reluctantly walked up the stairs. Gone were the days when Sylvie looked forward to returning home from work in the evening. She stopped in front of their apartment door and glanced along the landing to where the second staircase used to be, now just a blank wall. She wished she could turn back the clock, on everything, and go back to the way things were when John was still in work, and the house was still a home. Sylvie seriously doubted anything good was going to come out of all this. After experiencing living in an apartment with John, Sylvie was feeling very anxious about where this was leading. She knew she couldn't carry on sleeping in the spare bedroom forever. But if they were going to stay together in their twilight years, if that's what John wanted too, then perhaps they needed some time apart to figure out how this was going to work.

Sylvie was considering whether to tell John she needed that time he had promised her in the garden apartment to iron out the wrinkles. Not for the sake of the new tenants, but for the sake of their marriage. However, she was still undecided if that was the right thing to do, or whether she needed to go and seek some professional help from a counsellor.

Sylvie opened the door to their apartment and stepped into the lobby. She kicked off her shoes and placed them neatly together on the shoe-rack John had recently purchased. She hung her coat on one of the coat pegs behind the door with her name above it. Sylvie frowned at the coat peg. Yet another one of John's ridiculous house rules that he insisted they observe. What difference did it make which coat peg she used? Sylvie had kept that thought to herself, along with how she really felt about all the other irksome little things he insisted they do to keep the apartment spotless. Now she just went along with everything in order to keep the peace.

Sylvie walked into the lounge. John was in his new study next door having a conversation on the phone. She could hear his voice through the thin partition wall as though he was having the conversation in the same room.

'Chloe, everything will be all right, I promise. I'll tell her as soon as she gets home.'

Oh god! Sylvie froze. Her first thought was that Chloe was pregnant. At the age of twenty-nine, Sylvie still didn't think her youngest daughter was mature enough for motherhood. She couldn't even settle down and make a commitment to a relationship. How in heaven's name would she cope with a baby?

Sylvie listened intently, a knot building up in the pit of her stomach. Whenever Chloe had some bad news, she always broke the news to Dad first. Sylvie didn't think it was relationship issues, not so soon after splitting up from her last boyfriend, surely.

'Yes, I understand, Chloe. You want a break from Declan.'

Sylvie exhaled. So it *was* relationship issues. It always started the same way: she just needed a break. Both Sylvie and John knew where that was inevitably leading.

Sylvie sighed. It was such a shame Chloe would never settle down, especially with Declan. He was such a nice young man. So nice in fact that Sylvie had visions of Chloe getting married. But by the sound of things, Sylvie could forget any thoughts of another wedding on the horizon.

'Yes Chloe, the apartment is ready.'

The apartment? Sylvie looked bemused. *What apartment?*

'I agree that it would be a good idea to have somebody downstairs for a little while to iron out the wrinkles.'

What was John saying? Sylvie frowned as she walked through the lounge towards the study hoping she had misheard and John wasn't about to . . .

'Yes, of course you can move in downstairs.'

Sylvie stopped dead in the middle of the lounge.

'Oh, don't worry about that, Chloe. Yes, I know I mentioned it to your mother first, but she's never going to move into the garden apartment on her own.' John guffawed. 'She wouldn't last five minutes without me.'

Sylvie glared at the study door. What did he mean: I wouldn't last five minutes without him?

'Besides, I need somebody I can rely on who won't fall to pieces if something does go wrong – like you, Chloe. You've lived on your own. It will be a real help. Yes, I'll tell Mum as soon as I get off the phone. It's settled then. When do you want to move in? After the party? That's fine by me.'

Sylvie's mouth dropped open. It took all her self-control not to march right into the study and have it out with John. Instead, Sylvie turned on her heel, walked into the kitchenette and calmly made herself a cup of tea while she waited for John to emerge from the study.

'Who was that on the phone?' asked Sylvie, as soon as he walked into the lounge. She sat down on the sofa with her mug of tea, acting as though she had not heard a word of John's conversation, which would be pretty difficult in a place this size.

'Oh, just Chloe,' said John casually, not making eye contact Sylvie noticed.

'Is everything all right?' Sylvie asked.

'Yes fine, fine.'

Sylvie sat sipping her tea waiting for John to spill the beans and tell her that he had arranged for Chloe to move into the garden apartment without talking it over between them first. 'Was she phoning about anything in particular?' prompted Sylvie.

'Er no . . . not really.' Again, no eye-contact. 'Just the usual boyfriend issues – you know Chloe.' John rolled his eyes in feigned exasperation.

'I see,' Sylvie said coolly. She eyed John as he walked over to sit on the sofa next to her. As soon as he sat down, Sylvie got up. She walked through the lounge with her mug of tea, the soles of her feet feeling cold as she crossed from the carpeted lounge to the tiled floor of the small kitchenette. She stopped to look at the plates of party food lined up along the kitchen worktop ready for this evening. John had spent the entire day preparing for the party.

Suddenly, Sylvie had the impulse to pick up one of those carefully arranged plates of nibbles and toss it at John. Sylvie resisted that urge and deposited her mug into the dishwasher. She closed the dishwasher door and stood by the sink staring forlornly out of the kitchen window. She missed her old worn basement kitchen downstairs where she used to spend many an hour sitting at the large oak table looking through the french doors into the garden. Sylvie missed her home.

It came as no surprise that John didn't involve her in the conversion, but Sylvie thought she might at least get a say in which apartment they chose to live in. She naively assumed that John would realise how much her garden meant to her and eventually relent. The fact that he wouldn't change his mind about moving in downstairs spoke volumes about how much he took Sylvie's needs into consideration. Especially now he had offered the garden apartment to Chloe behind her back.

Sylvie stood there staring out of kitchen window thinking, what about me? What about what I want?

She turned around to find John sitting on the sofa reading his newspaper. Sylvie glared at him across the room. She had been looking forward to telling John her one piece of good news today. A gentleman had called into the charity shop in response to the ad in the window. He had recently moved into the area and was looking for some voluntary work in the local community. He was starting work at the charity shop tomorrow.

The new volunteer seemed nice, especially nice since Sylvie had just been released from her six-day week commitment. Recently retired, he had agreed to work the latter part of the week and Saturdays. He was taking over John's hours, which meant Sylvie finally had some free time on her hands.

Sylvie didn't feel inclined to tell John this. In fact, Sylvie didn't feel inclined to tell John any of her plans.

17

Upstairs in the spare bedroom, Sylvie was busy packing two suitcases. She could hear John downstairs, classical music playing on the radio as he put the finishing touches to his preparations for the party. Sylvie checked the time. It wouldn't be long before the guests arrived.

Sylvie crossed the room and opened her bedroom door. She then zipped up both suitcases and heaved them off the bed, carrying them one at a time over to the open doorway ready for departure.

John bounded up the stairs, dishcloth in hand, saying, 'I've nearly got everything ready for the—' He stopped abruptly when he caught sight of Sylvie putting the second suitcase down on the floor outside the bedroom door. 'Are we going somewhere?'

Sylvie looked at John and then glanced at the two suitcases; that was well timed, she needed a hand.

'Help me with one of these, would you?' said Sylvie, ignoring his question. She picked up one of the suitcases and strode past John lingering outside the door. Sylvie glanced over her shoulder, raising her eyebrows at John to get a move on and do as she asked.

John shrugged, flipped the dishcloth over his shoulder, and picked up the other suitcase. He followed Sylvie down the stairs humming a tune.

John had an idea what she might be up to. She had booked a trip for the two of them. He had suggested it in the recent past although Sylvie had pooh-poohed the idea at the time. Maybe this was the reason. Sylvie had been planning a surprise trip all along. They were going away together after the party to celebrate the successful completion of the conversion. Perhaps it was a romantic getaway; Sylvie's way of saying she was finally moving out of the spare bedroom. Despite the fact that John wasn't particularly partial to surprises, he smiled at the thought. He had a few surprises of his own.

John was thinking about the right moment to tell Sylvie what he had in mind with the rental income. He couldn't wait to surprise her with all the things he had planned for them to do together. His original idea was to tell her at the party. However, now it appeared that they were going on a trip together, John thought it would be infinitely better to wait until after the party when they were alone to tell her his plans.

This trip would be the perfect opportunity. He could tell her on the way there, or over a romantic dinner for two in the hotel restaurant. John smiled mischievously with thoughts of the hotel room they'd undoubtedly be sharing. He could even tell her in bed after—

John suddenly remembered the party. He glanced at his watch. Surely they weren't going right now? Had Sylvie forgotten there were people arriving in less than ten minutes? Sylvie must have planned for them to leave straight after the party. John didn't think that was a good idea. He couldn't just walk out and leave the apartment in a mess. He would need plenty of time to clear up afterwards. The more John thought about it as he heaved the second suitcase down the stairs, the more it felt like a bad idea. He wished Sylvie had told him her plans. She knew he didn't like surprises. But more than that, he would have preferred to get involved in organising the trip.

Maybe they could have spent more time planning it together. John would have liked that. John would have liked something to look forward to, like a new project to occupy his time, when all this was over. Now the conversion was complete, he didn't have a clue what he was going to do with himself after the party tonight. He was already on the verge of feeling down in the dumps again at the prospect of having nothing to do and no plans for the future. He glanced at the suitcase on his way down the stairs. Perhaps this trip would cheer him up.

Sylvie reached the bottom of the stairs and placed her suitcase down on the parquet floor in the entrance hall. She turned around and watched John follow her down carrying the other suitcase.

He stopped beside her. 'Shall we put them over there?' John indicated the other side of the hall.

'Why?'

John looked at Sylvie puzzled. 'Well, so they won't be in the way of the stairs when people arrive,' he replied in a patronising tone of voice.

Sylvie ignored that remark. She slid her suitcase a few inches along the floor until she was standing in front of the door to the garden apartment with her suitcase at her feet.

John put the other suitcase down next to hers. He didn't get the rationale behind leaving the suitcases in there. They might as well have left them upstairs and brought them down later before they were due to leave. John was getting irritated. Sylvie was wasting his time when he was in the middle of making final preparations for the party. However, John didn't see the point of arguing about it. The suitcases were down here now, and he wasn't about to lug them back upstairs. John fumbled in his pocket for the key to the garden apartment. He went to put the key in the lock.

Sylvie stopped him and held out her hand.

John looked at her outstretched hand and glanced down at the suitcases by her feet. He stared at the door with growing unease wondering what Sylvie was up to. Reluctantly, he placed the key in her hand. He was still holding on to the key fob.

Sylvie gave him an exasperated look. He let go. She took the key and unlocked the door to the garden apartment. Pushing the door open, Sylvie picked up one of the suitcases and walked inside.

John was about to follow her inside with the other one when Sylvie turned around abruptly and stopped him. She took the suitcase out of his hand and, without another word, stepped back and shut the door.

Sylvie stood there behind the door her breathing laboured, not from carrying the suitcases but from the enormity of what she had just done. Over the course of the conversion, she had often imagined what it would be like to move in downstairs to get away from John. Sylvie didn't really think she would go through with it. However, overhearing that phone call between John and Chloe had spurred her into action. If she didn't do it now, tonight, before the party, then Chloe would arrive and commandeer the garden apartment first.

Sylvie was sick and tired of being taken for granted. She was always the last in the pecking order, as though her needs weren't important. It was time things changed. Sylvie was putting herself first for once. And it felt good.

John stood outside the apartment in the empty hallway for several minutes staring at the door, waiting for her to emerge. He was just wondering what was taking her so long, trying to ignore the uneasy feeling in the pit of his stomach that something was up, when the door opened.

'Oh I forgot,' said Sylvie, 'there's something we didn't discuss. Whose apartment are we having the party in – your place or mine?'

John, who always had everything planned, every contingency taken care of, stared at her in bewilderment – lost for words.

'John?'

They were interrupted by the sound of the doorbell.

18

The party that evening did not get off to a good start. Chloe arrived first with an overnight bag. And she arrived early. The doorbell rang while Sylvie was still standing at her apartment door asking John sarcastically where they were holding the party, making it abundantly clear – if the suitcases hadn't already – that she was moving downstairs.

After she had overheard John on the phone to Chloe, Sylvie thought, stuff counselling. I don't need somebody with a fancy degree telling me what to do.

What Sylvie needed was some time on her own, away from the likes of builders and John and the plan, in order to try and put things into perspective. Maybe then, converting the house wouldn't seem like a complete disaster.

John could think what he liked, that she was ironing out the wrinkles before the first tenants moved in, or that she was leaving him. If John asked, even Sylvie wasn't certain she could wholly answer that question.

In truth, the only thing Sylvie knew for sure was that moving downstairs was what was good for her, at the moment.

But Chloe was going to be a problem.

As soon as Chloe arrived, John whisked her and her over-night bag upstairs to, 'Have a chat.'

Once the coast was clear, Sylvie opened the door and stepped into the empty hall, locking the door behind her. She guessed the party would be upstairs after all. Sylvie walked up the stairs to find the door to John's apartment ajar. She overheard Chloe and John talking in the lounge.

'What do you mean: I can't move into the apartment?' Chloe was whining at John. 'I thought we agreed?'

'Chloe, the situation has changed.'

'How so?' said Chloe, sounding argumentative.

Sylvie was listening to this exchange, wondering what John was going to say next, when the doorbell rang downstairs. She turned around and walked back down the stairs to answer the front door.

Harriet and Dominic were standing side by side on the front steps. Their eldest daughter, Harriet, a tall, willowy blonde who took after John's side of the family, stooped to greet her mother with an affectionate hug. She nudged her husband who stepped forward and handed Sylvie a bunch of flowers and a bottle of wine.

Sylvie smiled gratefully at her son-in-law. She was thinking how nice the flowers would look in her glass vase on the kitchen table downstairs. The bottle of wine would come in handy to toast her own move later on when everyone had gone home.

Sylvie said, 'Excuse me for just a moment.' She left them standing in the hall and quickly nipped into her apartment and down to the basement kitchen to put the flowers in some water in the butler sink. She left the bottle of wine on the kitchen table. When Sylvie walked out of the apartment and locked the door, she turned around to find Harriet and Dominic staring at her.

'Everything all right, Mum?' asked Harriet with a quizzical expression.

'Just perfect,' replied Sylvie, grinning like a Cheshire cat.

Harriet and Dominic exchanged glances as she led them up the stairs.

In the lounge, Chloe was still whining at John. Sylvie could hear Chloe's high-pitched whine before she even stepped foot in John's apartment. From the door, Sylvie could see through to the lounge where Chloe was sitting on the sofa, her overnight bag propped on her lap, a sulky expression etched on her features.

Chloe was slim and blonde like her eldest sister, Harriet, but Chloe did not have her stature. She had stopped growing when she was just an inch or so taller than Sylvie. Consequently, Chloe always looked younger than her years. And there were times she acted a lot younger too. Sylvie sighed. It could have been a petulant teenager sitting on the sofa arguing with her parent, not a grown woman of twenty-nine. Chloe would always be the baby of the family, but there were times Sylvie wished she would stop acting like one and just grow up.

'But I thought she wasn't moving downstairs,' complained Chloe. 'I don't understand what's going on.'

'Neither do I,' added John gravely. 'Look, I don't think now is the time to—'

Sylvie walked into the lounge closely followed by Harriet and Dominic.

'Mum!' Chloe bounced off the sofa, dropping her overnight bag on the floor. 'What's this about you moving into the garden apartment?'

Sylvie frowned across the room at John. He should have sorted this out by now. Sylvie decided she wasn't getting involved.

She stole a glance at Chloe. Her daughter's bottom lip quivered at the prospect of not getting her own way for once in her life.

Sylvie tried to remain detached even though she knew it wasn't Chloe's fault that John had made a promise he couldn't keep. John should never have offered Chloe the apartment without consulting her first. She knew why he did it. Sylvie always gave in when it came to the children. She always put them first. And didn't they know it. When it came to her family, the word *no* never entered her vocabulary. For that very reason, Sylvie was not looking forward to the possibility that John and Chloe might ask for the key back.

'Mum?' Harriet glanced at Dominic before continuing. 'What's this about you moving downstairs? Is something wrong?'

'Yes,' admitted Sylvie almost in tandem with John replying, 'No.'

Harriet raised her eyebrows. 'Well, which is it?'

'Daddy said I could use the garden apartment,' began Chloe, 'but Mum has moved in, instead.'

'To iron out the wrinkles before we get new tenants,' John quickly added. 'That's all there is to it, Harriet.'

'I thought I was doing that,' moaned Chloe.

Ignoring her sister, Harriet asked, 'Mum, is that *really* all there is to it?'

They were all staring at her.

Chloe looking angry.

Harriet looking worried.

John looking confused.

And Dominic looking uncomfortable. He gazed around the room in embarrassment and settled on studying his shoes.

Sylvie could hear her heart drumming in her chest in the

deafening silence that followed. Unfortunately, she realised her mistake too late. She should have had it out with John the minute he got off the phone after overhearing him offering Chloe the apartment. However, she was so incensed at the time that it was all she could do not to pack her bags and walk out. Sylvie saved that game-plan until later. But she didn't expect to face the Spanish Inquisition over it.

Sylvie looked at each one of them in turn. She didn't want to explain herself. Why should she? None of them had been living with John, confined to a small apartment, for the last three months. If she wasn't going to pack her bags and walk out permanently, then Sylvie needed some time living apart to figure out how this was going to work in the long run. She didn't think she had to explain all this to Harriet, Chloe and Dominic.

Chloe broke the silence with an unexpected question. 'Mum, are you and Daddy getting a divorce?'

'Don't be ridiculous,' said Harriet, looking to her parents to reassure her that Chloe was talking crap – as usual.

Sylvie didn't say a word. She couldn't honestly answer that question right now. This didn't surprise her. What did surprise her was that John wasn't able to answer that question either. She glanced his way. John was standing there in muted silence.

The front doorbell rang.

'I'll get that,' said John.

Sylvie was closest to the door and got there first. She shot out of the apartment and down the stairs, tears welling up in her eyes. At the bottom of the stairs, Sylvie paused outside the door to the garden apartment. She looked across the hall. Through the frosted pane of glass in the front door, she could see the faint outline of people waiting outside; they were some of John's work colleagues from his old job that he had invited to the grand opening party. Sylvie hesitated. She knew she should answer the door. It was extremely rude not. But for Sylvie, the party was well and truly over. She really didn't think she could face anybody right now.

Sylvie reached into her pocket for the key to the garden apartment. She was trying to put the key in the lock when the doorbell chimed again making her jump. Sylvie dropped the key.

'Oh for goodness sake,' she hissed, venting her frustration. Sylvie retrieved the key, opened the door, and launched herself inside slamming the door behind her. She could barely see where she was going because her eyes were so full of tears. Sylvie came to a halt just inside the apartment with her back to the door. She heard the doorbell chime for the third time and then John's irritable voice right outside her door.

'Sylvie, why didn't you answer the front door?'

'I don't want a party!'

'What do you mean, you don't want a party? What am I supposed to tell our guests?'

Sylvie turned around. 'Tell them what you like,' she shouted at the door. Sylvie couldn't care less. 'Or better still, tell them to go away!'

Sylvie listened to John's footsteps on the parquet flooring outside her door as he crossed the hall. She heard John open the front door and greet his guests.

'Sorry to keep you, but I'm afraid Sylvie isn't feeling well.'

She hoped John was going to send them all away.

'Yes of course the party is still going ahead.'

Sylvie stared at the door in disbelief. She couldn't believe what she was hearing.

'No, no, I insist. Come in, come in . . . that's right, straight up the stairs.'

Sylvie heard several pairs of footsteps walking up the stairs. She sensed someone hanging back, lingering in the hall outside – John. She could hear the shuffling of feet right outside her door. She knew it was him.

Sylvie stood staring at the door with conflicting emotions. On the one hand she wanted him to go away, leave her be, and return to his party. However, Sylvie remained rooted to the spot thinking about Chloe's unexpected question: are you and Daddy getting a divorce? The question had taken her by surprise, so much so that now Sylvie was seeking some reassurance from John that he didn't really want them to separate, even though she was the one who was standing on the wrong side of that door.

Sylvie listened intently waiting for John to say something. She knew she had surprised him today. Heaven knows she had surprised herself. She wasn't normally this single-minded. And she wouldn't normally leave people standing outside their house and refuse to answer the door. Sylvie was almost too embarrassed to show her face. She put her ear to the door wondering if he was still there.

John was still there standing at the bottom of the stairs outside the door to the garden apartment. He glanced upstairs and thought of the party he had organised for this evening. It was meant to be the grand opening; a chance to show off the two apartments and what a success the conversion turned out to be. They should both be celebrating tonight, but Sylvie wasn't in the mood for a party – that much was obvious.

John turned his attention to the door in front of him and stood there lost in thought. He was thinking about the house conversion. Unlike the original building work on the house thirty-odd years ago, the renovations to convert the property had gone so smoothly that the work was completed ahead of schedule. This should have pleased John no end, especially after all the horror stories he'd read about which he had spared Sylvie. Apparently, some house conversions dragged on for months, encountering all sorts of problems with the builders and the local planning office. They had been lucky in that respect.

However, as the day of the party approached, John didn't feel particularly pleased or lucky. All he felt was trepidation at what lay ahead. And all he could think about was his daughter Jessica's parting words during their last phone conversation when she had caught him off-guard with a ludicrous suggestion, "What if, when the apartments are completed, she moves into one on her own – and stays there?"

John had instantly dismissed that idea as absurd. Nonetheless, something had been bothering John. In all the time it had taken to carry out the conversion, Sylvie still insisted on sleeping in the spare bedroom. He thought this trial separation would have been over weeks ago.

He knew it was his idea for Sylvie to spend some time, if she wanted to, in the garden apartment. He even encouraged her, suggesting that it might be a good idea to iron out any wrinkles, so to speak, before the first tenants arrived. But that had simply been a ruse John had thought up on the spot to get her to agree to the conversion. By the time the two apartments were finished, he believed all this spare bedroom trial separation malarkey would have blown over and they'd be back together living as husband and wife. The last thing he expected was Sylvie to actually go through with it and move downstairs – alone.

Standing outside the garden apartment, John suspected that Sylvie wasn't simply moving in to iron out the wrinkles, as he had so stupidly suggested. She hadn't even mentioned that. All she did was ask for the key. John frowned. He had already given her some space, acting as though it was perfectly normal that his wife was sleeping in the spare bedroom. What he hadn't anticipated, all these weeks later, was that she was still intent on having a break from us, as she put it. He had no idea her break in the spare bedroom would extend to a whole apartment.

He realised rather belatedly that converting the house had provided the perfect opportunity for Sylvie to do just that. And to think, he had even helped her carry those suitcases down the stairs in the misguided belief that they were going away on a trip together to celebrate the beginning of their new lives living in the apartment upstairs.

What bothered John was where all this was leading. He raised a hand, about to knock on the door and ask her to answer Chloe's question: are we getting a divorce? John hesitated. What if he asked her to move back in with him and she said no? What if she said that what she really wanted was a divorce? Was he prepared for that? John slowly lowered his hand. Prepared or not, it seemed pointless to say anything. She was already the other side of that door, and that said it all. John's shoulders sagged in defeat.

On his way upstairs, another scenario occurred to John which made him wonder if he was making a mountain out of a molehill. Perhaps Sylvie was taking him at his word and using the apartment because she still needed some time on her own to process all these recent changes in her life, and she was acting up because he had offered the apartment to Chloe. That was understandable. He had promised Sylvie that she could use the downstairs apartment when it was completed if she felt the need. He should have taken that into account before he went ahead and said yes to Chloe without even thinking. He was feeling rather foolish over this blunder but optimistic that, given time, Sylvie would come round and move back upstairs.

By the time John reached the top of the stairs he was convinced there was absolutely nothing to worry about, and he should go ahead and enjoy the party. John walked back into his apartment with a spring in his step and a renewed sense of optimism. He closed the door behind him and joined the party.

Sylvie was still standing behind the door in the garden apartment when she heard footfalls on the stairs and the door to the apartment upstairs click shut.

He was gone.

Sylvie could hear faint conversation above her in John's apartment and the occasional sound of laughter. Sylvie's bottom lip quivered as she raised her eyes to the ceiling imagining everybody upstairs having a good time without her. She was upset that John hadn't cancelled the stupid party and stopped to consider that perhaps it was more important to sit down with his wife and ask her what was wrong. At the very least, it would have shown he cared more for her than following through on his stupid plans for a grand opening party.

Sylvie thought about marching upstairs and making a scene so that everybody would clear off home. John would pay attention to her then. But that wasn't Sylvie's style. She'd die of embarrassment if she did something like that. Besides, she had no idea what she was dealing with. John didn't exactly answer Chloe's question: are we were getting a divorce? He didn't say no, did he? What if she marched upstairs right now and asked him that question outright. And he replied that it was true, he wanted a divorce. Was she prepared for that?

Sylvie slowly backed away from the door. Prepared or not, it seemed pointless to confront him now. He didn't exactly beg her not to leave him. He didn't say a word. On the contrary, he just returned to his party as though nothing was amiss. That said it all.

Sylvie locked the door to the apartment and went downstairs to the basement kitchen where she wouldn't have to listen to the party going on right above her head. She saw the bottle of wine on the kitchen table and was immediately struck with an idea. She was going to have her own party. An exclusive party of one. Why ever not? She had the run of the place. She could do what she liked. Sylvie opened a kitchen cupboard and reached for a wine glass.

After four glasses of wine, downed in quick succession, she wanted food – and lots of it. Sylvie knew it was late, but she hadn't eaten since lunchtime. She found the yellow pages at the back of a kitchen drawer, picked up the phone, and dialled the number of the first Chinese takeaway she could find. John never let them have takeaway food because it was too smelly, too messy and too greasy. Sylvie ordered a lot. And she intended to eat it in the lounge, on the sofa, in front of the television; something John would never dream of doing.

Sylvie needed one more thing to make her party complete. She dialled Julia's mobile phone number and left a garbled message hoping her best friend could come over and make her party of one, a party of two.

Julia obviously didn't pick up on her message because she didn't turn up. Either that or Sylvie had inadvertently left the message on someone else's phone by mistake. That wouldn't surprise her. She was feeling rather tipsy after drinking nearly half a bottle of wine on an empty stomach. Sylvie didn't mind if Julia – or whoever might have got the message – couldn't make it. She was quite content to enjoy her evening in, even if it was on her own. At least she could do exactly what she wanted, when she wanted. That was the whole point.

After taking delivery of three large bags of Chinese takeaway, Sylvie spread all the boxes on the coffee table in the lounge, picked up the remote control and switched on the television. She turned the volume up high enough to drown out the noise from the party upstairs. Sylvie found an old black and white film she hadn't seen in ages and rather fancied staying up late to watch. John never stayed up to catch a late night film, and so neither did Sylvie – until tonight.

Sylvie piled her plate with a selection of Chinese food from every box and then poured the remains of the bottle of wine into her empty glass. She sat back on the sofa with the plate on her lap. She had a large glass of wine in one hand and the television remote control in the other. Sylvie smiled to herself. She was feeling rather pleased with John's decision to rent out the garden apartment furnished. It was all coming in rather handy.

Sylvie put her feet up on the sofa and raised her glass. A party of one, she decided, was just perfect.

19

Chloe didn't stick around at the party for long once she realised she wasn't getting her own way and no amount of sulking or whining at John was going to change that. She was the first to leave, taking her overnight bag and sulky face with her.

Harriet sidled up to John as he watched her storm out, and managed to get a dig in about her spoilt little sister. 'Isn't it about time Chloe started acting like a grown up and faced her problems head-on rather than running back to Mum and Dad like she always does?'

For once, John was inclined to agree. He was always too quick to give in to any of his daughter's demands. But on this occasion he hadn't stopped to consider the ramifications: if Chloe moved in downstairs, when would she move out? Strangely, Chloe hadn't mentioned that.

John spent the rest of the party preoccupied with thoughts of Sylvie residing in the garden apartment, wondering how long her sojourn downstairs was going to last.

Eventually, the party wound down. Harriet and Dominic were the last to leave once John had reassured Harriet everything was fine. He stood on the front steps and watched them walk to their car. Harriet turned around and waved before they set off. John waved back with a smile before closing the front door. When he turned towards the stairs, his smile faded rapidly. Despite attempting to put a positive spin on the situation, more for his own benefit than theirs, the fact that Sylvie had moved downstairs was still playing on his mind.

As if he didn't need reminding of that fact, John could hear the television on in the garden apartment quite distinctly from where he was standing by the front door. John raised an eyebrow. Was it really necessary to have the volume up that high in order to drown out the party noise? He didn't think his party was that loud. On the contrary, John had been most considerate to his neighbours by only having some classical music playing softly in the background. Besides, John abhorred parties where you couldn't even hear yourself think, let alone have a conversation with the fellow next to you.

He frowned at Sylvie's door as he passed by and felt like shouting out to tell her to turn the volume down, not that she'd hear him above that infernal noise. John didn't bother. He continued up the stairs to his apartment trying to ignore it.

John got undressed and changed into his pyjamas. He felt shattered. John was not a night owl; going to bed the wrong side of midnight did not agree with him. That's why he had a bedtime routine, and he liked to stick to it. He was normally in bed by half-past nine to read a book and always switched off the lights by half-past ten at the latest. This evening John had to make an exception for the party, so he dispensed with his routine and left the book unopened on the bedside table.

John switched off the bedside table lamp and wormed his way under the duvet. He closed his eyes and tried not to think about Sylvie in the garden apartment downstairs. Instead, he thought about the party this evening that he had spent so much time and effort organising, which Sylvie had nearly ruined because she was out of sorts.

The party had gone very well indeed even though everyone was disappointed that Sylvie would not be joining them. She had a headache and was lying down in the apartment downstairs; that was John's explanation for her absence and the fact that they could only see half the conversion. John's grand opening wasn't quite so grand considering nobody saw the rental apartment.

John was feeling put out that he couldn't show people around downstairs. Suddenly he had a brilliant idea. He could organise another grand opening once Sylvie had sorted herself out and moved back upstairs. They could have the second party in the garden apartment. John liked that idea a lot, especially as it would give him something to do in the coming weeks along with instructing a letting agent to find a tenant.

John was just thinking about how he could make the party in the garden apartment a little different, when he finally lost patience with that infernal noise. John opened his eyes and stared at the ceiling. He had been trying to ignore it, hoping it would eventually go quiet. John lay there a moment longer and then reached over and switched on the bedside table lamp to look at the time. He did a double-take when he saw it was getting on for two o'clock in the morning. John had no idea he'd been lying awake for so long with that noise disturbing his sleep. He had a pretty good idea where it was coming from but decided to get up and investigate nevertheless.

He slipped his feet into the slippers by his bed and padded downstairs to the lounge. He didn't have to go all the way down the stairs to confirm his suspicions that it was the television in the apartment below. John shook his head in disbelief. He didn't know what surprised him the most, the fact that Sylvie was still watching television at this hour, or that he could hear it quite distinctly from his bedroom two floors up.

John wished he hadn't left their old furniture downstairs in order to rent out the apartment furnished. He thought it would be less disruptive if tenants weren't moving in and out with van loads of furniture, little realising it was an open invitation for Sylvie to pack her bags and move downstairs.

She wouldn't have been all that eager to go if she had nothing to sit on, nothing to sleep on and nothing to watch. John had left their old tube television downstairs because it was large, it was bulky, and it was eons old. He was looking for an excuse to get rid of it to buy what he really wanted which was a small brand new flat screen television for the apartment upstairs.

Right now, John was wishing he had not left that infernal television downstairs. It was his own fault because he couldn't be bothered to cart it off to the dump.

John walked into the study and opened a drawer in his desk to retrieve the little black book inside. Closing the door on the study, John marched through his lounge to the kitchenette to pour himself a glass of water before heading back to bed. He set the glass of water down on the bedside table, climbed back into bed, and opened the little black book. It contained blank sheets of lined paper. John had already purchased the little hard-bound book in order to keep a note of any unexpected issues that may arise in either apartment post-conversion. Declan had suggested it. John thought a snag list was an excellent idea.

Turning to the first page where he had already written a

heading, *problems to be rectified*, he picked up a pen and wrote the name *Sylvie* underneath. John underlined her name twice. His attention drifted to the noise downstairs; had she forgotten to turn the television off before she went to bed or was she doing it on purpose just to irritate him?

John resisted the urge to go downstairs and bang on her door just in case that was her intention all along – to elicit a reaction from her husband. He wasn't going to give her the satisfaction. Instead, he calmly wrote in his little black book, *I must find out how to set the volume control on the television!* He knew it was possible because they did it in some hotels where the volume could only be turned up so high to avoid disturbing the other guests. That wouldn't solve the noise issue if tenants brought their own televisions, but John didn't want to think about that. John was going to approach one problem at a time. And right now his problem was residing downstairs.

He closed the little black book, switched off the table lamp, and lay down again to listen to the constant drone of the television. His mind drifted on to another potential problem he hadn't foreseen. For the first time since the idea of the house conversion entered John's head, he started to think about the reality of being a landlord. What was it really going to be like living with tenants downstairs? John was starting to worry about what he had got himself into.

John did not sleep well.

20

Sylvie did not sleep well. She watched two late-night films back-to-back, ate far too much takeaway food, and eventually fell asleep on the sofa. She awoke sometime in the early hours and realised she had left the television on.

Sylvie sat up to switch it off and a wave of nausea hit her. She darted downstairs for the wet room with a hand clamped over her mouth, making it just in time.

Afterwards, she flushed the toilet and turned on the tap by the sink, sluicing her face with cold water. 'No more takeaway food or bottles of wine,' Sylvie admonished her reflection in the bathroom mirror. 'Honestly, I'm acting like someone half my age,' said Sylvie aghast. She was thinking of her youngest daughter, Chloe. She had seen the state of Chloe, not to mention her flat, on a Sunday morning or most any day when she happened to stop by.

Sylvie pictured the empty bottles of wine and discarded takeaway boxes littering the coffee table upstairs, reminiscent of Chloe's flat. Fortunately, John wasn't here to see it otherwise he'd be on at her to clear it up. Sylvie rolled her eyes at the thought. Maybe she was getting an appreciation as to why Chloe's relationships kept falling apart. She wasn't exactly the tidiest person in the world either. If her boyfriends were anything like John, perhaps she simply got tired of being henpecked all the time and wanted her own space.

Emerging from the wet room, Sylvie glanced out of the french doors as she walked over to the sink to pour herself a glass of water. She could hear the birds outside singing their dawn chorus. Although she was wide awake, Sylvie decided it was far too early to get up, even though she hadn't technically gone to bed yet. She carried the glass of water back upstairs to the lounge and, ignoring the mess, stopped to switch off the television before making her way to bed.

Sylvie opened the door in the lounge which led into the inner-hallway and the bedrooms and bathroom beyond. Both bedroom doors were open. Sylvie stood in the hall debating which bedroom she fancied sleeping in. The big double bed in the main bedroom looked more inviting than the single bed in the small second bedroom next door. Sylvie fetched her suitcase from the lounge and carried it into the main bedroom. She unzipped it and rifled through her clothes until she found her nightie. Sylvie undressed and slipped under the cool covers on the same side of the double bed she usually slept on.

Sylvie had finally moved out of the spare bedroom.

Despite swapping the sofa for a comfortable double bed, once again Sylvie did not sleep well. After only a couple of hours of fitful sleep, Sylvie had woken with a start to find she was suffering from an attack of the collywobbles. Sylvie's stomach churned, not because she had eaten too much greasy food, but because the enormity of what she'd done had suddenly hit home. And she was afraid it was irreversible. What if John didn't want her back even if she changed her mind and decided to move back upstairs? Sylvie was in a panic over where all this was leading. Afraid for her future. Afraid she would end up alone. When the euphoria of having the apartment all to herself had finally worn off, along with the effects of drinking an entire bottle of wine, Sylvie had never felt as lonely as she did at that moment.

'Things will look better in the morning,' Sylvie said to the empty room. It was already morning, albeit very early, so she changed her mantra to, 'Things will look better *later* in the morning.'

Eventually, Sylvie managed to get back to sleep. She was woken later that morning by the muffled sound of her mobile phone. Sylvie kicked back the covers and got out of bed feeling surprisingly refreshed despite the late night. She hurriedly searched the room until she eventually found her phone on the floor beside her suitcase, by which time the phone had stopped ringing. Sylvie picked it up and discovered that somebody had left a voice message.

It was Julia apologising that she couldn't make it to her party last night and, not only that; she had left Sylvie her new address. There was more. She wanted Sylvie to come and see her new place today.

Today! Sylvie was so surprised when she heard Julia's message that she nearly dropped her phone. She had to replay the message just to be sure she wasn't mistaken. She had waited so long to see Julia's new home that she was almost felt it was never going to happen. Sylvie was over the moon with this unexpected news. This was just what she needed, a day out catching up with her best friend.

She raced down to the kitchen to put the kettle on and caught herself involuntarily getting two mugs out of the kitchen cupboard. Sylvie looked at the second mug and thought of John in the apartment upstairs. She knew John would confront her about yesterday, the way she had moved downstairs before the party without telling him what she was up to. She was surprised he had helped her carry the suitcases down the stairs. What did he think they were doing – going on a trip? He obviously had his precious party on his mind and wasn't paying attention to what was going on right under his nose.

Sylvie put the second mug back in the kitchen cupboard. She wasn't in the mood to see John this morning. And she wasn't in the mood for an argument over the fact that he couldn't show off his rental apartment during the party. Sylvie still had a thumping headache; a not-so-gentle reminder of that entire bottle of wine she had consumed last night. All she wanted to do was get out of the house and away from it all for a few hours to clear her head. Julia couldn't have timed it better, especially as Sylvie suspected she might need to get away from the house for more than just a few hours. She knew Julia wouldn't hesitate to extend an invitation to stay with her for a few days.

Sylvie sat down at the kitchen table with a cup of tea and wrote down Julia's new address in her diary. 'Little Venice,' mused Sylvie as she was writing it down. Small wonder Julia had wanted to keep it a secret. Sylvie was feeling a bit envious. Little Venice was one of Sylvie's favourite parts of London and a lovely area in which to live. It was also very expensive. Consequently, it was somewhere Sylvie and John could never afford to move to. She wondered how Julia could afford it. Sylvie finished writing down the address and smiled. She couldn't wait to see

Julia's new home; she already knew she would adore it. Sylvie resisted the temptation to pack an overnight bag otherwise Julia might find herself with a permanent house guest.

Sylvie sat on the bus, on her way to Julia's new home, thinking about her childhood friend and how much their lives had diverged over the years. Unlike Sylvie, Julia passed the 11+ and went to grammar school then on to university, qualifying as a primary school teacher in the mid-seventies. After university, Julia went travelling. She eventually returned to London where she secured a permanent teaching post and worked until she retired.

Just like Sylvie and John, she bought a run-down property in London that was so cheap they were practically giving them away. However, she did not buy a family home all those years ago like Sylvie and John. Julia bought a flat. Sylvie wasn't sure whether that was because it was all she could afford on her teaching salary, or she wanted some money over to spend on other things, like travel – a luxury John and Sylvie couldn't afford.

Sylvie suspected it was the latter. Julia often went away for the entire school summer break. And when she was home, Julia liked nothing more than to entertain all her friends by throwing house-parties at the weekend. Julia's parties back then were infamous, and her relationships were numerous. She never settled down with anybody for long. She had a few long-term relationships, but she never reached the point where she considered moving in with any of her partners permanently. Sylvie always wondered if that's why she never married. How could a relationship possibly work if Julia wouldn't compromise and give up her own place to move in together?

Sylvie brought up the issue of having children once. She was afraid her best friend would come to regret not settling down with someone and starting a family. Julia reassured her that wasn't the case. She explained that the school community was her family and teaching other people's children was her life. She was quite happy to leave the children behind at the end of her working day. Sylvie couldn't deny the fact that Julia always seemed happy living alone in her flat.

But all that was in the past. Julia had moved on and the flat was now a not-too-distant memory. Sylvie glanced out of the bus window. The Indian summer that had stretched right through September into the first week of October had finally given way to typical wet autumnal weather. Sylvie watched the rain outside drizzle down the window pane as she sat there trying to imagine what Julia's new home in Little Venice would be like. Her thoughts inevitably drifted back to Julia's previous home.

Julia had sold her flat for an obscene amount of money, which was ironic considering she had spent next to nothing on it over the years, choosing to spend the money on herself and having a good time. Julia told Sylvie she was going to be sensible with the proceeds of the sale and intended to put some of the money into her retirement fund. The rest she would use to buy a dream. It turned out her dream was to retire in Little Venice.

Sylvie smiled thinking that perhaps Julia hadn't been quite so sensible with the money after all; buying a property in Little Venice wouldn't come cheap. However, Sylvie knew there was another possible explanation. Julia and her brother had recently come into a sizeable inheritance. Their parents passed away last year. Julia had received quite a windfall from the sale of the detached house she grew up in.

Sylvie stared wistfully out of the window. She wondered what it would feel like to have a windfall, in the shape of a sizeable inheritance, fall into her lap. Sylvie sighed. It was an experience that was never on the cards for either herself or John, unless they won the lottery. The chances of that happening were zilch because they never bought lottery tickets.

The bus pulled up at Sylvie's stop. She stepped off the bus and wrestled with her umbrella in the blustery wind. She was aware it would have been quicker to take the tube to Warwick Avenue Tube Station. However, Sylvie preferred the bus even if it did involve a longer walk to Little Venice.

After an hour walking around Little Venice, Sylvie's feet ached, and she was feeling decidedly fed-up. Julia said it was only a ten minute-walk at most from the bus stop. She didn't know why she was having such a problem finding Julia's address. At least the rain had subsided to an intermittent drizzle before she got soaked.

Sylvie stopped to close her umbrella. She was standing on the pavement outside a grand terrace of pristine Victorian properties that formed a stunning crescent overlooking one of the canals in Little Venice. Sylvie looked up and down the street, and scratched her head in confusion. She knew she was in the right street because she had written it down in her diary. Sylvie double-checked the entry in her pocket diary. Julia had only given her the name of the house —Mandalay — but not the house number. That was proving a problem. Sylvie opened her handbag, found her mobile phone, and punched in Julia's number.

Julia answered immediately. 'Oh darling, where are you? I was expecting you half an hour ago.'

'I know. The problem is, Julia, I can't seem to find Mandalay.'

Sylvie stared at the elegant homes in front of her. 'Perhaps if you gave me the house number . . . ?'

'No need,' interrupted Julia.

'That's odd,' remarked Sylvie. She could hear an echo every time Julia spoke. It almost sounded as though she was—

'Turn around, darling.'

Sylvie slowly turned around.

'That's right, all the way round, darling. I'm right behind you.'

Sylvie turned around to face the black metal railings dividing the street from the canal below. She squinted at a woman a few feet away waving at her. 'Julia?' What was she doing down there?

Julia was sitting outside on the deck of a brightly coloured green and yellow houseboat. Matching hand-painted green and yellow pots lined the deck with winter flowers. An old-fashioned bike, with a large wicker shopping basket on the front, was propped up to one side. It turned out that Julia had bought a dream, or a houseboat to be precise, on the water in Little Venice.

Sylvie stood at the railings and stared down at her best friend in dismay. So this was what Julia had moved into. Sylvie wished she hadn't. It wasn't that she begrudged Julia following her dreams – far from it. It's just that Sylvie was not very good on boats, even if they weren't in transit and moored right next to the towpath. She couldn't seem to find her sea-legs.

Sylvie waved back and reluctantly made her way down the short flight of concrete steps that led from the street above to the narrow towpath along the canal front. A few paces along the towpath, Sylvie finally arrived at her destination. She grimaced. Even in the calm waters of Little Venice, Sylvie nervously stood in front of the houseboat dreading the thought of climbing on board.

Julia's boat was one of many packed in tight little rows like colourful Sardines lined up one beside the other along the banks of the canal. They were all moored with their nose right up against the canal towpath. An agile person could just hop aboard. That didn't make Sylvie feel any better. She glanced at the block of two wooden steps that Julia had left outside, presumably for her benefit.

Julia was standing on the deck within arm's reach. She held out her hand.

Sylvie was staring at the wooden steps when Julia pointed out what a lucky coincidence that Sylvie had been standing on the street directly above Julia's houseboat when she phoned.

Sylvie didn't feel particularly lucky that she had found Julia's new home – quite the reverse.

Julia was still holding out her hand.

Sylvie frowned at her best friend. Now she knew why Julia had kept this a secret. Julia was well aware that she didn't have much of a fondness for boats, to put it mildly. Julia probably guessed what would happen if Sylvie found out what she was moving into. Sylvie would have put off paying her a visit.

'Come on Sylvie,' said Julia impatiently.

Reluctantly, Sylvie took her hand and walked up the two wooden steps. She put her toe out at the top as though she was about to dip it in water rather than step on board.

'It won't bite,' Julia said jokingly.

Sylvie didn't look convinced.

'Darling, there's nothing to worry about – watch this.' Julia let go of Sylvie's hand and started rocking from side to side.

'Don't do that!' yelped Sylvie in alarm, even though the boat hadn't moved an inch.

'These things are incredibly stable,' Julia reassured her. 'We're not going anywhere, I promise you.'

Sylvie set a tentative foot down on the open deck.

'Unless you fancy going for a cruise down the canal,' added Julia as an afterthought.

'No!' cried Sylvie, although she wouldn't put it past Julia to twist her arm one of these days and do just that.

Sylvie grasped Julia's hand as she planted both feet on the deck. She glanced back longingly at the towpath; Sylvie knew where she would rather be right now.

'There, that wasn't so bad – was it,' Julia chuckled as she let go of Sylvie's hand.

Sylvie wasn't so sure. She still felt her legs turn to jelly the moment she stepped on board.

'I'll show you around,' said Julia enthusiastically.

Sylvie nodded even though what she really wanted was Julia to show her to the nearest seat. She eyed the small bistro table with two matching chairs where Julia had been sitting awaiting her arrival. If it wasn't for the wind and the drizzle, Sylvie would have been quite content to remain outside and leave the tour below for another time. Unfortunately, the weather scuppered that idea.

She ducked her head and followed Julia down the wooden stairs to the cabin below. Sylvie had never been inside a canal boat before. She paused at the bottom of the stairs to take it all in. Her immediate impression was that it was like a Tardis. The boat looked narrow and compact from the outside. However once inside, Sylvie was pleasantly surprised by how spacious it was. If it wasn't for the fact that it was still a boat, Sylvie could see the attraction. The cabin was not unlike the inside of a

Scandinavian pine lodge, with its soft pine tongue and groove on the walls and ceiling, making the interior feel warm and welcoming and cavernous.

Sylvie was standing at the bottom of the stairs. Her eyes drifted from Julia's reception room to the open-plan galley kitchen. It was even more compact than John's Kitchenette at home. There was still enough room for integrated appliances. Julia pointed out the dishwasher, washer-dryer and fridge-freezer. Julia's new home had been fully modernised and updated. Sylvie was impressed.

She politely declined Julia's invitation to explore any further, preferring not to move around too much. Her legs felt so wobbly she still needed to sit down. Besides, she could see everything just fine from where she was.

Julia opened the two cabin doors at the far end so Sylvie could see through to a cosy bedroom with a double bed, which had Julia's favourite multi-coloured patchwork quilt spread on top.

The narrow room next door was a bright, modern bathroom with all mod-cons. The tongue and groove panelling in the bathroom was painted a shade of pastel blue that Sylvie recognised; it was the same colour as her shed in the back garden. When she pointed that out, Julia smiled and admitted that the colour of Sylvie's garden shed had inspired her to paint the bathroom pastel blue.

'Why don't you take a seat while I make some tea?'

Sylvie didn't need to be asked twice. She made her way over to the comfortable beige Laura Ashley sofa and quickly sat down before she lost her balance.

The sofa was set back against the wall under two small round porthole windows looking out on to the water. Sylvie made the mistake of glancing out of one of the porthole windows before she sat down. She spotted the water lapping against the side of the boat and suddenly felt queasy. Sylvie took some deep breaths and tried not to think about the fact that she was inside a boat.

From her vantage point on the sofa, Sylvie looked around Julia's new lounge. It already felt so homely and lived in that it was hard to believe Julia had only been living here a matter of days. Sylvie managed a smile. The way it was furnished and decorated was very Julia. The lounge was a chaotic jumble of colour and cushions, furniture and bric-a-brac. Julia had insisted on bringing it all with her when she sold the flat even though theoretically she was downsizing.

There were two Persian rugs covering the floor when one would do, and lots of trinkets dotted about the room that Julia had picked up over the years from travelling and teaching abroad. A small flat screen television stood in one corner of the lounge and a painting easel in the other. Julia loved to paint. It was her second great love after teaching.

It surprised Sylvie that Julia had taken early retirement from a job she loved, even though it would give her more time to paint. She recalled Julia pointedly remarking, "We don't stay the same over time. We grow and change. Inevitably, that means we have to let go of some things in order to make room for new things in our lives." Sylvie looked around her lounge and thought that perhaps Julia should apply that bit of logic to all her clutter.

Julia came over to sit beside Sylvie on the sofa. She turned to her best friend and said, 'When I've made a pot of tea, you are going to tell me all about it, darling.

Sylvie gave Julia a blank look. 'Tell you all about what?'

'This,' said Julia, holding up her mobile phone. She punched in a number, listened for a brief moment, and then handed the phone to Sylvie.

Sylvie still didn't know what Julia was talking about, but she took the phone and put it to her ear as she watched Julia get up from the sofa and walk through to the galley kitchen to make tea. 'Oh, Lord!' Sylvie's face coloured as she listened to the message.

By the time Julia returned with a tea tray, Sylvie had listened to the whole cringeworthy phone message she had drunkenly left on Julia's phone last night. Sylvie had forgotten all about it.

'Well, that was embarrassing,' admitted Sylvie, still feeling flushed as she gave the phone back to Julia.

Julia grinned as she handed Sylvie a cup of tea. 'I take it you were having a good time last night.'

Sylvie nodded, avoiding Julia's gaze.

'I'm sorry I couldn't make it, darling. I would have loved to have been there. It sounds as though you were throwing yourself quite a party.'

'Enough already,' said Sylvie, slapping her arm playfully. 'I hope you're going to delete that message.' Sylvie couldn't remember ever being that drunk or coming out with such utter clap-trap. 'Just as well I don't do that very often,' she remarked.

'Oh, I disagree, Sylvie. Sometimes it's good to let your hair down and have some fun once in a while.'

Sylvie gave Julia a sideways glance as she sipped her tea. Julia knew all about letting your hair down; she loved to party. Perhaps she was right. It did feel good to do something silly for a change. Nonetheless, Sylvie still felt embarrassed. She had never done anything like that before. That was usually Julia's forte. No wonder Julia found it highly entertaining.

Julia sat down in the single armchair opposite Sylvie and scrutinized her best friend. 'Joking aside, you must tell me all about it because I got the gist from the phone message that you moved into the garden apartment on your own.' She studied Sylvie intently, adding, 'You left him – didn't you.'

'Oh, I wouldn't go so far as to say that.' Sylvie shook her head wishing Julia wouldn't jump to conclusions. 'I just needed a break – that's all.' Sylvie frowned wondering why that remark sounded strangely familiar; wasn't that something Chloe said every time she was on the verge of dumping a boyfriend?

Julia put her cup down on the side table and sat back in her chair regarding Sylvie thoughtfully.

Sylvie turned away from Julia's penetrating gaze and had no option but to look out of a porthole window. 'My, what lovely views you have,' said Sylvie in a lame attempt to change the subject.

Julia didn't take the bait.

Sylvie continued to gaze out of the window. Like her best friend, Julia, Sylvie wanted to make changes in her life. The more Sylvie thought about it, the more she understood what Julia was getting at when she said, ". . . we have to let go of some things in order to make room for new things in our lives." Julia had let go of her job and her flat to make way for her dream of living on a houseboat and spending her time painting.

Sylvie also dreamt of doing something different with her life, even though she didn't know what that *something* was yet. Sylvie thought she was making room in her life for new things when she let go of her job, but all she was left with was the frightening feeling that this was just the beginning. What bothered Sylvie was what else in her life she might have to cast aside on her journey of self-discovery – her marriage to John? Was she prepared to let go of their life together for a dream she couldn't even quantify? Was that what she really wanted? Perhaps she should just accept the status quo, be satisfied with the life she had, and quash the feeling that there should be something more.

'What is it, Sylvie?' Julia spoke softly, sensing her friend's anguish.

'Something doesn't feel right.'

'About the apartment?'

'About everything,' replied Sylvie turning from the window. In the early hours of this morning when she had the collywobbles over moving downstairs, Sylvie was having second thoughts about whether she had done the right thing. It certainly didn't feel like she had moved downstairs in order to test-run the apartment. It felt like something else. It felt like she had left John. Sylvie wasn't sure she was ready to give up on her marriage just yet.

Unlike Julia, who always seemed to know what she wanted in life, what would make her happy, Sylvie did not. Sylvie was confused. If she wasn't careful, she had a feeling she would start making decisions that she would later come to regret. Perhaps she already had.

'I don't think I should have moved downstairs,' confessed Sylvie. In the cold light of day, before Sylvie found her phone and listened to Julia's message inviting her over this morning, she just felt like packing her bags and moving back upstairs – if John would have her back.

'Oh Julia, I think I've made a terrible mistake.'

'Nonsense.'

That's exactly what Sylvie expected her to say. She never did like John. Next, Julia would be trying to fix her up with one of her single acquaintances.

'I have an idea,' said Julia bouncing out of her chair. She walked through the cabin at a brisk pace into her bedroom at the far end.

Sylvie grasped the arm of the sofa anticipating the boat to start rocking from the sudden movement. Nothing happened. Sylvie breathed a sigh of relief. On top of everything else, she didn't fancy a dip in the canal after capsizing.

A few moments later Julia emerged from her bedroom with a coat and a long hand-knitted scarf draped around her slender shoulders. She was carrying her handbag.

Sylvie rose from her seat. 'Are we going somewhere?'

'Indeed we are.' Julia handed Sylvie her coat and bag. 'Let's go shopping.'

Sylvie knew what she was up to. Shopping was the perfect antidote. Sylvie could forget all about her problems for an afternoon and enjoy visiting some of Julia's favourite haunts, like the chintzy shops and market stalls filled with all sorts of colourful paraphernalia from exotic, far-flung places. Just the thought of it lifted Sylvie's spirits, especially as it meant they were getting off the boat and back on dry land.

Sylvie offered up a smile. Her best friend always knew how to cheer a girl up.

Julia returned her smile. 'Good, that's settled then. Come on.' Julia led the way back up the narrow wooden stairs and out on to the open deck.

They had just stepped off the houseboat on to the towpath when Julia turned to Sylvie and said, 'Afterwards, we could go over to your place. I'd love to see your apartment.'

Sylvie felt down in the dumps again. 'It's not *my* apartment,' she said irritably.

Julia knew that. That's why she had suggested the shopping trip. Julia knew what was wrong with Sylvie: she didn't feel at home in her new place. Julia had every intention of helping Sylvie rectify that problem, starting right now.

After all, what were best friends for?

21

After a restless night, John had woken up in the early hours afraid this was it – Sylvie had left him. He eventually got back to sleep, and things looked a lot brighter in the morning.

After thinking things through in the cold light of day, once again John chose to believe that Sylvie was doing the agreed test-run on the garden apartment. All this cloak-and-dagger stuff was simply because she was upset with him for offering the apartment to Chloe without talking it over with her first. In fact, he wouldn't be at all surprised if Sylvie had moved in downstairs before the party last night just to make a point. Well, point taken thought John. He also thought he owed Sylvie an apology.

John had every intention of going downstairs to knock on Sylvie's door first thing in the morning and apologise. However, he had woken up too late and missed her. John was still in his pyjamas, making a cup of tea in the kitchenette, when he heard the sound of the front door downstairs. In the lounge, he glanced out the window and spotted Sylvie practically skipping down the garden path. She certainly had a spring in her step and seemed in high spirits. He even caught the wisp of a smile when she turned around to close the front gate.

As he watched her set off down the street in the direction of the bus stop, he was wondering where she was off to so early on a Sunday morning. Disappointingly, it meant there was nothing he could do right now about making that apology. He was pretty sure she would not appreciate him running down the street after her in nothing but his stripy blue pyjamas. Although the thought had crossed his mind.

Turning from the window, John decided to call on her as soon as she returned home. He hoped she wouldn't be gone long.

Sylvie was gone most of the day.

John was sitting in his lounge reading the newspaper when he heard the sound of a car driving down the street. He stood up, stretched and walked over to the window wondering when Sylvie would arrive home. It was dusk, and he was starting to worry. John looked out of the window at the street below and saw a black taxi cab pull up at the kerb outside their house. Two women exited the cab laden with shopping bags. John recognised Sylvie in the hue of the street lamp.

He was just about to rush downstairs and help Sylvie with her shopping bags when the woman with her turned around and looked up at the house. John recognised her instantly – Julia. John frowned at her until his attention was diverted by the taxi-driver hauling something out of the back of the cab. John pressed his nose up against the window pane and could just make out what appeared to be a rolled up piece of carpet, or perhaps a rug.

The taxi driver walked up the garden path carrying it over one shoulder, followed by Julia balancing a pile of cushions in her arms. Sylvie brought up the rear with a slew of shopping bags. One-by-one they disappeared from view up the front steps into the house.

John raised an eyebrow wondering what they were up to. Sylvie was meant to be having some time to herself, not inviting friends over and making herself at home down there. John scowled. Trust Julia to be up to no good. Sylvie had obviously spent the day shopping with Julia and bought god-knows-what for the apartment. He hoped Julia was leaving with the taxi.

John watched the taxi driver returned to his cab alone. 'Damn,' John muttered under his breath. 'There goes my apology.'

Julia gave the taxi driver a large tip for going the extra mile and carrying the Persian rug into Sylvie's apartment. They couldn't have managed it by themselves, and neither Julia nor Sylvie wanted to call on John upstairs to give them a hand. It wouldn't have been worth the aggravation when John discovered it was for the garden apartment. He'd hate the rug. Sylvie knew John didn't like bright colours or outlandish patterns.

Julia knew he'd hate the rug, if for no other reason than the fact that she had bought it.

'I love it,' squealed Sylvie when Julia shifted the furniture and unrolled the rug across the floor.

'That's a start,' said Julia, standing back and admiring the rug. She cast her eye around the apartment. It was just as she had feared; the apartment was decorated in magnolia with white paintwork. Not a speck of colour. Not a hint of something interesting. It was bland. It was boring. It was John. He had even got rid of the stripped wooden doors in favour of new white panelled internal doors. The original wide wooden floorboards that Julia thought was one of the best features of the lounge were now covered up with modern laminate flooring in a pale pine wishy-washy colour. Sylvie was right: the property had been transformed. Julia was not prepared for the devastation John had wrought. Where were all the beautiful period features that she used to love about this house?

Julia glanced at Sylvie standing next to her. No wonder Sylvie said something didn't feel right. The house no longer felt like Sylvie's home.

Sylvie stood staring at the new rug that Julia had rolled out over John's nondescript laminate flooring. Although she never particularly liked the décor John had chosen when he first decorated the house years ago, what they both did agree on was preserving the original features. Unfortunately, all that changed with the conversion. John wanted two modernised apartments. According to John, the conversion was the ideal opportunity to bring the house into the twenty-first century. Sylvie disagreed. She missed her period features.

Julia tossed six pastel-coloured cushions on the old plain beige sofa that John had left downstairs, presumably for tenants, and then turned to Sylvie. 'I think you need some throws,' said Julia, pointing to a bright crimson stain on one arm of the sofa where Sylvie had spilt some wine last night.

'Oh dear, John isn't going to be pleased about that,' observed Sylvie, not sounding at all bothered by it. She had no intention of buying throws for her apartment.

Julia delved down the remaining shopping bags and lifted out some ornaments she had bought for Sylvie. She dotted them around the apartment. Two found a home on the modern mantel shelf above the wall-mounted electric fire. Julia stopped abruptly and pointed at the fire. 'What happened to your fireplace?'

Sylvie rolled her eyes. 'Don't remind me.' During the original renovation work on the house, back in the late seventies, they had prized off a painted square of plywood stuck to the wall in the lounge, behind which they found the original cast-iron fireplace with its patterned tiles and grate still intact. Sylvie remembered their elation when they made that discovery. It was as though they had found some long-lost treasure.

Three decades on, Sylvie was horrified when she discovered that John had gone ahead and had it covered up again in order to install that eyesore. Sylvie hated John's modern wall-mounted electric fire. When she first saw it, it made her wonder if in years to come there would be a young couple prizing off John's electric fire to discover what lay beneath.

'Well, what do you think?' Julia had finished unpacking all the shopping bags while Sylvie was lost in thought.

They both stood back and cast their eyes around the room. Julia liked the items she had bought when they were sitting on the shop shelf in Camden Market, but for some reason they weren't doing anything for her now she had placed them around the apartment. She glanced at Sylvie and could tell by the look on her face that she felt the same way, but was too polite to say so.

Sylvie turned to Julia and said, 'I'm going downstairs to put the kettle on.'

Julia took a moment alone in the lounge to try and figure out what was wrong. By the time Sylvie called her down to the kitchen for tea, Julia had the answer.

'Je-sus!' exclaimed Julia as soon as she stepped into the kitchen.

'Please don't swear.' Sylvie would much rather people didn't use swear words, although she did think of a few choice words herself when she first saw the brand new kitchen cabinets John had installed in the basement kitchen. After years of living with her wooden farmhouse-style kitchen, Sylvie still couldn't quite get over the shock of the very bright, very white modern cabinets that had been put up in their place. Sylvie didn't like them one bit. She felt like she was in a hospital operating theatre, not a kitchen.

Julia stared at the new kitchen lost for words.

'At least I still have my butler sink,' commented Sylvie, placing her hand on the cool white enamel. That wasn't because John had let her keep it, but rather the fact that John had discovered their butler sink which was all the rage when they had the original wooden kitchen cabinets installed years ago had come back into fashion. At least that's what John told Sylvie. However, Sylvie suspected it had more to do with the fact that it saved him money installing a new sink, and of course it matched John's new white kitchen units. That's why it stayed and all Sylvie's wooden kitchen cupboards had not.

Unfortunately, that wasn't the worst of it. Not only had her original kitchen disappeared, so had half the cupboard space. John decided the new tenants would not require as many kitchen cupboards in a two bedroom apartment, which also rather conveniently saved John money. Consequently, Sylvie's kitchen had shrunk to half its original size. The kitchen units stopped halfway along one wall, leaving a bare wall where the original kitchen cupboards used to be.

Sylvie thought it looked hideous as though they had forgotten to finish the kitchen. She stared forlornly around the room.

Sylvie always loved her basement kitchen. She used to spend a lot of time down there, but all that changed once John installed the new kitchen. It no longer had that homely lived-in feel.

Julia walked up to one of the kitchen cabinets and ran a hand over the surface. To her surprise, they were not laminated cupboard doors, but more expensive wooden kitchen cabinets painted white. That made all the difference. Taking a closer look at the panelled door fronts, Julia had an idea. 'It might just work.'

'What are you talking about, Julia?'

Julia voiced her idea. 'You could paint these.'

Sylvie looked at the kitchen cupboards. 'Really?'

Julia nodded. 'They're wooden. They've just been painted a glossy white. But look here at the style of the door fronts.' Julia motioned for Sylvie to step forward and take a closer look. 'Now, if the kitchen cupboards were a different colour . . . perhaps a vintage green? Wouldn't the cupboards look more in keeping with your butler sink? Wouldn't the kitchen look more—' Julia was searching for the right word.

'—Rustic?' volunteered Sylvie.

'That's right!' agreed Julia.

'Such a shame they didn't fit units along the entire length of the wall like my old kitchen,' observed Sylvie, standing by the wall staring at the empty space where her kitchen cupboards used to be.

Julia had another idea. 'What about a Welsh dresser?'

Sylvie looked up.

'I'm sure one would fit,' continued Julia. 'I bet it would look really nice and prove quite useful. You could keep your fine china out on display. You could even paint it the same colour as your kitchen?'

Julia could tell by the expression on Sylvie's face that she liked the idea – a lot. So she asked Sylvie, 'Why don't we go shopping for some paint?'

'Oh, I couldn't possibly do that,' said Sylvie, biting her lower lip and casting her eyes heavenward alluding to her husband upstairs. 'Could I?' She shifted her gaze and stared at Julia with a mischievous glint in her eye.

Julia grinned at her best friend. 'While we are on the subject of making some changes, let's go back upstairs.'

They took their mugs of tea upstairs and stood in the lounge once more. It was going to take more than a Persian rug, cushions, and some well-placed ornaments for Sylvie to put her own stamp on the place and feel at home.

'The apartment needs redecorating for a start,' said Julia. 'I'd even go so far as to suggest redesigning the living space. This lounge is really small, but if you did away with the second bedroom it would provide more living space.' Julia turned to Sylvie. 'I know a really good interior designer. He's retired now, although he does take on the occasional job. I'm sure I could make a phone call and arrange—'

Sylvie stopped her right there. Painting the kitchen cabinets was one thing, but what she was suggesting . . . Sylvie shook her head. 'Julia, I don't think that's a good idea. You see, John and I . . . well the thing is we would need to agree on—'

'Who's *we?*' Julia cut in. 'I only see one person living here – and that's you.'

'But it's not part of the plan.'

Julia rolled her eyes. 'Screw the plan! Right now, this is your apartment. What do *you* want, Sylvie?'

Sylvie blinked. Nobody had asked her what she wanted in a

long, long time. Sylvie tentatively smiled. 'I have got a small lump sum from my early retirement package so I wouldn't have to ask John for the money,' said Sylvie, thinking aloud. She was a bit reticent at the thought of spending her lump sum, but it wasn't as though they were strapped for cash. Besides, she *had* moved downstairs. Perhaps Julia was right: why stop there?

'You know what . . .' said Sylvie, swept along with Julia's ideas for redesigning her apartment. 'Let's do it!'

22

John was standing in the small kitchenette wearing an oven glove when the timer on the oven pinged. He carefully removed the pie from the oven. It smelt delicious. Nothing could beat home cooking, thought John. He was rather chuffed with his first homemade chicken pie. The table was set for dinner, and he had already opened a bottle of wine. She would be home any minute. John waited patiently for her return.

He had left his apartment door ajar. It wasn't long before he heard the front door open in the communal hall downstairs, heels clicking on the wooden parquet floor. She was home at last.

John put the pie on the table and made his way through the lounge into the lobby where he shut the door to his apartment. He returned to the kitchenette and checked the time. He raised an eyebrow. John wondered what Sylvie was up to that had kept her out later than usual. John was still mulling this over when he sat down at the kitchen table. He picked up his knife and fork and cut slowly into his chicken pie. Gathering a tasty chunk on the end of his fork, he popped it into his mouth and ate slowly, savouring the flavour.

'Hmm delicious,' he congratulated himself.

In fact, it had turned out so well that John decided next time he would bake a larger pie and freeze half for another meal. I could get into this cooking malarkey, thought John as he poured himself a glass of wine.

John was about to take another bite when he heard Sylvie's voice from the apartment below. Was she talking to Jasper again? John remembered the neighbour's cat, an orange tomcat called Jasper. The cat often wandered into the basement kitchen from their garden, bold as brass. Sometimes he even appeared upstairs in the lounge. He'd make himself at home on one of the deep-cushioned sofas until John, catching the sleeping cat unawares, would toss him off the sofa – a little too exuberantly – and chase him out of the house. John could not abide animals indoors with their fleas and hairs and odours.

He had just raised his fork when he heard another voice, deeper this time. John dropped his fork in surprise. Last time he checked, cats didn't answer back! It didn't sound like the TV, which meant only one thing: Sylvie had company. *Male Company!*

John threw his napkin over his unfinished chicken pie and darted out of his chair. He listened intently, following the sound of their voices right below him in Sylvie's lounge. Although he couldn't make out what they were saying, he could determine where they were in her apartment.

John followed their voices to the door of his apartment and opened it. He stepped outside on to the landing just as Sylvie opened her door downstairs. John watched as a gentleman walked out of her apartment.

'I think that would be an excellent idea,' said Sylvie as she stood in her doorway with some paperwork in her hands.

John shifted his gaze from Sylvie to the man standing in the hall downstairs outside her door. He appeared older than John with thin greying hair and a noticeable paunch. He was smartly dressed in black suit trousers, a pale blue shirt and a conservative tie.

John glanced down at the jeans he was wearing that probably pre-dated Chloe. They had been through so many wash cycles; they gave new meaning to the word *faded*. His jumper was no different, with the added bonus of holes where there shouldn't be. John frowned. He missed wearing his smart suits to work. John turned his attention to Sylvie's visitor downstairs and saw her shake the gentleman's hand. It appeared to be a business call, not a social visit. John exhaled in relief as Sylvie walked him across the communal hall to the front door.

John was still watching Sylvie as she closed the front door. He was just pondering who her visitor might be when she turned around and unexpectedly looked up, catching him unawares. He didn't have time to duck into his apartment out of sight.

She stopped and glared at him, clearly annoyed to discover her husband standing on the landing upstairs spying on her. She turned on her heel and walked back inside her apartment, slamming the door shut behind her.

'Bugger it!' John strode back into his apartment and shut the door wondering what Sylvie was up to. He couldn't exactly knock on her door and ask her; they hadn't spoken since the party when she moved in downstairs. He knew who he had to thank for that. Over the last two weeks, Julia had been in and out of the garden apartment so frequently that John couldn't find the right moment to speak to Sylvie alone to apologise. He didn't relish the thought of calling downstairs when Julia was there. And he most certainly did not want to apologise in front of Julia.

As the days dragged on, John started to wonder why he

should apologise at all. Until eventually he decided Sylvie should be the one apologising. After all, she was the one who had taken the key to the garden apartment with no explanation and just moved in. She was the one who had nearly ruined his party by throwing a strop. John thought he had been very reasonable under the circumstances. He had nothing to apologise for. In fact, now the boot was on the other foot; he was waiting for Sylvie to apologise to him.

John returned to the kitchenette, finished his chicken pie and cleared away the dishes into the dishwasher. He wiped the entire kitchen surfaces and cleaned the oven hob until it sparkled. John spent the rest of the evening ensconced on the sofa reading a John le Carré novel, his mind drifting to the packet of chocolate biscuits in the kitchen cupboard. He fancied one. John resisted. He didn't want to leave biscuit crumbs on the sofa.

He made a pit stop in the kitchenette, before taking himself off to bed, and scoffed several chocolate biscuits with a plate strategically positioned under his chin. Unfortunately, boredom and food cravings had returned with a vengeance since the conversion on the house was completed.

Half a packet of biscuits later, John had to undo the top button of his jeans. This didn't particularly bother him as he was on his way upstairs to get undressed for bed anyway.

John was woken up the next morning by strange noises coming from the apartment downstairs. He sat up in bed and glanced at his alarm clock. Although it was a weekday, he hadn't set the alarm because he was no longer at work. Even so, John was an early riser. And it was still early – for a retired person at any rate.

John reluctantly hauled himself out of bed. He missed Sylvie bringing him up a cup of tea in bed first thing in the morning. It was very tiresome having to get up and make it himself.

As he walked down the stairs and into the kitchenette, he could hear the strange noises quite distinctly. John cocked his head to one side to listen before filling the kettle with water. He left the kettle to boil while he made his way through the lounge. John was intending to nip downstairs and find out what was going on, until he walked into the lobby before exiting his apartment and caught sight of himself in the wall-hung mirror. John was still wearing his pyjamas. What if she had company? He couldn't very well wander downstairs without getting dressed first.

For a moment there, John had forgotten that his house was no longer a private home. Anybody could be on their way in or out of the house visiting the apartment downstairs. People he didn't know. People he did know – like Julia.

In hindsight, he wished that he hadn't been inflexible with his plans for the house conversion. He should have listened to Declan rather than going ahead with his own idea to have a shared front door into a communal entrance hall. He wanted this arrangement so he could keep an eye on the comings and goings of the tenants.

The flip-side, he soon discovered, was that he didn't know who might be milling around in the hall downstairs when he exited his apartment. Declan did warn him that he might come to regret that decision. Now he could see why. What appeared a good idea, in theory, wasn't turning out quite so agreeable in practice; perhaps his wife moving downstairs had something to do with it. She kept inviting people round like Julia. And if that wasn't bad enough there were the people he didn't know, like the man in the conservative suit and tie who visited Sylvie yesterday and left her with some paperwork. John still wanted to know what she was up to down there.

John returned to the kitchenette and tried to ignore the odd noises emanating from the garden apartment. He made a cup of tea and walked into his study. John shut the door, trying unsuccessfully to shut out the noise, and sat down at his desk. He placed his cup of tea on a coaster on his desk, picked out a pen from the stationery organiser, and opened the desk drawer to retrieve the little black book. John flicked through the pages. There were now several entries. Each one had Sylvie's name scrawled at the top of the page.

John wrote Sylvie's name at the top of a fresh page, adding the date. He checked the time and wrote that down too. It was only eight o'clock in the morning, and it sounded as though Sylvie was moving furniture around downstairs.

He was just about to write a new entry down in his little black book when a sudden thought occurred to him: what if she wasn't moving furniture around but having some new furniture delivered? He thought back to Sylvie's shopping spree with Julia a little over a fortnight ago and wondered if cushions and rugs weren't the only things she had bought.

John darted out of his chair, threw open the study door and raced over to the bay window in the lounge to see if there was a tell-tale delivery van parked outside the house. If she was having some furniture delivered, John had every intention of putting his boot in and sending it back. He had set that apartment up for tenants. As far as he was concerned the furnishings he had left down there were quite adequate.

John looked out of the window, up and down the street.

There was no sign of a delivery van. What John did see was a nondescript white van with no markings parked right outside the house and two beefy men piling out wearing paint-splattered jeans, heavy boots and torn tee-shirts. He didn't recognise them personally, but he recognised the type: builders. He watched them saunter up the garden path and disappear from his line of vision up the front steps and into the house.

His first thought was that Sylvie had encountered some problem in the apartment downstairs and called in a builder to fix it. John wasn't pleased about that. It wasn't just the fact that there might be a burst pipe or faulty wiring – he didn't relish the expense of putting it right – what bothered John more was that Sylvie had gone ahead and called in a builder without consulting him first. That's not the way things normally worked in the Baxter household. When it came to the house, John always, always had the final say – at least he used to. John had an uneasy feeling in the pit of his stomach that Sylvie was up to something.

Anxious to find out what was going on, John was just about to race downstairs when he looked down at his stripy-blue pyjamas. 'Blast!' John raced across the lounge instead, intending to go upstairs and get dressed, but in his haste he stubbed his big toe on the large glass coffee table in the centre of the room. John yelped in surprise as his big toe made contact.

John had insisted on moving the glass table into the upstairs apartment. It had cost a lot of money and he was loath to leave his expensive coffee table downstairs for tenants. He wouldn't get rid of it because then he'd have to admit to an expensive mistake, which it was. It was an even bigger mistake when he shifted it upstairs. It swallowed up a good proportion of the floor-space in the lounge and looked at odds with the new furniture John had purchased for the apartment. He had bought a compact two-seater sofa, in starch-white machine-washable covers, and a matching single upholstered chair. They were the smallest sofa set that John could find to fit the room.

He cursed and hobbled up the stairs to his bedroom trying to ignore the pain in his big toe. John dressed quickly and headed back down the stairs, by which time his toe wasn't smarting quite so much. Walking through the lounge into the small lobby, John briefly stopped in front of the wall-hung mirror to smooth his hair down in an attempt to make himself look more presentable before he came face-to-face with Sylvie.

John unlocked his apartment door and quickly made his way down the main staircase to the entrance hallway. He slowed as he neared the bottom of the stairs. The front door was wide open. The builders had already been back and forward to their van leaving a trail of dust in their wake. John paused on the bottom stair looking at the trail of dusty footprints that led across the hall from the front door into the garden apartment. They'd left the apartment door slightly ajar.

John stepped off the stair and reached for the door. He was about to push the door wide open and find out what was going on in there when he was rudely accosted by one of the workmen.

'Mate! Excuse me, mate!' He stepped in front of John and pulled the door to, keeping hold of the door handle.

John turned around and said, 'I am not your mate. Now, will you please let go of the door.'

'Can't do that mate,' he said flatly.

'Why not?'

'We were left with strict instructions not to let anybody into the apartment.'

John called out, '*Sylvie!*'

'If you are after Mrs Baxter, she has gone out for the day. She's a nice lady, said we could help ourselves to tea and biscuits.'

John frowned. 'Just what do you think you're doing in there?'

'You'll have to ask Mrs Baxter.'

John shook his head in exasperation. 'Now look here, I am the owner of this house and I demand to know what's going on. Now let me in!'

'She said you'd say that.'

John turned around at the sound of the other workman right behind him. 'I'll have you know,' said John, 'I am her husband!'

'She said you'd say that, too.'

'Are you insinuating that I'm not telling the truth?' John glared at them.

'Look, mate, we don't want any trouble.'

'Then let me into—'

'Don't press you're luck, mate.' They both folded their large muscular arms forming a human barricade in front of the door.

'Okay, okay. I'm going.' John stepped back holding up his hands in defeat. 'Can you at least tell me how long you're going to be here?'

'Just for the day, mate, and then we're finished.'

'Fine,' said John turning towards the stairs, although it wasn't fine – far from it. A whole day meant Sylvie hadn't called them in to fix a leaky pipe or some other household emergency; they were here to do a job. But what job exactly?

He slowly walked up the stairs and overheard an exchange between the two workmen.

'Mrs Baxter said her neighbour upstairs could be a nuisance.'

'Too right, mate.'

John whirled around to give them a piece of his mind now they weren't in spitting distance. But they were already gone, the apartment door closing behind them.

John stood on the stairs staring at the door. He narrowed his eyes. He could just imagine who had put Sylvie up to this. Julia had been poking her nose in and out of the garden apartment for the last two weeks. John wouldn't be at all surprised if it was Julia's idea to have the builders in. At least he could console himself with the thought that the builders were clearing off by the end of the day. Surely there wasn't an awful lot they could do in one day that couldn't be undone?

John turned around and walked back upstairs. Looking around at his modern, comfortable apartment, John thought about the sparsely furnished apartment downstairs set up as a rental for tenants. It was devoid of any personal effects apart from some of their old furniture. He could quite understand why Sylvie would want to make herself feel more at home living downstairs, even if it was just for a short time. However, buying some new cushions and a rug for the apartment was one thing, but having builders in to do heaven-knows-what was quite another.

It was making him feel uneasy. Why didn't Sylvie approach him to discuss her intentions? He was left wondering if Sylvie's was at it again: going ahead with something without divulging her plans just to make a point. It was reminiscent of when, without warning, she upped and moved downstairs. He had a good idea what it was all about this time. She was getting back at him for not letting her get involved at any stage during the conversion of the house. John realised belatedly that was probably a mistake.

John knew why he wouldn't let Sylvie get involved; they had

very different tastes. This was what was on his mind right now as he listened to that racket downstairs. What were the workmen up to? And more to the point would he like the end result? He doubted it. John was no longer dismissive about the fact that the builders were only down there for one day. On the contrary, the more he thought about it, the more he believed they could do an awful lot of damage in just one day.

He was standing in the kitchenette making another brew, trying not to think about the builders downstairs denying him access to his own property. Not to mention what they were getting up to, right beneath his feet, at this very moment. Instead, his mind drifted back to the first round of building work they had done to the house.

Not long after they moved in, John remembered they had sat down together and looked through some magazines for ideas on decorating their new home. That was when he had made the surprising discovery that their choice of interior décor was not at all compatible. As a result, during the original renovation work, he didn't let Sylvie near the inside of the house with so much as a feather duster. However, he relented when it came to the garden. What a mistake that turned out to be.

John wanted a neat lawn and simple borders. What he hadn't bargained for was a veritable overgrown kitchen garden that was reminiscent of some country cottage in the back of beyond. It was not in keeping with the style of their London home. John had to suffer that disorderly jungle of flowers that passed for a garden for all these years – not anymore.

Declan had helped John draw up plans for a new layout in the garden that would be far easier for a tenant to maintain. Declan's new plan turned out to be surprisingly similar to John's original idea, a low-maintenance garden, mainly laid-to-lawn with neat narrow borders. It was just the way John had imagined it before he let Sylvie loose on the garden all those years ago.

Then Declan had asked John one day, as the conversion was progressing, if he wanted him to go ahead with clearing the garden ready for the lawn to be laid.

Without consulting Sylvie, John said yes.

John stared out of the kitchen window at the neat square lawn below wondering if that had been a step too far. He recalled that Sylvie didn't say a word when she returned home from work in the charity shop to discover her garden had been transformed in just one day.

Not a word.

John could still hear the builders hard at work downstairs.

23

Sylvie put her paintbrush down on the old newspaper spread out in front of her and glanced across the room at Julia. They had both finished at the same time. Sylvie got off her knees as Julia climbed down the wooden step-ladder.

Julia had spent many hours over the past two weeks in the garden apartment with a paintbrush in hand. Sylvie thought of Julia's painting easel on her houseboat and joked that this probably wasn't the sort of painting Julia had in mind when she retired. It had taken almost two weeks to paint the kitchen cupboards. Sylvie couldn't have done it without her. They stood side by side to survey their handiwork.

'The cupboards look fantastic,' said Julia. 'It looks like you've got a brand new kitchen.'

'I know,' Sylvie agreed, turning full circle to take it all in. When they started painting the kitchen cupboards, Sylvie had daubed her first bit of green paint on the white cupboard doors and doubted that Julia's idea was going to work.

Looking at them now, the kitchen cupboards had turned out looking much, much better than Sylvie could have imagined possible with just a lick of paint. In fact, the kitchen looked so different that anyone would be forgiven for thinking they had ripped out the white cupboard units and had the whole kitchen replaced. Sylvie smiled at the thought. She'd like to see the look on John's face when he discovered that his glossy white kitchen was now a vibrant shade of vintage green.

The transformation of the kitchen wasn't the only thing that pleased Sylvie no end. The builders had finished the changes she wanted to the apartment in one day and, by the sound of it, succeeded in keeping her upstairs neighbour out of harm's way. The builders told Sylvie they had followed her instructions to the letter and not let anybody into the apartment, no matter who they claimed to be. That was just as well because Sylvie knew John would kick up a tremendous fuss if he found out what the builders were up to.

Sylvie had arrived home yesterday evening from another shopping expedition with Julia to find the work was complete. Very happy with the results, Sylvie had written the builders out a cheque there and then, and slipped them some extra cash as a thank you for handling her nuisance neighbour upstairs. She didn't want to think about the money that was *not* left in her bank account, especially after her latest shopping expedition with Julia. She was beginning to suspect her best friend was a bad influence.

With Julia's encouragement, Sylvie had spent far too much money yesterday on one item for the apartment – which pretty much swallowed up what was left of her retirement lump sum. Julia said she wouldn't regret it. Sylvie hoped not. She was expecting to take delivery today.

The store had promised to make a note on their delivery sheet to park the van around the corner in the side street. Sylvie and Julia agreed that it would be easier if the delivery men used the side gate into the back garden, and brought Sylvie's new purchase through the french doors straight into the kitchen. This wasn't the only reason Sylvie did not want them to park out front. She didn't want any chance that John spotted the van and tried to put a stop to the delivery.

They had just cleared away the paint pots and washed out the paintbrushes when Sylvie got a phone call. The delivery truck had left the depot and was on its way. Sylvie unlocked the french doors to the garden and threw them wide open in readiness for their arrival. She wrapped her cream woollen cardigan tightly around her against the chilly October breeze and stood in the open doorway staring forlornly into the garden. Sylvie didn't venture out there much of late because there was simply no need. All her plants and flowers were gone, replaced with a dull green lawn and year-round shrubs filling the narrow borders.

"Low maintenance," was John's buzzword when Sylvie found out what he had done to her garden.

She would never forget that day . . .

Sylvie had just returned home from a day working in the charity shop. She was walking down the street from the bus stop when she saw a skip sitting in the driveway where the car was normally parked.

Sylvie hardly gave it a second thought as she passed by on her way up the garden path to the front door. Although she did wonder where those dead plants had come from that had been tossed in the skip like yesterday's rubbish. It crossed her mind that perhaps a neighbour was surreptitiously dumping some garden waste in the builder's skip.

As soon as she walked into the upstairs apartment, John barely gave her time to take off her coat and shoes before herding her through the lounge towards the kitchenette saying, 'I've got something to show you, Sylvie.'

'Does it have to be right now?' Sylvie pushed past John to get a glass out of the kitchen cupboard. She was tired and she wasn't in the mood for games.

Sylvie turned around to the sink under the window to fill her glass with cold water, and happened to glance out of the kitchen window to her garden below. Except it wasn't her garden. Sylvie squeezed her eyes shut several times to try and focus. She must be seeing things.

'Great isn't it!' beamed John. 'I wanted to surprise you.'

The tap was still on and her glass was over-flowing. Sylvie could feel the sleeve of her blouse getting wet. She didn't move a muscle. Frozen, as if in suspended animation, she stared vacantly at the garden until the dreadful truth hit home – she was looking at John's god-awful surprise.

'What do you think?' asked John, clearly delighted. 'I think it's bloody marvellous – don't you? A low-maintenance garden is just what we need for tenants.'

Sylvie couldn't find the words to express how she was feeling; it was beyond words.

'I kept the tree though,' said John, not sounding entirely happy about it.

Sylvie knew why the tree had got a reprieve. People from the local council were in and out inspecting the alterations being carried out on the house. John couldn't afford to rock the boat over felling one old elm tree with a preservation order. If it wasn't for that, the tree would most probably be gone too.

Sylvie tried to push the memory of that awful day to the furthest reaches of her mind as she stood in the doorway waiting for her delivery. She stared at the tree that was all that was left of her garden. Was it her imagination or were the autumn leaves less colourful, less vibrant this year? To Sylvie, the old elm tree no longer stood as tall and proud as it once had. Its branches appeared to droop as though weighed down by sorrow, grieving for the plant kingdom it once watched over now decimated, torn up, bulldozed to make way for John and the plan.

Sylvie empathised. The garden used to fill Sylvie with joy. Now all she felt was sadness as it marked yet another great loss in her life.

'How about a cup of tea, Sylvie?' Julia called from inside the kitchen.

Sylvie turned her head and smiled across the room at Julia. Sylvie was very thankful for Julia's help with making the changes she wanted to the apartment. But there was one area that her well-meaning best friend could do nothing about – the garden.

It had taken years to nurture that garden. Over time Sylvie realised the garden she had created reminded her of somewhere familiar. It was not unlike the garden of the cottage in Cornwall where Sylvie had fond memories of spending her summers as a child. Sylvie had unwittingly created a little corner of Cornwall right here in the heart of London. That's why the garden had a special place in her heart and she had been so devastated by its loss.

No matter what she did to the apartment now, the garden was the one thing she couldn't change. There was no point even trying. Sylvie no longer had the years ahead of her to do that all over again. The painful truth was that her garden was gone, lost to her forever. Now all that was left behind was the sad elm tree. She thought John understood how important the garden was to her. God knows she had spent enough time nurturing that garden over the years. But there was more to it than that. What John didn't realise was that Sylvie had plans for her garden – very personal plans.

Sylvie had thought about it long and hard, and come to a decision: if she was unable to find the cottage in Cornwall with the garden where her mother wanted her ashes scattered, then Sylvie intended to do the next best thing. She planned to scatter her mother's ashes and finally lay her to rest in Sylvie's own little corner of Cornwall – in the garden of their London home. Sylvie hoped it wouldn't come to that, but at least she had something up her sleeve, somewhere that she felt confident her mother would have approved. Sylvie knew this for a fact because of the happy times they had shared in her garden.

In the beginning, when Sylvie and John first moved into the house, her mother used to pop in to see her grandchildren and help Sylvie in the garden. They would often be found on their hands and knees, side by side, digging up the weeds and planting new flowers. Together they created Sylvie's cottage garden.

Towards the end, before her mother was too old and frail to leave the nursing home, she had spent many hours sitting in the garden, a blanket tucked around her knees, just content to watch Sylvie tending the plants.

Sylvie would often glance at her mother sitting under the old elm tree. Sometimes she would catch her staring pensively at the garden with an unmistakable air of melancholy. Sylvie often wondered what she was thinking; perhaps the garden reminded her of those holidays in Cornwall and the cottage by the sea where they stayed each summer, now but a distant memory.

Thinking about the cottage in Cornwall reminded Sylvie of her mother's last wish to have her ashes scattered there. She knew she couldn't keep putting it off. At some point soon she would have to try and find that cottage, and hope the garden still existed just as they had left it nearly fifty years ago.

Sylvie stood there staring at the garden she no longer recognised and felt a sudden pang of anxiety. Her own garden had gone in a single day. It made Sylvie feel less optimistic that she would find what she was looking for. And now, thanks to John, she didn't even have a back-up plan if that turned out the case.

Julia walked over with two mugs of tea and stood beside her. 'No sign of the van, yet,' she remarked, handing Sylvie a mug.

Sylvie shook her head and silently took the tea.

Julia glanced at Sylvie; she looked preoccupied. Julia followed her gaze out on to the neatly laid lawn.

It had surprised Julia when she first visited the apartment, after their shopping trip together, and saw how Sylvie's garden had been transformed. It had John written all over it. It was very neat and tidy, and very like thousands of other gardens up and down the country. Sylvie's garden wasn't like that. Sylvie's garden was special. At least it used to be.

Gardens were never really Julia's thing. She had lived in a flat without a garden most of her adult life and now she would live the rest of her days on a houseboat. However, Julia always had several lovely gardens at her disposal if she felt the need to smell the roses. They were called public parks. It was one of the things Julia loved about living in a city. She didn't need her own private garden to enjoy the great outdoors. But Sylvie did. That's why Julia was so surprised to discover the dramatic change in Sylvie's garden. She thought Sylvie preferred all those flowers and shrubbery to a lawn. Her garden always reminded Julia of a wild garden, untamed and free. Over the years, Julia often wondered if it was the only thing Sylvie really loved about the house.

The fact that Sylvie hadn't mentioned the transformation had given Julia pause before she blurted out, *Bloody hell, Sylvie, what happened to your garden?* Julia didn't do that. Julia kept her mouth firmly shut. She didn't even bring up the subject of the garden in conversation, not once in all the time they had been painting the kitchen together.

And neither did Sylvie.

It made her wonder if John had done the unthinkable: destroyed Sylvie's garden without her knowledge. Julia had a feeling that's exactly what had happened because she knew, without a shadow of a doubt, that Sylvie would never, ever have agreed to it. A thing like that could spell the beginning of the end of a marriage, pondered Julia as she finished her mug of tea. She shifted her gaze from the garden, surreptitiously glancing at Sylvie's profile wondering if this was it – Sylvie had left him for good.

'It's here!' Sylvie exclaimed excitedly. She had spotted the delivery van. Sylvie turned to Julia. 'Look.' The roof of a van could just be seen above the six-foot-high garden wall which ran the length of the garden separating their property from the street outside.

Sylvie handed Julia her empty mug and stepped out on to the patio. She walked diagonally across the lawn aiming for the garden gate that was inset halfway along the red brick garden wall.

Sylvie opened the gate and waved at the two men sitting in the van on the street outside.

They both got out of the van and approached Sylvie, one holding a clipboard and pen. 'Mrs Baxter?'

'That's right.'

'We have a delivery for you.' He checked his paperwork. 'There's a note here that says you want it delivered through the rear of the house. Is that correct?'

'Yes, please. It's for the kitchen, you see, and I thought it would be much easier if you brought it straight through here . . .' Sylvie led the way.

He followed Sylvie through the garden gate and across the lawn to the back of the house, to assess the entrance into the kitchen. 'That won't be a problem,' he said, examining the width of the french doors. 'I'll just go and help my mate bring it in.'

Sylvie and Julia waited in the kitchen.

Ever since she purchased it, Sylvie felt uneasy about the amount of money she had spent on just one item for the apartment. Julia had persuaded her to buy it, reassuring her that it would make her kitchen complete. Sylvie hoped she was right.

When Sylvie caught sight of them heaving it through the gate and into the garden, her first reaction was, *Oh no, I've made a terrible mistake*. However, as soon as they brought it into the kitchen and carefully set it into position against the blank wall, slotting it neatly into the gap where the kitchen units abruptly ended, she knew it wasn't a mistake – far from it. It fitted so perfectly into that space it was as though it had been handmade for Sylvie's kitchen – which it hadn't.

Even the two delivery men remarked on it. 'It's a perfect fit. You'd think you had it made special.'

Sylvie grinned at them. She couldn't agree more.

The delivery van driver handed her the clipboard and pen. 'Just there please,' he said, indicating the space for her signature.

She signed her name and returned the clipboard.

'Nice kitchen by the way,' he said, giving her kitchen the once over as he walked out the door.

Sylvie shut the french doors behind them and turned to Julia who was looking a bit worried.

'Well?' said Julia anxiously. 'Do you like it?'

Sylvie thought it was the most beautiful Welsh dresser she had ever seen. 'I adore it,' Sylvie enthused.

Sylvie had always wanted one. She imagined her fine bone china out on display. The problem was there was never any room to have one in the basement kitchen until John fitted new kitchen units, leaving a large space where the old cupboards used to be. That space just happened to be the perfect size. It was as though it was meant.

Sylvie smiled. She always thought a dresser would complete her kitchen. Not everybody would agree with her. Some people, like John, wouldn't want it cluttering up their kitchen. But Sylvie did, and that's what mattered. It felt good to please herself for a change. Really good.

After they made a pot of coffee and sat admiring the Welsh dresser until there was no more coffee left in the pot, Julia turned to Sylvie and said, 'Where's your stuff?'

'Huh?' Sylvie stared at Julia blankly.

'You know . . .' Julia gestured at the Welsh dresser. 'Where's your china?'

'Oh – that.' Sylvie hadn't thought that far ahead. She had been too preoccupied with whether the dresser would look any good in her kitchen. Never mind what she was actually going to put in it. However, she did know exactly where to find her best china. Sylvie lifted her chin and raised her eyes heavenward: it was all upstairs.

'I take it,' said Julia, 'that you don't mean it's upstairs in *your* apartment.'

Sylvie slowly nodded her head, no.

'Oh dear.' Julia rolled her eyes. 'That's going to be a problem.'

Sylvie nodded. 'I know.'

As much as Sylvie wanted to see what her Welsh dresser looked like with her best china plates on the shelves and her best china mugs hanging from the little hooks above, Sylvie didn't want to go upstairs and get them.

And neither did Julia.

The both heaved a sigh of disappointment.

Sylvie had been avoiding John this past fortnight, with good reason. After all the things that had been done to the apartment, Sylvie wasn't looking forward to the inevitable confrontation with John when he found out exactly what they'd been up to.

They were sitting in silence looking at each other across the kitchen table, wondering how they could get hold of Sylvie's stuff without involving John, when the doorbell chimed.

Sylvie remained in her seat.

'There's someone at your door,' said Julia unnecessarily.

Sylvie knew who it was and she wasn't in the mood to talk to him.

It chimed again.

'Shall I answer that?' offered Julia.

Sylvie reluctantly rose from the table. 'No, I'll get it.' On the third chime, Sylvie sighed heavily and opened the door.

'Mum, what in god's name took you so long?'

'Chloe, please don't swear,' admonished Sylvie. She looked over Chloe's shoulder into the empty hall. There was no sign of John. Thank goodness. Sylvie turned her attention back to Chloe and looked at her puzzled. 'Did I leave the front door open?' Sylvie glanced into the communal hall wondering how Chloe got into the house.

'No. Dad gave me and Harriet a key to the house.'

'I see.' As usual, John hadn't thought to discuss it with her first.

Chloe lingered in the hall outside the door.

Sylvie didn't want to invite her in because she was afraid Chloe was going to have another gripe about not moving into the garden apartment. She suspected Chloe was here on a mission to persuade her to move back upstairs. Sylvie knew her youngest daughter's modus operandi; if she turned on the charm, she almost always succeeded in getting her own way. It would be very difficult not to give in to Chloe's demands.

However, from what Sylvie could see, Chloe wasn't standing at her door with an overnight bag and a chip on her shoulder. All she had was a small handbag in one hand and a laptop in the other, suggesting she had called in straight from work.

Chloe glanced at her laptop. 'I promised Dad I would install Wi-Fi in the apartment. I did that because I thought I would be moving in here for a little while and there's no way I could live here without the internet.'

At least she was honest, thought Sylvie.

'I guess a promise is a promise,' Chloe sighed, not looking too happy about it. 'May I come in?'

Sylvie opened the door wide and stepped aside wondering

what Chloe's reaction would be when she walked into the apartment and saw—

'Bloody hell!'

'Don't swear.'

'Sorry Mum,' Chloe apologised. 'You know Dad's going to go mental when he sees what you've done to this apartment?'

Of course Sylvie knew that, that's why she was avoiding him.

Chloe dropped her handbag on the sofa and did a circuit of the lounge. She suddenly looked down at her feet. 'I thought Dad had the old floorboards covered up with laminate flooring?'

'He did, but I didn't like it.' Sylvie looked down at the original floorboards freshly stained by the builders only yesterday.

'Neither did I,' admitted Chloe, surprising Sylvie. She thought youngsters these days preferred everything modern.

'I like the rug,' commented Chloe. 'It's so colourful.'

'Me too,' said Sylvie, catching Julia's eye. She was standing off to one side watching Chloe make a slow circuit of the room.

'That's nice.' Chloe picked up one of the ornaments Julia had bought for the apartment. It had found a home on the warm rattan furniture that Sylvie had picked out for the lounge.

Yesterday evening, after the builders finished up and left, Sylvie had arranged for another delivery. She paid a premium to have her new furniture delivered when John was tucked up in bed fast asleep. It was a necessary precaution because they were also taking away all the old furniture which John had left downstairs for tenants. Sylvie had donated it to charity. She imagined John would not be best pleased when he found out, hence the rather clandestine delivery. Although there wasn't a lot John could do about it now because, as Julia quite rightly pointed out, when it's gone – it's gone.

243

Sylvie had no money left in the kitty to buy one of those snazzy flat screen televisions like the one John had bought for the apartment upstairs, so the large old tube television stayed. Sylvie wasn't all that upset about it when Julia pointed out what great sound that old television had compared to her own flat-screen television.

Chloe put the ornament back where she found it and continued doing a circuit of the room, watched avidly by two pairs of eyes. She walked past the mustard yellow sofa, her hand brushing the array of brightly patterned cushions and the chenille throw draped casually over one arm that Julia had persuaded Sylvie to buy.

Sylvie didn't regret purchasing the throw because she had found a rather novel use for it. It was so soft and cosy that she liked nothing more than to curl up on the sofa watching a late night film tucked up all nice and toasty under that throw.

Chloe arrived at the fireplace. Studying it for a long moment, she turned around with a question, 'I thought Dad was going to—' She stopped abruptly and stared at Sylvie. 'You didn't!'

Sylvie loved that old fireplace. She stood and watched her lovely decorative old fireplace being covered up still intact – it was the first task John had set the builder to do as part of the conversion – then she watched early yesterday morning as the two builders she had employed set to work disconnecting and removing John's new wall-mounted electric fire. They uncovered the old fireplace beneath, restoring it to its proper place as the focal point of the room.

Chloe stood for a moment in front of the fireplace regarding Sylvie thoughtfully before casting her eyes around the room once more. Apart from the original floorboards and the old fireplace, everything else – from the buttercup yellow paint on the walls, to the patterned cushions, Persian rugs and Julia's eclectic mix of ornaments – were not at all what Chloe was used to seeing at Mum and Dad's house. Sylvie had transformed the garden apartment, and now it looked completely different to John's apartment upstairs.

Sylvie shifted nervously from one foot to the other. She glanced in Julia's direction.

It was Julia who asked the question first. 'What do you think?'

'What do I think?' Chloe's blue eyes were round with wonder. 'I totally love it!' Chloe added, 'Now I really want you to move back upstairs.'

Sylvie's face dropped at the mention of moving back upstairs. Was Chloe joking or was this the reason she was really here, using the Wi-Fi as an excuse to pop round and pester her to move out?

'There's just one thing . . .' said Chloe as she walked over to the sofa and sat down.

Here it comes, thought Sylvie preparing herself.

'I love it so much that if I moved in here, I might never move out!' Chloe tittered into her hand. 'And then what would Daddy do about his plan to find a tenant?'

'If you like all this . . .' said Julia, ignoring that comment about John, 'wait until you see the kitchen!' Julia grinned, took Chloe's hand, and led her downstairs.

Sylvie followed them down the stairs frowning at Chloe for reminding her about John's plan to rent out the garden apartment. Sylvie had got so carried away with Julia's ideas of how to make her feel at home in the apartment that it had completely slipped her mind this was meant to be someone else's home.

As soon as Chloe saw the green kitchen cupboards, she said, 'I can't believe you ripped out a brand new kitchen!'

'Actually, I didn't.' Sylvie smiled mischievously at Julia. 'They're painted.'

'Never!' Chloe stepped forward to take a closer look. 'This is amazing. I can't believe how a lick of paint can transform a kitchen. The white units were so—'

'—Bland?' offered Julia.

Chloe nodded emphatically. 'I much prefer it to Daddy's kitchen in the apartment upstairs.'

Sylvie smiled. Those were her sentiments exactly.

'It makes the room feel so homely,' Chloe continued, taking it all in. Her eyes settled on the Welsh dresser. 'Oh wow, look at that.' She hurried over and ran a hand along the smooth wooden surface. 'Where did you find it?'

'Julia found it,' replied Sylvie, 'when we went shopping at the Camden Antiques Market.'

'It's really something,' said Chloe, standing back to admire it. She frowned.

'What is it?' said Julia and Sylvie in unison, sensing a problem.

'The Welsh dresser looks kind of . . . empty.'

Sylvie and Julia looked at each other. A silent question passed between them: are you thinking what I'm thinking? They exchanged a knowing smile and moved as one towards her.

Julia sidled up to Chloe and wrapped a friendly arm around her slender shoulders.

'Chloe,' Sylvie began, taking her hand and smiling sweetly at her daughter. 'We have a little favour to ask.'

Chloe listened intently as they explained what they wanted her to do.

Sylvie stood outside her apartment door and waited for Chloe to emerge from upstairs with the boxes of china. She hoped Chloe could manage to walk down the stairs without dropping them en route. Sylvie had told her to be sure to let John know that Julia was downstairs for the evening.

Chloe cheekily called Julia a friend with benefits, presumably referring to the fact that John would steer clear of them if he knew Julia was anywhere in the vicinity. Everybody, including Chloe, knew they didn't get along.

Sylvie was standing at the door to her apartment waiting for the boxes of china when she heard an exchange between John and Chloe at the top of the stairs.

'Dad, don't worry. Mum's done a great job downstairs. The apartment looks really nice.'

'Nice – how?'

John was giving Chloe the third degree over what she had done to the apartment. Thank goodness Chloe was being evasive and sparing John the grizzly details. Sylvie didn't fancy a perfectly lovely day spoiled by John having a temper-tantrum when he found out the truth.

'Turncoat,' John said sulkily.

'Oh don't be like that, Dad. Look, I'm sure it won't be long now.'

Sylvie wondered what Chloe meant by that. She didn't have to wait long to find out. Chloe continued the conversation right outside John's door, oblivious to the fact that Sylvie was standing in her doorway at the bottom of the stairs and could hear every word.

'I'm only helping because the sooner Mum has her fun, the sooner she'll get bored and move back upstairs.'

And the sooner you'll have the garden apartment all to yourself, thought Sylvie narrowing her eyes.

'Come on, Dad. You know Mum, I'm sure everything will be back to normal very soon – just you wait and see.'

John said something Sylvie didn't quite catch. Then she heard Chloe laugh nervously. 'No, I haven't got an ulterior motive helping Mum, if that's what you're thinking, Daddy.'

Sylvie slowly shook her head from side to side. She could always tell when her daughter wasn't entirely truthful with John because *Dad* became *Daddy*, and her voice always went up an octave with every fib.

Sylvie folded her arms and watched Chloe struggle down the stairs with a box. 'I'll take that,' said Sylvie, eyeing her daughter.

Chloe handed over the box. 'Do you need some help unpacking the china?'

'No, thank you,' said Sylvie coolly. 'Haven't you got the Wi-Fi to sort out?'

Chloe looked at her mother. She was picking up a vibe that for some inexplicable reason she was in her mum's bad books. Chloe shrugged it off. 'I'll fetch the other boxes then and get on with installing the internet.'

'Fair enough,' said Sylvie. She turned around and carried the first box of china through the lounge and down the stairs into the basement kitchen. Her thoughts drifted back to when she had packed up these boxes for storage.

Before the building work on the conversion got underway, Sylvie had carefully wrapped up her fine china and temporarily packed it all away in cardboard storage boxes for safekeeping. However, when the time came to unpack the boxes once they moved into the apartment upstairs, Sylvie discovered there was no room in the small kitchenette for her fine china. Unbeknown to Sylvie, John had already purchased a plain white sixteen-piece crockery set to match his plain white kitchen. Sylvie had no choice but to leave her china packed away in storage boxes – until she upped and moved downstairs.

Sylvie fetched two more boxes of china from the lounge where Chloe had deposited them. With Julia's help, she set to work unpacking and arranging the china on the Welsh dresser. This was something Sylvie wanted to do for years, but John didn't want a large dresser cluttering up the kitchen. Sylvie suspected it was not so much the dresser that was the problem; what he really didn't want to see was her fine china out on display.

Julia flattened three empty boxes while Sylvie stood back to inspect the Welsh dresser. It now looked dressed. Sylvie was very happy with the results. It was as though, after all these years, her best china had finally found a home.

Sylvie glanced at her watch. It was already early evening and she wanted to invite Julia to stay for dinner. The problem was she didn't have much in the way of groceries to whip up a meal. Sylvie had been so busy redecorating the apartment over the last two weeks that she had neglected to do a proper shop. She had been surviving on takeaways and ready-meals.

Sylvie couldn't stomach the thought of another Chinese takeaway. She opened the fridge. 'I've got pizza,' she said hopefully.

'And I've got wine,' added Chloe, appearing at the bottom of the stairs holding up a bottle of wine in each hand.

Sylvie didn't think to ask where the wine materialised from.

Chloe didn't mention that she had nipped into Daddy's apartment and raided his kitchen when he wasn't looking.

'Sounds perfect,' said Julia.

Sylvie opened the oven door and slipped two large pizzas out of their boxes straight into the oven while Julia found three wine glasses in one of Sylvie's kitchen cupboards.

They all walked back upstairs to the lounge.

Chloe was just saying that she had finished setting up Wi-Fi when Sylvie spotted three more boxes on the rug in front of the fireplace. She pointed at them and looked at Chloe with a question.

'I did as you asked and brought down the boxes.' Chloe shrugged. 'Perhaps it's more china?'

'I thought we unpacked all the china,' said Julia, walking into the lounge and setting three wine glasses down on the coffee table.

'We did,' Sylvie confirmed.

Chloe squatted down in front of the boxes. 'Then I wonder what's inside these?'

24

Sylvie blew a thick film of dust off the top of one of the boxes. The dust made her sneeze. She examined the box and could just make out her name written on one side in bold black lettering that had faded over time. Sylvie couldn't even remember packing these boxes. They must have been stored in that cupboard for years – decades even.

'The pizzas are ready,' said Chloe, returning from the kitchen where Sylvie had sent her to fetch a pair of scissors.

'Be a dear and get them out of the oven, would you?' said Sylvie, taking the scissors from Chloe's outstretched hand.

Sylvie turned her attention to the box in front of her. She knelt down on the rug and cut the dusty tape, peeling it back from the top of the box before opening the flaps to look inside.

Julia, who was sitting on the sofa in front of Sylvie – wine glass in hand – leaned forward to take a closer look. It wasn't china inside. The box was brim full of notebooks.

Sylvie recognised them instantly. She picked one out of the box and looked up at Julia. 'These are my old diaries from years ago!'

'You kept all those?' said Julia in surprise.

'I'd forgotten all about them.' Soon after they moved into the house, Sylvie had packed them all up in boxes and stored them in the cupboard on the landing. That cupboard had remained untouched until just recently when John had suggested it as the ideal place to store Sylvie's china during the conversion. It was one of the few places in the house that would not be disturbed by the builders once they set to work.

Once John had put the boxes of china in the cupboard, he kept the cupboard locked and the key in the desk in his study. Lucky for Sylvie that Chloe had turned up when she did and agreed to fetch the key from John to retrieve the boxes of china. The only problem was Sylvie had forgotten there was more than china stored in that cupboard. Chloe had brought down every box, unaware that the last three didn't contain Sylvie's best china. If it wasn't for Chloe, those boxes full of Sylvie's old diaries would have remained there gathering dust and forgotten for years to come.

Sylvie picked out an old worn notebook, its pages yellow with age. She opened it and read the first entry dated September 1964. Sylvie was nine years old. According to the diary entry, she'd had another fight with one of her siblings. Sylvie had been sitting alone, quite happily minding her own business and writing in her diary, when one of them had crept up behind her and grabbed the diary out of her hand. The top right-hand corner of the page was torn where she had tried to keep hold of it in the ensuing struggle.

She finished reading that entry which ended with the words: *I wish they would all go away and leave me alone.*

Sylvie couldn't remember which one of her brothers and sisters were being mean to her on that occasion. It happened so often, it could have been any one of them. She often wrote her diaries in bed under a sheet by torchlight, until her brothers and sisters pounced on her and stole her diary. That happened most nights. The only time she really got a chance to write her diaries in peace was during the summer holidays she spent in Cornwall without her siblings.

Sylvie sighed and put that diary to one side. She started to rummage through the box in front of her.

Julia had been busy undoing the other two boxes when she noticed Sylvie picking through the notebooks searching for something. Julia eyed her best friend. 'Are you looking for anything in particular, Sylvie?'

Sylvie looked up. 'I'm trying to find the diaries that I wrote during those summer holidays I spent in Cornwall with my mother. I thought they would make fascinating reading after all these years.'

'Do you want me to help you look for them?'

Sylvie sat back and looked at the three boxes, all chock-full of notebooks. 'Yes, if you wouldn't mind, Julia.' It would take some time to search through the boxes on her own.

The smell of oven-baked pizza wafted into the room along with Chloe. She was carrying two large serving dishes, one in each hand. 'Dinner is served,' announced Chloe, placing the dishes on the coffee table in front of Sylvie and Julia. Three plates and paper serviettes were already on the table.

Chloe helped herself to a large slice of pizza. 'That's not china, is it,' remarked Chloe gazing down at the open boxes. 'I suppose you'll want me to cart those boxes back upstairs and put them back where I found them.'

'No, that won't be necessary,' said Sylvie.

Chloe looked at her mother. 'So, what's inside the boxes?'

Sylvie turned around and got up from her knees. 'These are my old diaries.'

'Really?' Chloe took her place on the rug and sat down crossed-legged in front of an open box to take a closer look. 'I didn't know you used to write diaries.' Chloe took a bite of pizza and studied her mother.

Sylvie explained, 'I used to write all the time, up until . . . well . . . I suppose until I met your father and got married.'

Sylvie took a plate and a serviette off the coffee table and helped herself to a slice of pizza. She sat down on the sofa and spread out the serviette on her lap. 'Julia is going to help me search through the boxes to find some of the diaries I wrote during my summer holidays in Cornwall.'

'Can I help?' asked Chloe, quickly polishing off her slice of pizza and wiping her hands on a serviette.

Sylvie smiled. 'Of course you can.'

Chloe got them organised. She went back downstairs to the kitchen and retrieved the two flattened boxes that had been used to store Sylvie's best china. She taped the bottom of the boxes up again. When they had finished eating, she cleared the plates away and placed the empty boxes on the coffee table. 'So here's the plan . . .'

Sylvie looked over at her daughter and sighed. How many times had the girls heard John use those two words growing up? John always had various incarnations of *the plan*: the plan for renovating the house; the plan for his career; the plan for the girl's education. And most recently, the plan for converting the house and renting out the garden apartment, which didn't exactly go according to plan when Sylvie decamped downstairs.

After all those years living with John and the plan, Sylvie's eyes glazed over at the mere mention of those two words.

'Mum, are you listening?'

Sylvie fixed her gaze on Chloe. 'Of course I am, sweetheart. Do carry on with *the plan.*'

Chloe glanced at her mother before continuing, 'As we search through the notebooks, I suggest we put the Cornwall diaries you want to read to one side, over there.' Chloe pointed at the empty bookcase in the alcove beside the fireplace. 'The rest we can pack up in these boxes.' Chloe pointed at the empty boxes lining the coffee table.

'Works for me,' said Julia.

Sylvie nodded enthusiastically. 'Sounds like a good—' Sylvie thought *plan* and said, '—Idea.'

They each took a box full of Sylvie's diaries and made a start.

One hour passed in silence as Sylvie, Julia and Chloe took one diary at a time, first of all checking the year in which it was written. Any diaries written after Sylvie's twelfth birthday, when the summer holidays in Cornwall stopped, were discarded in one of the empty cardboard boxes on the coffee table. Any diaries written before Sylvie's twelfth birthday were then leafed through to check in which month the diary entries were made. If they were not from Sylvie's summer holidays, then those too were consigned to one of the empty boxes.

So far, they hadn't found a single one of Sylvie's Cornwall diaries. They enthusiastically ploughed on, each wanting to be the first to shout out victoriously that they had found one.

Chloe was the first to break the silence. She had picked out another diary from the box and turned to a page at random. She knew immediately it wasn't one of the diaries Sylvie was looking for because of the date; her mother would have been around seventeen years old. But something caught her eye. Chloe read the diary entry and gave Sylvie a sideways glance. 'Who's Simon?'

Sylvie and Julia looked up.

'Pardon me?' Sylvie had been so engrossed in the task at hand that she needed Chloe to repeat the question.

'It says right here,' Chloe read from a page in Sylvie's diary, "I think Simon is very dishy and I hope to see him again soon." Chloe held the diary up and pointed. 'Look, it's followed by lots of little kisses.'

'Give me that!' exclaimed Sylvie, exchanging a look with Julia as she reached over and grabbed the diary out of Chloe's hand. 'You're meant to be looking for the diaries I wrote *before* my twelfth birthday, remember?'

'Yes – but who's Simon?'

Sylvie rolled her eyes and stole a glance at Julia. 'It was just a silly teenage crush.'

'Was he like an old boyfriend or something?'

'That was before I met your father. It's ancient history now.' Sylvie closed the diary and put it in one of the boxes on the coffee table. She caught Julia staring at her. 'What?'

'Nothing.' Julia quickly turned her attention back to the box in front of her.

Sylvie turned to Chloe. 'Now come on, chop, chop,' she clapped her hands. 'Let's stick to the plan.' Sylvie winced at her choice of words. 'Please discard the ones we don't want, without reading them first, Chloe. Otherwise, we're going to be here all night.'

All three of them put their heads down and continued searching through the boxes in front of them.

A little over an hour later Chloe's box was empty. 'I can't believe I didn't find a single one.' Chloe held up her empty box. 'If they were in some sort of date order and I had a box of diaries you'd written *after* your twelfth birthday I'd understand. But they weren't.' Chloe stared at her empty box for a moment longer and then got up from the floor. 'I'm going to make some coffee.'

Sylvie watched Chloe cross the lounge and disappear down the stairs. She turned to Julia. 'Why don't we take a break?'

'That is an excellent idea.' Julia stiffly got up from the rug and sat down on the sofa. 'I think I've got cramp,' commented Julia, rubbing one of her knees as she stretched her legs out in front of her. She still had one of Sylvie's diaries in her hand. Julia opened it and flicked through the pages.

Sylvie sat next to her on the sofa. She could hear Chloe downstairs in the basement kitchen putting the kettle on and opening cupboards and drawers.

Julia put the diary down and turned to Sylvie. 'Don't you ever think about him?'

'Who?'

'Simon.'

Sylvie frowned. 'Why would I do that?'

'Don't you ever wonder what your life might have been like if you'd waited for him?'

Sylvie looked at Julia and then cast her eye around the apartment. Was this what it was really all about – regrets? Is that what Julia thought was behind her move downstairs: regrets about the past? Regrets about whom she had spent the last thirty-nine years married to?

'I wonder where he is now?' pondered Julia.

Sylvie hadn't thought about Simon in a very long time. She didn't want to start now. As she'd said to Chloe, it was ancient history. And she wanted it to stay that way.

Thankfully, Julia changed the subject. 'Now you've finished the apartment, have you thought about what you're going to do next?'

Sylvie looked at her blankly.

Julia held up a diary. 'What about renewing old interests?'

Chloe walked into the room carrying a tea tray containing a fresh pot of coffee, a small jug of cream and three coffee mugs.

'I haven't really thought about it,' replied Sylvie, watching Chloe place the tea tray on the coffee table in front of them. Although Sylvie's hours had been reduced at the charity shop, all her spare time had been taken up with redecorating the apartment and shopping with Julia. She hadn't stopped to consider what she would do, besides the charity work, once the apartment was finished.

Chloe poured the coffee and handed Sylvie a mug. 'Whatever you're thinking of doing, Mum, you're going to need a computer.'

Sylvie disagreed. 'What do I need a new computer for? I've already got one.'

'You mean the one upstairs in Dad's apartment,' Chloe reminded her as she poured two more mugs of coffee. She handed one to Julia and then settled herself down in the single rattan chair opposite them with her mug of coffee. Chloe looked at her mother expectantly.

Sylvie knew that look. Chloe was waiting for her to change her mind and give in. Sylvie rolled her eyes. 'I still don't see why I need one, Chloe.' And more to the point, could she afford one? Sylvie had been putting off checking her bank balance, worried about how much money she was spending on the apartment. She hadn't been keeping a tally. Sylvie was afraid that she had not only spent all her retirement lump sum but gone into overdraft.

Chloe put her coffee mug down on the new rattan side table, picked up her laptop and placed it on her lap. She flipped open the lid. 'I'm just checking you are connected.'

Sylvie and Julia sipped their coffee and watched Chloe in fascination as she set to work, her fingers dancing over the computer keys.

Sylvie sat there thinking that her youngest daughter was the epitome of a Generation Y. She had read it in a magazine in the hairdressers all about the computer-literate generation that Chloe, in her late twenties, belonged to. The article called them *Gen Y* for short. Chloe had always been fascinated by computers ever since she was a little girl. It didn't surprise Sylvie and John that she studied for a computer science degree at university. She breezed through her degree and continued her studies to be awarded a Master's degree with distinction, before establishing herself in the world of work as a talented computer software engineer.

'You're online,' Chloe whooped punching the air. 'Now all we need to do is buy you a—'

'Chloe!' Sylvie interrupted, her voice held a warning note. 'I really don't think I need a computer, at the moment.'

Chloe gave her a look that said, *you are joking?* Chloe, a typical Gen Y, couldn't imagine life without being connected.

'Besides, I really haven't got the room,' added Sylvie. 'John has got his study upstairs for a computer.'

Chloe looked around the apartment taking in what she said. 'You're right,' she agreed. 'You don't need a computer.'

Sylvie breathed a sigh of relief. She really didn't want Chloe badgering her to buy something she didn't want and couldn't afford.

'What you need is a laptop.' Chloe grinned. Staring avidly at the laptop screen, Chloe's fingers danced across her keyboard once more.

Sylvie groaned. 'Chloe, I don't want to buy a laptop.'

'Too late!'

'What do you mean – too late?' Sylvie said in exasperation.

'I've already bought one,' said Chloe, closing the lid on her laptop. She looked exceptionally pleased with herself as she reached for her mug of coffee.

Sylvie sighed heavily. The trouble with Chloe was that sometimes she was just like her father; once she got an idea into her head, there was no stopping her. Sylvie was too tired to argue. Instead, she wondered how much Chloe's idea was going to cost her.

'It's just something basic.' Chloe caught Sylvie's worried expression. 'Don't worry, Mum. It didn't cost a lot. In fact, it's my treat.' Chloe glanced around the apartment. 'Let's call it a moving-in present.'

'A moving-in present,' echoed Julia thoughtfully. Chloe had just given her a marvellous idea.

'The laptop will be delivered in the next few days. I'll come over and set it up for you.'

'What on earth am I going to do with a laptop?' Sylvie glanced at Julia who shrugged her shoulders.

'You could surf the web,' Chloe offered. 'I'll show you how.'

'Perhaps you could set me up with email,' suggested Sylvie, warming to the idea. In the past, when she used the computer that was now sitting in John's new study upstairs, Sylvie had enjoyed sending emails to Jess in Australia, keeping her up to date with all the family news.

Julia smiled at Chloe. 'It sounds as though the laptop is going to come in handy, after all.' Julia put her empty coffee mug to one side. She knelt down beside the box of old diaries that she had been searching through before they stopped for a coffee break. She glanced over her shoulder at Sylvie. 'Do you think you'll start writing again?'

Sylvie joined her on the rug and picked out a notebook from one of the boxes. Sylvie used to write her diaries religiously. But that was years ago, before marriage and children, when she had some time to herself. Time to *be* herself.

'I suppose I could try,' said Sylvie, turning over the notebook in her hand wondering where all the intervening years had gone since she had last put pen to paper. How frighteningly quickly time passed. She was sixty this year, and yet those childhood summers were still so fresh and vivid in her memory that it was hard to believe it was almost fifty years since she had left Cornwall, never to return.

Sylvie sighed. Discovering her old diaries reminded her of the reason she would finally be returning to Cornwall after all these years. Under different circumstances, she would be looking forward to the trip. Sylvie wished she had found the time to return to Cornwall with her mother when she was still alive.

Sylvie recalled that soon after her father passed away, her mother had surprised her by suggesting they take a trip to Cornwall together, just the two of them, like they used to when she was a child. Sylvie's mother hadn't spoken of those holidays for years. The problem was Sylvie had three teenage daughters, a part-time job and a household to run. It was never the right time to drop everything and leave John and the girls for a trip down memory lane. And before Sylvie knew it, time had flown and her mother was too old and frail to make the journey.

Sylvie stared at the notebook in her hand. She hated regrets. It was the worst kind of feeling, knowing you let an opportunity slip through your fingers and realising, in hindsight, that you should have done things differently. Unfortunately, she realised too late that there was never going to be a right time to make that trip. Sylvie consoled herself with the thought that she could still do one last thing for her mother by returning to Cornwall to scatter her ashes. At least she still had the memories of their summers together in Cornwall, and those diaries recounting her childhood adventures at the cottage by the sea. Sylvie was looking forward to reading them more than she let on.

Sylvie opened the notebook in her hand and briefly perused it to find, once again, that it wasn't one of the diaries she was looking for. With a sigh, she discarded it in one of the cardboard boxes on the coffee table. She happened to glance in Julia's box and was surprised to discover her box was almost empty too. They still hadn't come across a single diary from those summers in Cornwall. This surprised her. She recalled spending long summer evenings in the cottage writing voraciously, filling many, many notebooks with tales of her Cornish summer adventures. Where had they disappeared to?

'You know what you could do, Mum.'

Sylvie turned around and looked at Chloe.

Chloe leaned forward in her chair. 'You could use your new laptop to write a blog.'

Noting her Mum's blank look at the mention of the word

blog, Chloe took a moment to explain, 'In plain English please, Chloe,' just what a blog was . . .

'. . . and a blog can be whatever you want it to be,' concluded Chloe. 'It could be kind of like a diary. You could write all about yourself and what's going on in your life, that sort of thing.'

'Oh, I couldn't possibly do that,' said Sylvie, absently flicking through another old notebook before casting it aside. Sylvie had heard all about those social networking sites. She couldn't imagine putting anything of a personal nature on a website for all to see.

Chloe tried to explain that it wasn't like that. 'A blog isn't the same as a social networking site.'

Even so, Sylvie told Chloe she was still worried about her personal life being out there.

Chloe keeled over with laughter. 'Mum, don't take this the wrong way, but I don't think you've got anything to worry about on that score. Seriously, nobody is going to read your blog.'

'Why not?' Sylvie shot back defensively feeling offended, which was absurd because she didn't really want anybody to read her blog. She hadn't even decided she was going to write one yet.

'Mum, it's nothing personal. The fact is people blog all the time. There are gazillions of blogs out there, so I'm pretty confident nobody is going to take much notice of yours.'

Chloe quickly added, 'And I mean that in the nicest possible way, of course.'

'I'll think about it.'

'Chloe looked at her watch. 'God, is that the time?' She quickly finished her coffee in three large gulps and stood up, gathering up her laptop and bag. 'Mum, I have to go. I'll pop round in a couple of days when your laptop arrives to set it up.'

Chloe was already striding to the door. 'I'll sort out the blog as well, just in case you decide it's something you want to do.' She stopped short and turned around. 'Do you need me to stay and help you look through the rest of those notebooks?'

'Unfortunately not,' said Sylvie, closing the last notebook in her box and casting it to one side. She glanced at Julia who was holding up an empty box.

Julia shrugged. 'I'm sorry, Sylvie. I didn't find any either. It doesn't make sense. You're bound to have mislaid a few note-books over the years, but not to find a single one amongst all these?' Julia sounded as disappointed as Sylvie felt.

Sylvie stood up and glanced at the empty bookshelves in the alcove by the fireplace where she was going to put those diaries. She had been looking forward to reading them and revisiting the summers of her youth. Sylvie thought they would have been especially poignant now her mother had passed away.

Sylvie turned from the bookcase and shrugged. 'There's no use crying over spilt milk. They're gone and there's nothing we can do about it.'

'What do you think happened to them?' asked Chloe.

Sylvie walked over to join her by the door. 'I haven't a clue.' Sylvie was just as perplexed as they were. Julia was right: it didn't make any sense.

Chloe opened the door to the apartment and turned around to say goodbye.

Sylvie gave her little girl a big hug. 'Thank you, my sweet.' Chloe had been surprisingly helpful this evening. Not at all what Sylvie had expected from her youngest daughter.

As the archetypal baby of the family, Sylvie and John would never admit they spoiled their youngest child rotten. But ever since word dot Chloe always got what she wanted. And rarely, in Sylvie's experience, did she do something for nothing.

Chloe lingered outside the door.

Sylvie could tell there was something on her mind. 'What is it, Chloe?'

Chloe stared over her mother's shoulder. She could see into her bright, colourful lounge through the open doorway. Chloe shifted her attention to the bland communal hallway outside before glancing upstairs at the door to the other apartment. Finally, Chloe fixed her gaze on Sylvie. 'Everything *is* all right, Mum – isn't it?'

Sylvie looked at Chloe in surprise. How can everything be all right if she was living downstairs and John was living upstairs in a separate apartment? If Chloe couldn't see that, then Sylvie had no intention of upsetting her by telling her the truth.

'Everything is just fine, sweetheart,' said Sylvie, lying through her teeth and crossing her fingers behind her back.

Chloe smiled in relief. She was confident everything was all right at home. Chloe knew her mum. She never swore and she *always* told the truth. Chloe kissed her goodbye.

Sylvie waved at the front door. Her smile faded as soon as Chloe was gone.

Sylvie walked back into the apartment feeling utterly wretched that she had lied to her daughter, right to her face.

'I think someone needs cheering up,' remarked Julia, catching the look on Sylvie's face as she walked in and closed the door. 'I know just the thing. I've had the most brilliant idea, darling.'

Sylvie didn't feel in the mood for company, or cheering up, but Julia was still ensconced on the sofa eagerly waiting to share her brilliant idea.

Sylvie looked at her best friend and didn't have the heart to tell her to leave. 'Shall I put the kettle on?'

'No, it's late. I won't keep you long.' Julia smiled. 'Sylvie, do you remember those parties I used to throw at my flat?' She paused. 'No, of course you don't – what was I thinking?' Julia tapped her temple. 'As I recall, you never once came to one of my parties because John said he didn't like parties. To be honest, I suspected he just didn't want to come to *my* parties.'

Sylvie rolled her eyes and slumped down in the rattan chair opposite Julia. She wondered when Julia and John would settle their differences or at least act civilly towards each other.

'Well, to cut a long story short,' continued Julia. 'I want to throw you a party.'

Just the thought of eating party food and drinking alcohol on a boat was enough to make Sylvie's stomach churn. 'Julia, you know I'm not exactly fond of boats.'

Julia laughed. 'I don't mean on my houseboat, darling.' She stood up. 'I want to throw you a party right here.' Julia threw her arms wide indicating Sylvie's apartment.

Sylvie shook head. 'Julia, I really don't think—'

'It will be a housewarming party with a difference!' Julia wasn't going to take no for an answer.

Sylvie felt too tired to argue, although she did wonder what Julia meant by, "a housewarming party with a difference." She had never been to one of Julia's parties, but she had heard the rumours – who hadn't? Back in the seventies, Julia's house parties were legend.

'I was thinking of a seventies-themed party,' said Julia enthusiastically, as she opened the apartment door and stepped into the communal hall outside. She glanced at Sylvie still seated in the lounge. 'You won't regret it, darling. You know my parties used to be famous, back in the day.'

'Don't you mean infamous?' Sylvie said dryly.

'Oh, I'm not giving anything away,' Julia replied cryptically. 'You'll have to find out for yourself.' And with that, she winked at Sylvie and shut the door.

Sylvie stared at the door trying to work out if she had just agreed to a party right here in the apartment.

25

Soon after Julia left, the eventful day caught up with Sylvie so she decided to retire early. She nipped down to the kitchen to switch off the lights and lingered a moment to admire her new Welsh dresser before she took herself off to bed.

She walked back upstairs thinking about Julia's suggestion to get rid of the second bedroom in the garden apartment and extend the size of the lounge. The trouble with Julia's idea was that Sylvie liked the lounge just the way it was: small and cosy. On the other hand, she wasn't that fussed about having a spare bedroom.

Julia's suggestion had given Sylvie an idea. She missed the large master bedroom upstairs that she and John used to share when the house was still a home. What Sylvie loved about that bedroom was that it had not one, but two large sash windows. Sylvie liked nothing more than to wake up in a bright bedroom with sunlight streaming through both bedroom windows first thing in the morning.

Fortunately, there was only a partition wall separating the two bedrooms in the garden apartment. And now there wasn't. Sylvie didn't take on board the fact that by removing the partition wall she had turned John's two-bedroomed rental apartment into a one bed. Sylvie couldn't care less. All she thought was that the builders had done a grand job in just one day. Now she had her wish: a large, bright, airy bedroom with two sash windows to let in the light.

Sylvie walked into the bedroom and pulled down the Roman blinds hanging at each window. The handmade blinds had cost a small fortune, but Sylvie thought they were worth it.

Sylvie glanced at the notebook in her hand which she had randomly selected from one of the boxes on the coffee table in the lounge. She intended to take it to bed, to leaf through before settling down to sleep; that turned out not to be one of her better ideas. Sylvie couldn't settle down or get to sleep. The more she thought about it, the more upset she became over the fact that they were unable to find a single diary she had written during those summers she spent in Cornwall.

She left the notebook unopened on the bedside table and lay down in bed. Sylvie wished she hadn't discovered those boxes full of her old diaries after all these years. Sylvie was of the opinion that nothing good ever came from dredging up the past. Her old diaries were a case in point. Now all Sylvie could think about were the notebooks that had inexplicably gone missing and that diary entry Chloe discovered about a young man she hadn't thought about in years – Simon.

They met Simon at a dance when they were seventeen. He had moved to London with his father who was stationed at RAF Northolt. Simon was a forces brat. He had travelled and attended school all over the world, wherever his father was posted.

Julia was infatuated with him from the moment she laid eyes on him. Unlike Sylvie, Julia wasn't looking for an ordinary, dependable kind of guy. She wanted excitement, she wanted adventure . . .

'I want *him*,' Julia had whispered in Sylvie's ear at the back of the dance hall as soon as he walked in.

It turned out that Simon wasn't interested in the Julia's of this world with their porcelain skin, silky strawberry-blonde hair and tall, slender frames. He only had eyes for a young woman with olive skin, wild untamed dark hair and a short hourglass figure.

Sylvie had tried to act disinterested as Simon chatted to her about his plans for university and beyond. He wanted to follow in his father's footsteps and join the RAF to become a pilot.

'Of course, any wife of mine would have to be prepared to travel and live all over the world.'

Sylvie could positively feel Julia salivating over her shoulder. This was the life she wanted. This was Julia's dream come true. A handsome young man whisking her away from her dull cardboard existence, living with her conservative mum and dad in the suburbs, to find a life of adventure and fun.

Sylvie couldn't remember if it was because Julia's curiosity and interest in Simon was so infectious that Sylvie was drawn to this young man.

Or was it her first kiss?

The memory came flooding back. At the dance, Simon sent Julia off to get them some lemonade. She had disappeared before you could say abracadabra – so eager to please. Sylvie gazed after her. When she turned to Simon, he caught her completely off-guard by planting a hot kiss smack on her lips.

That kiss had been totally unexpected but not unwelcome. Sylvie didn't exactly complain. On the contrary, she closed her eyes and kissed him back.

When she told Julia about her first kiss, and that Simon had asked her out on a proper date, Julia was genuinely pleased. She encouraged Sylvie to go out with him. Julia wanted Sylvie to give him a chance; she believed they had a future together.

Simon had gone away to university as planned. They continued to see each other as often as they could over the course of the next three years.

Sylvie recalled one meeting in particular. He had just finished university and was leaving for RAF Valley on the Island of Anglesey in Wales to spend several months training to be a pilot. On his return, when he qualified, he was going to ask for her hand in marriage. In the meantime, he asked Sylvie if she would wait for him. Sylvie said yes.

Then along came John. It was when Simon was away in Wales that Sylvie literally bumped into John on the way to work one day. He had apologised profusely even though they both knew it was Sylvie's fault; she had been walking along in a daydream, not watching where she was going.

He invited her for a cup of coffee at the local tearoom by way of apology, although it was completely unnecessary.

Sylvie had surprised herself by saying yes without hesitation. She discovered he was easy to talk to, calm and self-assured. And he had *the plan*. That's what had impressed her the most. He knew exactly where he was going in life.

With Simon, it was different. Although his career was all mapped out, he didn't know where in the world he would be posted, or where they would be living from one year to the next.

But what he did tell Sylvie was that their life together would be exciting and fun. In hindsight, Sylvie realised that word *fun* had sounded the death knell for their future together. You couldn't build a marriage, a future, on just having fun together. At least that's what Sylvie thought at the time.

Sylvie had grown up in a household full of fun and laughter. More sensitive and introspective than her older siblings, Sylvie always sensed that deep down her mother wasn't entirely happy, as though what she had wasn't enough. Perhaps it was the melancholy expression Sylvie caught on her mother's face when she thought no one was looking, that gave her away.

Sylvie had no idea why her mother felt sad, but she knew whatever it was she didn't want to repeat the same mistake. That's what was on her mind when she met John. Sylvie didn't simply want to have fun together like her parents. She wanted something more, and John's concrete plans for the future appeared to be the answer.

From the moment Sylvie introduced her new fiancé to Julia, it was as though Julia had already made up her mind about John even though she didn't know him. Over the years, despite getting to know each other, nothing changed; there was always this friction between them. Sylvie had a good idea why. Julia no doubt believed that if John hadn't come along, then her best friend would have been happily married to Simon for all these years, not hiding in the downstairs apartment avoiding her husband.

She knew what Julia was thinking: she had made the wrong decision all those years ago, when she broke up with Simon in order to marry John, and now it was coming home to roost.

Sylvie sighed. She wished Chloe had never read that diary entry. Now she was wide awake, unable to sleep, and all she could think about was Simon and that kiss. Sylvie hadn't thought about her first kiss in a long, long time. What if Julia was right and she *had* spent the last thirty-nine years married to the wrong person?

Julia always blamed John for getting in the way of Sylvie's one true love. Sylvie remembered telling Julia years ago, soon after she married John, that she was never sure Simon was her one true love. How could a seventeen-year-old possibly know that? How could a seventeen-year-old be sure of anything?

Sylvie would never forget the way Julia had turned on her with such venom. Julia had never, ever spoken to her like that before, or since. At the time, Sylvie couldn't understand what she had said to make her best friend so angry. Sylvie only discovered later, through a mutual friend, that soon after she broke it off with Simon, Julia had asked Simon out on a date. He turned her down. She had been inconsolable. It was only then that Sylvie finally understood; Julia was secretly in love with Simon. If Simon was her one true love, little wonder she would never understand how Sylvie had chosen John over him.

But she *had* chosen John. Maybe it was that, that was making Sylvie unhappy and spurring her on to make changes in her life. Simon might not have been her one true love, but it didn't mean the man she married was her one true love either. It certainly felt that way now the cracks in their marriage were starting to appear. It didn't occur all of a sudden. Sylvie hadn't taken on board all those small hairline cracks in the fabric of their marriage. What Sylvie was afraid of, was that over the years this had been building up to a giant fissure in their relationship, making it glaringly obvious that she could no longer live with John.

Was this the truth of the matter and she was making herself unhappy by not accepting it and moving on with her life? Or was it something else? Was she unhappy because she had never found a fulfilling career like her three daughters? Was it simply that she had lost her sense of self, the young woman who once had hopes and dreams and aspirations, smothered by years of marriage and motherhood. She was always taking care of her husband and her children. Perhaps somewhere along the way she had forgotten to take care to nurture herself.

Sylvie didn't want to chuck in the towel on thirty-nine years of marriage simply because she was unfulfilled as a person and she was projecting that failure on to her marriage. It didn't mean she had made the wrong decision all those years ago when she walked down the aisle with John and should have married someone else. But if John knocked on her apartment door right now and asked her if she wanted to move back upstairs, Sylvie wasn't ready to answer that question – not yet.

Sylvie turned over in bed and tried to think about something else other than her neighbour upstairs. She thought about Chloe's spot of impromptu internet shopping this evening. Despite her initial reservations, Sylvie was rather looking forward to taking delivery of her new laptop, even though she wasn't quite sure what she was going to do with it. She thought about Chloe's suggestion of starting a blog. Sylvie mulled that over until her thoughts drifted on to Julia's plans for a seventies-themed party in the apartment.

Although she still wasn't convinced it was a good idea, Sylvie started a mental shopping list of all the items she might need to buy for the party. She was still thinking about that list when she drifted off to sleep.

26

They were late. Sylvie and Chloe had arranged to meet Julia on her houseboat for morning coffee at half-past ten. However, Chloe insisted on picking Sylvie up in her car and driving to Little Venice. It didn't take long to drive there, but finding a parking space was proving a problem.

Chloe still drove the old second-hand Volkswagen Polo that John had bought her for her twenty-first birthday. Sylvie wasn't surprised Chloe hadn't replaced the old rust-bucket. It wasn't for lack of money. She could easily afford a new car. The fact was Chloe, like her parents, was a saver and loved a bargain. So did Julia. This was the reason Sylvie had organised a shopping trip with Julia today. She knew it would be right up Chloe's street – if they ever got parked.

They eventually found a space above the canal in Bloomfield Street. Fortunately, Chloe had a small car. After several tries and much crunching of gears, she managed to squeeze her car into a tight space between two parked cars.

Chloe turned off the engine and got out of the car. She stood on the pavement admiring her parking.

Sylvie opened the passenger door and frowned at her

daughter. She didn't see what Chloe was congratulating herself for; the car was parked at an odd angle with the back wheel up on the pavement and the nose of the car wide of the kerb. Even so, she supposed Chloe deserved brownie points for getting it parked at all. Sylvie had visions of spending half the morning trying to find a parking space, not to mention having an almighty *I told you so* row with Chloe because Sylvie knew it would have been far less hassle to take the bus.

'Come on, Mum, let's go. I can't wait to see Julia's houseboat.'

Pity Sylvie did not feel the same way.

Chloe ran up to the railings and peered down at the canal.

Sylvie shook her head and couldn't help but smile at her youngest daughter. She was a young woman on the cusp of turning thirty, and yet she still had the energy, enthusiasm and giddy excitement of a teenager. More often than not she was mistaken for one too. She had inherited John's slender frame and Sylvie's small stature; coupled with her blonde pigtails, she looked far younger than her years. This didn't please Chloe when she was out clubbing with her friends in London and was the only one asked for ID, apparently.

Sylvie didn't think her dress sense was helping matters. Chloe didn't exactly dress like a sophisticated young professional woman. Sylvie looked her up and down. Today was a case in point. She was wearing a short floral dress under a sleeveless padded jacket, which would have been okay if it wasn't for the multi-coloured woollen tights that clashed horribly with the dress.

Her eyes drifted down to Chloe's trade-mark sheepskin boots, or UGG boots as Chloe called them, which she'd worn for years. Chloe hadn't grown out of the boho style she had adopted as a teenager in the noughties. The problem was that once that trend had dissipated and moved on, Chloe didn't follow. To this day, not one to follow the crowd, Chloe always did what made her happy. That extended to her wardrobe. Sylvie had given up trying to give her fashion advice years ago.

Sylvie knew Chloe would jump at the chance to go shopping with Julia because the kind of kitsch shops Julia loved meant she would be in boho heaven.

It turned out Chloe had been so excited about their planned shopping expedition with Julia that she had hardly slept a wink all night. Sylvie was only thankful she hadn't told her this before she got behind the wheel of the car and drove them to Little Venice.

Sylvie suspected her daughter's infectious enthusiasm for life sprang in part from being able to do whatever she pleased whenever she felt like it because she didn't have responsibilities. By the time Sylvie was Chloe's age, she'd been married for almost ten years, had three children, and the commitment of a large four-storey property they were in the throes of renovating.

Chloe's life was far simpler at the moment. All she had to do was look after herself. Sylvie had a feeling she liked it that way. The word commitment tended to be way down her list of priorities. That didn't worry Sylvie as long as Chloe was happy. If anything, Sylvie was more concerned about her new boyfriend. Chloe had left several broken hearts in her wake. As soon as things got too serious, Chloe moved on. This time Sylvie hoped things would be different. It certainly seemed that way now that Chloe had committed to buying her first place. Sylvie was delighted it was with the nice young man who had converted their house into two apartments.

Sylvie thought back to when she first saw Declan arriving at their house to discuss John's plans for the conversion. She remembered thinking that he would make a lovely suitor for her youngest daughter, Chloe. However, Sylvie wouldn't dream of interfering in her personal life. Although, she did happen to ask Chloe to pop in to see her one afternoon when she knew Declan would be there, making up some story about John's computer not working.

They were living downstairs at the time while the conversion work was being carried out on the top two floors of the house. Declan always called in to see John every day and update him on their progress. On that occasion, Sylvie sent John out on an unnecessary errand. She asked Chloe to go downstairs to the basement kitchen and let Declan in when he arrived.

From her vantage point on the sofa in the lounge, Sylvie had heard Chloe and Declan talking in the kitchen below. When they finally walked upstairs, and Declan gave Sylvie an update on how things were progressing, she noticed Declan couldn't take his eyes off Chloe. He was smitten. Sylvie recalled the look on Chloe's face suggesting she felt the same way about Declan. Sylvie was delighted that her spot of matchmaking had paid off.

Chloe and Declan's relationship had moved very fast indeed considering they had already bought their first home together. Sylvie couldn't be happier, especially after that wobble when it appeared things weren't going so well between them. It hadn't been long after they moved in together when Chloe approached John to ask him if she could stay in the garden apartment. Sylvie was afraid that Chloe was on the verge of dumping yet another boyfriend. Sylvie would have been very upset if things hadn't worked out between them. They just seemed so right for each other. Fortunately, Declan and Chloe resolved their differences.

Sylvie wondered if that was in no small part down to the fact that, for once in her life, Chloe couldn't run away from her problems back to Mum and Dad.

Chloe was very excited about the property she had bought with Declan; it was all she talked about. Sylvie knew this was a huge step for her youngest daughter. It marked a turning point. Chloe was finally growing up and moving on with her life.

'Oh look, there she is!' Chloe waved enthusiastically at Julia who was sitting on the deck of her houseboat reading a book.

Julia looked up and spotted Chloe standing at the railings. She waved back.

Chloe turned around. 'Come on.'

Sylvie reluctantly followed Chloe along Bloomfield Street to the gap in the railings and started down the stone steps towards the canal. Sylvie slowed halfway down wishing that Julia's dream hadn't been to retire on a houseboat of all things. Gone were the days when she looked forward to visiting Julia at her place.

'Mum, hurry up!'

Sylvie rolled her eyes and picked up her pace. She was the only one in the family with an aversion to boats. At least she could console herself with the thought that after Chloe had a look around the houseboat, and they downed a quick cup of coffee, they would be back on dry land and off to do some shopping for Chloe and Declan's new home.

Sylvie continued down the stone steps to the canal towpath. She was thinking about the conversation with Chloe that had precipitated this shopping trip.

It wasn't long after Chloe and Declan moved into their new home together that Chloe confided in Sylvie that she wasn't happy. Chloe couldn't put her finger on why she felt this way until she called on Sylvie in the garden apartment. When Chloe saw the way Sylvie and Julia had transformed the apartment, she had an idea what the problem was at home – the décor.

The terraced house she and Declan had bought was an old Victorian property which had been renovated and stripped of all the original features. It was not unlike John's modern bland apartment. It wasn't what they were originally looking for. However, they were prepared to compromise because of the location; they both fell in love with Walthamstow Village in East London. Chloe thought she could get used to living in the house, but clearly something wasn't working for her.

Sylvie hoped that when Chloe sorted out the décor, she didn't find another problem on the home front. Sylvie hoped the problem wasn't Declan. Chloe seemed to get to a point in her relationships where the word commitment raised its head, and then things inevitably went wrong. Sylvie trusted that buying a house together was a good omen that Chloe had changed.

Chloe had rented with previous boyfriends in the past but one whiff they expected more and she had dropped them like a stone. One former boyfriend wanted to get engaged. Another one had gone a step further and asked John if he could marry his daughter.

John said yes.

Predictably, Chloe said no.

Sylvie recalled another young man Chloe was dating who had already saved up a deposit for a house. Unbeknown to Chloe, he started visiting estate agents, intending to surprise her with some property particulars and a suggestion that they buy a house together. It was he who was in for a surprise when Chloe dumped him, poor mite.

Sylvie imagined that walking away from a relationship in which you really hadn't invested anything concrete was easy; at least it appeared that way for Chloe. Each time Chloe walked out, she returned home – albeit temporarily – and then quickly settled herself into another rental property, on her own. And then the cycle started again with yet another new boyfriend – until she met Declan.

Of all her boyfriends, Sylvie concluded that there must be something special about Declan for Chloe to have got this far. It was unprecedented. For this reason, Sylvie was determined to help Chloe in any way she could to make things work this time. Sylvie was very fond of Declan and could just imagine him as her future son-in-law. Helping Chloe to redecorate their house was the least she could do if it would make Chloe feel happier in their new home together, even if it did involve another trip to Julia's houseboat.

'Welcome aboard!' exclaimed Julia, as Chloe stepped on to the houseboat.

Sylvie clambered aboard after Chloe and brushed past both of them at supersonic speed, heading straight for the stairs leading down to the cabin below. She wanted to get this over with so she could get back on dry land as soon as possible.

Julia rolled her eyes as Sylvie disappeared below and then winked at Chloe knowingly.

Chloe offered Julia a mischievous grin in return.

If Sylvie had caught that little exchange, she would have known they were up to something, but she didn't. Instead, she had already found a seat in the cabin below and was sitting tapping her fingers impatiently waiting for them to join her.

She glanced around the room and her eyes settled on Daisy,

Julia's golden cocker spaniel, who was sitting in her basket wagging her tail.

'Hello, old girl,' said Sylvie.

Daisy's ears pricked up at the sound of Sylvie's voice. She clambered out of her basket and padded over to say hello, passing Julia and Chloe coming down the wooden steps.

Sylvie smiled as the dog approached. She hadn't seen Daisy for some time. Daisy wasn't here on her last visit because Julia's brother had been looking after her, and for a good reason. The last thing Julia needed was an excitable cocker spaniel under her feet when she was trying to get organised on the houseboat.

Daisy jumped up, resting her two front paws on Sylvie's lap.

'Daisy, get down this instant!' Julia scolded.

'It's all right, Julia. I don't mind,' said Sylvie affectionately, as she stroked her soft velvety fur.

Julia walked over to the galley kitchen to put the kettle on.

Chloe stopped dead at the bottom of the stairs. 'Oh wow! Auntie Julia, this is amazing.'

Sylvie wasn't surprised by Chloe's reaction. The Persian rugs and bright cushions and kitsch furnishings wouldn't be to everybody's taste, but they both knew Chloe would love it. Sylvie hoped that Julia's houseboat would give Chloe some inspiration for what she could do to liven up her own home.

'Why don't I give you the grand tour?' Julia took Chloe's hand to show her around.

Sylvie smiled knowingly. Although all three girls were close to Auntie Julia, it was Chloe who had a special place in Julia's heart. Perhaps it was because they were so alike. If Julia had had a daughter of her own, Sylvie would not have been at all surprised if she turned out just like Chloe.

Chloe called her Auntie Julia even though she wasn't really her aunt, but she was the closest thing Sylvie had to a sister. Sylvie had little contact with her own sisters over the years, so Julia was the only auntie the girls had ever really known. All three girls grew up popping in and out of Auntie Julia's flat, and there were many dramas played out there. Sylvie recalled the number of times their daughter Jess had a teenage spat with one of her sisters and ran away from home. Nobody was unduly concerned because they all knew where they'd find her: having milk and cookies at Auntie Julia's flat.

Out of her three daughters, it was the teenage Chloe who was most often over at Julia's flat. She found every opportunity to visit Julia's home with its exotic, eclectic mix of neighbours and friends, furnishings and décor; so very different from her parents' home. Chloe even asked once if she could live with Julia, complaining that nothing exciting ever happened at their house.

Sylvie remembered that one particular instance when Chloe was fourteen and she had sneaked out of the house late at night to go to one of Julia's house parties. John and Sylvie had to drive over and collect her.

John was livid. He called it the last straw and attempted to ban Chloe from visiting Julia. However, John hadn't counted on the backlash. Chloe wouldn't speak to him. Sylvie gave him the silent treatment. Harriet and Jess sent him to Coventry.

John soon got the message and backed down realising that, whether he liked it or not, Auntie Julia was as much a part of their daughters' lives as Mum and Dad.

'In here is the master bedroom,' said Julia proudly, as she opened the door to show off her bedroom.

Chloe stepped inside followed by Daisy.

Sylvie heard Chloe ooohing and aaahing, and Daisy yapping excitedly. A few minutes later they emerged from the bedroom and walked into the bathroom where Chloe commented, 'Hey, that tongue-and-groove panelling is the same colour as Mum's shed in the back garden.'

Sylvie smiled. Chloe had spotted that too.

The tour didn't take long and a short time later Chloe was ensconced on the sofa next to Sylvie, still ooohing and aaahing. 'Isn't Julia's houseboat amazing? It seemed so small from the outside, yet it's so spacious once you get inside.'

Julia smiled at Chloe as she set the tea tray down on the small coffee table in front of Sylvie.

'I could almost live on one of these myself,' continued Chloe, clearly smitten with Julia's new living arrangements. 'I mentioned to Declan just the other day that I was coming to see Auntie Julia's houseboat. I had a feeling I was going to love it, so I suggested that perhaps we could go on one of those canal holidays together. I even had a look online to see if we could rent a barge for a week and cruise along the canals.'

Julia picked up the pot of coffee. 'Sounds like a wonderful idea, darling.'

'I thought so too, Julia. But he didn't seem enthusiastic about it. That's when I discovered Declan doesn't particularly like boats.' Chloe rolled her eyes. Her expression said she found that incomprehensible.

Sylvie, on the other hand, understood perfectly. 'A man after my own heart,' quipped Sylvie, rather pleased to hear she wasn't the only one who didn't get the attraction.

Chloe furrowed her brow. 'I better not discover other things we disagree on.

Sylvie exchanged a glance with Julia who had momentarily stopped pouring the coffee. Sylvie guessed they were both thinking the same thing: this was how it started with all the others, as though the least little thing made Chloe start to question her relationships.

Sylvie swiftly changed the subject. 'Julia, where do you think we should spend the afternoon shopping, do you have any ideas?'

'As a matter of fact, I do.' Julia grinned as she handed Sylvie a cup of coffee with cream and sugar.

Sylvie took the cup wondering why Julia was grinning like a Cheshire cat. 'Well? Don't keep me in suspense. Where are we going shopping?'

'Camden Market. It was Chloe's idea.'

Chloe perked up. 'Yes, I haven't been there for ages. Do you remember when I was little, you and Daddy used to take us there to look for things for the house?'

Sylvie remembered those trips to Camden Market on the weekend when they were in the throes of doing up the house. It turned out that the kind of things they sold at Camden Market was not John's cup of tea. Sylvie never did buy anything there for the house. Perhaps this time, without John in tow to veto anything she had her eye on, she could actually buy something. Sylvie was thinking of looking for something for the apartment, like a picture frame for a photo from the family album.

'Is that okay with you, Mum?'

'Yes Chloe, I think that's a marvellous idea.' Sylvie gulped down her coffee. She was looking forward to planting her feet back on dry land. Sylvie put her empty cup on the coffee table.

'My, that was quick,' commented Julia glancing at Sylvie's empty cup. 'Fancy a re-fill?'

'No, I'm fine. Shall we make a move?'

'Absolutely,' agreed Julia, surreptitiously glancing at Chloe. 'Before we leave there's something I need to do. I won't be a jiffy.' Julia put on her coat. She was on her way to the stairs when she had a thought. 'Chloe, I've got a stack of magazines you might like to leaf through to give you some ideas for your place.'

Chloe nodded. 'Sounds great.'

Julia rummaged in a cupboard under the stairs and retrieved a cardboard box stacked to the brim full of magazines. 'I'm afraid interior design has become a bit of an obsession since I retired and bought this houseboat.' Julia dumped the box by Chloe's feet. 'I must admit that I did feel at a loss once I had finished doing up my new home, so getting the chance to help Sylvie out with her apartment was a real bonus.'

Chloe and Sylvie both reached down and took a magazine each out of the box.

'We certainly had our work cut out for us,' remarked Julia, thinking of John's rather bland conversion.

Sylvie nodded her head in agreement.

'But I do so enjoy challenges,' Julia added.

'Well, in that case I think you're going to enjoy redecorating my house.' Chloe reached for the phone in the pocket of her dress to show Julia what she was up against. 'Here.'

Julia took the phone and scrolled through the photos. 'Oh my goodness, it looks just like Sylvie's apartment before we did the makeover – only worse.'

'Exactly,' said Chloe unhappily. 'I don't like it one bit. I've been dying to do something about it. I didn't know where to start until I saw what you and Mum have done with the garden apartment.'

Julia handed Chloe her phone.

'But here's the thing . . .' Chloe popped the phone back in the pocket of her dress, 'Declan is going up North to help out one of his mates with an extension. He's going to be away for a few days. I was kind of hoping you guys might be able to help me redecorate while he was away, so it's like a big surprise when he gets back.' She looked from Julia to Sylvie.

Sylvie was more than happy to help Chloe and Declan get settled in their new life together – whatever it took. 'I'm ready when you are.'

'You can definitely count me in,' said Julia enthusiastically. 'Oh boy, another interior design project. I can't wait!' Julia paused in mid-thought and looked at Chloe. 'I don't suppose you've got any friends who might need some help too?' Julia inquired only half-jokingly. She never thought she would find something she enjoyed as much as teaching.

Chloe looked at Julia thoughtfully. 'Have you considered turning your hobby into like a second career?'

Julia was about to head upstairs when she stopped abruptly and turned around. 'Do you mean as an interior designer?'

'Yes – why not?'

'I haven't got any qualifications. I'm a retired school teacher.'

'You could start a course,' suggested Sylvie. 'You've always been creative.'

'Yes I have, haven't I?'

'I could build a website advertising your new interior design business,' suggested Chloe. 'We can take some photos of Mum's apartment and your houseboat – and my house when it's finished – so we'll have some cool stuff to put on there.'

'An interior designer,' mused Julia. 'It never crossed my mind to start a second career when I retired. What an absolutely marvellous idea, darling. You can set up a website for me?'

'Of course I can – no problem.'

Julia stared wide-eyed at Chloe. 'I'll do it. I'm going to start my own interior design business.' Julia ran over and hugged Chloe for her brilliant idea. Sylvie got a hug too for being supportive as always.

Not to be left out, Daisy jumped up at Julia and got a cuddle too before pouncing on the sofa and settling down for a nap between Sylvie on Chloe.

'Gosh, this is turning out quite a day,' said Julia, clapping her hands in excitement. 'Now, I must nip upstairs otherwise we'll never leave for our shopping trip.'

'That sounds like a good idea,' agreed Sylvie, still anxious to make a move in the direction of dry land.

Julia wasn't gone long. Sylvie watched her return down the narrow flight of steps into the cabin and take off her coat.

'Is it warm outside?' asked Sylvie, wondering if she might not need her coat.

'Not particularly,' replied Julia, walking into the galley kitchen. 'I thought we'd start with some window shopping in Camden Market,' said Julia conversationally as she stacked the dishwasher with the dirty mugs. 'We can look at some colours and fabrics, and see if anything takes your fancy, Chloe. That will give us some idea of what you envisage for your house before redecorating.'

Sylvie glanced at Chloe who was sitting on the sofa next to her casually leafing through a magazine and nodding her head at Julia's suggestion. Sylvie turned in her seat to find Julia was busy in the kitchen filling the kettle with fresh water and placing some clean cups and saucers on the tea tray.

'I'm sure I had some biscuits around here somewhere,' said Julia rifling through a kitchen cupboard.

Sylvie glanced at her wristwatch. She didn't think they had time for tea. Sylvie stood up and put her coat on. 'If we don't leave now, there won't be much time left for shopping,' said Sylvie buttoning up her coat.

Julia's head popped up from behind a cupboard door with a packet of biscuits and three plates. 'Yes I know, Sylvie. That's what I told Pete.'

Sylvie frowned as Julia opened the packet of biscuits and poured the tea. 'I thought we were going out?' She paused. 'Who's Pete?'

'Oh yes, I forgot to mention that the reason I nipped out for a few minutes was to call on Pete. You see, I haven't got the hang of the locks yet. I think I need more practice.'

'Locks?' Sylvie shook her head. 'You've lost me, Julia. What are you talking about? And who's Pete?'

Chloe lowered her magazine. 'Julia, I think we're underway!'

'Underway?' Sylvie's head whirled from Julia to Chloe catching a conspiratorial smile pass between them. 'What do you mean – *underway?*'

Sylvie followed Chloe's gaze out of the porthole window where the towpath used to be. 'Good heavens!' Sylvie exclaimed in alarm.

'Don't worry, Sylvie,' Julia reassured her. 'Pete knows what he's doing. I'm just going to pop him up a mug of tea.'

Chloe giggled. 'Mum, don't look so worried.'

'That's easy for you to say. You know very well I've got no sea legs!' Sylvie grabbed the arm of the sofa and quickly sat down, quite shocked to discover she was now on a boat that was moving. She looked across the room at Julia, and screeched, 'Will someone please tell me who on earth is Pete?'

'Pete is my neighbour who is a dab hand at the locks. He's been taking his barge up and down Regent's canal for years. Today, he kindly agreed to take my boat out for a spin along the canal to Camden Lock. This way, we can get to Camden Market without moving a muscle. So just sit back and relax.'

'Relax?' Sylvie could murder Julia. 'You planned this all along.'

Julia and Chloe were grinning from ear to ear.

Sylvie looked from Julia to Chloe. She should have known they were both in it together. 'You're holding me captive against my will – on a boat!' She glared at them.

'Now, now, Sylvie, don't be so melodramatic,' said Julia, handing Sylvie a cup of tea and offering her a digestive biscuit. 'If I'd kept the curtains closed, you wouldn't even know we were moving – admit it.'

Sylvie grudgingly took the cup of tea and a digestive biscuit, but she wasn't about to admit anything, even though Julia was absolutely right: apart from the gentle *phut-phut* of the engine and the changing scenery from the porthole windows, Sylvie hardly felt the boat moving at all.

'This is so great!' Chloe jumped up from the sofa and darted from one side of the boat to the other looking through the porthole windows.

'You'll get a better view from outside. Why don't you go up top, Chloe?' suggested Julia.

'While we're moving?' Sylvie looked at Julia aghast. 'What if she falls in?'

Chloe rolled her eyes. 'Mum, I'm not five years old!'

Sylvie glanced at her blonde pigtails and stripy tights.

Chloe gathered up her coat. She was about to head upstairs when she turned around and said, 'Julia, may I drive?'

Sylvie yelped, 'No!' It took Chloe six attempts to pass her driving test, and that was on dry land. Sylvie still had reservations about letting Chloe loose behind the wheel of a car, let alone something she could sink!

'Go ask Pete. I'm sure he won't mind,' said Julia, ignoring Sylvie. 'Chloe, can you take this mug of tea up for him?'

Chloe disappeared up the stairs with the mug of tea.

Julia turned around and caught the look of horror on Sylvie's face. 'Don't worry, Sylvie. We pretty much go in a straight line. Pete will closely supervise Chloe.'

Sylvie relaxed a little as Julia sat down opposite her. Sylvie brushed biscuit crumbs off her lap and absently stroked the sleeping dog sprawled out on the sofa next to her. She eyed Julia. 'So, what's the deal with Pete – is he a person of interest?'

'A person of interest?' Julia smiled at Sylvie's turn of phrase. 'He's my neighbour a few boats down – that's all. Although he is a bit of a rascal inviting me out on a date. But before you get any ideas—' Julia was interrupted by the cabin door opening at the top of the stairs.

Pete popped his head inside the cabin. 'We're underway.'

'Talk of the devil,' said Julia, smiling up at him. 'Sylvie, this is Pete, our captain for the afternoon.'

'Hello,' said Sylvie, taking in his weather-beaten brown face and the old pipe lodged between his lips. He looked in his late seventies, too old for Julia, and he looked every inch the captain with his blue cotton cap and old worn navy jumper. Which reminded Sylvie, if the captain was standing at the cabin door smiling down at her and drinking his tea, then who was driving the boat? *Chloe!* Sylvie gripped the armrests of the sofa and barked at Julia, 'I thought you said Chloe would be closely supervised?'

'Don't worry, Chloe is doing marvellously,' said Pete. 'She's taken to it like a duck to water. I'm going to show her how to do the locks next.'

'There you see.' Julia turned to Sylvie as Pete closed the cabin door. 'There's absolutely nothing to worry about.' Julia grinned.

Sylvie's face was still a picture. This was not turning out to be one of her better days. She should have known Julia and Chloe would get up to something like this.

'Sylvie, I've got an idea. It will take around forty-five minutes to reach Camden Lock. In the meantime, I'm guessing you won't want to join Chloe and Pete up on deck . . . ?'

Sylvie shook her head vehemently no.

'You don't know what you're missing . . .' chided Julia.

'I do know what I'm missing, Julia. I have walked along the canal towpath all the way to Camden Lock with John when the girls were small. It's very picturesque.'

'Yes, but it is really rather special when you see it cruising down the canal on the open deck of a houseboat.'

Sylvie wasn't budging from the sofa. 'I'll take your word for it.'

'Well, maybe next time,' Julia commented under her breath.

'Pardon me?' Sylvie looked at Julia sharply.

'As I can't tempt you outside,' continued Julia evenly, 'why don't I make another pot of tea and we can go over the details of your forthcoming party?'

Sylvie nodded. 'All right.'

'I've already started to make a guest list.' Julia reached for her diary and opened it at the date she had pencilled in for the party.

Sylvie stared at the page. It seemed like an awfully long list. Just how many people was Julia inviting?

Julia gathered up her pen. 'Now, who else can you think of to invite to your party?'

Sylvie couldn't very well go ahead with the party without inviting her immediate neighbours.

Julia wrote down Sylvie's next door neighbours. She looked up. 'Anybody else?'

Sylvie sighed and muttered, 'John.'

27

John had just finished breakfast. He was loading the dishwasher with his dirty dishes when he heard the doorbell chime downstairs. John wiped his hands on the dishcloth, walked through the lounge and opened the door to his apartment. The doorbell chimed again. Sylvie obviously wasn't answering it, so John walked down the stairs and opened the front door.

A friendly young man, sporting a bright red shirt, was standing on the doorstep holding a large box. 'I have a delivery for you,' he said jovially.

John glanced at the Royal Mail delivery van parked outside at the kerb. He wasn't expecting a delivery.

The postman noted John's confused expression. 'This *is* number 67 Penfold Place?' he asked, reading the address on the parcel.

John nodded. It was in actual fact numbers 67a and 67b, to be precise, but John didn't bother correcting him. It would obviously take some time for the PO to catch up with the changes.

'I have a delivery for Mrs Sylvia Baxter,' he said, holding up the box.

'Ah, just a moment, I'll go and see if she's home.' John nipped across the hall and tentatively knocked on the door to the garden apartment. He waited nervously outside her door wondering what sort of reception he would receive when she answered. They hadn't said a word to each other since she moved downstairs. John supposed it had turned into a stand-off over who was going to apologise first.

John knocked again. He then put his ear to the door and listened.

'I think she's out,' said John, returning to the front door and making no move to take the box.

The postman looked puzzled. 'Er . . . do you mind taking it in for her?'

John looked at the box. For a split second, he felt like being awkward and refusing to take the delivery. He knew Sylvie had been avoiding him since she moved downstairs and John felt peeved. But that wasn't the postman's fault. He had a job to do.

'I'll take it,' said John, relieving him of the parcel.

John closed the front door behind him and was about to leave it outside her door when a thought occurred to him. This would be the perfect excuse to knock on Sylvie's door and find out when she was moving back upstairs. She had been in that apartment for almost a month. As far as John was concerned, she'd had enough time on her own to sort herself out. It was time for things to get back to normal. Apart from anything else, John wanted to finish the plan and rent out the garden apartment. However, before a tenant moved in, there was something John wanted to do in the garden apartment first.

John had kept himself busy over the past month planning all the details. He was looking forward to telling Sylvie his brilliant idea. John was going ahead with his plan to host another housewarming party. This time his plan was to have the party in the apartment downstairs. He had even drawn up a tentative guest list. As with the original grand opening party, the guest list wasn't very long because he didn't know a lot of people. He was hoping Sylvie might help him out by inviting some of her friends. Not Julia though. Definitely not Julia.

John stood outside the door to the garden apartment holding the box. He wouldn't dream of telling Sylvie outright to move back upstairs. With the way she had been acting lately, he wouldn't be at all surprised if she did the exact opposite just to be difficult. But he could ask her nicely, and that's exactly what he intended to do. If she wanted to, John had no objections to Sylvie moving back upstairs after his party.

John was confident everything would go according to plan. After all, he had Sylvie's box and that was going to set the wheels in motion. John made up his mind to take the box upstairs and deliver it personally as soon as she returned home. He reasoned that when he knocked on her door she might not be happy to see him, but at least he would have the parcel to break the ice. She would be pleased he had taken it in for her. That might put things on a good footing before he asked her nicely to move back upstairs. John hoped so.

He walked into his apartment and set the box down on the kitchen table, wondering what was inside. John left the box where it was and busied himself around the apartment dusting and vacuuming. Almost an hour later, when John was satisfied everything was ship-shape, he walked back into the kitchenette and put the kettle on. He glanced at the box as he spooned some coffee into a mug, still wondering what was inside.

While John waited for the kettle to boil he circled the kitchen table. Starting to feel dizzy, he stopped and pulled out a chair. John sat down with the box in front of him and drummed his fingertips on the glass table top studying the box intently. He couldn't see any writing or pictures on the box to indicate what Sylvie had bought. John had half-a-mind to pick it up and give it a shake. He reconsidered. What if there was something fragile inside?

By the time the kettle boiled, John couldn't stand it any longer. He bounced out of his chair, pulled open a kitchen drawer and picked out a pair of scissors. John turned on his heel to face the table. Scissors in hand, he approached the box.

Five minutes later John was standing in front of the open box, scratching his head, wondering why Sylvie had bought a laptop. He turned around to put the scissors back in the kitchen drawer and walked back to the table. John groaned loudly. The kitchen table was now covered with the entire contents of the box, most of which was packing material. The place looked a mess. Worse still, when John was in the throes of tossing out the reams of cardboard and plastic and polystyrene, dying to know what was under all that packaging, he did not stop to consider that everything that came out of the box had to go back in – just the way he found it.

John panicked. What if Sylvie came home right now and walked straight up to his apartment only to discover that he had taken in her delivery and opened it? It was an unlikely scenario. Nevertheless, John quickly set to work trying to pack the laptop back in the box with every bit of packaging that came with it. He thought it would be straightforward, but after thirty minutes, and several attempts, John was at his wits end.

He stopped and scratched his head thinking that if all the stuff came out of the box, it should all go back in, and he should be able to close the flaps sufficiently to tape up the blasted box. But he couldn't. 'Oh for pities sake!' John threw up his hands in frustration. 'Serves me right for unpacking it in the first place.'

After one more attempt, John swore and then discarded some of the packaging. He taped up the box hoping Sylvie wouldn't notice it had been tampered with. By this time John was so sick of the sight of it, he wanted to forget the plan, leave the box outside her door and be done with it. John shook his head. Perhaps if he had just asked Sylvie what was in the damn box, she might have told him. At least he would have saved himself some grief and a precious hour of his life.

He was about to take the box downstairs, and leave it outside her door, when he heard footsteps on the wooden parquet flooring in the communal hall downstairs. Sylvie was home.

John looked at the box. 'Now or never,' he said, scooping it up and heading to the door, relieved to be rid of it.

John made his way downstairs and knocked on Sylvie's door. He held up the box in front of him to be sure it was the first thing Sylvie saw as soon as she opened the door.

'Oh there it is,' said Chloe, as soon as she opened the door. She took it straight out of John's hands before he could stop her.

John frowned. He intended to carry it inside the apartment for Sylvie himself. It was quite a large box; he was going to use that to his advantage to get inside the flat and have a look around. Chloe had just scuppered that plan.

'Mum home?' John inquired innocently.

'Yes.'

'Well, can I come in?'

Chloe didn't budge out of the doorway.

John was getting tired of these games, first Sylvie's builders refusing to let him into his own property, now Chloe.

She was about to shut the door.

'What's in the box?' asked John, feigning ignorance. He was trying to keep the conversation going in the hope that Sylvie might overhear them and come to the door.

'It's a laptop. It says so on the box.'

'Where?' John thought Chloe was having him on.

Chloe turned the box over. On the bottom of the box was a large picture of a laptop with the word *laptop* scrawled across the width of the box in big, black, bold lettering.

Oh, you have got to be kidding me! 'So it does,' observed John with a tight smile realising he must have put the box down on the kitchen table the wrong way up. 'What does your mother want with a laptop?'

Chloe cocked her head to one side, a familiar gesture John recognised meaning that, as far as Chloe was concerned, the conversation was over.

'Can I come in?' John tried again.

'Sorry Dad, no can do. We're busy.'

'Busy doing what?'

Chloe shut the door.

Sylvie walked into the lounge with two cups of tea and a plate of ginger biscuits on a tea tray. She spotted the box on the coffee table. 'It's arrived!'

She set the tea tray down next to the box and fetched a pair of scissors to unpack her brand new laptop. Sylvie was so excited she didn't stop to ask where it had materialised from while she had been busy downstairs in the basement kitchen making tea.

Chloe looked at the packaging strewn all over the floor. 'Shall I get a rubbish bag to clear this up?'

'No, that can wait until later.' Sylvie didn't want to get rid of the packaging just yet in case they had to send the laptop back for any reason. She hoped not because she couldn't imagine packing all of it back in the box.

Chloe got to work setting up Sylvie's new laptop. It was much smaller and lighter than Sylvie had expected. She was now feeling rather pleased that Chloe had talked her into having one. She was less pleased with the fact that Julia had talked her into having a party right here in the apartment.

Sylvie took her cup of tea and a ginger biscuit, and sat down opposite Chloe. She wondered what Chloe would think about Julia's idea. 'Julia wants to throw me a party right here in the apartment. I'm not sure it's such a good idea.' Sylvie spooned some sugar into her tea. 'What do you think?'

Chloe shifted her gaze from the laptop. 'Mum, I think it's a brilliant idea.' She thought about it some more. 'It would be like a second housewarming party for your apartment. Now it's all finished and looks so nice, everyone is going to be dying to see it.'

That's what was really bothering Sylvie. Everyone will want to see her apartment – including John. Unfortunately, Chloe wasn't making her feel any better about Julia's brilliant idea. Sylvie knew that sooner or later John was going to find out what she had been up to in the garden apartment. A party would be the perfect opportunity for John to finally get inside and look around. It's just that Sylvie didn't think it would be a particularly good idea for John to discover the true extent of the alterations at a party, in front of dozens of people.

Sylvie sipped her tea. She couldn't exactly stop him from

coming to the party. He would find out about it whether she invited him or not. Sylvie had seen Julia's guest list. There was going to be an awful lot of people and it would probably be very loud. Keeping it under wraps would be nigh on impossible. However, if the party was going ahead, there was a way out of her dilemma: she could still invite John to the party, but make sure he was the first to arrive. That way, Sylvie could give him a private tour and get any histrionics out of the way before the other guests arrived.

That could work, mused Sylvie picking up her ginger biscuit. She knew she couldn't keep John locked out of the apartment forever. One day soon he would find an excuse to walk down those stairs and knock on her door, catching her unawares. At least this way she could call the shots and be prepared.

'Are you going ahead with the party, Mum? Please say yes.'

The more Sylvie thought about it, the less sceptical she felt about the whole idea. She smiled at her daughter.

'Is that a yes?'

Sylvie nodded an affirmative as she ate her biscuit.

Chloe clapped her hands with glee and then stopped abruptly. 'I hope I'm getting an invite.' Chloe looked at her mother expectantly. 'Remember the last house party at Julia's flat that I snuck into years ago? It was when you and Daddy turned up and spoiled all the fun.'

Sylvie slowly nodded her head. It was, in actual fact, John who had spoiled all the fun. To this day, Sylvie believed that his behaviour was totally uncalled for under the circumstances. It wasn't Julia's fault that Chloe found out about the party and decided she'd invite herself. To Julia's credit, she did phone them straight away when she spotted Chloe. And to Chloe's credit, all she had done was help herself to a small glass of punch, which she was tentatively sipping in the corner while browsing Julia's record collection. That didn't stop John going off on one and causing a scene in front of Julia and all her guests as soon as he arrived. Sylvie didn't exactly help the situation by suggesting they stay for a drink. She didn't see the harm. Like Chloe, she had always been curious about Julia's parties. Unfortunately, John didn't feel the same way.

Sylvie remembered the almighty row on the way home in the car when John had, without foundation, accused Julia of being a bad influence; he even came up with the ridiculous notion that next Chloe would be smoking pot and getting up to god-knows-what, thanks to Julia.

'What is *pot*?' Chloe had asked innocently from the back seat of the car.

'It's Marijuana, sometimes called weed or grass – among other things. Your father and I used to smoke it quite regularly before we got married and he morphed into a stuffed shirt.'

That shut John up.

That shut Chloe up too because on the way home in the car Chloe had learned something about her parents that made her look at them in a whole new light; it was quite possible that once upon a time, they used to be just as cool as Julia.

'I wouldn't want to miss one of Julia's parties again.' Chloe was still angling for a party invitation. 'I think it will be quite an event.'

So did Sylvie. But she wasn't thinking of the party. She was thinking of John and that private tour she intended to give him before the party started.

'Well?' Chloe pestered. 'Am I getting an invite – or not?'

Sylvie brushed some biscuit crumbs off her lap. 'Yes Chloe, you'll receive a party invitation.' She regarded her daughter thoughtfully. Chloe seemed so excited about the party that she didn't want to dampen her enthusiasm. All the same, Sylvie thought she better add a caveat. 'Chloe, I have to warn you that Julia is organising a seventies-themed party, which means there's going to be an awful lot of people of advancing years wearing garish outfits and doing embarrassing moves to disco music.'

Chloe giggled. 'Now this I have got to see.' Her expression suddenly changed. She regarded Sylvie solemnly.

Sylvie knew that look: something was on her mind.

'Are you inviting Dad?'

'Yes, I'm inviting your father, that's all taken care of.' Sylvie smiled to herself as she finished her tea.

Chloe looked around Sylvie's lounge and jokingly said, 'I think you better have the paramedics on standby when Dad arrives, in case he passes out with the shock.'

Sylvie looked at her daughter sharply. 'That's not funny, Chloe.' She had enough anxieties as it was over the thought of John's reaction to the apartment, without piling any more on her plate.

Chloe was still sniggering into her hand.

Sylvie couldn't help but smile. 'Okay Chloe, I'll admit that was funny.' She cast an eye around her lounge and suddenly burst out laughing. It was more than funny: it was hilarious. Sylvie was starting to think the party wasn't such a bad idea after all. In fact, she was rather looking forward to it.

When they had both recovered from their fit of giggles, Sylvie said, 'Julia is making all the arrangements. All I have to do is shop for the party food. I was going to pop to M&S in the morning.' Sylvie was thinking aloud. She glanced at Chloe. 'Is there anything, in particular, you want me to get for party nibbles?'

Chloe wiggled her nose and thought about it until her eyes lit up with an idea. 'What about seventies-themed party food like cheese and pineapple on sticks and—'

'What a wonderful idea,' Sylvie interrupted. 'Hold that thought. I'll write a list.'

Sylvie nipped down to the kitchen and returned with a pen and notepad. She smiled. This was turning out such fun. She sat down on the sofa next to Chloe and flipped open her notepad. 'Now, let's start again. Cheese and pineapple on sticks . . . '

28

John had just finished breakfast. He was loading the dishwasher with his dirty dishes when he heard the doorbell chime downstairs. John wiped his hands on the dishcloth, walked through the lounge and opened the door to his apartment. The doorbell chimed again. John paused in the doorway with a distinct feeling of *déjà vu*, as though this was yesterday all over again.

Sylvie obviously wasn't answering it, so John walked down the stairs and opened the front door.

A friendly young man, sporting a bright red shirt, was standing on the doorstep holding a large box. 'I have a delivery for you,' he said jovially.

John glanced at the Royal Mail delivery van parked outside at the kerb. John was, in actual fact, expecting a delivery. 'That was quick,' remarked John, taking the large box off his hands.

'Talk about *déjà vu!*' said the postman as John shut the door.

John had paid for special delivery so that he would get his parcel as soon as possible, but he wasn't expecting it to be delivered the very next day. He glanced at Sylvie's door as he zoomed past and up the stairs with his box. In the kitchen, John set the box down on the table and got out a pair of scissors from the drawer. He was about to open the box when he stopped abruptly realising he had forgotten something. John opened a kitchen cupboard and took out a roll of black sacks. He tore one off the roll. Now he was prepared.

John walked back to the table and turned the box the right way up. He glanced at the large picture on the box with the bold black lettering underneath before cutting off the tape and undoing the flaps. He carefully lifted out all the packaging and deposited it straight into the black sack, so he wasn't left with a gigantic mess to clear up like the last time. Finally, John lifted out the brand new laptop and placed it on the kitchen table. It was identical to the one he had unpacked only yesterday.

He was surprised how small and light it was. John thought of his old desktop computer with the clunky CRT monitor that was sitting on his desk in the study. He decided there and then to ditch the old computer. Chloe had been on at them for years to buy a new computer. Now he could see why. Compared to this, their old computer was out of the ark.

John hurried into his study and quickly removed his old computer. Everything, including the monitor, keyboard and mouse, was discarded in a pile on the floor by his desk ready to be dumped. He returned to the kitchen and retrieved his laptop.

Back in the study, he carefully set it down on the desk and admired his purchase. It was small, it was neat, and it took up very little space. He opened the lid and flexed his fingers above the keyboard. John sat there for a full minute staring at it, then stood up and went into the kitchen to make a cup of tea while he tried to figure out what he was going to do with his brand new laptop. Since leaving work, he didn't really have much use for a computer. John hadn't stopped to think about that when he had eagerly ordered it online yesterday. All he could think about was that if Sylvie had one, then he had to have one too. He wished he knew what Sylvie was doing with hers downstairs.

John returned to his study, sat down at his desk, and placed his cup of tea on a coaster beside him. He decided first things first: he would switch the laptop on and then go from there. John flexed his fingers above the keyboard once more and reached out to switch it on. His finger hovered in mid-air for several seconds moving first to the left, then to the right, as though he was using an imaginary Ouija-board rather than trying to locate the button to switch on his laptop.

'Oh, this is ridiculous!' John was getting frustrated.

He tried pressing some keys at random. Nothing happened. He knew he had plugged it in properly because a blue indicator light had lit up beside the power outlet on the side of the laptop. John thought about calling the customer helpline but dismissed that idea almost immediately. He didn't fancy talking to a youngster on the phone making him feel like a laughingstock because he couldn't figure out how to switch his laptop on. John had his pride. Besides, he had his own youngster who was quite capable of doing that. And she would make a personal visit to tell him to his face, "Dad you're an idiot," while she showed him how it works. If all else fails, John was going to phone Chloe.

John had one more idea before he resorted to phoning Chloe. John sat forward in his chair. 'On!' he commanded. He'd seen stuff like this on television. Perhaps they were now voice-activated. After several attempts at talking to his laptop, including the words, 'I'd like to do some work now, please,' because he really had no idea how sophisticated these things had become, John was starting to feel rather foolish and gave up.

He reached for the phone to call Chloe and happened to glance at the clock on the wall. It was only five past nine on a weekday morning. Chloe was probably at work. John sighed and replaced the handset. The phone call would have to wait. John wished he was at work too. He sat there staring at the clock on the wall wondering what he was going to do with the rest of his day.

Sylvie would know what to do. Thinking about his wife, John was just contemplating for the umpteenth time how he might go about asking her to move back upstairs, when he heard the sound of the front door bang shut downstairs. John jumped up and ran out of his study into the lounge to look out of the bay window. He spotted Sylvie walking down the front path carrying her M&S re-usable shopping bag.

John's first impulse was to race down the street to catch her up and say, 'Well, what a coincidence, I was on my way to the shops too. We could go together.' Anything was preferable to sitting in his study, staring at the clock on the wall, watching the minutes tick by.

Then all of a sudden John had a better idea. Sylvie was going shopping which meant she would be gone for some time. He hadn't seen anybody else turn up at the house this morning. For once the apartment downstairs was empty. Sylvie seemed to have so many people back and forward lately – what with the builders and Chloe and Julia – that John had to bide his time and wait for an opportunity. John's patience had finally paid off. This was the chance he'd been waiting for.

It had been at the back of his mind ever since the builders refused him entry into the apartment downstairs; one way or another he was going to get inside that apartment and find out what Sylvie had been up to. John didn't need anybody's permission, not Sylvie's, and certainly not the builders. And he discovered he didn't even need a key to the garden apartment. John had found a spare key to the french doors that led into the basement kitchen.

When John had delivered Sylvie's laptop yesterday morning, he had asked Chloe politely to let him into the apartment. Now it was time to take matters into his own hands.

John raced back into his study, pulled open the desk drawer and reached inside for the key. He was about to walk out of the study when it occurred to him that he might need his little black book. It could come in handy to jot down any small jobs that my need doing to get the apartment back to its original condition in readiness for letting. He had already considered letting it out to two tenants – like a house share – in order to make more money on his two-bedroomed apartment. John opened his desk drawer once more and reached inside.

With the key in one hand and his little black book in the other, John was ready for his expedition downstairs. John crept out of his apartment and softly closed the door, wondering why he was suddenly creeping around his own house.

He checked his watch. He didn't know how long Sylvie would be out shopping, but he was giving himself fifteen minutes tops. John couldn't imagine it would take that long to nose around the apartment downstairs and write the odd thing down in his little black book. John walked out of the house, locked the front door, and made his way down the garden path. He paused at the front gate and glanced up and down the street checking for any sign of Sylvie heading back because she had forgotten something.

The coast was clear. John opened the gate and ambled along the pavement whistling a tune. He stopped at the intersection to make one last sweep of the street and then darted around the corner. He made his way along the side of his house aiming straight for the gate into the back garden. How many times had he told Sylvie to lock that gate in case of burglars? Now he wished he hadn't made such a fuss about it because if the gate was locked, John's plans were scuppered. Fortunately for him, she hadn't listened. John breathed a sigh of relief as he opened the gate. He wouldn't have got very far if he had to clamber over a six-foot wall to get into the back garden.

John checked the street one more time before disappearing into the garden, closing the gate behind him. Hurrying down the garden towards the back of the house, John nearly dropped his key in his haste to unlock the french doors and get inside before Sylvie arrived home. He couldn't imagine it would go down well, asking her to move back in with him, if she found out he'd been snooping around the apartment while she was out.

John unlocked the door and glanced anxiously over his shoulder. He was still worried that Sylvie would come back any minute and discover what he was up to.

He stepped inside and hurriedly closed the door behind him before marching straight through the kitchen, heading for the stairs to the lounge. The apartment wasn't that big so this wouldn't take long, reasoned John. Although he already had a pen and his little black book to hand, John was hopeful that the builders couldn't have done that much damage in just one day. What bothered him more was what Julia had been up to, in and out of the apartment, since Sylvie moved in.

John was halfway up the stairs when he stopped abruptly and

slowly turned around; something wasn't right. He turned on his heel and walked back down the stairs to the kitchen.

'*What the blazes!*' John dropped his little black book on the kitchen floor in astonishment.

John's first thought was that the builders had ripped out his brand new kitchen and replaced it with . . . with *that!* But on closer inspection, John discovered it was much, much worse. His crisp, white kitchen cabinets had turned a definite shade of green. 'Ugh!' John shuddered and backed away in disgust, knocking straight into the new addition to the kitchen.

John turned around. 'What the hell is that?' John knew what it was. What he was really asking himself was what the hell is it doing here? And worse still, John couldn't believe she had dressed the damn thing with her hideous flowery crockery. He thought he had seen the last of that stuff when he bought the plain white crockery set for upstairs, making sure Sylvie had no cupboard space left for her china in the kitchenette.

John picked up one of the plates on display and arched an eyebrow. 'So this is what Chloe was up to when she asked for the key to the landing cupboard the other day.'

John put the plate back where he found it and stood staring at the kitchen in dismay. Turning full circle to take it all in, John suddenly stopped in front of the french doors. His eyes settled on the garden. He knew what this was all about. It was payback for what he had done to her garden. John turned around with a sinking feeling in the pit of his stomach at what lay in wait at the top of those stairs.

As John slowly opened the door at the top of the kitchen stairs and saw the lounge, his first thought was that he'd just stepped into an episode of *Changing Rooms*, the television programme where neighbours swapped houses for a day and redecorated a room in each other's homes as a surprise.

What John used to love about that show were the instances when things went wrong because their neighbour's taste in décor was completely different to their own. John couldn't wait to see the look on their faces when they discovered just what their neighbour had done to one of their rooms. John used to find it hilarious. He wasn't laughing now.

As John stood in the doorway and gaped at the lounge, he bet his face was a picture worthy of a *Changing Rooms* episode gone wrong. He had anticipated some minor changes, but nothing had prepared him for this. Gone was the subtle magnolia paint, the walls repainted vibrant mustard yellow. Gone was the light pine-effect laminate flooring, removed in favour of the original wide oak floorboards. John was sure they had been varnished a darker shade. Gone were the neutral plain cream curtains John had chosen to hang at the window, replaced by a roman blind in bright yellow and green stripes. Gone was the modern wall-mounted flame-effect electric fire inset in the wall.

John did a double-take. When he saw that, he had to walk over and touch the old fireplace just to make sure he wasn't seeing things. He couldn't believe Sylvie had told her builder to rip out his brand new fire in favour of that old thing. He had no idea Sylvie liked it so much. John shook his head. He still couldn't quite believe what he was seeing. John's neutral colour scheme and modern inset fire – which he had chosen specifically with the intention of letting out to tenants – had been obliterated.

The change in the décor obviously bothered John a great deal, but as he gazed around the room it struck him that what he was looking at was something far more worrying. What was once a sparsely furnished lounge with an old two-seater sofa, single chair, a coffee table, television and empty bookshelves – totally devoid of anything personal – had been transformed into someone's home. Sylvie's home. There were rugs, cushions, lamps, and ornaments dotted around the room and a brand new Rattan three-piece suite with a matching coffee table.

John stared at the new furniture wondering what the blazes had happened to the stuff he had left down here for tenants. All that remained was the old tube television. That wasn't the worst of it. There were also lots of personal items dotted around. John's eyes drifted from the framed photographs of the girls, and Gertie their granddaughter, to that box containing her mother's ashes on a bookshelf in the alcove beside the fireplace.

This was more serious than he thought. Sylvie had settled into the garden apartment, and it was looking less and less like a temporary arrangement. Sylvie had made the place her own. How was he going to get her to move back upstairs now? He had a feeling that simply asking her nicely wasn't going to cut it.

John stood beside the fireplace taking it all in, shaking his head solemnly, totally unprepared for what he was seeing. Heaving a sigh, he glanced at his watch and thought he really ought to get going. John didn't see much point looking around the rest of the apartment. It couldn't get much worse than this. However, John always liked to follow through with a plan. And the plan was to look around Sylvie's apartment – all of it.

John walked through the lounge and opened the door to the inner hall that led to the two bedrooms and the bathroom. Something struck John as odd the moment he stepped into the hall, but he couldn't put his finger on it.

He walked down the hall scratching his chin and stopped to

open the bathroom door. He glanced inside the bathroom and was relieved to find Sylvie had not changed a thing. The brand new white bathroom suite was still there, along with the white tiles that John had chosen with small border tiles in blue. She had even left the walls above the tiles painted magnolia. The simple chrome fixtures and fittings were all present and accounted for. John smiled approvingly pleased to discover that, after the shock of the kitchen and the lounge, things couldn't get any worse - thank god.

John closed the bathroom door and stepped forward two paces to the door opposite that led into the main bedroom. John put his hand on the doorknob and glanced down the hall.

'That's odd,' muttered John. All he could see was a blank wall with a picture hanging in almost the same spot where the door to the second bedroom used to be.

'That *is* odd.'

Still confused, John opened the door to the main bedroom and stepped inside. 'What the . . .!?'

29

John sat in the kitchenette drumming his fingertips on the kitchen table trying to think. John was in a quandary. If he confronted Sylvie over what she'd done downstairs then she would find out that he'd been inside the apartment without her knowledge, which would only make matters worse.

Since moving downstairs, Sylvie had made it crystal clear that for the time being it was *her* apartment and John wasn't invited. If she discovered he had sneaked in there while she was out, well . . . the consequences didn't bear thinking about. John wasn't going to dwell on that; there was no way she'd discover what he'd been up to. That didn't make him feel any better. John had got himself up the proverbial gum tree. In hindsight, it would have been far better if he had just waited for an invitation. She couldn't keep him out forever. At least that way he wouldn't be angsting over what he had just seen.

He picked up his mug of coffee and brought it to his lips, taking a sip. 'Ugh!' The coffee was stone cold. John didn't realise how long he had been sitting at the kitchen table pondering this conundrum. And to think, he had even brought along his little black book imagining he could write down a snag list of all the odds and ends Sylvie had done to the apartment that, in his naivety, he thought he could simply undo.

The problem was far more than repainting walls and clearing clutter, or even erecting a new partition wall to recreate the second bedroom. John realised the problem was far bigger than that. The problem was Sylvie. John reached into his pocket for his little black book, intending to write Sylvie's name down for the umpteenth time under the snag list, but came up empty. He stood up and tried the other pocket with no luck. John scanned the room. It wasn't on the table or under the table, or on the kitchen counter where he'd made himself a cup of coffee.

John scratched his head and walked out of the kitchenette wondering if he had been so preoccupied on his return that he had put it back in the desk drawer in his study without even realising it. He walked into the study confident that's exactly what had happened. He opened the drawer. Empty. John stood there staring into space trying to think where he might have left his little black book. With a start, he remembered. 'Oh Lord!'

He flew out of his apartment and down the stairs, thanking his lucky stars that he hadn't heard the sound of Sylvie's footsteps on the parquet flooring in the hall downstairs signally she had returned from her shopping trip. John glanced at the door to her apartment as he whizzed across the hall. He threw open the front door and slammed it shut behind him.

Racing down the front steps and through the front gate at full pelt, John nearly collided with his wife who was fumbling in her purse for the front door key as she strolled along the street towards the house.

John made a quick sidestep as Sylvie looked up. 'Must dash,' he said, avoiding eye contact. John didn't want to get into a conversation with Sylvie, which was a ridiculous thought as they were barely on speaking terms.

'Where are you off to in such a hurry?' asked Sylvie, looking up at the house thinking, where's the fire?

John turned around and replied nonchalantly, 'Oh, you know . . . things to do . . . places to be.' He smiled nervously.

Sylvie stared at him and narrowed her eyes. He was up to something, she could tell. However, she didn't feel inclined to get into a conversation with John in case he saw that as an opportunity to invite himself back to her apartment, perhaps offering to help her in with the shopping bags. Sylvie kept her mouth shut and turned towards the house, keys in hand.

As soon as her back was turned, John made his move. He darted around the corner, flung open the garden gate, and dashed across the lawn to the french doors. Cupping his hands to the glass, John immediately spotted the little black book on the kitchen floor where he had dropped it and forgotten to pick it up on his way out. John rolled his eyes. Of all the stupid, idiotic things to do, he had to leave *that* behind.

John unlocked the french doors and glanced in the direction of the stairs. Sylvie had been shopping which meant she would be heading straight down to the kitchen with the shopping bags. John hesitated. He was debating which was worse: Sylvie discovering him in the kitchen, or Sylvie discovering his little black book and what was written inside?

With that thought in mind, John threw caution to the wind and launched himself into the kitchen to retrieve the book. It could not, under any circumstances, fall into the wrong hands. As he bent down to retrieve the book from the kitchen floor, John thought he heard the familiar creak of the top stair. He froze.

John's heart raced at the thought of Sylvie discovering him standing right here in her kitchen.

Sylvie had already taken five more steps down the stairs – John had been counting each one – when he suddenly sprang into action and leapt towards the french doors, forcing himself not to look back.

Sylvie walked into the kitchen, straight past the french doors, and didn't notice John in plain sight surreptitiously locking the doors from the outside.

Sylvie put her M&S shopping bag down on the worktop and was just starting to unpack the shopping when she suddenly had an irrational feeling that somebody had been in her apartment. Sylvie stopped what she was doing and took a cursory look around the kitchen, arriving at the french doors to check they were secure. She stood at the french doors staring into the garden.

Outside, John was standing with his back up against the wall a few inches from the french doors, clutching his little black book to his chest and breathing heavily – his heart racing. If Sylvie was unpacking the shopping at this very moment, which he suspected she was – what else would she be doing – then she would be standing at the kitchen cupboards with her back to the french doors and he could make a run for it. John eyed the gate halfway down the garden within plain sight of the kitchen.

Sylvie was still standing at the french doors. She eyed the gate halfway down the garden. John had told her time and time again to lock that gate in case of burglars. It was still shut but she knew it wasn't locked. Sylvie wondered whether she ought to nip outside right now and lock the gate. Sylvie turned around and walked over to a kitchen drawer to fetch the key. She glanced at her shopping bag as she reached in the drawer for the key. On the other hand, thought Sylvie, the garden gate had been left unlocked this long surely it could wait until later. All the same, Sylvie dilly-dallied with the key in her hand. She looked over at the french doors knowing it would only take a couple of minutes to nip outside and lock the gate.

What made up Sylvie's mind was suddenly picturing John standing in her kitchen telling her in a patronising tone of voice, "How many times have I told you to lock that gate?"

Sylvie proceeded to unpack the party food.

Outside, John was trapped in a web of indecision. He was trying to estimate how long it would take Sylvie to unpack the shopping and go back upstairs, and whether he should just wait it out rather than risk getting caught making a run for it.

John was bored of waiting already. He was contemplating making a quick dash across the lawn to the garden gate until he thought, wouldn't it be Sod's law if Sylvie was passing the french doors and happened to glance outside when he made his move? John rolled his eyes. After all the trouble he'd gone to, returning to retrieve his little black book, why risk getting caught now just because he let his impatience get the better of him?

John remained rooted to the spot. It was another gloomy October day. John cast his eyes heavenward hoping it didn't rain. He had raced out of the house without putting on a coat, not expecting to find himself stuck on the patio beside the french doors with his back up against the wall. John was already feeling cold. To keep himself occupied, and his thoughts distracted from the chill air making him shiver, John opened his little black book and leafed through the pages to pass the time. It made for surprising reading.

It was originally meant to be a snag list for the downstairs apartment; all the things that might crop up and need to be put right before tenants moved in, like a leaky tap or a faulty plug. However, that little black book had turned into something else entirely. Each page contained a list – in most cases followed by a rant – of all the irritating things that were getting on John's nerves about his downstairs neighbour. Like the fact that she often had the television on until the early hours disturbing his sleep, or the way she neglected to wipe her shoes on the doormat before she came into the house. She always left a trail of dirty footprints in the hall downstairs which John had to sweep up every evening.

There was page after page of her annoying little traits. What John couldn't fathom was why he hadn't noticed all these irksome little things about Sylvie before. Was it because he had hit the big Six O and suddenly turned into a grumpy old man overnight, and everything was just getting on his nerves? Or was it because Sylvie had upset his plans for the garden apartment? John's thoughts turned to his plan to rent out the garden apartment. Leafing through his little black book was making him anxious about what it was going to be like having a tenant living downstairs for real. What if, after they moved in, John didn't like his new neighbour?

John found a pen in his pocket, turned to a blank page and wrote, *Sylvie*. He underlined her name twice. Underneath, he added the words, *How to evict a problem tenant*. John stared at the new entry and thought about Sylvie's odd behaviour of late. She never used to stay up late watching the television and gorge on takeaway food – he had seen the empty boxes in the rubbish bin – or have friends visiting at all hours. From what he had seen today, her apartment looked chaotic; there was too much stuff, too much clutter. And it wasn't tidy.

John had congratulated himself on resisting the urge to tidy up when he had been nosing around her apartment, but it did get him thinking. This wasn't what Sylvie was really like – untidy, disorganised, chaotic – was it? John shook his head with a definitive no. This wasn't the person he had lived with for the past thirty-nine years. She never behaved like that when they were together. So what had changed?

As far as John was concerned the answer was clear and not totally unexpected: Sylvie was lost without him. He could forgive her what she had done to the apartment because he knew exactly what had happened in his absence. The bright garish colours, the rugs, the cushions and the rattan furniture had Julia written all over it. The home they shared together never looked like that. John knew what was going on here. Sylvie wasn't coping on her own – that much was obvious. Her life, like her apartment, was a total shambles. She needed someone to step in and sort her out.

The other side of the wall, Sylvie was sitting at the kitchen table munching on a tasty ploughman's sandwich which she bought in M&S during her shopping trip. Sylvie was feeling satisfied with her morning. She nearly had everything organised for the party. Sylvie had already written out the party invitations which were sitting in a neat pile in front of her on the kitchen table. She had delivered the first party invitation as soon as she returned home from shopping. She didn't dally; she just slipped it under his door before she changed her mind. She knew he would say yes. After all, what other way was John going to get inside the apartment to nose around? Sylvie sighed. She still wasn't looking forward to it, but at least the party wasn't until the weekend and she had plenty of time to prepare herself.

Sylvie's thoughts drifted to what she had planned for this afternoon. She had already organised her laptop upstairs so she could start doing some research on the internet, or googling as Chloe called it. Sylvie needed to find out some information on the area in Cornwall where she used to spend her summer holidays as a child. Sylvie intended to spend the afternoon doing just that – googling.

Sylvie finished her sandwich and got up from the table. She deposited her empty plate in the sink and spotted the key she had left on the kitchen counter. Sylvie picked it up and turned in over in her hand. She was debating whether she ought to nip outside and lock that gate before retiring upstairs to the lounge.

Still rooted to the spot inches from the french doors, John thought he heard something. Was that Sylvie getting up from the table? He listened intently and was rewarded by the sound of her footsteps as she moved around the kitchen. Lucky for him, Sylvie was still wearing her shoes. John waited patiently. He was eagerly anticipating the moment Sylvie finally went upstairs.

John closed his little black book thinking about the last entry. From what he could see, there was only one solution: Sylvie needed to move back in with him for her own good. John raised an eyebrow. How was he going to make that happen? And happen soon? For the second time that morning John realised this wasn't going to be as simple as just asking Sylvie to move back in with him. John needed a plan.

Suddenly all went quiet indoors. It sounded as though Sylvie was no longer in the kitchen. John breathed a sigh of relief. He felt his legs would give way if he had to stand there for a moment longer. Even so, John didn't want to take any chances. He turned around and slowly inched his face towards the french doors to take a peek inside, praying that Sylvie wasn't sitting at the kitchen table or, heaven forbid, standing at the french doors looking back at him. Or worse still, on her way out into the garden to finally lock that gate. Oh the irony, thought John, after he had been on at her in the past for not locking that gate, if she chose right now to finally listen.

John held his breath and stole a look. She wasn't sitting at the table, or standing at the french doors about to step outside. In fact, she wasn't anywhere in the kitchen. John took himself and his little black book straight home to his apartment.

On his way back upstairs, John thought about the past thirty minutes he had spent trapped on the patio. He congratulated himself on using the time wisely. Going back over all the entries in his little black book, John was convinced that Sylvie was in trouble and all this odd behaviour – John glanced at his little black book – was clearly a cry for help. From the moment she took those suitcases and moved in downstairs, Sylvie's behaviour was so out of character that, as far as John was concerned, there was no other possible explanation. And with Julia's influence, things had obviously escalated beyond her control and quickly got out of hand.

Like a knight in shining armour, John was going to come to her rescue and find a way to save his wife and their marriage. All John wanted was for things to return to normal in the Baxter household. That wasn't too much to ask for was it? John didn't think so. To that end, John already had a plan in-the-making. He was intending to invite Sylvie to the party he was organising. It would be a grand opening exclusively for the garden apartment. He had already bought some party invitation cards. The first thing he was going to do when he got in was write one to Sylvie and slip it under her door as a surprise.

He knew he was being presumptuous. She didn't have to agree to a party in the garden apartment. However John was pretty confident Sylvie wouldn't object. He knew this for certain because one day soon Sylvie would have to show him the apartment. What better way to do it than during a party when he couldn't exactly kick-off and embarrass her in front of family and friends?

By the time John reached the door to his apartment, he thought he had come up with a pretty solid plan. A second party consisting of a small get-together for close family and friends to show off the rental apartment was a brilliant idea, especially as Sylvie would not be expecting his reaction – or lack of – to what she had been up to down there.

That was the beauty of his plan. He had already seen the garden apartment. He had freaked out – fortunately not in front of Sylvie – and now all that was left to do was show her that he could be grown up about it. Pretend it was no big deal. Tell her that all was forgiven. And invite her to move back upstairs – no hard feelings. John smiled confidently. It was the perfect plan. What could possibly go wrong?

John opened the door to his apartment and immediately spotted the hand-delivered envelope from Sylvie that had appeared on his doormat. He bent down to pick it up. John was about to find out what could go wrong with his perfect plan.

30

Sylvie stood in front of the long mirror in her bedroom unsure what she thought of her outfit. It was the evening of the party and there wasn't a lot she could do about it now. Even so, she still stood there for some minutes turning this way and that trying to convince herself she looked okay. Sylvie frowned at her reflection. Perhaps it wasn't the outfit that was the problem. If her thighs were just a few inches smaller, and her bust a few inches larger, maybe her ensemble would work.

Sylvie knew she was lucky to have found an outfit at all. Shopping for something suitable to wear to a seventies-themed party had proved quite a headache. Sylvie got to the point where she regretted agreeing so readily to a fancy-dress party.

She had started by browsing in some charity shops feeling confident she would find something that might pass for a seventies outfit. That turned out a gigantic waste of time. Next stop was some vintage clothes shops on the Kings Road, which was Chloe's suggestion. Chloe found a couple of pretty retro dresses for the summer. Sylvie made the mistake of joining the queue for the checkout holding the dresses, at which point Chloe and her purse inexplicably disappeared, only to reappear when

Sylvie had paid for them. Disappointingly, there was nothing particularly suitable for the party. Sylvie and Chloe had run out of ideas.

It was during Sylvie's unexpected cruise down Regent's Canal to Camden Market on Julia's houseboat, when they had started to discuss plans for the party, that Julia came up with a novel idea; rather than buy something for the party, they could hire an outfit. After shopping in Camden Market, Chloe left her purchases on Julia's boat so they wouldn't be lumbered with shopping bags when they went in search of a fancy-dress shop. They had no idea how long it would take to choose some outfits for the party, so Pete took Julia's houseboat back to Little Venice on his own.

Sylvie remembered feeling extremely happy standing on the canal towpath below Camden Market waving goodbye to Pete, and Julia's houseboat. She had not been looking forward to the return trip. For Sylvie, the journey on the canal had been the low point of her day. But that was more than made up for when they found a costume hire shop. Julia's idea turned out to be the highlight of their shopping expedition.

When Sylvie stepped inside that shop, her original problem of finding one suitable outfit for the party morphed into a problem of choosing which outfit, out of literally dozens and dozens, she wanted to wear. They all agreed it had turned out fortuitous that the three of them were together to provide a second opinion.

However, once they started trying on the outfits, they could barely string a coherent sentence together before keeling over with laughter every time one of them stepped out of the changing room in another psychedelic disco dolly dress, or a bright satin jumpsuit.

At one point all three of them disappeared into the changing rooms, only to reappear looking as though they were auditioning for an Abba tribute band.

Sylvie couldn't remember the last time she'd had so much fun. It made her feel young again and reminded her of those carefree days with Julia when they were children. She had almost forgotten the simple joy of being spontaneous and doing something silly just because you felt like it. Julia was absolutely right when she said that sometimes it was good to let your hair down and have some fun once in a while. Unfortunately, living with John and his godforsaken plans seemed to suck the life out of anything remotely spontaneous or fun.

When Julia caught Sylvie looking down in the mouth again, she wagged her finger at Sylvie and told her to stop thinking about John.

Sylvie did as she was told. After all, she had a party to think about and an outfit to choose.

Sylvie tried on dresses down to the ankles, dresses up to the bum, disco diva dresses, and disco queen dresses. There were fringed dresses, fringed waistcoats, catsuits, and jumpsuits. You name it – they had it. The choice was overwhelming. And that was before they experimented with the accessories. Chloe started it when she walked out of the changing rooms in a pair of platform shoes, a headscarf, and huge sunglasses. She had even found a seventies-style blonde wig which, together with her large blue eyes and delicate features, instantly transformed Chloe into a surprisingly good Farrah Fawcett lookalike.

Once they'd had their fun, they all got down to the serious business of choosing a costume and accessories for the evening, which wasn't easy – not the choosing part, but being serious. In the end, they all chose completely different outfits. Chloe settled on a paisley go-go halter dress, which looked really pretty with a matching headscarf. Julia was more adventurous and went with a psychedelic jumpsuit complete with bell bottoms and huge flared sleeves. Only Julia could get away with wearing an outrageous outfit like that without feeling completely ridiculous because she was such an extrovert. Julia also wore the blonde wig which, coupled with her stature and slim build, made her look like a Hollywood film star. Jane Fonda came to mind.

Sylvie thought they both looked fantastic. Unfortunately for Sylvie, despite all this choice, she still couldn't choose an outfit she felt comfortable wearing. All the dresses were either too long, which made Sylvie feel like a munchkin in *The Wizard of Oz*, or far too short which just accentuated her thighs. Skin-tight jumpsuits or catsuits were out of the question with her figure. Long flowing dresses made Sylvie look as though she was trying to hide up her figure. Sylvie wanted to feel attractive in her outfit. She wanted to enjoy the party and not spend the evening feeling self-conscious.

The manageress of the shop came up with a solution by pairing a short pink and yellow psychedelic dress with a pair of dark satin trousers. She found some platform shoes to give Sylvie some height. The outfit was rounded off by a large pair of sunglasses and a hippie-style satin headscarf that wouldn't have looked out of place at Woodstock back in the late sixties.

Sylvie liked her outfit a lot in the shop, but now she had it on at home on the evening of the party it was a different story. Sylvie's enthusiasm for the party had waned considerably since their visit to the costume hire shop. For one thing, she was worried that the three of them had overdone it and they would be the only ones at the party dressed head-to-toe in fancy dress. She felt foolish enough as it was in her costume, without discovering all the other guests were acting their age and had dressed sensibly for the party with perhaps only a token alluding to the seventies, like a flower in a lapel, a psychedelic purse, or funky shoes.

Sylvie sighed. She wished that was all she had to worry about. What was really putting a dampener on Sylvie's party spirit wasn't her outfit, but the thought of John turning up at any minute for his private tour of the apartment before the party. Sylvie now regretted that she had even invited him, let alone asked him to arrive early. It seemed like a good idea at the time. In hindsight, Sylvie now believed it would have been far better if he had arrived with the other guests; perhaps he wouldn't lift off quite so much in front of other people.

Sylvie was nervously glancing at her wristwatch when the doorbell rang. She looked up with a start. Oh god! Here we go, thought Sylvie as she tottered out of the bedroom in her platform shoes and made her way along the hall into the lounge. She wasn't looking forward to the confrontation with John one bit. Sylvie approached the door with trepidation. She put her hand on the doorknob recalling Chloe's joke about John having a heart attack when he saw what Sylvie had done to the garden apartment. Sylvie no longer thought it was funny.

She cast a long look back into her lounge. The seventies-themed decorations weren't helping any. Julia had persuaded Sylvie to decorate the lounge for the party with some seventies kitsch they found at Camden Market. John wasn't going to like it one bit. But all that was going to pale into insignificance when John found out his two-bed rental apartment was now a one-bed.

Sylvie took a deep breath and opened the door.

'Chloe?' Sylvie scanned the hall behind her looking for John. She even poked her head around the doorframe to see if he was on his way down the stairs. There was no sign of him.

'Chloe, you're early. The party doesn't start for another half an hour.' And John was late. Sylvie was so distracted by thoughts of John appearing at any moment that she had barely glanced at her daughter.

'I know I'm early,' Chloe sniffed, wiping a tear-streaked face with the sleeve of her party dress. 'Declan and I had like a massive row.'

'Oh dear.' On hearing this, Sylvie stepped forward and put a protective arm around Chloe's shoulders. She guided her inside and closed the door behind them, but not before she stole a glance upstairs. John's door was still firmly shut. Sylvie checked the time by her wristwatch and frowned.

'Mum, have you got any tissues?'

Sylvie looked at Chloe's mascara-smudged cheeks and went to fetch a box of Kleenex tissues from the kitchen. When she returned, she handed Chloe the box and sat down on the sofa.

Chloe hovered by the door. She plucked a Kleenex tissue from the box and wiped some of the mascara from her face.

Sylvie patted the empty seat next to her. 'Why don't you sit down and tell me all about it.' Sylvie was all too familiar with Chloe's little dramas on the relationship front. Her previous boyfriends seemed nice enough, but inevitably things went south. Chloe seemed to lurch from one relationship disaster to another. Sylvie thought with Declan that things would be different. In fact, she was sure of it, especially as they had just recently got over one wobble. But one look at Chloe's face said that wasn't the case.

Chloe ambled over with the box of tissues and slumped on the sofa beside her.

Sylvie turned to look at Chloe's profile and sighed. 'What's he done this time?' Sylvie didn't really think Declan had done anything. "He" was just a euphemism for each and every boyfriend she'd ever had. Sylvie knew her daughter all too well; the beginning of the end always started with the small things that got on Chloe's nerves. It was often the kind of thing that, in most relationships, involved compromise if you were going to share your life with someone. Unfortunately, the word *compromise* was not part of Chloe's vocabulary.

'I got all dressed up for the party. Declan was due home from up North.'

'Let me guess. Declan has been held up and can't make it to the party.' Sylvie really didn't have time for this. She had one eye on her watch and an ear out for the doorbell. All she could think about was John.

'I wish it was that, Mum. I really do.' Chloe wiped a tear from her puffy red eyes. 'He arrived home earlier than I expected. I was so excited. I couldn't wait to show him my surprise.'

Sylvie was preoccupied with the thought of John turning up and lifting off in front of Chloe. 'Surprise?' repeated Sylvie distracted.

'Our house, don't you remember?' Chloe paused. 'Mum, are you listening?'

Sylvie instantly stopped looking at her watch and turned to Chloe, giving her a reassuring smile. 'Chloe, you have my full attention.'

'As I was saying, I was so excited at the thought of Declan walking through the door and seeing what we'd done to the house while he was away. I'd bought some scented candles and even tidied up. You know I'm not exactly the tidiest person in the world.'

Sylvie nodded thinking, like mother, like daughter. She gazed around her own apartment recalling the effort she had gone to, to make it look presentable for the party.

'I wanted everything to be perfect when Declan arrived home. I couldn't wait to see the look on his face when he found out what I'd been up to.'

Sylvie's smile faded. She had an idea what was coming next.

'He hated it,' said Chloe with tears in her eyes. 'He thought it was some kind of prank, as though he'd stepped into an episode of *Changing Rooms*. Any minute he thought one of his mates was going to jump out and say it was all a big joke and put it back the way it was.'

Chloe paused to wipe a tear from her eye before continuing, 'Once he'd got over the shock, we had a shouting match. The way he saw it, I'd done exactly what I wanted as though it was *my* house and not ours. I told him that I did it for him as a surprise, that I love it and thought he would too. I was wrong. The way he looked at the house . . . the way he looked at me . . .' Chloe's face crumpled. 'I think he hates me.'

Sylvie reached over and hugged her daughter, feeling terribly guilty that this was all her fault. In hindsight, it should have occurred to her that something like this might happen. Especially in light of what she had been up to herself and what she imagined John's reaction would be to his newly-refurbished garden apartment.

All Sylvie wanted to do was help Chloe settle into her new home. The problem was she got carried away with Chloe's idea of doing up the house when Declan was away as a surprise. She hadn't stopped to consider the possibility that Declan might not appreciate Chloe going ahead and redecorating without at least discussing it with him first. Poor Chloe. Her plan to surprise Declan had backfired spectacularly.

'Oh dear, oh dear,' said Sylvie repeatedly, wondering what on earth she could do to put things right.

Unfortunately for Chloe, she had found out the hard way that she didn't know Declan quite as well as she thought she did. It reminded Sylvie of a particular instance when she and John were first married, and they had just moved into this house. It wasn't long before they were making plans to do up the house and disagreeing on almost everything.

Chloe shook her head sadly. 'I can't believe we've fallen out over something as trivial as the colour I painted the walls!'

Sylvie tried to remain positive. 'Chloe, I'm sure it will blow over. Perhaps when you get home, you can both sit down and—'

'He won't be there when I get home. I told him to get out – it's over.'

'Oh, Chloe.' Sylvie couldn't hide her disappointment. She rather hoped that Chloe could get past these petty differences over décor and find it in her heart to give Declan another chance.

'Don't "Oh, Chloe," me!' Chloe said defensively. 'It's not my fault we're different. I tried. I really tried this time. I wanted it to work with Declan. I genuinely thought he'd love what I've done to the house. It wasn't the reaction I was expecting.' Chloe paused thoughtfully. 'It makes me wonder how well I really know him.'

Sylvie sighed heavily. She remembered having those exact same thoughts about John when they started doing up this house, except Sylvie was married and already pregnant with their first child. At least Chloe could back out now, put the house on the market, and start over before the best years of her life were swallowed up in the wrong relationship, if she discovered there was more to it than simply their different tastes in décor. Sylvie still hoped this wasn't the case, but then again this wasn't exactly a good omen.

'I thought I knew Declan, I really did,' repeated Chloe. 'Now all I'm thinking is that we moved too fast and we should never have bought a house together.'

Sylvie was beginning to wonder that herself. Maybe that was part of the problem. If they had taken things slowly, it would have given them a chance to get to know each other a little better first.

'Julia was even going to help me organise a housewarming party,' said Chloe miserably.

The mention of the word *party* reminded Sylvie of her first guest who hadn't arrived yet. She furtively glanced at her watch. He was late. In John's party invitation she had made a point of asking him to arrive early before the other guests. It was making her wonder whether this was his intention all along, to turn up late on purpose just to be awkward.

Sylvie anxiously glanced at the door praying that John had decided not to come at all. The last thing Sylvie needed right now was for Chloe to see John lift off over what she had done to the garden apartment. Chloe might have found that funny when they talked about Daddy's reaction on her last visit, but she certainly wouldn't find it amusing now. Sylvie was listening for footfalls on the stairs alerting her that John was on his way, but in the midst of Chloe still whingeing about Declan, she couldn't hear a thing.

She turned to Chloe, gave her hand an affectionate squeeze, and said, 'At least things can't get any worse.'

There was a loud knock at the apartment door.

Sylvie froze.

'Shall I answer that?' offered Chloe, wiping her eyes dry. She stood up. 'To be honest, Mum, I don't feel in the mood for a party.' Chloe gathered up her bag to leave.

Sylvie stared wide-eyed at the door. She didn't feel in the mood for a party either. Sylvie grabbed her hand. 'I'll go.'

'It's no trouble. I'm on my way out.'

'No, I better handle this.' Sylvie darted out of her seat and sprang for the door.

'Handle what?' asked Chloe walking up to Sylvie as she opened the door.

'Hey, Sylvie – what's up? This is meant to be a party, not a wake!' exclaimed Julia, peering at her best friend.

Sylvie was standing in the doorway of her apartment with a dead-serious expression. She said, 'Julia – you're early.' And John *still* hadn't turned up. 'How did you . . . ?'

'Your front door was open.' Julia pointed across the hall.

'Sorry, Mum. I forgot to close it when I turned up at yours.'

'Darling, whatever is the matter?' asked Julia, taking in Chloe's puffy red eyes and mascara-streaked face.

Chloe's face crumpled. 'Declan didn't like what we'd done to the house and we had like the biggest row ever. I told him to get out and . . . and I never want to see him again. He's spoilt everything.'

'You poor thing.' Julia stepped forward and gave Chloe a comforting hug.

Chloe started to cry again.

Julia exchanged a worried look with Sylvie. 'This is all my fault, Sylvie.'

'It's not your fault,' said Chloe, her voice muffled in Julia's embrace. 'I had to find out sometime it wasn't going to work out.'

Julia gave her one last affectionate squeeze and then let go, only then noticing that Chloe was clutching her bag intending to leave. Julia wiped a tear from her cheek and said, 'I've come early to help Sylvie prepare the party food.'

'Oh crumbs – the food!' exclaimed Sylvie. It was still in the fridge. She hadn't laid out a thing for the guests.

'I'll be going then,' said Chloe. 'I'm not in the mood for a party.'

'Of course you're not,' Julia sympathised, 'but I could do with a hand arranging the party food and mixing the cocktails. Can you help me?' Julia smiled sweetly at Chloe. 'Pretty please?'

Chloe cocked her head to one side thinking it over. 'Okay.'

Julia smiled warmly. 'Good girl.'

Chloe walked back inside the apartment and threw her bag on the sofa.

Sylvie mouthed, 'Thank you,' to Julia. They both knew the last thing Sylvie wanted was for Chloe to go home to her empty house and spend the evening alone.

Julia squeezed Sylvie's arm as she passed by, and whispered, 'She'll be okay. I'll get her in the party spirit – you'll see.' Julia held up a bottle of bubbly and winked at Sylvie before following Chloe down the stairs to the kitchen to start the preparations for the party.

Sylvie checked the time. The guests would be arriving any minute. Sylvie was still thinking about one guest in particular as she walked over to the coffee table and picked up a laminated sign that Chloe had remembered to bring with her for the party. Sylvie looked at it wistfully. She had done a smashing job.

In her spare time, Chloe loved to draw. She had used her hidden talent to produce a sign for Sylvie's party. It was a colourful, eye-catching montage of seventies icons surrounding the words *Party This Way*, with a large thick arrow painted in the colours of the rainbow. The sign was Sylvie's idea. John's communal entrance hall, while all well and good, in theory, was not turning out quite so agreeable in practice. Sylvie first discovered this when she caught John upstairs spying on her the day she had the architect round to assess removing the partition wall between the bedrooms. It made her feel as though she couldn't do anything downstairs without involving John. This evening was a case in point.

Sylvie glanced at the sign in her hand and sighed. She couldn't imagine that once John finished his quick tour of the garden apartment, he would want to stay for the party, and Sylvie didn't want any chance that when her guests arrived they accidentally paid a visit to her crotchety neighbour upstairs.

Sylvie picked up a packet of Blu-Tack and wandered out of the apartment. Glancing around the hall, Sylvie decided to stick the laminated sign to the stair post so it was directly in everyone's line of vision as soon as they walked into the house. She hoped the vibrant multi-coloured arrow pointing to the door on the right at the bottom of the stairs would circumvent anybody making a wrong turn.

She tied three helium balloons to the bannister and had to catch one that nearly floated upstairs. After securely tying the last helium balloon, Sylvie glanced upstairs and frowned. She could see the door to John's apartment was still shut. If this was John's way of expressing his disapproval that she was having a party, by boycotting the party, then that was fine by her.

She would be more than happy if he decided not to come. The last thing she needed was John arriving and making a scene in front of Julia otherwise sparks really would fly. There was a reason Sylvie didn't want Julia and John in the same room together when he finally discovered what they'd done to his rental apartment.

Sylvie lingered at the bottom of the stairs staring up at his door, wondering if he had decided to go out for the evening. Or better still, if he had booked into a hotel room for the night. More than anything, she wished she knew his plans. At this rate, she was going to spend the entire evening in limbo speculating when or even if he was going to turn up. Sylvie sighed. Perhaps that was his intention.

She turned on her heel and walked over to the front door, propping it open in readiness for the guests to arrive. Several black taxi-cabs had already pulled up in the street outside offloading the first partygoers. Sylvie adjusted her party dress. She was just fixing a smile on her face, hoping John didn't choose right now to make an appearance and flip-out, when she saw Chloe walk out of the apartment.

'Chloe, please stay for the party,' pleaded Sylvie.

'I'm not going anywhere,' said Chloe cheerfully. She held up her mobile phone. 'Declan phoned me and apologised for overreacting. He told me that our relationship is far more important than our difference in opinion over the décor. He said he could live without magnolia walls, but he can't live without me.'

Sylvie sighed in relief. 'Oh that's wonderful – isn't it?' She sincerely hoped Chloe was going to give him another chance.

'Yes. I told him, "Apology accepted". He's getting ready to come to the party as we speak.'

'He is?' Sylvie clapped her hands together, very pleased to hear it. She gave Chloe a hug before sending her back inside the apartment to turn the music on.

By the time the first guests walked through the door, Sylvie was smiling warmly and genuinely looking forward to the party.

There was still no sign of John.

31

John was sitting in his study when the music started. He could hear it quite clearly coming from the garden apartment below – it was that loud. John checked his watch. 'Right on time,' he remarked as he glanced at the party invitation on his desk. He picked it up and turned it over in his hand.

John cast his mind back to this time last week when he discovered the envelope that had been slipped under his door . . .

He had just returned from that fun-filled escapade downstairs to retrieve his little black book from Sylvie's kitchen, and there it was. When he opened the envelope, the last thing John expected was Sylvie to be throwing a party downstairs. It didn't take him long to figure out who had put her up to it: Julia. In fact, he wouldn't be at all surprised if the party was Julia's idea.

What had surprised him was receiving an invitation to the party. Then again, Sylvie couldn't very well have a party down-stairs and not tell her neighbour upstairs, running the risk that said neighbour would gate-crash her little soiree and ruin it. John would have preferred Sylvie to have told him about the party personally instead of slipping an invitation under his door because he would have tried his best to talk her out of it. But Sylvie probably knew that. John didn't like parties with loud music. Sylvie knew that too.

In with the invitation, Sylvie had included a personal note. John unfolded the note and read it. Sylvie wanted him to arrive early so she could show him around the apartment; a private tour, no less, before the other guests arrived.

Bugger that, thought John. He knew what she was up to. Sylvie didn't want him spoiling her party by kicking off and embarrassing her in front of her friends. And was it little wonder? He had seen her apartment. He knew she must be worried about what his reaction might be. She had obviously thought this through. Wasn't this just perfect timing? He could hardly have a rant over what she had done if there were other people arriving and she had guests to see too. Very clever. Not so clever if he didn't turn up. John wasn't going to give her the satisfaction.

When John first read the note, he had a good mind to tear up the party invitation and bin it. Instead, John marched downstairs to have it out with Sylvie. This party was not going ahead under any circumstances. Apart from anything else, John was worried about the neighbours. John liked to think they had always been perfect neighbours, quiet and considerate.

Their neighbours had already voiced their concerns to John and Sylvie over converting their house into two apartments and taking in tenants downstairs. He could well imagine this party would be just the sort of thing they were worried about, living next door to tenants. And now John was worried too. It had never crossed his mind that a tenant might play loud music and have parties until Sylvie moved downstairs.

They lived in a quiet street, and some might even say a rather boring existence, but John liked it that way. He didn't want things to change. He liked his staid, predictable life. John rolled his eyes. Perhaps he should have thought of that before he converted the house. John felt like kicking himself. He wanted his old life back. He wanted the old Sylvie back who was neat and tidy and predictable, and didn't watch television until the early hours, eat takeaway food, or organise surprise parties behind his back.

As John headed downstairs to confront Sylvie about her plans to host a party in the garden apartment, he made a mental note to write all this down in his little black book. There must be some sort of clause that could be written into a tenancy agreement prohibiting a tenant from playing loud music inside the apartment. That would put a stop to any potential parties. However, John already knew the problem was much bigger than that. Not for the first time, John reminded himself that the problem was residing downstairs. They hadn't spoken in over a month, and he didn't even know if she was in, but that didn't stop him from tearing downstairs on a mission to stop the party before she sent out any more party invitations.

He was standing outside the garden apartment summoning up the courage to knock when, to John's surprise, she opened the door. He guessed Sylvie heard him stomping down the stairs.

'We need to discuss *this!*' John had just held up the invitation in front of her nose when the doorbell rang. He glanced over his shoulder at the front door and frowned at the interruption. He was in the middle of something important here, namely trying to put a stop to Sylvie's plans for a party.

'Well, aren't you going to answer that? You're closest.' Sylvie tapped her foot impatiently.

John whirled around in frustration and strode across the hall to open the front door. He hoped it wasn't Julia; she was the last person he wanted to see at this moment.

'Hi Dad,' Chloe walked straight in as soon as John opened the door. 'I've come to sort out your new laptop.' She noted his bemused expression. 'Remember you phoned and asked me to come over because you couldn't work out how to switch it on?' Chloe shook her head at silly Dad.

Sylvie looked at John in surprise. For years he point-blank refused to spend any money replacing their archaic computer because it was still in perfect working order. 'You bought a new laptop?' Sylvie wondered what had brought on the sudden change of heart.

John's head bobbed up and down in answer to Sylvie's question. 'Chloe, I wasn't expecting you until later.'

'I know, but I finished work early and thought I'd pop straight round.' She smiled brightly looking from John to Sylvie and back again. 'Am I interrupting something?'

John glanced at Sylvie. This was awkward.

'Well?' Sylvie looked at John and folded her arms. 'You had something you wanted to say to me about the party?'

'Dad, you've got your party invitation!' exclaimed Chloe, noticing the party invitation in John's hand.

'Yes, that's what I'm here to—'

'Mum, I haven't got mine yet.'

'Just a moment, Chloe, I'll go and fetch it.' Sylvie trotted back inside her apartment.

John noticed she pulled the door to behind her. He turned to Chloe. 'You're coming to the party?'

'Of course I am.' Chloe frowned at John. 'You're not coming. That's what you came downstairs to tell Mum, isn't it.'

John hesitated. 'I'm a bit concerned about the neighbours and the noise.' John added, 'That's all,' even though that wasn't *all*.

'Oh Dad, you needn't worry about them.'

'Worry about whom?' asked Sylvie, walking out of the apartment and handing Chloe an envelope identical to the one she had slipped under John's door.

Chloe took her party invitation. 'Dad's worried about the neighbours and the noise.'

'Really,' said Sylvie flatly, eyeing John.

'I was just going to tell Dad that he needn't worry because you have already invited the neighbours.' Chloe turned to her Mum with a smile and linked one arm in hers. Chloe held up the party invitation and said, 'I'm coming, so I don't need to RSVP.'

John stood staring at them and realised the chances of putting a stop to Sylvie's party were receding rapidly. Sylvie had obviously covered all her bases. As for Chloe, she couldn't have timed her arrival better, providing the perfect ally. John frowned.

'Now, I mustn't keep you both,' said Sylvie, taking Chloe's arm from hers and patting her hand. She paused to look at John. 'Unless there was something else you wanted to say to me?'

John glanced at Chloe. She had already opened her envelope and was looking mighty pleased with the party invitation inside. John rolled his eyes. He looked back at Sylvie and mumbled, 'No.' He shook his head in defeat and started up the stairs.

Chloe followed him upstairs. 'So. Dad. Are you coming to the party – or what?'

John wished that he had called the laptop customer helpline instead. His youngest daughter could, at times, be a royal pain in the behind.

As soon as Chloe had finished setting up his laptop and making him feel like an idiot into the bargain – 'Dad. Seriously. You couldn't even figure out how to switch it on? Even Mum could do that!' – Chloe didn't hang around. She offered to call in downstairs on her way out and tell Mum that he was coming to the party.

'No thank you, Chloe,' John replied.

'Is that, "No thank you", you're going to tell her yourself, or "No thank you" because you're not coming to the party?'

John walked Chloe to the door and saw her out, smiling tightly and refusing to utter another word on the subject. What remained of John's convivial mood had evaporated when he found out a small detail about the party that Sylvie had neglected to mention in the invitation. According to Chloe, it was a housewarming party.

Housewarming party! John baulked when he heard those words. It was bad enough that he had been in the middle of planning another party to show off the apartment downstairs, only to discover Julia had stolen his idea and beaten him to it. Worse still, he found out courtesy of Chloe that this was no ordinary party. Sylvie was having her very own housewarming party to celebrate moving in downstairs. John was now officially worried.

As soon as he closed the door on Chloe, John disappeared into his study; he had a phone call to make. He knew when he was outgunned and outmanoeuvred. John needed reinforcements. But what he needed above all was *a plan*, and John knew just the person. Unfortunately his brother Dave, the person in question, was on holiday in the Caribbean with his wife. He wouldn't return for another week, landing back the day after the party.

John wasn't happy about that. He was intending to phone him up and ask him to come over as a matter of urgency. At least John was able to contact him on his mobile phone. It gave John an opportunity to tell Dave all about what had been happening in the Baxter household in recent weeks.

Dave had some sage words of advice. He told John to hold tight and that he was not, under any circumstances, to show his face in the downstairs apartment until Dave got back from holiday and had a chance to come over and see him. Dave's immediate take on the situation was that it sounded serious. John needed to put a stop to these antics and get the apartment back once and for all. And crucially, John needed *a plan.*

Listening to his big brother tell him that he needed a plan was like manna from heaven. John got off the phone feeling as though he was finally getting somewhere. He was confident that all he needed was a plan to get Sylvie out of the apartment. John was looking forward to Sylvie moving back upstairs and getting tenants lined up to move into the garden apartment.

Dave promised to spend some time on the remainder of his holiday trying to figure out what that plan might be. John couldn't wait for Dave to get back from holiday with *the plan.* In the meantime, he was going to stick rigidly to Dave's advice and avoid Sylvie at all costs until his return.

Avoid Sylvie at all costs, thought John recalling Dave's advice from the phone call last week as he tried his level best to ignore the thumping seventies disco music assaulting his eardrums from the party downstairs. He turned the invitation over in his hand and then dropped it into the waste paper bin beside his desk.

John shifted his attention to the laptop in front of him. Chloe had shown him how to google and that's exactly what John had planned for the evening. He was going to do some research on the internet, if he could find a way to concentrate with that din. John had already brought the radio in from the kitchen and placed it on the desk in his study. He tweaked the dial on the front to turn up the volume. It was now doing a pretty good job of drowning out the disco music downstairs with Chopin.

John had momentarily closed his eyes to listen to the classical music on the radio when he thought he heard voices in the communal hallway downstairs. He opened his eyes. It sounded as though the first guests had arrived.

John got up from his desk, stretched, and walked over to the study window to look outside. In the street below, people were arriving for Sylvie's party. John hoped Sylvie was feeling anxious right about now, wondering when her upstairs neighbour would make an appearance. John smiled knowingly. He might not be able to spoil her party by turning up and causing a scene in front of her friends – John realised he wasn't that good of an actor – but he could make her feel on edge for the entire evening wondering when he would finally make an appearance. And then make her anxious speculating why he hadn't come – even better.

Glancing out of the window, John was only too pleased he wasn't going to the party. He could see people arriving dressed in psychedelic seventies outfits. John arched an eyebrow. Did they have any idea how completely ridiculous they looked? He tutted. People his generation should be acting their age, not trying to relive their youth and have fun. How immature. They weren't kids; they were grown-ups, well past middle-age, who should know better. John slowly shook his head from side to side as he

347

stood there staring at them. It was all rather embarrassing.

Watching the dozens of people arriving, John was still concerned about the neighbours; they had no idea what they were in for. John had heard about Julia's parties back in the seventies. Who in London hadn't? Apparently, her house parties were legendary. John wondered what exactly Julia's parties were legendary for. He remembered that one time he nearly had the displeasure of finding out for himself when the then-teenage Chloe discovered Julia was throwing another one of her infamous parties back in the noughties. Fortunately, after fetching Chloe from the party, he didn't hang around. Apart from that, John was just thankful he had never had the misfortune to experience one first hand – until today.

He dropped his gaze to the floor beneath his feet and frowned. Goodness only knows what was going on down there. John considered that perhaps he would be better off booking into a hotel overnight. On the other hand, he thought why should I have to get out of my own house?

He knew full well why it had crossed his mind. Watching the steady stream of people arriving at the party – none of whom John recognised – he suspected this housewarming party was going to be nothing like the one he had organised for close friends and family a few weeks ago when the conversion finished. His party was a calm, mature, dignified affair. It was more akin to a dinner party, without any of these childish antics like dressing up or playing loud disco music. John sighed. He seriously hoped he wasn't going to regret not booking that hotel room.

John closed the curtains. He'd had enough of watching badly dressed baby boomers beating a path to his door. He returned to his desk and sat down in front of his laptop. John had some research to do. Opening his little black book on the desk in front of him, he turned to the last entry and typed into the Google search engine the words: *How to evict a problem tenant*. He knew that wasn't exactly the circumstances he found himself in at the moment. What he really wanted to type in was: *How to evict a problem wife*. But that was a stupid idea – even for him.

John sat reading through some of the web pages on the subject of evicting tenants. Although it didn't apply to his own situation – thank goodness – all this going on downstairs had given John pause for thought. It was making him aware of the potential pitfalls of renting out the garden apartment that, in his naivety, he had not even considered before converting the house into two apartments. At the time, all that had been on John's mind was money. John read on believing that forewarned is forearmed. Besides, it might give him some useful pointers as to how to deal with his nuisance neighbour downstairs. And her nuisance friend Julia.

He was busy reading an article on his laptop screen when he suddenly looked up and grimaced. Did someone just turn the music up? John adjusted the volume on his radio to compensate and sat back in his chair massaging his temples. He had a feeling this was going to be a long night. However, despite the party downstairs, John had already decided that he was not going to let it disrupt his usual bedtime routine.

At nine o'clock John closed down his laptop and switched off the radio. John groaned as the full extent of the party noise hit him. At least he could console himself with the thought that it was hardly going to go on all night. With the exception of Chloe and her boyfriend Declan, the party-goers weren't exactly spring chickens. John imagined it would probably quieten down by eleven or so. Once in bed, he knew there would still be a good hour or so to go until that interminable racket subsided, but this was his house and he was determined to carry on as normal. With that in mind, John walked into the kitchen to make a cup of Horlicks, his milky drink of choice before bedtime.

He was standing by the cooker waiting for the milk to boil in the pan, and trying to ignore the sound of blaring disco music, when the security light outside was triggered by something in the garden. Normally the culprit was the neighbours orange tomcat, Jasper. John glanced out of the kitchen window at the floodlit lawn below and was astonished to see the party had spilled outside into the garden. Some of the party revellers were dancing on his lawn. John gaped at them. How many people had Sylvie invited to this party?

John's first reaction was to rush downstairs and tell them to get off his lawn. Did they have any idea how much new turf cost these days? Then John remembered the conversation on the phone with Dave last week who cautioned him not to show his face downstairs under any circumstances. John intended to follow Dave's advice to the letter. He rolled down the kitchen blind, so he wouldn't have to see what they were doing on his expensive new lawn, and finished making himself a cup of Horlicks. John picked up a novel from the coffee table in the lounge and made his way upstairs.

Sitting in bed with his cup of Horlicks, John checked the time by the clock radio on the bedside table. It was half-past nine. John opened his book and began to read. Fifteen minutes later, he was sitting there staring at the page unable to concentrate. John kept thinking, is it me or is the party noise getting louder? He assumed that by now the party would be winding down, not going the other way. John gave up, put the book to one side, and just sat there in bed listening to it. 'Good grief. Thank goodness it's my wife down there and not a tenant.' John didn't think he'd ever say that in a month of Sundays. But at least with Sylvie downstairs, he knew this party was just a one-off. He didn't think he could take much more of this.

John climbed out of bed and started rummaging through his bedroom cupboards and drawers. All he wanted was some peace and quiet – and some ear-plugs. He was sure there was some in a travel pack they had bought for those holidays they never seemed to get around to. John couldn't find them. He had no intention of going downstairs and asking Sylvie where they were, so he gave up and climbed back into bed.

He checked the time before switching off his bedside table lamp. It was now half-past ten. John was confident it wouldn't be long and they'd all be clearing off home. In the meantime, he reached across the bed and snatched up the other pillow, putting it over his head in an attempt to muffle the noise. It worked to a degree if he wanted to suffocate himself. John threw the pillow across the room and pulled the duvet over his head instead.

Closing his eyes, John tried not to think about the party downstairs. He would just have to put up with it until things quietened down. It wouldn't be long now, John told himself yet again. He eventually drifted off to sleep in spite of the party downstairs carrying on well into the night.

In the early hours, drifting in and out of sleep, John thought he heard someone outside his apartment door shouting, their words slurred, 'Who do you think lives in there?' And he was pretty sure he heard someone else reply in an equally loud, equally slurred voice, 'That's the nuisance neighbour, apparently.'

'I'm the nuisance neighbour?' John shouted back sarcastically.

John had woken from his slumber wondering if that was just a dream and then promptly fallen back to sleep.

Although John dozed off surprisingly quickly, he had a fitful night's sleep. He experienced nightmarish dreams that strangers were gathering outside his apartment trying to break in because there wasn't enough room downstairs, and there wasn't enough room on the lawn in the back garden, so they all spilled into his apartment. They kept coming and coming, more and more people, all dressed in hideous psychedelic outfits.

And John couldn't stop them.

32

John woke up with a start. Was that just a dream or did the party really spill over into his own apartment last night while he slept upstairs oblivious to it all?

John hastily got out of bed, his heart racing as he walked down the stairs imagining all sorts of horrors that lay in wait, like wine stains on his upholstery, party food trodden into his new carpet, cigarette burns on his wooden coffee table and baby boomers sleeping it off on his new sofa.

John could scarcely bring himself to look as he reached the bottom of stairs and walked into the lounge. His hand flew to his chest in utter relief. All was just as he had left it last night. The lounge was neat and tidy, with absolutely no evidence that anybody – apart from John – had been in the apartment last night. All the same, he did a quick circuit of the entire apartment starting with the kitchenette. John popped his head around the door to his study before walking into the small lobby where he checked the front door was locked. Finally, he nipped back upstairs to check the bathroom and spare bedroom. John sighed. It was all just a bad dream.

John returned to the kitchenette to make himself a cup of

tea. While he waited for the kettle to boil, he pulled up the blind at the kitchen window and squinted as the sunlight broke through the cloud cover. Standing in front of the window, John closed his eyes for a moment letting the warmth of the morning sunshine wash over his face. A smile played on his lips. John was convinced things could only get better. The party was over. Dave was on his way home with a plan to get Sylvie out of the garden apartment. John was determined to put all this behind him and make a fresh start with Sylvie. He didn't want to fight; he didn't want to argue. There was no reason why they couldn't act like two reasonable, mature grown-ups, and just bury the hatchet and work things out.

John no longer felt the warmth of the morning sun on his face. He opened his eyes to see storm clouds gathering. It looked as though it was going to turn out another dismal autumnal day. The kettle boiled. John turned from the window to make himself a cup of tea. As was his routine every morning, John took his first few sips of tea as he looked out of the kitchen window to admire his expensive newly turfed lawn, now littered with crisp packets and wine glasses and beer cans and bottles of coke and—

John spluttered into his tea, spilling it down his pyjama top.

What the fu—

John didn't even finish that thought as he dashed upstairs and hastily pulled on trousers and a jumper over his pyjamas.

'Someone is going to clear up that mess on my lawn!' John exploded. 'Otherwise, they're gonna have some explaining to do – goddammit!' John was seething. This wasn't some teenage house party that had been gate-crashed by a hoard of youngsters who had read all about it on *Facebook* or *Twitter*.

That thought stopped John in his tracks. Was that possible? He shook his head dismissing that idea as totally absurd. Why would they want to gate-crash some old fogies' party? No self-respecting teenager would be seen dead at a party with people dressed in silly outfits, most of whom were old enough to be their grandparents for heaven's sake. On the other hand, John might have preferred it if a mob of teenagers *had* gate-crashed Sylvie's party. At least that would explain the litter strewn all over the lawn.

John walked over to the bedroom window as he did up the button on his trousers and glanced at the garden below. He was thinking about the strangers he had seen arriving at the party last night. Who were they? John's brow furrowed. He knew exactly who they were: Julia's friends.

Ignoring his brother's advice, John was going to march downstairs and give Sylvie a piece of his mind. This had to stop. She'd had her fun. Playtime was over. Now it was time to get down to the serious business of renting out the apartment. But first, somebody was going to clear up that mess in his back garden. John stopped briefly in the kitchen to pick up some black refuse sacks on his way out. He was in no way intending to clear up that mess himself, but he would come prepared so there would be no excuses along the lines of, *I haven't got anything to put the rubbish in.*

John was trying to decide how many black refuse sacks were needed to do the job when he thought *sod it,* and just took the roll. He stormed out of his apartment and nearly slipped on an empty beer bottle discarded on the floor outside his door. Stooping to pick it up, John counted five others lying empty on the floor outside his apartment. He stared at the beer bottle in his hand. John was thinking about a conversation between two drunken strangers outside his door last night that he thought was just a dream but, as it turned out, wasn't a dream at all.

John picked up all six bottles, deposited them in a refuse sack, and then proceeded down the stairs picking up coke cans, more beer bottles, crisp packets, and a paper plate with some half-eaten party food. John stopped and looked at the paper plate in his hand. He picked up some cheese and pineapple on a stick and held it up; was that seventies party food? John shook his head, ate the pineapple and cheese which was rather tasty, and dumped the empty plate into the refuse sack.

On his way down, he continued to fill up the refuse sack with more party debris left discarded on the stairs until he reached the communal hallway downstairs. John put the bulging refuse sack on the floor and picked up an empty pizza box that said Domino's Pizza on the lid. John tossed it in with the other rubbish and turned to Sylvie's door. It was slightly ajar.

He reached out and pushed the door wide open. John took an involuntary step backwards at the scene that greeted him therein. It was not unlike his worst nightmare. In actual fact it was his worst nightmare; the one he had experienced last night. Except it hadn't happened in his apartment, it had happened in Sylvie's – thank the heavens.

If this was a horror film – John really didn't go in for that sort of thing, although he was quite partial to Hitchcock – the camera would be capturing the scene and zooming in, for the benefit of the audience, as jump scare sound-effects punctuated the silence with each jerk of the camera. John's eyes darted around the room like a camera lens zooming in on the horrifying scene: on the wine stains on Sylvie's sofa, on the crushed party food in Sylvie's brand new rug, on another black refuse sack's worth of party debris littering her lounge.

And then there were the bodies; people dead to the world crashing out in Sylvie's flat. One was lying motionless on Sylvie's sofa, arms and legs splayed all over her new upholstery, still wearing their shoes. Four were asleep on her rug, snoring softly into cushions used as pillows and sharing the throws as make-shift blankets. Two had even fallen asleep sitting up, their backs propped up against the wall either side of the fireplace – heads resting on double chins – like a pair of baby boomer sentinels guarding Sylvie's precious fireplace.

Good grief. John shook his head in dismay. This was worse than he could ever have imagined. If this was a bunch of teenagers, at least they could be sent home with a flea in their ear after a good telling off. What on earth was Sylvie going to do with this lot?

'Cook them breakfast when they wake up – if you must know,' said Sylvie, picking her way across the assault-course of bodies towards John.

Unless Sylvie had suddenly acquired the power of telepathy, John didn't realise he had just spoken out loud.

As he watched Sylvie approach, he was thinking sarcastically and rather ungenerously that, considering the aftermath, he hoped she thought the party was worth it.

'Oh John,' she gushed, 'you should have been here. It was tremendous. I never knew parties could be such fun. I wish I'd been to one of Julia's parties in the past. They must have been fantas—'

John stopped listening at the mention of Julia's name. So that's what this was all about: John had refused every party invite they had ever received from Julia over the years, and so Julia had brought the party to Sylvie, right here in his very own house. Well whoop-de-do, wasn't she clever. John was not sharing Sylvie's enthusiasm one bit. She obviously hadn't seen the state of the back garden yet.

John stood in the doorway and folded his arms waiting for Sylvie to come back down to earth. She was still talking incessantly about her so-called fantastic party and gesticulating wildly. He raised an eyebrow. Did she even realise that she had an empty wine glass in her hand? And look at those dark rings under her eyes; did she get *any* sleep last night?

'. . . and I can't wait to throw another party.'

'Pardon me?' John blinked. Did she just mention *another party?*

Sylvie tapped him on the shoulder unnecessarily. 'I said that I can't wait to throw another party.'

'I heard you the first time, Sylvie.' Surely, she can't be serious. 'Have you seen the state of the apartment!' exclaimed John, pointing at her lounge and nearly poking Sylvie in the eye accidentally.

Sylvie tottered backwards. 'Yeah – so!'

'And have you seen the state of the garden?'

'Of course I have!' Sylvie raised her glass as though she was about to make a toast. 'You pulled up my bloody plants to put in a bloody lawn for your bloody tenants.'

John gaped at her. Of course the bloody garden was for the bloody tenants, they were meant to be renting out the garden apartment, weren't they? At least that was the plan until all this nonsense. 'Look, Sylvie, this has got to stop.'

'I know that! The party finished hours ago,' she said glumly, not catching his meaning.

'No Sylvie, I'm not just talking about the party. I'm talking about all of it. The apartment, your friends, whatever the hell you do all day on your laptop,' he blurted.

Sylvie looked him up and down. 'How do you know I've got a laptop?'

He hadn't meant to say that. John hastily backtracked. 'Look, I'm just trying to be reasonable. It's all got to stop.'

'But this is my life, John,' she said, prodding herself in the chest. 'Are you telling me I can't be myself, John? Are you saying you don't like the real me?'

John was getting in a muddle. Now she was just confusing the issue. John moved in closer, cupped his hands together as if in prayer, and tried to explain, 'This isn't the real you, Sylvie. This is Julia's influence.' He was staring at her intently trying to get his point across, hoping she would understand.

Sylvie was grinning back at him.

John got the distinct whiff of drink on her breath. He stepped back and looked her over. 'Are you drunk?'

'Who me?' said Sylvie, still grinning. 'Course not.' Only then did Sylvie notice the empty wine glass in her hand. 'Oops.' She giggled as she held it up in front of her nose. 'Where did that come from?'

John was leaning casually against the doorframe watching Sylvie – drunk or stoned or both – trying to put the glass on the sideboard without dropping it, when he saw something out of the corner of his eye scurrying across the floor towards him.

It landed on his foot.

John yelped and jumped back in surprise. 'What the heck is *that*?'

Sylvie put the wine glass down on the third attempt and

looked at the floor where John was pointing. 'Oh, didn't I mention that Julia bought me a moving-in present?' Sylvie pointedly looked at John and remarked, 'She said he would make a lovely companion.'

'But it's a . . . it's a . . .'

Sylvie rolled her eyes. 'It's called a *puppy*, John.' She bent down and scooped up the black wriggly cocker spaniel pup in her arms.

'I can see that!' John backed away from the messy mass of fur and a slobbery pink tongue trying to make a pass for his nose.

'Isn't he adorable?'

John didn't think so. All he wanted to know was, 'What the heck is it doing here?'

Sylvie looked at John with an expression that said he'd just asked a really dumb question. 'Alfie lives here.'

'Alfie?' John stared at the puppy in astonishment. 'But . . . but we never had pets,' said John, backing into the hall. 'We didn't like pets!'

'No, John, *you* didn't like pets.' Sylvie slammed the apartment door shut.

John stared at the door. 'You know that you're not allowed pets in apartments.'

'Says *who*?' shouted Sylvie from behind the door.

'Well . . . I'm sure there's some law against it.'

Sylvie didn't answer.

Standing in the hall, staring at Sylvie's door, it occurred to John that perhaps he should have drawn up some ground rules before Sylvie moved in downstairs. People living in apartment buildings must have rules regarding what they could and couldn't do in their apartments, surely. It's just that he never imagined this situation would go on for so long that they would even need ground rules. John glanced at the bulging refuse sack of rubbish he had collected on his way downstairs. He felt like leaving it outside her door just to make a point, but he couldn't do that unless he didn't mind the stench of decaying party food permeating the entrance hallway.

John sighed and picked up the rubbish. The wheelie bins were in the back garden. It would be quicker to take the refuse sack straight through Sylvie's apartment and out the garden. John didn't bother knocking on her door. After that heated exchange, Sylvie wasn't about to open the door and let him in – John wasn't a complete idiot.

He turned from her door and walked out of the house, taking the bulging refuse sack with him. John made his way around the corner into the adjacent side street alongside their end terrace house. A little further along was the side gate into the back garden. Fortunately, the gate was still unlocked. After depositing the rubbish in the wheelie bin just inside the gate, John stood staring at the lawn in dismay. He couldn't believe Sylvie was talking about throwing another party. John frowned. She really hadn't seen the state of the back garden.

John held up the roll of black refuse sacks and tore off two, no three, make it five black sacks, and set to work clearing all the rubbish off his expensive back lawn, and the patio, and the borders. While he was at it, just to make him feel worse, John thought about his brother Dave and his wife arriving back at Heathrow airport right about now from their Caribbean cruise together. John wondered why that wasn't him and Sylvie arriving home this morning after a happy holiday together. Instead, he was in his back garden, on all fours, cleaning up after Sylvie's housewarming party and trying to figure out where it had all gone wrong.

Despite all that, the thought of Dave returning home lifted his spirits considerably. John was confident that Dave would return with a plan to get Sylvie out of the apartment and things back to normal in the Baxter household. In fact, he was counting on it because just lately John was beginning to despair of things ever returning to the way they were.

'This breakfast is delicious, Sylvie,' commented Julia.

There were murmurs of approval around the table. The party stragglers, who had not made it home last night, were hungry too and appreciated Sylvie cooking them breakfast.

Sylvie dished up the last of the bacon, eggs, waffles and fried bread from the frying-pan on to her plate. She picked up her plate and turned around smiling at her new friends gathered around the kitchen table.

Her smile faltered as she stood there wondering where she was going to sit. Her kitchen table comfortably seated six, but there were ten people squeezed around it, some sitting on deck-chairs. However, she needn't have worried. Julia had found an old stool from the pantry.

They all shuffled along to make room for Sylvie as she carried her plate over to the table.

Before she sat down, Sylvie said, 'If everybody is up for it, I'd like to pull the curtains to let in some sunlight.'

Once again there were murmurs of approval from around the table.

Sylvie pulled the curtains at the french doors. Bright sunlight flooded the room eliciting a collective groan. They had all drunk far too much last night and were suffering the after-effects, Sylvie included. She sat down on the stool next to Julia, rubbing her temples. The natural light hurt her eyes and wasn't helping her headache any. Sylvie had a hangover. She vaguely recollected smoking something last night that probably wasn't legal.

'Who's that?' asked one of Julia's friends, jabbing his fork in the direction of the french doors.

Sylvie looked up as everybody turned in their seats to look out the garden. They sat watching a man on all fours with a black rubbish sack picking up the party debris from the lawn. He was talking animatedly, as though he was having a heated argument with somebody who wasn't there.

Sylvie rolled her eyes. 'That's my husband, John.'

Julia laughed. 'I don't think John realises he's got an audience.'

Sylvie considered inviting him in for breakfast and then thought the better of it. The party had been a night to remember – for all the right reasons – and she wasn't about to end it on the wrong note by inviting the party-pooper to join them, especially after his reaction to Alfie. She glanced at her new puppy asleep in his basket and smiled.

Sylvie shifted her attention to the plate of food in front of her and picked up her knife and fork. She glanced around the table to find everybody busy tucking into their breakfasts, apart from Julia who was staring steadfastly at her.

Sylvie leaned towards Julia and whispered, 'What is it?'

'I don't want to bring it up, Sylvie, but I was wondering . . .'

'Yes?'

'You've done up the apartment. You've had your housewarming party – what's next?'

'Oh, that's easy.' Sylvie smiled. 'I've still got to find that cottage in Cornwall and carry out my mother's last request. And now I've got a laptop, I was thinking about Chloe's idea of starting a blog—'

'I'm not talking about that,' interrupted Julia, glancing out of the french doors at the garden beyond. She lowered her voice. 'What about John?'

Sylvie followed her gaze. John was still on all fours in the back garden furiously filling up another black refuse sack.

In the back garden, John paused to take a breath. As he wiped his brow, he glanced in the direction of the house and caught sight of Sylvie sitting at the kitchen table staring back at him, surrounded by her new friends. John held her gaze. There was a question hanging between them. A question they had both been avoiding. A question as yet unanswered. What about *us*?

The story continues in

It Takes 2 to Tango

For further details visit:

www.elisedarcy.com

Please feel free to add your email to the mailing list for updates
on forthcoming book releases in the author's e-newsletter.

And finally . . .

If you enjoyed this book, and have a spare moment, please
consider leaving some feedback for other readers by writing a
quick review on Amazon. Great reviews spread the word and
help readers like you choose books they enjoy.